Child
OF THE LIGHT

JANET

BERLINER

AND

GEORGE
•
GUTHRIDGE

Cover Illustration: Matt Manley
Cover Design: Michelle Prahler

White Wolf Publishing
780 Park North Boulevard, Suite 100
Clarkston, GA 30021

Printed in Canada

to the survivors

PART I

"But every shadow is in the final analysis also child of the light, and only he who has experienced light and dark, war and peace, ascent and descent, has really lived."

—Stefan Zweig

Die Welt von Gestern

(The World of Yesterday)

CHAPTER ONE

Nine-year-old Solomon Freund removed his glasses and pressed his face against the wrought-iron bars of his open bedroom window. Without the wire rims digging into his nose he felt more comfortable, but no less impatient. He had been at the window since sundown, waiting for the evening star, the wishing star, to take its place beside the moon, and watching the soldier guarding the fur shop that adjoined the Freund-Weisser tobacco shop across the street.

The star had not yet appeared, the soldier had lost his appeal, and Solomon had grown weary of waiting.

Earlier, his sister, Recha, had cored apples for the sauce

that went with the potato pancakes his mother was making for tonight's birthday-Chanukah-Christmas celebration with the Weisser family upstairs; he had grated the potatoes. Now he could hear the *latkes* sizzling in the heavy frying pan his mother kept salted and greased for her specialty. The smell of browning butter wafted into his room and his stomach growled in anticipation. The soldier must be cold, and hungry, too, he thought.

He glanced up at the ceiling that separated him from his best friend, Erich Weisser. Here, on the ground floor, the Chanukah Menorah had been lit and the smell of butter and applesauce filled the air; up in the Weissers' second-story flat, there was the scent of pine and the glow of Christmas candles—and Erich, furious that once again his parents had said no to his birthday and Christmas wish: a dog of his own. He *needed* a dog, he said, the way Sol *needed* glasses. Besides, he said, Sol could talk to his sister when he got lonely. Whom did *he* have? At least if he had a dog he would have someone to talk to, he said. Strange how he always talked about dogs as if they were people. He swore he could talk to them and that they answered him—which wasn't all that crazy, Sol thought, not if their friend Beadle Cohen was right and anything the mind could conceive of was possible.

It didn't matter. What *did* matter was that Erich get over his sulk by the time the party started.

What a party this was going to be—the first night of Chanukah, Christmas Eve, Erich's tenth birthday. Best of all, Papa was back from the Front for good, recovered from influenza without infecting the rest of the family.

A true miracle, Mama called it.

Maybe the glow of Christmas and Chanukah candles together would make another miracle and stop Erich's papa from drinking too much tonight. Then he would not make all those snide comments about Jews, and Frau Weisser would not go on about all the things she wanted and could not have, all the while looking at Mama accusingly, as if she—and not Herr Weisser's gambling—were responsible for their reduced circumstances. Herr Weisser would keep off Erich's back, and—

Across the street, the soldier shook his fist at the moon.

Was he blaming the moon for keeping him from his family on this Christmas Eve? Sol replaced his glasses and waited to see if any of the people milling around Friedrich Ebert Strasse had noticed the soldier's strange action.

Nobody seemed to care.

A crowd had gathered at the corner, around a hurdy-gurdy man grinding out a polka on his barrel organ. Several beer-drunk locals had grabbed their fat, frumpish wives and begun to dance. Two women in ragtag coats begged at the door of the butcher shop whose shelves had long since held only black-market horse meat and a skinned cat or two; a couple of street vendors hawked indoor fireworks and sugar-coated ginger cookies. They stepped delicately around the beggars to approach a passing coterie of laughing Fräuleins in their fashionable calf-length holiday skirts. Having sampled the spicy cookies, the ladies boldly offered a taste to a trio of cadets walking stiffly upright to balance the weight of their gold-mounted Pickelhauben helmets.

The cadets ignored them and continued to make their way toward a group of men in uniform who stood at the far corner, beneath skeletal trees. Arms crossed, they listened to a Freikorps band play a solemn Lohengrin medley.

The scene held endless fascination for Sol. It was as if his entire pewter soldier collection had come alive in the street: Cuirassiers in armored breastplates, Death's Head Hussars, Foot Artillery, Hasans—

He thought about his little army, so proud and smart in the closet he carefully kept locked. Though he knew that daydreaming could bring the voices again and leave him shaking, he let his mind drift. He resisted the urge to imagine himself in the Great War. Papa had said the fighting had been too terrible to contemplate—and no glory in it, despite the Kaiser's decrees to the contrary— so Solomon imagined himself...*saw* himself...among his soldiers outside Paris forty-five years earlier, the great city surrounded, he with saber in hand, leading a heroic charge against a *mitrailleusse* machine gun. Bullets whizzed past his ears. He called out encouragement to his men and they in turn invoked the name of the Fatherland. The French abandoned their posts and scattered before the brave Prussians racing through the field.

The battle froze as if caught in a photograph. Everyone stopped running. The artillery bursts stayed in place, as though the sky were permanently bruised, yet light, a different light, flashed before Sol's eyes, spangling like a foil pinwheel. The flashes brightened, got bigger...seemed to swallow him. He no longer saw either the battlefield or the street of Berlin. Only a cobalt-blue twilight surrounded him—the world without form, without substance. He tried to shut his eyes, but the glow held him. A man's voice cried out from the twilight—shrill, plaintive, filled with pain:

"Is this your season of madness, Solomon Freund? Is this your season of sadness?"

A *real* machine gun rattled, cutting off the twilight voice—another of the voices he had been hearing off and on for at least as long as he'd been wearing glasses…which seemed like forever.

Solomon blinked. The cobalt-blue light dissipated as the music and the strollers along Friedrich Ebert Strasse paused. Rifle fire filled the momentary silence. Couldn't people, he wondered, trembling and angry with himself for hearing another of the voices again, at least stop shooting for the holidays? Sometimes he had a hard time remembering what things were like before the start of the Communist revolution. Seven weeks was not forever, but it was too long to be confined to the apartment house, where he had been since the Great War ended and the revolt in Berlin's streets began.

"Snipers!" A man dressed as St. Nicholas ran down the street, waving his arms. "They've positioned themselves atop the Brandenburg Gate!"

Two or three people turned and stared in the direction of the Siegesallee—the Victory Alley. Then the music began again, the barrel organ and the Freikorps band, and people continued to saunter down the boulevard as if they had heard and seen nothing more unusual than a man shooting wooden ducks at a carnival stand.

The shooting must have something to do with the Kiel sailors holed up in the Imperial Palace, Sol decided, vaguely remembering a discussion between his father and Herr Weisser about some mutinous sailors who had sacked the Royal Palace, "under the guise of socialism," whatever that meant.

Grownups often said things he and Erich didn't understand, he thought. Like Papa, getting agitated about Herr Lubov, the furrier, calling his shop *Das Ostleute Haus* because *Ostleute* meant "people of the East." The Lubovs were rumored to be Communist sympathizers who waved what Papa called "the red flag of revolt." Then he and Mama turned right around and talked about Rosa Luxemburg as if she were a heroine in a book—yet she was one of the founders of the new Communist Party in Germany. It was all just too confusing!

Taking a deep breath to calm himself and put the twilight voice from his mind, he refocused his attention on the soldier.

One by one, as dusk turned into night, shopkeepers doused their lights and closed up for the day. Finally, all the stores were dark except the furrier's. Mannequins dressed in sable and centered in blue-white light stared at Sol from behind the plate-glass windows. He squinted, distorting the image until the windows across the street became the irises of a Persian cat, a royal Eastern princess whose gleaming eyes hid ambition and avarice. *Prinzessin Ostleute*.

Intensified shooting again pulled him back to reality. He gripped the wrought-iron grill and leaned away from his open window, as much to give his nose a chance to warm up as to remove himself from the sound of the guns.

Staying home and playing with Erich all day had been fun at first, but he was beginning to miss school, and he and Erich were getting on each other's nerves. They needed something special to do, something different, like going back to the hideaway they had discovered just before all the trouble started. They had been sent down to clean the shop's cellar, a job that in the past had been done by hired help. While moving a crate to one side, they had noticed a rusty drain-grate that led into a section of ancient brick sewer, sealed off from Berlin's modern system. Though fetid and damp, the sewer ran beneath both the furrier's and their shop, and made a perfect hideaway.

Best of all, it was *their* sewer. Their secret.

"Tonight will be like old times," Sol's mother said.

He turned to look at her. She stood framed in the doorway of his room, wiping her hands on her apron. Her face was flushed, her hairline damp from the heat of the kitchen.

"Come, Sol. You must be hungry. Wash your hands and face and help me carry the food upstairs."

Sol glanced at his hands. "I'm starving."

"Wash," his mother said. "Even if you think you're clean."

Frowning, Sol moved away from the window.

His mother laughed. "Watch out—your face might stay ugly," she said. "And close that window, Solly, or there'll be icicles on your bed when we come home. Already in here it's like Siberia."

CHAPTER TWO

"Aren't you going to help us put this on the tree?" Erich's mother held out a handful of tinsel.

Erich shook his head and went on rocking in the chair he had placed as far away from the tree as possible. He hated Christmas. Mama knew that! He hated his birthday, too, because it was Christmas Eve and he always lost out. He had liked them both all right until he was about six, when his parents started lumping everything together, cheating him, giving him one present instead of two. Sure, the present was bigger, but that still meant he only had one package to open.

"Here, Friedrich, you do it. I have other things to do before they come."

Inge Weisser handed the tinsel to her husband. He took it from her and threw it at the tree. "There! Is that good enough for them?"

"What do you mean *for them?* It's for *us*, Friedrich, and for the boy."

"Jews—what do they know about Christmas! Not even a tree in the shop—*he* wouldn't allow it—"

It's almost as though he wishes Herr Freund had died in the trenches, Erich thought. One of these days he's going to forget himself in front of Herr Freund and say something even Sol's papa—for all his niceness—cannot excuse, and then what will happen to us?

"I hear them coming up the stairs." His mother set her face in a smile and looked at her husband as if she hoped it were contagious. "Quick, Erich, open the door."

He let the Freunds in and for a while it was like old times. The two families sat on the Weissers' astrakhan rug, among stray tinsel and pine needles. There were warmed schnapps, potato pancakes, and easy laughter in front of a roaring fire. And songs—not religious ones of Jesus or God particularly—just nonsecular, happy, holiday ones.

When the stories began about the children when they were little and Germany was at peace, Recha climbed onto her father's lap and snuggled against him. "Tell us about when *you* were little, Papa."

Jacob Freund smiled. Reaching into his pocket, he took out a tiny, four-sided brass top. "This *dreidel* is even older than I am. Can you imagine that, children? My grandfather brought it all the way from Russia."

Erich and Sol grinned at each other. This was their favorite story, the one about Sol's great-grandfather Moshe, who was both a rabbi and a horse thief. Why didn't *he* have an interesting family like that, Erich thought.

Holding the *dreidel*, Jacob said, "We'll never be sure which of his two occupations made it necessary for him to leave Russia in the middle of the night, but—"

"Couldn't you spare us the story of your illustrious ancestors just this one time?"

Friedrich Weisser downed another schnapps and Erich felt as if a cold wind had blown through the room. There were hours to go before midnight and the opening of presents. An argument now would spoil everything.

"I'm first," he said, hoping to avert a quarrel. Taking the *dreidel* from Herr Freund's hand, he spun it hard. "*Nun, gimel, he, shin,*" he chanted, repeating the letters of the Hebrew alphabet that were engraved on the old brass surface of the *dreidel*. He had learned the words from the Freunds; maybe being the first to say them tonight would make up for his father's rudeness.

Recha, whose eyelids had begun to droop, got her second wind. She climbed off her father's lap and joined in the game, yelling loudly as the top slowed down and she, too, tried to guess which letter would be visible when the spinning stopped and the *dreidel* finally lay still.

"Ridiculous game!" Herr Weisser placed his rough hand over the top and stopped its spinning.

Ella Freund's face hardened. "All right, children," she said, standing up. "It's getting late. I think it's time to leave."

"Don't be so sensitive, Ellie." Her husband took out a fresh cigar. "Fred's just had a little too much schnapps. He doesn't mean anything by it."

Oh doesn't he, Erich thought, watching his father pace up and down the room.

"You Jews all think you're so special—" Friedrich Weisser stopped in his tracks and glared at Herr Freund.

He's done it! He's gone too far, Erich thought. "Let's go to my room, Sol," he whispered, embarrassed for his father. "You, too, Recha, if you like."

"Recha?" Sol asked.

Erich saw the worried look on Sol's face. True, Erich hardly ever voluntarily included Recha in anything—not that he didn't like her, but she *was* only seven.

"Come, Friedrich!" Jacob Freund said, his voice firm. "You don't really mean any of that. We are friends, all of us. Old friends." He put out his hand. "Let us put an end to this at once. For all of our sakes."

"Papa, please—"

Erich was cut short by a knock at the front door.

"The beadle." Frau Freund looked flustered. "I forgot. I invited him for a glass of schnapps. I didn't think you would mind—"

"Well, I do mind!" Friedrich Weisser jammed the cork into the bottle. "And so does my good wife!"

"Sol." Erich tugged at Sol's arm, pulling him toward his bedroom. "I have something for you."

"Bring it out here."

"No. It's private. Come now, before—"

There was a second knock at the door, louder this time.

"Do I let him in?" Ella Freund asked quietly. Sol's father gave her an *it's not our home* look.

"Please, Papa, he's a nice man. Let him come in," Erich said. He could feel that his face had turned red.

"Go on, go on!" His papa waved his hand. "Open the door. But only one drink—"

As graciously as if she had sent him a gilt-edged invitation, Frau Weisser ushered Beadle Cohen into her home. He was a short, rotund man with thinning hair and a limp that got better or worse depending on the weather. His built-in barometer, he called it, impressing the boys no end with the accuracy of his predictions. He spent all of his time around the synagogue, where he was a glorified janitor, or surrounded by musty books which he foisted upon the mostly unwilling boys who attended the Hebrew School attached to the *shul*.

Sol was one of the exceptions—not only willing but anxious to get his hands on as many books as he could. He loved to read. Most of all he loved to discuss what he had read with the beadle, who made no bones about either his poverty or his intellect. He had a particular fondness for Sol and, strangely enough, for Erich, who was not much of a reader—certainly not of Jewish literature. Often, when Erich was through with sports, he would walk past the Hebrew school and wait for Sol so they could walk home together. Sometimes the beadle would walk with them. He made a point of talking about things like astronomy, which interested Erich as well as Sol.

"Happy Chanukah." The beadle accepted a glass of schnapps and an invitation to be seated. "And a merry Christmas, too." He sipped at the drink with obvious enjoyment. "So kind of you to include me. Most kind."

"We have potato pancakes left over, if you're hungry," Sol's mother said.

"Hungry? One needs to be hungry to eat *latkes*, especially Ella Freund's *latkes?*" The beadle glanced down at his stomach and laughed. "But I can't stay long. I have other stops to make."

Erich saw a look of relief on his friend's face. He felt the same way; he wanted the beadle to stay, but who knew how long Papa would control himself?

"I have no gifts for the adults," the beadle said, "but I was able to manage a little something for each of the children. Recha!" He dug in his pocket and pulled out an old sepia photograph. "Because you love to dance, I brought you a photograph of Anna Pavlova. This was taken when she was just your age. Now she's the most famous ballerina in the whole world."

Recha took the photograph and stared at it, her dark eyes sparkling.

"Say thank you to Beadle Cohen." Ella Freund smiled at her daughter.

"Thank you, Beadle Cohen." Recha performed a little curtsy.

"I'd prefer a kiss, right here." Pretending great seriousness, the beadle pointed at his cheek.

Recha obliged.

"Would it be too much to ask for one on the other cheek, too?" The beadle was enjoying himself.

Recha shook her head and, instead, kissed the photograph.

"Well, I suppose that will have to do," the beadle said, with mock sadness. "Erich! I believe today is also your birthday. Happy birthday, my boy."

Erich saw his papa's expression harden. Hurry up, beadle, he thought. There's not much time left.

"One day you will get that dog you want so badly,"

the beadle said, "and you will have to know how to look after him. I talked to a man I know who knows *everything* about dogs. He gave me this for you." He pulled a worn leather leash out of his pocket and held it out to Erich.

"This is foolishness," Herr Weisser said. "I have told the boy he cannot have a dog. He nags me about it enough, now he will double his efforts. We cannot have that. The way he embarrasses me, telling people he knows what dogs are thinking—!"

"But Papa—"

"No!"

The beadle stood up. Stuffing the leash into his pocket, he gave the boys a broad wink. "Perhaps I can find a temporary use for it," he said. "Thank you for your hospitality."

"Your *latkes*, beadle." Ella Freund emerged from the kitchen with a plate in her hands.

"Perhaps you will be kind enough to repeat the offer some other time."

The beadle seemed calm enough, but Erich knew he was upset. Why else would he have forgotten to give Sol his present? Papa always spoiled everything, and *he* had to make excuses!

"Look, I'm sorry, Sol," Erich said, as soon as they were in his room. "My father, he..."

"Not your fault." Sol sounded close to tears.

"Here!" Erich handed Sol the dog collar he had kept hidden under the bed. "I made this for you—for us—in leather craft at school. We'll have a puppy soon. It'll be just ours, yours and mine, and no one else will even be allowed to pet him...'cept maybe Recha, sometimes."

"Boys, come out of the bedroom. Everything is all right," Jacob Freund called from the hallway. "We're all friends again."

"We'd better go—" Sol began.

"Don't you like it?"

"It's great, Erich. But—"

"I don't know when or how, but we'll do it, Sol," Erich said. "If we stick together, we can get whatever we want. We're blood brothers, right?" Remembering something he had seen in a film, he held up his arm, wrist toward Sol, who touched his wrist to Erich's and reached for the collar with his other hand.

"Wait!" Erich placed the collar carefully around their arms and closed it tightly. "Nothing can separate us now!"

"Ow! You made it too tight!"

"Okay, pull! One, two, three."

Laughing, the boys tugged in opposite directions and the collar dropped to the floor. Sol picked it up, examined it briefly, and stuffed it into his pocket. "Thanks."

"*Solll!*" Recha wailed outside the door. "Sol!"

Patting his pocket, Sol opened the door to a tearful Recha.

"You always leave me out. Always."

Sol crouched and gave his sister a hug. She was okay—for a girl, Erich thought. "What happened in there, Recha?" he asked.

Recha handed her brother a book bound in soft black leather. "Beadle Cohen went away. He left this for you."

Sol took the book and read the title out loud. "*Toledot

ha-Ari. Life of the Ari...the Lion. Look, Erich, it's the biography of Isaac ben Solomon Luria!"

Erich had no idea who that was but he could see that his friend was pleased.

Sol's mother came walking down the hallway toward them. "He said to tell you he was given this very book when he was your age," she told Sol. "He wants you to have it. Your papa said you were much too young to understand anything about the Kabbalah, but our beadle is a stubborn man. The Lurianic Kabbalah must be part of your education, he says, and to understand the philosophy you must first understand the man."

The book was small enough to fit in Sol's pocket with the dog collar. Erich saw him slip it inside and pat his pants. "I tried reading this once," Sol said. "It's about a man who saw things inside his head that other people couldn't see. He was a mystic, whatever that is."

"Ask your papa," Erich said.

"I did. He said, 'leave the study of mysticism to the *Hasids*—'" Sol looked at Erich and laughed. "They're *very* religious," he explained, "like the Pope and the Cardinals—"

"Beadle Cohen says that when you are ready, the understanding will come." His mother took Recha's hand and led the little girl back into the living room. Sol started to follow but Erich stopped him.

"When we get the dog, we'll keep it in the sewer," he whispered. "We'll take turns going down to feed him and—"

"Boys!" his papa called out pleasantly. "We've decided to start opening the presents early."

Erich looked at Sol, raised his wrist one more time, and grinned. "Brothers," he said again. "Forever and ever."

CHAPTER THREE

"Liebknecht and Luxemburg! Both killed!" Jacob Freund removed his glasses and dangled them from his fingers over the newspaper headlines. "What is Germany coming to?"

Though this was one of those rare times that all the members of the Freund and Weisser families were in the shop together, Sol knew from his papa's tone that he was thinking aloud and did not expect an answer to his question.

"How did they die, Papa?" he asked from the back of the shop. Since the table was occupied, he and Erich were playing chess on the linoleum floor.

"What does it matter how," Friedrich Weisser said. "Dead is dead! Things will quiet down and we can get back to business."

"Ella, more and more I think you and the children

should go to your sister. You'll be safer in Amsterdam with Hertl." Jacob Freund sounded agitated.

"Look here, Recha." Ella Freund pointedly ignored her husband and gestured at the newspaper. "It says here this pretty little girl loves to dance, just like you." She leaned closer to the paper. "Miriam Rathenau, granddaughter of industrialist Emil Rathenau, is being sent to the United States to study the new modern forms of dance that have become so popular over there," she read aloud. "Poor thing. Her parents were killed in an automobile accident."

"Such a poor little thing I should like to be," Frau Weisser said. "They say her father left her a fortune in art in Switzerland, and it's just waiting for her to be old enough to collect it."

"Is money all you can think of, Inge? The child's an orphan—"

Sol stopped listening. Not that he didn't feel sorry for the girl, but right now he felt sorrier for himself. He was tired of staring out of his window and of reading about Isaac ben Solomon Luria. He was even more tired of listening to the four adults bicker about things that seemed entirely unimportant, or talk endlessly of danger and revolution. Already it was past the middle of January and there was no end in sight. He would probably never see the inside of a classroom again—

Erich sat up so abruptly that he knocked over his king's rook. He did not seem to notice it, though he usually went to great lengths not to lose his castles, even sacrificing knights and bishops. His face was turned toward the door, his head cocked like that of a bird. The adults went on talking; Erich gestured, palms close to the floor, as though wishing he could will the conversation to stop. It was interrupting his concentration—whatever it was he was listening to.

"Erich?" Sol asked in a low breath.

Erich shook his head and went on listening.

Then he leaned conspiratorially across the chessboard. His blue eyes shone with excitement. "We need to go. *Now*. Make up some excuse."

"Why! Go where!" Sol whispered.

Again Erich shook his head.

"*You* make up the excuse," Sol said.

But Erich was back to listening to something outside. Besides, Sol knew why he would have to be the one to ask. Herr Weisser inevitably denied any request Erich made, no matter how innocent or rational. It was a matter of course. Oddly, despite his obvious feelings concerning anything Jewish, the father always responded to Sol's opinions and requests, as though the boy were an extension of the man to whom, like it or not, Herr Weisser was indebted. *He respects intelligence*, Sol's mother had said once of the shop's co-owner.

He's stupid, Erich had insisted when Sol relayed his mother's remark. Sol argued that no one should say such a thing about one's papa, but Erich would not be deterred. Stupid and...*and* selfish, Erich added.

"Do something." Erich poked Sol's forearm.

"I need to go...for extra lessons." Sol stood and held up his Luria book.

"You're going to the Grünewald? Now?" Sol's mother asked, wiping her hands on her apron as though ridding herself of imaginary dough.

"Yes. Me too," Erich piped in, rising so quickly that

he bumped over more chess pieces. "Beadle Cohen promised to explain more about Mister Einstein's ideas."

"That damn beadle…teaching *my* boy," Herr Weisser muttered, "…Jewish science."

"You want instruction outside of school," Inge Weisser said, "you should go see Father…" she looked at her husband as if for confirmation about the name, "Father Dahns."

"Fast as he is, the boy should be looking for someone to teach him track-and-field," Herr Weisser said. "Not thinking about stars and psychics and God knows what else."

"*Physics*," Erich said, then added as if in afterthought: "Papa."

Herr Weisser's features clouded as he looked at his son, yet Sol could see light in the man's eyes. It's true what Mama said, he thought. He does admire intelligence— just doesn't want to admit it. Particularly in Erich's case.

"I'm going," Erich said stiffly.

"You be careful on the trolley," Sol's mother said to the boys.

"Of course, Mama." Sol leaned forward to peck her cheek, a motion guaranteed, he knew, to get him *almost* anything.

Erich hurried outside. Sol put the chessmen away, avoiding the adults' eyes for fear they might change their minds, and backed through the door, smiling a simpering smile.

"I hate lying," Sol said as they hustled down the sidewalk, dodging passersby. "Especially where Luria is concerned." He patted the book in his pocket to assure himself it was still there.

"Some things are more important than lying." Erich trotted across the street at a diagonal, Sol beside him. They rounded a corner and Erich gestured for Sol to follow him down an alley, a look of fear and anticipation apparent in Erich's face. He stopped behind a pyramid of garbage cans.

"There." He pointed down toward where the alley ended in a brick wall. "You see?"

Tied beneath a lattice of small filthy windows was a bull terrier, whimpering. Beside him stood a stack of crates crammed with chickens, clucking uproariously. A calico cat lay on the top crate, asleep in the slant of sunlight, seemingly oblivious to the birds below.

"The pup called to me," Erich said.

"Sure he did. Three blocks away. Next you'll be telling me that the Kaiser sends you mental messages from Holland."

Erich eyed him sternly. "Don't mock me, Solomon. Just because you can't—"

A barrel-chested man in a bloodstained apron emerged from the building. He carried a cleaver. A cigarette dangled from his lip as if it were glued there. He opened a cage and gripped a chicken by the neck. While it hung flapping he chopped the twine that had kept the cat tied against the crate, and lifted the animal by its collar. It dangled forlornly, as though surrendered to its fate. Holding both animals, the man went inside, kicking the door closed with his heel.

"Butcher," Erich said.

"I know that. I'm not stupid," Sol said.

"Not stupid. Just not smart." Erich sat down, his back against a garbage can. "Not smart *here*. In your heart."

He tapped his chest with his forefinger. "Peer between the cans. Watch the pup. I'll show you what I can do. I won't even look at him."

Erich closed his eyes; his face tightened. Sol could tell he was thinking hard.

As if it had received some kind of message, the pup began mewling, straining so much against its rope that the forepaws scrabbled ineffectually against the pavement.

"His name's Bull," Erich said.

"I suppose he told you that."

"He's telling me...a lot of things."

"Like what."

"*Private* things," Erich said. "If I told you, he wouldn't trust me."

"He smells us, is all."

"All he can smell is death, right now." Erich stood and crept around the garbage cans, keeping close to the wall.

"If you can speak to him so easily," Sol said, "teach him to untie the rope himself."

Erich waved him off and continued on. Sol went around the cans but feared going farther. "That butcher comes out and finds you with his dog, he'll chop you up instead," he whispered.

"You want me just to let Bull be someone's dinner?"

The comment caught Solomon so off guard that he consciously closed his mouth. He hadn't thought about the reality. Maybe Erich's right, he thought. Maybe I *am* smart yet stupid.

He ran to help his friend.

"Hurry up!" he whispered, as Erich fumbled with the knot. Erich bundled the dog into his arms and raced back toward the street. Sol looked at the thin rope…at the chicken cages.

He tied one end of the rope to the shop door and the other to the crates, which he unlatched but did not open. When the butcher opened the shop door, he would free the chickens himself. Life—and death—must go on, but perhaps having to chase after his chickens would make him think twice about stuffing so many into a cage.

Besides, Sol thought, why should only the dog go free?

CHAPTER FOUR

"This is crazy," Sol said, looking at the puppy Erich held wrapped in a piece of old blanket they had found in another alley. "We'll get...*caught*."

He had started to say *scolded*, but knew it would spark Erich's always-sarcastic laughter. What did a scolding matter, when a puppy was at stake?

His back against the tobacco shop, Erich craned his neck and peered in through the door's window. "Your papa's busy with a customer. I can't see anyone else inside," he whispered.

"What if they're in the cellar?"

"They're probably over at the apartment. Go on, now. Do what we planned."

"What *you* planned," Sol said morosely, but opened the door. The bell jangled. Smiling deferentially to his father, he stepped inside. He did his best to block the view between the door and the curtain that led to the

30 JANET BERLINER AND GEORGE GUTHRIDGE

cellar stairs. Jacob Freund was busy showing a derby-hatted man a silver cigar-guillotine. He did not look toward the boys as Erich stole in behind Sol and disappeared behind the curtain.

"The beadle had other business, so we came right back. We'll be downstairs cleaning up," Sol announced.

His father nodded, gave him a cursory smile, and went back to his customer. A silver guillotine, Sol knew, would easily equal the value of whatever other products his father sold this day—or for the week, for that matter. Sol was angry with himself for having interrupted.

He went behind the curtain but paused at the cellar door. He wanted to go down there and yet he did not. If his papa or Herr Weisser caught them playing in the sewer, they would be punished and he would be right back where he had been for so many weeks—in his room—alone.

By the time he descended the steps into the cellar, however, he could hardly wait to push aside the crate they had left guarding the entrance to the sewer. Their *magical* place, fearful yet inviting…especially after all the months cooped up across the street.

While Erich stood holding and kissing the puppy, the dog squirming against the confinement, Sol heaved the crate away from the sewer's grate. It was blood-brown with corrosion and recessed into a limestone floor discolored by a century of cellar moisture seeping into the drain. Taking hold of the crowbar they had hidden there, he jammed it beneath the lip of the grate and, using the tool as a lever, pressed down on it with all his might. The grate did not budge.

"Hurry up!" Erich said, hopping from one foot to the

other as though he needed to use a bathroom. "Get the thing open."

"I can't!"

"*I* always open it easily," Erich said.

"You do it, then! I'll hold the dog." Solomon was getting annoyed. He was confident of his brains but not his muscle, which was why he usually left feats of strength to Erich, even though Erich was the smaller of the two.

Footsteps sounded above them.

"The customer's leaving. Wonder if he bought the guillotine," Sol said.

"Someone else," Erich said. "Coming *into* the shop."

They kept quiet and listened. There was movement in the shop upstairs, more footsteps, the faint echo of raised voices.

"Your papa," Sol said. "Hope he doesn't come down here for supplies."

Erich glanced anxiously toward the cellar steps, then sharply nodded toward the crowbar. "Get it done." His lips looked tight.

Holding down the crowbar with his foot, Sol gripped the edge of the grate and, grunting with the effort, began to lift. This time the grate creaked open. He gave it one last push and it thudded back against the limestone wall. After making sure the wire stems of his glasses were snugged behind his ears, he lowered himself into the hole.

The cylindrical sewer was three meters deep—a long drop. The last time they had come down, the boys had worked two bricks loose from each side of the sewer wall, at midpoint, and jammed in a two-by-four to serve as a step. Still, it was farther down than Sol remembered. His feet dangled in midair and panic seized him. What if—

His toes found the board and he reached for the dog. The action was premature. He lost his balance and had to jump onto the partially dismantled packing crates they had used to cover the slick sewer floor.

The blackness smelled stale. He stayed crouched, his ears keened to the sound of dripping water and his eyes searching the darkness for—

For what?

Chiding himself for being afraid, he climbed onto the board. Balancing precariously, he reached up for the dog. He smiled as he dropped back down and cradled the puppy against his cheek. It felt warm and alive and somehow reassuring. When it licked his nose, he laughed and scratched it behind the ear.

"Watch out below," Erich whispered. Quick-footed as he was quick-tempered, he lowered himself onto the two-by-four, dropped deftly, and sprang to his feet.

"Give me that." Erich took the dog. He kissed the puppy on the nose and held the animal up at eye level to admire it. "The pup doesn't like the dark," he said. "Why didn't you light the candle?"

"I haven't had a chance," Sol said, choosing to ignore Erich's supposed knowledge of the workings of puppies' minds.

Served Erich right if he had to wait! Who did he think he was, treating everything like a military operation, with each of them allotted specific, immutable tasks— assigned by Erich, of course.

Scowling, Sol grabbed the jar of matches from the

shelf they had fashioned by attaching the bottom of a cardboard box to coat-hanger wire and jamming the ends into cracks between the mildewed bricks. The candle on the shelf was burned down to a wick and melted wax. Beneath the shelf hung a sailor's bag containing such treasures as some of Sol's books and his extra harmonica, the gunsight Erich had found, the dried frog Erich had put in Ursula Müller's hair. From the bag Sol reluctantly retrieved the glass-encased *Yahrzeit* candle he had hoped never to use.

It took five matches before one of them yielded a flame. When he finally got the candle lit, it guttered and flickered. He had not wanted to bring it down here in the first place; a *Yahrzeit* candle was only meant to be used to commemorate the anniversary of the death of a close family member. That was its purpose. That, and that alone; to burn until there was no more candle. To mourn the dead. But because it was encased in a glass holder and fatter than an ordinary candle, Erich insisted it was far more practical for their purposes than the skinny Christmas candles at his house. True, a single *Yahrzeit* candle burned for a whole night and day—but Sol, for one, had no intention of being down here that long.

He stared beyond the small circle of light he had created, into the sewer's nether realms where anything could be lurking. He could not see the walls or the sewer's other entrance, which was a padlocked grate that led into the furrier's subbasement.

"Erich?"

"What!"

"I—" Solomon, about to share his feelings about the

darkness, changed his mind. "Will the puppy be all right here?"

"Why shouldn't he be?" Erich stooped and righted one of the packing crates. He lined it with the blanket and set the puppy inside. "We'll stuff some old rags in the grates so if he whines no one will hear. We'll visit him every day." He stroked the puppy's head. The dog was standing with its forepaws on the edge of the box, its tiny tail wagging. "Won't we, boy!"

"What if we can't get down to see him every day or if our papas see—"

"They won't be able to see anything. We'll put the boxes back over the grate." Erich pursed his lips and made little kissy sounds in front of the dog. "He'll be a real scrapper when he grows up. Like me. Right, Bull?" He scratched the puppy under the chin. "Better bring our own collar with you next time we come down."

"If we're staying down here for a while, we'd better close the grate," Sol said, conceding the argument. "If one of our papas comes down to the cellar—"

"I guess you're right." Erich stopped playing with the puppy. "Give me a boost."

Solomon braced himself and cupped his hands in readiness. He was not enjoying himself. The *Yahrzeit* candle bothered him, Erich's attitude bothered him, and he felt bad about leaving the puppy alone in the sewer. The candle would go out eventually and the little thing would be scared. Hungry, too. What if they came back and found it dead and stiff and covered with mildew?

Eyeing the open drain like an acrobat about to somersault toward an oncoming trapeze bar, Erich placed one foot in Sol's hands and hoisted himself onto the two-by-four. With Sol holding his legs to steady him, he poked his head and shoulders through the hole in the cellar floor. Then, snaking his hand through, he patted around for the crowbar.

"Whatever you do, don't let go, *Spatz*."

"Maybe you'll grow longer if I leave you hanging for a while. Maybe then you'll stop calling me 'Sparrow.'"

"I might do that if you ever stop feeding the little buggers." Erich inserted the crowbar through the slats of the grate, and tugged.

The grate creaked but did not move.

"Damn this! What did you do to it?" He tugged harder, his body straining with the effort.

"Do to it? Nothing," Sol said. He had developed a crick in his neck from trying to see upward. "There! You've got it! No! Wait—something's wrong!"

Something *was* wrong—Sol could feel it. But what? He watched the grate come away from the wall and move to an upright position. As it teetered, he saw the problem.

Erich was balancing himself by holding onto the lip of the hole. His hand—

"Let go!"

Even as Sol yelled, he knew it was too late. The grate clunked down, followed a split-second later by the thud of the crowbar hitting the boards on the sewer floor.

Erich's scream died to a choking gurgle as he pawed at the grate. Light, slanting through the bars, cast pale stripes across his face, and blood curled down his arm. He kicked spastically.

"Erich!" Not knowing what else to do, Solomon held onto Erich's legs.

"Help me!" Erich screamed hysterically.

"Papa!" Sol shouted, as Erich stopped to take a breath between convulsive sobs. "Papa, help us!"

He waited, listening for footsteps, for a voice. At his feet, the puppy softly whimpered.

"Papa!"

A woman's voice answered him, floating out of the sewer's darkness.

Oh God, let me die. I did not know...I did not know.

CHAPTER FIVE

"It hurts! Sol, help me!" Erich tried to take a deep breath between sobs, but the pain was too great. "M-my hand. It's st-stuck! The crowbar! Open the grate. It hurts—it hurts!"

Sol let go of his legs. Erich could vaguely hear Sol rummaging around below. His own body weight was dragging him down, wrenching at his armpit. Oh God, he thought. What if my hand busts right off and my fingers stay up there and—

He heard himself screaming again. His heart was beating so hard, he knew it was about to burst open and fly right out of his body. He forced himself to stop screaming.

"Erich? Are you alive? Answer me!"

Sol's voice came from somewhere outside of Erich's cocoon of pain.

"I'll get there!" Sol was yelling desperately. "I'm trying to pull myself up!"

Why is he crying! Erich wondered, feeling a strange numbness creep over him. Why doesn't he just reach up here and help me? He doesn't have the strength and balance to get past you and shift the grate, some other part of him answered.

"Papa!" Sol shouted again.

Erich could hear him clawing at the slimy walls of the cellar. "Papa!" he screamed, in unison with his friend.

"Solomon? Erich? For God's sake, boys, where are you? What's happened?"

"Papa! Down here!" Sol shouted. "Erich's hurt!"

"Herr Freund! Help me, please!"

"*Gott in Himmel!*" Jacob's voice pleading for God's help came from directly above Erich's head. "I have to find something heavy to pry open this grate. I'll be as quick as I can, boys!"

There was the sound of running footsteps up and down the stairs. Then Herr Freund's voice again. "A moment and you'll be out."

Within seconds, he pried open the grate and hauled Erich out of the sewer like a sack of potatoes. "My hand!" Sobbing, he cupped his injured hand with his good one and blew on it. The ridge where the edge of the grate had flattened his fingers was like raw meat after his mama pounded it in the kitchen. The flesh around the ridge was puffed and red and swollen. He felt sick to his stomach.

"Friedrich!" Jacob Freund called. "Come down here. Your son has been hurt."

He cradled Erich gently and led him to the stairs.

"Wait!" Erich said. "Sol n-needs help getting out."

Herr Freund set Erich down gingerly on the bottom step and went back to the grating. "Here, take hold of me," he told Sol.

He reached into the drain and pulled Sol up through the hole. Sol collapsed onto his knees beside Erich. "You're alive—you're alive!" He was crying.

"He's alive," Jacob said quietly.

"Thank you, Papa!" Sol said. "Thank you. Oh God…what if Erich had died…and nobody knew where we were…and—!"

Jacob put his arm around his son. "Did you think I didn't know about this place? And the dog?"

"You saw?" Erich whispered.

Jacob nodded. "I didn't have the heart to say anything—"

"Erich! What have you done now?" Erich's papa shouted, charging down the stairs and almost tripping over his son. "*Mein Gott*, your hand! Did Solomon do this? I'll—"

"The boys got into the sewer—"

"The sewer!" Breathing hard, his papa bent over Erich. "Idiot! This will break your mama's heart!" He turned to Jacob. "It's all your fault. You should have sealed the drain!"

"Calm down, Friedrich. It was an accident," Jacob Freund said. "Let's leave recriminations for later, shall we, and attend to your son. We must get him to the hospital."

"It hurts, Papa," Erich said, trying not to cry and keeping a tight grip on his injured hand.

His father helped him to his feet. "Let's go," he said.

"But I promise you, when I get back I'm going to seal that place so tight not even a cockroach will be able to get in!"

"I'll take care of it," Jacob said softly. "Now go. And don't worry about the dog, Erich, I'll—"

"Dog? What dog!"

Erich cringed at the look on his papa's face.

"A puppy," Herr Freund said matter-of-factly. "The boys have a puppy down—"

"You insist on disobeying me!" Erich's father shouted.

"Friedrich! This is not the time for anger! I told you, I will take care of everything."

"*No!*" Erich's father shouted. "No! No! No! *You* take him to the hospital. I'm going to take care of this grate, right now, this minute—"

"Sol! Don't let him seal Bull in there!"

Erich had begun to shake uncontrollably.

"The boy's going into shock," Herr Freund said. "He must be kept warm."

He took off his jacket and wrapped it around Erich.

"He's having one of his seizures, Papa," Erich heard Sol say.

Suddenly Erich felt as if a giant fist had punched him in the small of his back. He heard himself scream as his head jerked back tautly and his body arched into a hard bow. He heard his teeth chattering, felt something soft being wedged between his lips. Pinpoints of light exploded in his head and he saw trees layered upon more trees, thick and lush, like a jungle, and a moon—yellow and full and round. The edges of the moon began to melt, coating the leaves in moon-wax....

He lay in a tumbled heap at the bottom of the stairs.

There was pain coming from somewhere; he could feel it, yet it was distanced from him as if it belonged to somebody else. He could not understand why he was lying there, when he felt so strong. He tried to get up but the energy was trapped in his body—

"Erich?" Solomon bent over him.

"A moon," Erich whispered. "I saw a moon...melting like a candle. And trees...everywhere." He tried to reach for Sol. "I was scared—"

Sol pressed his wrist against Erich's. "Blood brothers," he said, sobbing.

CHAPTER SIX

As if he had momentarily forgotten that Erich's father was standing right there, Jacob Freund took the boy in his arms and rocked him. For a moment, Erich appeared to relax. Then he arched his back again, and shuddered convulsively. His eyes were wide open, his pupils so small that Sol expected them to disappear altogether. Instead, his eyes rolled upward. All Sol could see were the whites before they closed and Erich passed out.

Still Herr Weisser stood by, doing nothing.

"Either get help, or hold your boy and *I* will get help," Sol's father said. "Your son is in shock. He must be taken to the hospital."

"Is he going to be all right, Papa?" Solomon asked.

His father nodded. "I told you already, Solomon. He is going to be fine. Fine."

"May I go to the hospital with him?"

"You not only may," his father said, "you must." He laid Erich down on the floor and headed up the stairs. "I'll find help," he called down. "The two of you bring Erich up here. Keep him covered until I get back."

Sol and Herr Weisser labored up the stairs with their inert burden. They placed him on the floor with one jacket over him and another under his head like a pillow. After a few minutes of pacing, Erich's father grew impatient.

"You stupid boys," he said. To Sol's horror, he appeared to be working himself up into one of his tempers. "You have no sense, either of you." He paused for a second, then went on, voice rising as it grew louder. "You watch Erich. I'm going downstairs. I'll make sure this never happens again, you can be certain of that."

He stomped downstairs. Sol heard the yelping of the puppy, punctuated by the scraping of large crates being moved, until, what seemed like hours later, his father returned to the shop. He was followed inside by two burly men. One was shouldering a stretcher, the other carried two blankets and a medical bag.

"There was a shooting near the Reichstag, so there was no ambulance available. No taxis either when you need one." Jacob clutched the doorjamb for support while he struggled to catch his breath. "We had run halfway back from the hospital before—" He stopped and looked around, frowning as if he had just noticed that Friedrich was nowhere to be seen. "Where's Herr Weisser?"

"Down there," Sol said, pointing toward the cellar steps. "He…he's sealing up the sewer."

His father sighed loudly and shook his head. Marching

to the top of the stairs, he yelled down to his partner to come upstairs at once.

Face red from whatever physical effort he had been making, Herr Weisser appeared at the top of the stairs. "Well, Freund, you certainly took your time," he said ungraciously.

Jacob's own face reddened, and he opened his mouth as if to make an angry retort, but apparently thought better of it. "There were no taxis or ambulances available," he said quietly. "Herr Wohmann kindly stopped and brought us here on his wagon. He is waiting to take us to the hospital."

Sol looked up. Through the open doorway, he saw horses pawing uneasily. The closer nag had her head turned back, trying to look around her blinders at the leather-vested vegetable dealer on the back of the wagon, rearranging baskets, apparently making room for them.

"A *hamster* wagon!" Friedrich Weisser sounded outraged. His eyes had narrowed in a look of compressed fury. "I'm not going anywhere on a damn *hamster* wagon." He glanced toward the cellar curtain. "You take him, Jacob. I'll tend to...matters...here."

"For God's sake, Friedrich!" Jacob Freund stared at his partner with stunned incomprehension as the men took the boy from his father and laid him on the stretcher. With Jacob's help from below and Wohmann's from above, they hoisted it and themselves onto the wagon. They had reached down to pull Sol up when a taxi rounded the corner.

"Taxi!" Jacob called out. It came to a screeching halt behind the vegetable wagon.

Dangling halfway between the ground and the top of the wagon, Sol felt suddenly lightheaded. It was as if the reality of Erich's injury were only now taking hold of him. The hands holding him let go and he dropped to the ground, landing unsteadily on his feet.

"A taxi will be faster," Jacob said to the attendants. "Do you think it will harm the boy to move him again?"

"It won't help him," the burly one said. But he nodded at the other man and, together, they reversed the process and settled Erich, *sans* stretcher, onto the back seat. When they had folded the stretcher and placed it somehow in the trunk of the taxi, Solomon and one of the men squeezed in beside the boy, leaving the other medic and Jacob to maneuver themselves into the front seat beside the driver. Friedrich Weisser was nowhere to be seen.

"What about the father?" one of the medics asked.

"We have waited too long already," Sol's father said. His features looked strained. "Let's go."

Obediently but none too smoothly, the taxi driver pulled the car away from the curb. Jolted by the abrupt movement, Erich opened his eyes. Though he was wrapped in a blanket, he was shaking and seemed to be chilled. There was not enough light in the taxi for Sol to see if his pupils were still tiny pinpoints or if they had returned to normal.

The shaking worsened.

"Hope it's not another convulsion. Could affect the brain, too many convulsions," the attendant next to Sol said, almost absently. His white jacket rubbed against Sol; it smelled of disinfectant and ether. "Has he ever had anything like this before today, Herr Freund?"

JANET BERLINER AND GEORGE GUTHRIDGE

"The boy has epilepsy."

"Aha!"

"Not 'Aha,'" Jacob said, "He has small seizures. Not even seizures, really. Small episodes. I'm told the doctor calls them lightning seizures. He never passes out or anything. Just kind of shudders and then gets really sleepy."

The medic had wrapped Erich's fingers in cotton and gauze which was rapidly reddening. Sol watched, fascinated but queasy. The blood was seeping through and spreading like red ink on a blotter. He felt dizzy, as if everything hung at the edge of his consciousness. The voices around him sounded hollow, and his own thoughts felt apart from him. *Don't faint,* he told himself. *Don't look at the blood.*

He forced himself to look straight ahead. He could see the reflection of his father's eyes in the windshield. They looked old and tired. He took a deep breath and looked outside, as though needing to get away, at least until his mind and stomach settled.

They were on a side street, headed toward Unter den Linden. People and traffic moved past as if in a world he no longer inhabited. He wanted to put his head between his legs. Or worse, vomit. He was supposed to be helping his friend, but instead felt sick. What a baby he was, a baby sparrow, like Erich said; too helpless to fly.

He removed his glasses, put his head against the seat-back and tried to keep from passing out. His skin felt cold and clammy, and the world outside seemed to be composed of dots, like the French pointillist painting in the book his mother had shown him during one of the "culture sessions" she insisted upon. His heart was racing. He thought he saw people lined up for a block behind a milk cart, empty bottles in their hands waiting to be refilled.

He could not look away, and suddenly he was no longer in the taxi. He was in the queue. "Last week I waited for six hours," the elderly man behind him in line grumbled, talking to no one in particular. Sol turned around. The gray of the man's woolen beret seemed to bring out the deeply etched lines in his face. "Should have sent one of my grandchildren," he said, putting a beefy hand on Sol's shoulder. "Damn *goyim*," he muttered, watching the policeman near the cart screen the people in line and pull some out to the back of the line.

"Careful," the man behind him warned. "They hear you, we may never get milk. My daughter has children to feed."

There was heavy activity in front as people made a social event of their milk purchases and Jews were rerouted to the back of the line to make room for *real* Germans. Sol looked down at the strange canvas shoes he was wearing and began moving in place, faster and faster, like someone trying to stay warm or treading water. The sidewalk seemed to slip beneath him, like a conveyor belt. He was running in place when several boys in lederhosen trotted by, a familiar face among them.

"Erich!" Sol called out.

His friend halted. "We're off to Luna Park," he said. "They've added a new hall of mirrors to the Panoptikum. Come with us."

Sol shook his head. His feet kept moving. "I have to buy milk," he said, puffing with the effort.

"No problem," Erich said. "Give me the money. I'll get it for you."

Sol gave Erich the two bottles and a fistful of marks.

Erich and the other boys disappeared, to return in what seemed to be an instant, Erich holding a filled bottle in each hand. He held them just out of Sol's reach. "Here they are. Now let's go to Luna Park."

"Can't," Sol said, stretching for the bottles. "Mama—"

"Ma-ma, Ma-ma," Erich mimicked in a baby voice. He swung one of the bottles menacingly over the curb. "You coming with us, or are you going home with *one?*"

"I told you, I—"

Glass and milk splattered. Sol jerked backward to avoid both...and found himself pressing hard against the seat of the taxi, which was slowing as it neared the hospital. Light filtered through the car's window, foggy with the breath of its occupants.

"Moon...melting moon," Erich whispered, eyes open wide and staring upward. "Jungle..." Fur glistening wetly, two black-and-white long-muzzled monkeys hunched over him.

Sol blinked hard and put on his glasses. Quickly, the image vanished. No monkeys...only the attendants. *A dream*, he told himself. *Only a bad dream.*

But then, why was he still frightened?

CHAPTER SEVEN

MAY 1922

Solomon kicked off his shoes and stretched out on top of his eiderdown. He was so tired—and shaken. A few minutes of sleep and he would start studying again, he promised himself. In less than two months it would be his bar mitzvah. He had studying for that and schoolwork and—

His eyes closed.

"Studying dreams, again, *Spatz?*"

"Wha—who—oh, it's you." Sol could feel sweat running down the back of his neck. He shifted his position slightly and glanced at the bed to make sure there were no damp patches. Erich knew nothing about the bedwetting; Sol wanted to keep it that way.

"Still having nightmares?" Erich narrowed his eyes and stared at Sol.

Sol nodded. "What about you?"

"The Bull dream," Erich said. "If it's the last thing I do, I'll pay my father back—"

It had been three-and-a-half years since the accident and, though they were less frequent, the nightmares had not stopped. The day after the accident, groggy with painkillers, Erich swore he could hear Bull gurgling as Herr Weisser drowned him in the canal. He had been dreaming about it ever since. Sol's nightmares were also always the same: Erich screaming; Erich hanging limply from the grate, blood curling down his arm; the woman begging God to let her die; and the monkeys—always the monkeys. Superimposed over all of it, swollen and bloody and bruised, Erich's three crushed fingers—

He looked at Erich's hand, at the pale flesh and the scars, red and raised, like symbiotic vines that had wound themselves around his fingers and taken root. Eventually the scars would turn white, the doctor said. Whiter than the flesh—

"Want to go for a walk—feed the birds—make trouble?" Erich asked.

"I have to study."

Erich perched on the edge of the bed. "Look, *Spatz*, I have an idea. Remember when Karl almost drowned at the swimming meet? Remember how he was terrified of water after that, until they *made* him go swimming again?"

"What's that got to do with me?"

"Saturday, you and your papa went to synagogue and

I was helping in the shop. I got into the furrier's subbasement—"

"How?"

"I have my ways." He took a key chain from his hip pocket. Attached to the chain was a small book-shaped leather pouch which Sol knew contained Erich's lock picks. "There's a padlocked sewer-entrance down there—"

"You went inside!"

"I went looking for that woman you told me about." He raised his voice and mimicked a woman's voice. *"Oh God, let me die. I did not know ...I did not know."*

A thin shiver ran down Sol's spine—the kind his mama said meant a goose had walked on his grave. The nightmares, the fear—how foolish he had been! Maybe there had never been a woman's voice! He should have thought of this before, after the accident and Erich's grand mal seizure, when the doctor told them about some of the strange things that happened to people who had seizures. Sometimes they could not remember anything about what had happened before and after the seizure, and sometimes—during the seizure—they spoke in tongues. Erich's seizure must have been coming on when he was hanging from the grating. He could have mimicked a woman, like now, Sol thought. The sound could easily have been distorted by the sewer's weird acoustics.

Since Erich hated talking about his seizures, Sol decided to keep his latest theory about the voice to himself—at least for now. "You didn't go down by yourself," he said.

"Yes, I did." Erich looked at him and relented. "No. I didn't go down. But we're going down there tonight. I've decided."

Sol got up and walked over to his window. Two workmen were erecting an awning above the entrance into what had been the furrier's basement and was now about to become a cabaret. From where he stood, he could not see the steps leading down; the awning looked like it was at street level.

Once down those steps and through the door, there was a circular flight of metal stairs. After the basement—the cabaret—came a low-ceilinged subbasement, on the same level as the cellar beneath the tobacco shop. And beneath both shops...the sewer.

"Forget it," Sol said. "We're not going down there."

"You're afraid." Erich joined him at the window.

"I am not!" Sol knew he didn't sound convincing. Even if it had been Erich's voice playing tricks on him, the boys had promised on their honor never to play in sewers again—and their fathers had welded the tobacco shop's grate shut just in case. "Our papas will kill us if they catch us. The watchman could see us—"

"The construction-crew watchman won't be there tonight." Erich's eyes shone expectantly. "I saw him earlier this afternoon outside a Schultheiss. He was holding a quart of Pilsner and bragging to some girl about how his crew is so ahead of schedule he's been assigned to another project."

"I still don't think..."

"Tell you what." Erich sounded as if he'd just had an idea, but judging from the look on his face, Sol suspected his friend had worked out the answers to all of Sol's possible objections ahead of time. "Bet your pewter soldiers against my bike there's no woman in the sewer."

Erich's voice had that *it's no use arguing about this one* tone to it that Solomon knew only too well.

"You might as well hand over the soldiers right now. Voices come attached to bodies. If there ever was a real woman in the sewer, Papa would've found her."

Erich's face darkened in anger and Sol guessed his friend was thinking about Bull. Neither of them was sure what Herr Weisser had done with the puppy; he had refused to talk to them about it. But Erich knew. Or so he said.

"I have to hear her…the woman…or you lose." Erich dangled the lock-pick pouch in front of Solomon's face.

"That's dumb! Your bike against my soldiers? Dumb!"

Erich grinned and pushed a hand through his sandy hair. "I only bet on sure things. The voice was all in your mind. The trouble with you is, you read too much."

Sol watched the sparrows pecking at cracks in the sidewalk. They were not nearly as bad as the pigeons everyone hated—Berlin's second-worst enemy, the city council called them. What perversity kept him feeding the sparrows, he did not know. Habit, maybe. He had been taking them bags of crumbs since Recha was a baby. There were times, he thought, when he wished they would repay him by flying overhead and decorating his friend's hair. That would cure Erich of some of his arrogance!

The cabaret's awning slapped and heaved in the breeze. Startled, the sparrows took wing. The black-, red-, and gold-striped canvas billowed like a flag honoring the

Republic; beneath it, newly installed hand and guard rails—painted the hue of ripe bananas—shone in the weak afternoon light. A door veneered with sculpted ceramics had replaced the mass of rusted iron and enormous locks and bolts that had formerly marked the entrance. It led into a basement likewise transformed, for the furriers had moved all their inventory—wardrobe crates, odorous with mothballs and filled with coats of leopard, mink, and seal—from there to the building's upper two levels.

During the past month, he and Erich had watched the nightclub take shape. Sol enjoyed listening to the sawing and hammering, and he liked the smell of the new lumber. Leather-aproned carpenters and chalk-faced plasterers scuttled up and down the steps. He and Erich snickered at the effeminate gray-haired decorator in purple plus-fours who stood on the sidewalk, frenetically waving his arms whenever things seemed to be going wrong. Any day now, according to Solomon's mother, trucks would arrive with furniture—God should only grant her such elegant things as she had heard were coming, she said.

The door of the tobacco shop opened and Sol's father stepped out.

Jacob Freund was a thin, bespectacled man whose neck, constricted in his high starched collar, made him look rather like a rooster. He shielded his eyes from the sun and gestured to Sol to come outside.

"See. Even your papa thinks you should get some fresh air," Erich said. "Let's go outside. You can study after supper. There will be plenty of time before we meet to go down there."

"I haven't agreed to go, yet," Sol said, though by now he knew—and so did Erich—that it was as good as done.

Chapter Eight

"Well, boys—it seems as if it's actually going to happen." Jacob put a hand lightly on each of the boys' shoulders as they joined him on the sidewalk outside the shop. He smiled, and the crows' feet around his eyes deepened.

"Do you really think the nightclub will help the furriers all that much, Herr Freund?" Erich asked.

"It's bound to."

All of Berlin's businesses had been hurt by the rising inflation that had seized the city following the war, especially luxury shops like *Das Ostleute Haus*. Frau Rathenau's offer to buy their basement and subbasement had been a double blessing. Not only would the money help keep the furrier shop afloat, Sol's father explained, but the kinds of people who would frequent the cabaret were also those who could afford life's other amenities.

"It will help the whole street." There was a soberly

thankful tone to Jacob's voice. "Our business is sure to boom, not to mention that the cabaret will afford us the opportunity to meet and mingle with people such as the Rathenaus and their peers." He looked seriously at Erich and then at Solomon. "People whose decisions spell the future not only of Berlin but of the entire Fatherland—"

The pounding of a hammer interrupted him as a workman, standing on a ladder at the bottom of the basement stairs, unceremoniously nailed up a rectangular, mahogany-stained plaque above the door. The edges of the plaque were trimmed with a delicate gilt band, and the graceful lettering stood out black and bold:

KAVERNE

The sign gave Solomon a sense of satisfaction. He was proud of his neighborhood. Most of the store owners had moved to the more residential areas; he was glad his family had not—especially now. A cabaret, right here on his street! Papa said most of Berlin's nightclubs had sprung up after the war, when the Kaiser's *Tanzverbot*— the antidancing edict—was lifted. They were clustered along Leipziger Strasse, near the Kaiserhof Hotel and the Prussian State Theater. Many of them were known for the decadence of their patrons, whose outrageous behavior made for meaty reading in the weekend papers.

Frau Rathenau's purchase of the furrier's basement had made the newspapers, too. A columnist for *Der Weltspiegel*, Berlin's most widely read Sunday entertainment insert, had quoted her as saying that she had deliberately chosen to open her nightclub away from the riffraff. Kaverne was, she had said, part of her

"...crusade to bring respectability to Berlin's entertainment industry." The columnist had suggested that the real purpose of the cabaret was to showcase the talents of her granddaughter—Foreign Minister Walter Rathenau's niece, Miriam, who had recently returned from America.

"I'll be back, boys. Don't go away...I have something to show you." Jacob released the boys and went back into his shop.

"If we don't go down tonight, we may never get there," Erich said as soon as Sol's father was out of earshot. "If you're too scared, I'll go alone. Once the cabaret opens, there's no way we'll get in."

"I told you, I'm scared of getting caught, not of going down there," Sol said, gesturing emphatically.

"I'll bet there's a woman's body behind one of the walls at the end of the sewer," Erich said, as if trying to goad him into agreeing. "Maybe someone sealed her up back there, like the guy in that Poe story Herr Schoenfelder made us read."

In one of their many discussions about the subject, the boys had decided the sewer had probably once been a dungeon and that there were all kinds of bones shored up behind the wall. The idea of finding them might thrill his friend, Sol thought, but it was not his idea of a good time. "I still don't think—"

"If you're worried about the bet, forget it," Erich said. As if signaling for silence, he held up his crushed hand. "Tonight. We'll meet at—" He pulled up his sweater sleeve and checked his watch. "Midnight," he said, obviously carried away by his own sense of melodrama.

If only one of their papas had sealed off that

subbasement, Sol thought again, feeling less sure of his theory that the voice he had heard was Erich's. Something awful could be waiting for them down in that brick bowel.

"I—" Sol clamped his lips shut as the bell over the door of the tobacco shop jangled and his father reemerged, waving a card embossed with calligraphy.

"You see?" His father ran a thin, long-nailed finger along the lettering as if to prove the invitation was indeed a reality, then placed it carefully in the breast pocket of his three-piece suit. "Already our foot is in the door. Oma Rathenau has invited all of us, the Freunds and the Weissers, to a private dinner party in celebration of the cabaret's opening. Good thing she is not as stingy as her husband was. He would never have invited us!"

Though Sol had never met the Rathenau family, he had seen them occasionally at synagogue—not Walther, who did not deny he was a Jew but never went to *shul*— but Mathilde, Walther's mother; his father, Emil; and his younger sister. He knew that Emil, who'd died when Sol was little, had built an empire after using a small loan to buy the German rights to the Edison invention; everyone knew that.

"Mathilde Rathenau is the grand dame of the Allgemeine Elektrizitats Gesellschaft—the General Electric Company combine," Jacob Freund said. "She will insist on preserving the integrity of the Rathenau name. You watch. There will be only genteel people at her nightclub." He patted his pocket with pride. "Two weeks from tonight we shall dine with the cream of Berlin."

"I dine with the cream of Berlin every evening," Ella Freund said, coming out of the shop. "Now why don't you take care of the customers, Jacob, while I put supper on the table. You're welcome to join us, Erich."

The boy shook his head and mumbled his thanks. "Have to go. See you later, Sol."

"Later, he will be at his studies," Sol's mother said. "Why don't you two take a walk or something. Wake him up, Erich. He has a lot to do before bedtime. Have you practiced your cello?"

"Not yet, Mama."

"You had better not neglect your music." She turned to Jacob. "Have you told him?"

"Told me what, Mama?"

"To express our thanks to Mathilde Rathenau, Recha will dance and you will play your cello at the opening of the cabaret."

"But I'm not good enough to play for those people—"

"We do not ask you to be a genius—simply that you show you are a cultured young man."

Cultured, schmultured, Sol thought, a sick feeling settling in his stomach. Was it not enough that he loved music? Did he have to be forced to make a fool of himself in front of—what was it his father had called them, "...the cream of Berlin"?

Erich decided he did not have to leave quite yet, so the boys continued watching the construction. At the first sign of dusk, the workers started packing up their tools.

"Now," Sol said, making a decision. "We go down now or forget it."

"Are you crazy? It's light enough for them to see us!"

"They're used to us. If we wander in like we're just curious, they'll probably ignore us."

"You really mean it, don't you?" Erich looked dumbfounded. "Listen, you don't have to punish *me* just because your parents want you to make an idiot of yourself with your cello."

"Never mind about the cello. Do you want to do it— or not?" Sol enjoyed the shift in power. Suddenly he, and not Erich, was in command.

Sol was right. Nobody noticed them as they wandered into the half-finished cabaret and down into the subbasement.

"Over here." Erich knelt beside the padlocked drain.

"Well, open it." With a little luck, Sol thought, the padlock will be too rusty to budge and we won't have to go into the sewer.

However, it took Erich no time at all to pry the lock open. The grate was as heavy as the one in the tobacco shop, but Erich opened it easily.

"I'll go first," Sol said, deciding he might as well go all the way with his playing the leader. Besides, he was a lot taller than Erich; the drop would be shorter for him and he could help his friend down.

The sewer smelled damp and fetid. Hardly any light filtered down, but Erich's pocket, which always seemed to hold an endless array of surprises, yielded a candle.

"See, I told you." Erich lit the candle and held it up to extend the circle of light. "There's nothing here."

Erich's voice was a little tremulous. The place didn't exactly hold pleasant memories for him either, Sol reminded himself. And his friend was right. There was nothing down here—except slime and mold, he thought, touching the wall and wiping his fingers on his pants.

Herr Weisser had cleared out everything except the dismantled packing crates. Sol sat down and heaved a sigh of relief.

Erich laughed. "Did you really expect to find some woman hiding out? Lucky for you I took back the bet or you'd owe me one set of pewter soldiers. I'm going to search for bones. You coming?"

"Not yet." Sol was convinced now that his theory about Erich's voice was correct, but he was playing the game. He could soon hear Erich scratching around the bricks.

"Oh God, let me die!"

Sol went rigid with fear.

"I did not know...I did not know."

He waited, holding his breath. Then a man with a strange accent whispered something about blood, and another, his voice old and worn, rambled on about lice and corpses and cold, and pleaded for borscht to quiet his belly-pains.

"Erich!"

"What is it?" Erich held up the candle. "Bogeyman get you?"

Sol didn't answer. He knew without asking that Erich had not heard them—not the woman, or the man whispering, or the other one, who spoke of death and of hunger. They were speaking to him, to Solomon, in voices only he could hear.

C HAPTER NINE

Two weeks later, dressed and ready for the private opening of the cabaret, Sol returned to the sewer. He and Erich had come back several times together, but this was the first time Sol had come alone. They had left the padlock in place but unlocked, so he had no trouble opening the grate and climbing down. Though he had brought a candle, he did not light it.

He sat in the blackness and listened.

The voices would come, he knew that now. What he did not know was why he was stupid enough to come back, or why he would worsen the terror by sitting in the dark. He considered himself the brains of the Weisser-Freund team. Some brains!

Then again, he decided, he had reason to hide tonight. Not only did he loathe performing, he was terrible at it. And he got stage fright. But no amount of begging had changed his parents' minds about his cello performance at tonight's function. "The children of a cultured household," Jacob said, "must understand music and be ready and eager to perform at a moment's notice." It was tradition, he said; though why people should suffer for tradition's sake was never adequately explained. After hearing Gregor Piatigorsky play, he could harbor no illusions about his own ability. Gregor, who had fled Russia by swimming the Sbruch River, holding his cello over his head while border guards shot at him, had performed in the Freunds' music room, and had played like an angel.

If Sol lived to be a hundred, he would never play that well, nor would he forget his mortification when his father insisted he perform for Gregor. He had squeaked and sawed through part of Haydn's *Concerto in D Major*, bowed—cheeks burning at the guests' tolerant smiles— and retired to his bedroom before bursting into tears.

Tonight would be worse. One of the honored guests was Walther Rathenau, Germany's newly appointed Foreign Minister and heir to the Rathenau fortune.

He gazed forlornly up into the darkness, toward the cabaret. If only he had refused to play for Gregor, there would be no issue now—

A baby began to shriek.

Sol shuddered violently and jammed his hands over his ears.

The wailing grew louder.

Pressing his back against the bricks, he kicked his legs as if to drive away the sound. It made him think of the lambs at the slaughterhouse he had visited before Passover a few years ago, of a lost kitten, of an infant too young to put words to whatever terror it was feeling.

Hearing voices, words, that was one thing. But this was really crazy. "Go away!" he shouted. "Leave me alone."

He took his hands away from his ears. The crying had died to a sob and soon only his own breathing rasped in the darkness. He took a deep breath, let it out slowly, and thought about lighting the candle, but the dark was almost comforting—like when he removed his glasses and images were out of focus—his own special, personal world. It was the silence that was making him suffer: he kept expecting it to fill with voices. If some outside noise would only restore a sense of reality to the sewer, he would feel better.

Sitting perfectly still, he looked up through the sewer's opening into the subbasement. With over a hundred guests in the cabaret upstairs, the music, at least, should be filtering down from above. There—he could hear it now; first the melodious cry of a violin, then the tinkle of a piano. A timpani joined in.

Someone, probably a waiter, dropped a tray and, instinctively, Sol ducked.

Elbows on knees and head down, he examined his choices. He could stay in a hideaway that had probably once been part of a medieval torture chamber or enter a modern torture chamber, complete with audience and an instrument of terror—his cello.

"Solomon?"

"Erich?" Sol rose to help his friend descend by guiding his feet to the two-by-twelve they had installed as a step at this—the cabaret—end. "Am I ever glad it's you."

"Expecting one of your ghosts?" Erich hopped down. Using the cigarette lighter he had taken from the shop, he lit a candle he had stolen from the Seifenvogel laundry opposite Bellevue Station. "Your papa sent me to look for you. He's pretty upset that you aren't there yet," he said.

"I'm not exactly happy myself," Sol said, though now that Erich was here he felt a little stupid at his reaction to what was probably only a stray kitten up in the subbasement.

He transferred his gaze to Erich, saw what his friend was wearing, and suppressed the urge to laugh. His amusement did not escape his friend.

"None of this was my idea." Erich touched his slicked-back hair. He had on pressed trousers, a white shirt with starched, rounded collar, and his father's silk paisley cravat. "At least I'm at the party, not hiding in the dark like a cockroach."

"You're not at the party. You're here with me."

"You know what I mean!" Erich raised the candle and looked at Solomon's face. "You been crying?"

"Of course not!" Sol stared down at the crate boards on the floor.

"Worrying about ghosts again? Guess I was wrong—I shouldn't have talked you into coming back down here. God, you're a baby!"

Shoving past Sol, Erich walked over to a clothes rod they had set up. Dangling from a coat hanger were a white shirt, a black tie, and suspenders: the uniform of his Freikorps-Youth unit.

"Pull yourself together, *Spatz*." He picked lint and dust off the outfit. "Fears are for queers."

"It's the cello. You know how much I hate performing. I can't go up there. I just can't!"

"Then don't perform," Erich said coolly. "If your papa says you have to play, tell him to—" He paused. "Just tell him no."

"Easy for you to say. You do whatever you want these days."

"That's right." Erich clenched his fist and narrowed his eyes. "They say I can't have a dog? I'll have any dog I want, and Papa won't be able to stop me. No one's ever again going to drown something I own. And no one tells me what to do! Like they said I couldn't join the Freikorps. 'Not until you're fifteen!'" He did a whining imitation of his mother. "What an idiot."

"You shouldn't talk about your mother like that," Sol muttered. Erich had secretly joined the Freikorps the morning after he and Sol picked the lock of the cabaret and reentered the sewer that first time. Since then, he seemed to think of himself as older, wiser, more daring than ever, as if joining the movement had turned him into some kind of hero.

"I wish she could see me in this." Erich was admiring his uniform again.

"Your mother?"

Erich eyed Solomon with disdain. "Miriam. Rathenau's niece. She's really something." He made a slurping noise as if he were about to wolf down a piece of his mother's plum cake. Setting down the candle, he slid the suspenders off the shirt and held it across his chest. "Girls love uniforms."

"Clean uniforms, maybe. I wish you'd wash that thing. It stinks of dogs."

"One of the bitches at the camp just had puppies." Erich's voice was heavy with longing. "They'll keep the perfect ones and destroy the rest. If it weren't for my parents…"

"*You'd* take a reject?"

Staring off into the shadows, Erich did not seem to notice the implied insult. "I could give one of the puppies to Rathenau's niece. Papa said her dog died in the accident that killed her parents. Can you see me arriving at Miriam Rathenau's house in my uniform? With a puppy…maybe even two?"

His friend talked about girls as though he were Romeo, Sol thought, but if he had to choose between a dog and a girl, he would almost certainly choose the animal. "She probably wouldn't even speak to you if you went there dressed in that thing," he said.

"Her uncle financed a Freikorps unit during the war. Everyone knows that."

"That was before things changed. Besides, you're in the Freikorps-*Youth*. That's different. People in her part of society look down on you. The *Berliner Tageblatt* called you and your pals 'pawns in short pants.'"

"Who cares about that conservative rag!"

"Which of your precious Freikorps leaders said *that?*" Sol asked. Erich parroted them more and more. "Your parents read the *Tageblatt*, you know."

"I told you, they're idiots."

"Maybe you're the idiot."

For a moment there was fierce anger in Erich's eyes. Then he said, "Just forget it." He replaced the suspenders on the hanger. "Want to go to the matinee tomorrow? *The Cabinet of Doctor Caligari* is playing at the Marmorhaus."

Sol shook his head. "I don't know why you enjoy films

about murder and madness. I'd rather save my money for one of Elizabeth Bergner's plays."

"You really are a baby! No wonder you don't care about meeting Miriam Rathenau. You wouldn't know what to do with her."

"And you do?"

Before Erich could answer, a girl began singing in the cabaret.

"*Glühwürmchen, Glühwürmchen, glimm're...*" Shine little glowworm, glimmer, glimmer...

"Glowworm" was one of Sol's favorite songs. The composer, Paul Lincke, often visited his two spinster nieces late at night in their flat in the building next door to the Freunds to try out his latest melodies on them. The sound of their old piano would fill Sol's room. When he fell asleep to the strains of *Lady Moon*, his dreams were enchanted. But Lincke's music had never sounded like this—innocent, earthy, a firefly love song that filled Sol with feelings he did not understand.

The song ended to applause. "That was *her* singing," Erich said. "I'm going back up. I'll tell your papa I couldn't find you, but you don't know what you're missing!"

Sol tried to imagine what Rathenau's niece looked like. If she were half as wonderful as her voice—

"Someday I'll be a man and wear what I want and do what I want all the time," Erich said in a hoarse whisper. "Papa won't be able to order me around anymore." He boosted himself onto the plank and crawled up through the drain.

Sol stepped onto the board and poked his head

through the hole. Erich, guided by the light seeping through the gap beneath the door upstairs, was climbing the steps to the cabaret. Miriam Rathenau had begun a second song. If he stayed in the sewer, Sol thought, the voices would return—and even if they did not, the fear would. He spat on his fingers, snuffed the candle, and crawled out. Closing the grate behind him, he ascended the steps and stretched out on his stomach across the top several stairs.

With his cheek pressed against the top landing, he tried to peer through the gap beneath the door.

Finding it hard to focus, he pushed his glasses as high as he could up his nose and held them there with his index finger. Now he could see plush red carpet, a metal table leg, three pairs of trousers resting on shiny black shoes, and white high heels festooned with seed pearls. But nothing resembling a beautiful young girl.

He stood and inched open the door.

"Wenn der weisse Flieder wieder blüht," Miriam Rathenau sang. "When the white lilac blooms again…" She held the microphone lightly with one hand. The other was slightly raised. There was about her a combination of delicacy and boldness—her face expressive, her body graceful and lean.

Something inside Solomon exploded. Standing there in the middle of the dance floor beneath a spotlight, the girl created a new universe for him. For an instant nothing existed except white tights, a form-fitting tunic, a knee-length swirl of pale pink niñon. Gradually he began to notice other things: the rose-colored shawl that draped her shoulders; her dark hair, pinned in a dancer's chignon and decorated with a spray of white lilac; the piano player, dressed in sequined tails and top hat and smiling up at her from the Blüthner baby grand.

It wasn't until she turned her head slightly to return the piano player's smile that reality intruded. Until that moment she had been facing Sol, and though he knew he was hidden in the dark of the stairway, he had felt she was singing for him alone.

He looked around the cabaret. Twenty tables ringed the dance floor. Each was set with an ecru tablecloth and a spray of lilac. It was easy to see his mother's hand in the decorating, for while some of the flowers were white, most were that shade between pink and white that was her favorite. Fine crystal, silverware, and gold-rimmed china gleamed beneath chandeliers fit for the palace of the Kaiser. Waiters in black tie and tails moved among the guests, offering a fish course. Silver platters were laden with exquisitely poached salmon, filet of sole, and sturgeon embellished with olive-green capers; there was even beluga caviar, sprinkled with chopped eggs and served on tiny rounds of pumpernickel.

The guests were arrayed in diamonds and lace, taffeta and ostrich feathers. White tuxedos trimmed in magenta vied for attention with chiffon and brocade cut from patterns designed to conceal or reveal secrets of the flesh. Smoke from cigarettes in silver holders curled into the glow of the spotlight. Everyone eyed Miriam Rathenau with rapt attention.

Erich was no exception. He and his parents were seated at Walther Rathenau's table, but right now it was not the Foreign Minister who impressed him. Face alive with nervous energy and anticipation, eyes bright, Erich focused on Miriam Rathenau as if he also felt she were performing only for him.

Chapter Ten

"*Wenn der weisse Flieder wieder.*" Miriam paused and dropped her voice. "*Blüht,*" she ended softly.

She curtsied and listened to the applause.

With a few exceptions, it was what she had expected from an audience that measured its responses with care even after a virtuoso performance at the Berlin Opera. They were boring, the Germans, always controlled and disciplined—so unlike the Americans, with their wild enthusiasms and their appreciation for anything the least bit extraordinary.

Well, let them try to be neutral about this next number, she thought. She nodded to the piano player, who struck up a lively tune, his fingers springing across the keys.

Smiling, she flung aside her shawl and broke into a modified cancan, whirling, kicking—low at first, then higher—until her foot was above her head...repeating the routine until, with a suddenness calculated to send an ache through the groin of the shy-looking young man who had just crept into the room, the music ended and she dropped into a split.

The boy stared at her with his mouth open, as if she were a fairy princess and he the frog prince. The audience, less restrained, clapped louder; someone even called, "Brava!"

Resting easily in the split, Miriam touched one knee with her forehead, bent the other leg under her and used it to propel herself back onto her feet.

The boy seated at her Uncle Walther's table, evidently unable to contain himself, jumped to his feet and began clapping wildly.

Her uncle raised a black eyebrow in apparent amusement at the boy's excitement, and smiled at her. Easing his narrow shoulders against the back of the chair, he stroked his goatee, removed his cigar from his mouth, and blew a perfect smoke ring into the air. Despite his obvious pride in his niece, he took the time to flick a stray piece of ash from the sleeve of his finely tailored evening suit and replaced the cigar in his mouth before applauding.

After curtsying a second time, Miriam threaded her way to her uncle's table. She was almost there when her grandmother held out a gloved hand and touched her arm.

"You have given me much pleasure, my child. You never knew your Uncle Walther's brother. He died when he was fourteen…a little younger than you are now. He had the same delicacy you have…the same way of holding his head—"

As if contact with her granddaughter's young body had made her feel young and beautiful again and she no longer needed to hide her wrinkles, the elderly woman removed her gloves. Her hands were heavy with diamonds. Miriam glanced at them and then back into her grandmother's eyes. They held a sadness that spoke of more than the death of her asthmatic second son.

Miriam smiled prettily and bent to hug her grandmother. "Thank you, Oma. What a wonderful way to welcome me home from the United States."

"The delight is all mine, Miriam. Now go and have fun. That young man at your table will burst if you don't get there soon."

The band had begun to play and couples were gravitating toward the dance floor as Miriam approached her uncle's table. The boy's mother said something to him and, with a sickly, silly grin, he bowed formally and pulled out a chair for Miriam.

Wondering how he had injured his hand, she started to sit. Her uncle half-rose expectantly and, knowing what he wanted, she leaned over and kissed his cheek. Then she took her seat and smiled her thanks to the boy.

"I'm Erich Weisser." He beamed as he scooted his chair closer to hers.

"Hello, Erich Weisser." She looked toward the other boy. "And who's he? Your brother?"

"My best friend, *Spatz*."

"*Spatz*? What kind of name is that?"

Erich laughed nervously. "I call him 'Sparrow' because he's always feeding the darn things. His name's Solomon Freund. His sister Recha is the one over there at the table next to us, staring at you. Those are his parents next to her."

"Why aren't they sitting with us?" Miriam smiled across at the young girl named Recha, who appeared transfixed.

"There wasn't room for all of us at this table so our papas—" He hesitated.

"They did what?"

"Rolled dice for who'd get to sit here," Erich said.

Though Miriam tried not to laugh, she could not help herself. "Did you hear that, Uncle Walther? They—"

"Don't say anything. Please." Erich's face was red.

Miriam stopped. She really hadn't meant to embarrass the boy. It was just so typical—so German!

Stretching out her hand, she introduced herself to Erich's parents and exchanged a few pleasantries with them. That ought to make the boy feel better, she thought, not particularly taken by Herr and Frau Weisser. The woman looked nervous; the man, at best, uncomfortable. His nose was red, as if he had been drinking too much, and his eyes were hard. Clearly, they were not enjoying themselves.

She glanced sideways at the boy; he had his father's square jaw but, unlike either of his parents, he had light hair and was quite good looking.

She turned her attention back to the Freunds. Recha's mother was removing a lace handkerchief from her evening bag and handing it to the girl. While she blew her nose, her father tugged nervously at his shirt cuffs and glanced anxiously about the room as if he thought the blowing might be offensive. Sol's mother leaned over and whispered something in her husband's ear. His eyes flashed angrily behind his thick lenses as he turned toward the frog prince, who had finally stepped all the way into the room.

By now, the waiters had begun to ladle out the entrée of sauerbraten and dumplings, which her uncle had requested. It was plebeian fare, but he had declared himself tired of foreign foods after his recent journey across the Atlantic. Reluctantly, for she missed America, whose chefs ironically prided themselves on producing superb European cuisines, Miriam lifted her fork.

"Your friend looks lonely," she said. "Why not ask him to sit with us?"

"Later. " Erich spoke without conviction. "Right now he's got stage fright. His papa wants his little sparrow to entertain us."

Miriam looked from one boy to the other. How very different they seemed! She liked Erich's Aryan good looks but there was something about Sparrow—

What had Erich said the boy's real name was? Solomon. Solomon Freund...wise friend. He looked more like his nickname, a sparrow hoping for tidbits of congeniality, for someone to reach out a hand or offer a crust of conversation and draw him in among the crowd. Something about him reminded her of the boys in her ballet class—not homosexual, but sensitive. That appealed to her as well; he seemed forlorn as he stood gazing at the cello that stood like a sentinel amid the shadows in the corner of the room. By the looks of him, he would rather face a firing squad than perform in public, and seemed about to retreat down the stairs.

"I'm going to ask him to join us," she told Erich.

She got up and walked toward Solomon, but she was

too late. His father had seen him and was holding up a hand in a gesture that warned Sol to stay where he was. Pushing himself from the table, he gave a peremptory bow to the guests near him and made his way toward his son. Smiling and nodding in greeting to several guests who glanced up curiously, he guided Sol through the doorway.

Miriam followed them. Herr Freund had left the door slightly ajar. She pushed at it gently, let herself through, and found herself standing in the shadows at the top of a flight of stairs. There appeared to be a storage room at the bottom of the steps, and she could hear voices.

She went down just far enough to be able to see Solomon and his father; they stood under a dangling naked lightbulb.

"Sit down." Herr Freund gestured toward a wooden box next to a pair of ancient, discolored laundry sinks.

Sol did as he was told. The bare light swung to and fro as, scowling, his father stood over him.

"So, and where have you been?" Jacob clicked open an engraved gold watchcase that hung from a chain across his waist. "You're such an important fellow that you need not show up on time for a party at which our Foreign Minister is present?"

Sol started to answer, apparently thought better of it, and sat with his eyes downcast.

Jacob put a foot on an adjacent box. "Poor Miriam Rathenau had to do an encore for which she was quite unprepared."

Unprepared! She controlled a giggle as Herr Freund wiped dust from his shoes with a handkerchief he took from his trouser pocket. The popular Reichsbanner handkerchief in the breast pocket of his pinstriped *Shabbas* suit was doubtless just for show, Miriam thought. The way Germans felt about their country, only a lout would soil a cloth that resembled the flag of the Fatherland.

"She looked prepared to me, Papa," Sol said in a low, weak voice. He reached for a rag on a packing crate and brushed the dust from his own shoes.

"Don't argue with me!" Jacob removed his glasses and, squinting angrily at Sol, wiped the lenses clean, refolded the handkerchief, and placed it back in his pocket. "She's a mature girl—too mature for her years—so she carried it off."

"Yes, Papa."

"It is rude to keep anyone waiting, you know that. But it is idiotic, Solomon Freund, to offend such as Walther Rathenau—and not just for business reasons."

"I know Herr Rathenau is an important man." Sol fidgeted, his head still lowered.

"Not merely an important man. An important Jew."

"You are an important Jew, Papa." Solomon looked up. "You won the Iron Cross, First Class."

"Ah, the Iron Cross!" Jacob chuckled sadly as he dusted off a box with his hand and sat down. "For that you would consider me another Rathenau? Look at me, Solomon." He turned his palms up in supplication. "I'm an ordinary Jew, forty-nine years old, a Berlin seller of tobacco. Hardly a Walther Rathenau."

Even at that distance, Miriam could sense that a sadness had displaced Herr Freund's wrath.

"One of every six German Jews fought in the Great

War, Solomon. One out of six! That means almost every young male German Jew served the Fatherland."

He paused, and when he spoke again his voice had taken on the quality of a man immersed in memory.

"A third of us were decorated, another twelve thousand died. So I was not alone—or special. When we stood in formation to receive our medals, the names of the Gentile recipients were read alphabetically, then came the Jews. That's how it went in every platoon and company in the army. We Jews who had fought and lived, and we who had fought and died—all those to be decorated—we were all at the bottom of the lists." He put a trembling hand on Solomon's shoulder. "That is why the respect and friendship of a man like Walther Rathenau, himself a Jew, is so important—so your surname will never be at the bottom of a list."

"But isn't the Foreign Minister only half-Jewish?" Sol asked.

"There is no such thing," Jacob Freund said, looking directly at his son, "as being half-Jewish."

A long silence followed as Solomon stared into his father's eyes. He seemed unnerved by his father's sudden vulnerability. Miriam thought about her uncle, the only older man she really knew. He had always seemed to her to be larger than life despite his small stature. She realized it would unnerve her too, if she were forced to look into the face of his humanness.

"I think you understand what I have been trying to say," Solomon's father said quietly, standing up. "Let us go upstairs."

Quickly Miriam scooted back into the cabaret and

waited near the door for father and son to reenter. They did so together. Then Jacob moved ahead though the crowd.

Crossing the dance floor, he removed the cello from its mahogany case and placed it against a chair where it could easily be reached. He stood before the band and raised his hands for quiet. There seemed a calmness, a surety in his actions, as though he, and not her uncle, were the honored guest—as if this were his party.

"We of the Freund family are honored to be the friends and guests of Walther Rathenau, our esteemed Foreign Minister; of his esteemed mother, Mathilde; and his lovely and talented niece, Miriam." Jacob bowed slightly to each in turn. "In our house we like to listen to our two children perform together." He watched Sol take the cello bow from its case and snap the lid shut. "Recha sings and dances, and Solomon accompanies her. Our little Recha has become the darling, if I may say so, of the Berlin Singakademia."

Jacob waited for the brief round of applause to end. "Both of our children were to perform tonight in small repayment to you, Frau Rathenau," he bowed in Oma's direction, "for the wonderful companionship and dinner we have so enjoyed. Unfortunately, Recha has a cold. Therefore, Solomon will do a solo."

He looked at Sol, who bowed slightly and managed a weak smile.

"Solomon has not had quite the musical training Recha has enjoyed, but we should all remember that, in the world of music, unlike in business," Jacob nodded toward Friedrich Weisser, "or even in politics," a nod toward Rathenau, "the very act of performing is often

JANET BERLINER AND GEORGE GUTHRIDGE

at least as important as the product." Gesturing toward Sol, Jacob stepped aside. "So now, it is with great pride that I give you my son...."

Walking as if his knees had turned to liquid, Solomon clutched the neck of the cello and moved into the spotlight. He bowed to the audience.

Feeling a mixture of empathy and amusement, Miriam waited for the first note. When it came, she was relieved to find herself not entirely unimpressed. His playing was tenuous, but the emotion was there, the caring which, for her, shifted technique to secondary importance. She closed her eyes and let the sweet strains of Haydn flow around her. When it was over, she opened her eyes and applauded loudly. She would introduce herself to Solomon and tell him that he was not nearly as poor a performer as he seemed to think.

She rose and walked toward him, but was not quick enough. Apparently terrified that he might be required to give an encore, he bowed and fled the room. Disappointed, Miriam headed back to her table.

"I really enjoyed that," she said to Erich, who had once again jumped up to pull out her chair. "Please ask him to come back."

"He won't."

Erich sat down. He had a strange expression on his face, like a swimmer on the verge of diving into icy water.

"He'd come back if...if...you asked him," the boy said. "We could go for a walk...maybe...until he calms down...and then look for him together—"

"I'm starving. I have to eat something first or I'll faint right into your arms in the street," Miriam said, teasing.

She wondered if Erich always stammered like that when he felt embarrassed. Or perhaps it was only when he did not feel in control of a situation, she thought. She had met men like that—grown men who had wanted her and were embarrassed by feeling that way about a fifteen-year-old.

"L-later? All right."

Seeing his crestfallen expression, Miriam relented. She took a slice of dark pumpernickel from a silver basket and bit into it hungrily. "Don't they feed the entertainers in Germany, Uncle Walther?" She motioned at the bare tablecloth in front of her.

"My profound apologies, Fräulein Rathenau," Erich's mother said. "I will rectify the situation immediately. You were—"

"Don't take me seriously, Frau…Weisser." At the last moment, she remembered the woman's name. "This will do just fine, thank you—as long as you save me some of those nonpareils they're serving with dessert. I crave them."

She took a second slice of bread and stood up.

"Let's take that walk, Erich."

Her uncle looked at Erich. "How old are you, son?"

"Fif—" Erich looked at his parents. "Thirteen, sir." He blushed.

"Just once around the block." The Foreign Minister barely suppressed a smile.

Miriam smiled openly at him. "Just once around the block. Promise!"

Erich led the way up the metal stairs, which gave Miriam a chance to see his outfit from the rear and to hope that he had not chosen it himself. Must have been his parents, she decided, wondering why she sometimes disliked people so intensely on first sight. She did not know Herr or Frau Weisser, yet something about them made her uncomfortable: the mother, obsequious and angry; the father arrogant, yet betrayed by a weakness around the mouth.

As soon as they were in the street, Miriam felt better. No matter how many German aristocrats she met, how many celebrities, she never felt quite comfortable being herself. They had a way of watching and judging, as if they measured everything anyone did on a scale of one to ten—one if you were Jewish, ten if you were an Aryan Berliner; anything else had to be earned, if that were even possible!

"Did they feed you, Konnie?" she called to her uncle's driver, who was lounging against their limousine, smoking a cigarette.

"Ja, Fräulein Rathenau. Thank you for inquiring." He quickly crushed the cigarette underfoot and stood up straight.

"Relax." Miriam waved her hand. "We're not leaving yet."

A few of her grandmother's guests, taking the air at the top of the steps, looked in her direction. Several other people craned their necks, trying to see into the cabaret. They glanced at her and at the limousine and, whispering and pointing, moved on. At the corner of the street, surrounded by a dozen locals, a barrel-organ man was grinding away.

Miriam stood for a moment and listened. Then she

executed a few dancing steps and grabbed Erich's hand. "Listen. He's playing 'Glowworm.' I never get enough of that song."

She lifted Erich's hand so that she could see it more clearly in the lamplight.

"Kiss it better!" she said. Impulsively, she kissed the red scars. "Tell me about it one day?"

Before he could answer, she let go and danced in the direction of the music.

"Glühwürmchen, Glühwürmchen, glimm're—"

She stopped abruptly. She had not realized she was singing aloud. People were staring at her—not that she cared, but it was not exactly smart to draw attention to herself like that, at night, in the middle of the street.

Someone started to applaud and others joined in.

"More!" a man yelled. "More!"

"Play, barrel-organ man!" another shouted. "Bring out the beer. We're going to have a real Saturday-night party now!"

The barrel-organ man grinned widely and patted the head of his monkey; it seemed to be grinning too. The stiff-necked upper crust could keep their genteel appreciation, Miriam thought as she curtsied and began to sing. This was more like it; this was the real thing.

CHAPTER ELEVEN

The clop of a leather dice-cup and the clicking of ivory dice against the glass counter lured Erich and Sol away from their Sunday job in the basement of their fathers' tobacco shop. From the top of the curtained-off basement stairs, they watched their fathers' customers come and go, hoping for a big sale that would provide them with pocket money for the week.

The two men playing dice asked for a box of Solomons, one of Herr Freund's first creations—a blend of cherry and Martinique tobaccos. After getting odds on the Dempsey-Hülering fight, they let the dice determine which man would pay for the purchase. Not for the first time, Erich wondered if there would ever be a cigar named after him, and dismissed the thought. Papa was and always would be nothing more than a junior partner in Herr Freund's shop.

If he were certain of nothing else, Erich thought

angrily, he was sure of one thing: he was not going to play second fiddle to anyone—not even if, as was true for Papa, there was justice in it. After all, Herr Freund was the original owner of the shop.

He glanced at Sol and then back at Herr Freund, who was quietly restocking the shelves. Their parents had it all worked out—after all, the two boys were such good friends. What could be more natural than the two of them taking over ownership of the shop one day? Not me, he thought. He was destined for better things. Last night at the cabaret—and being with Miriam—had convinced him of that.

Not that this place was so bad; it was actually fun because of the gambling license, which many of the more elegant tobacconists had.

Like all other Berlin stores, Die Zigarrenkiste, "The Cigar Box," was officially closed on Sundays. But the cost of maintaining the gambling license was high, the rent on the shop exorbitant; in these days of encroaching inflation, Herr Freund said, shopkeepers could ill afford to close for an hour, much less a day. There were always high rollers seeking action, dapper men craving good cigars, and finely fashionable women wanting cigarettes dyed to complement new outfits. Any of them might stop by their favorite tobacconist-bookie on Sundays "to see if the lights were on."

The shop was perfectly located, close to the train depot, the embassies, restaurants, and outdoor cafés, and surrounded by clothing and jewelry stores. Sunday strollers ambled along the wide boulevards of Unter den Linden, past Embassy Row, and on toward Pariser Platz. They turned into Friedrich Ebert Strasse at the

Brandenburg Gate, meandered past the Academy of Arts, the Tiergarten, and the zoo, and stopped to window-shop at the various stores that dotted the route to their fashionable destinations. It seemed quite natural that, on the pretext of saying hello, they should drop into Die Zigarrenkiste for a quick gambling fix and their weekend smoking supplies.

The men purchased cigars singly or in cedar boxes; they carried them home like chocolate soldiers in wooden coffins, transferred them to humidors, and gave the boxes to their children to use as treasure chests. For weekdays, they bought less expensive cigars; but on Friday and Saturday evenings at the theater and after large Sunday dinners, only Havanas would do.

Berlin's upper-crust ladies also frequented the shop. Erich loved to watch them make their selections. They purchased one or two at a time, agonizing over their choices. Right now, Turkish and Egyptian cigarettes were all the rage. Since most of the ladies smoked out of fashion rather than habit, nothing else would do but that their cigarettes be specially ordered: embossed with their own names or initials—or those of their tobacconist— or colored to match their outfits or their eyes.

On days when his own gambling losses were excessive, Erich's father complained about the expense of stocking goods to suit the whims of the rich. Papa could rant and rave all he liked, Erich thought, it did not take a mathematical genius to figure out that the profit was worth the investment. The bookie operation was no sure thing, so the shop's real profit lay neither in that nor in tobacco. Tobacco's accouterments, that was where the real money came from: gold and silver cigarette holders encrusted with gems that matched jeweled hatpins and tiepins; cigarette cases initialed or inscribed to husbands or wives or lovers; ivory and enameled guillotines for snipping cigar tips.

"There aren't as many customers as usual," Sol whispered.

"Maybe there'd be more customers if your papa weren't so stubborn," Erich said, referring to his father's contention that his partner was allowing street merchants to take profits rightfully theirs. *Why not*, Papa said, *cater to those who prefer the dreams brought by cocaine and morphine*.

And why not, Erich thought. It was legal, and would boost the shop's declining revenues. But Herr Freund inevitably dismissed the topic with words that brooked no further discussion. "We will leave such transactions to lesser men."

"Business will pick up after Kaverne opens," Sol said.

"Depends on how good the cabaret is. Papa says if Oma Rathenau thinks the rich will flock to her place just because *she* opened it, she's in for a surprise."

"My papa says they'll all come—the rich and famous."

"Your papa says a lot of things. People might come once, but after that Frau Rathenau has to make them *want* to come. They want excitement, not just elegance anymore."

Erich lifted his head and shoulders the way his new Freikorps-Youth leader, Otto Hempel, did when he was about to deliver a speech. Why couldn't *his* father look like that, Erich thought. Better yet, why couldn't he *be* like that. While his father was working here in the shop

during the war, drinking and playing the horses, Otto
Hempel was helping von Hindenburg decimate the
Russians at Tannenberg, earning a field commission for
gallantry. He had told them about it one night around
the campfire, silver hair shining in the firelight. He had
commanded the battery that fired those first shells of
liquid chlorine in Poland, only to have it fail to volatilize
in the frigid conditions. He had helped coordinate the
mustard-gas attack at Ypres, only to have the victory
that could have won the war snatched away because no
one believed him about the new weapon's wonderful
potential.

Now *there* was a hero—and he looked the part, too.
Said his hair had turned silver from the ardors of the
battlefield.

Erich glanced at himself in a cigarette case Herr
Freund had left lying on the counter to be polished. He
turned it this way and that, imagining himself with a
head of silver hair and a row of medals.

"Give people what they think they want, then make
sure they keep wanting what you give them," he said to
Sol. "Some cabarets have naked waitresses. Men can
touch them...anywhere they want."

Sol lifted his head and looked at Erich, who quickly
put down his makeshift mirror. "Where did you hear
that? At one of your stupid campfires?"

Erich narrowed his eyes. "You watch what you say
about my camp."

"Then you watch what you say about my papa. He
knows what he's doing." Sol raised himself to his full
height and looked down at Erich.

Erich clenched his fist. "If you really want to know, Miriam told me." He opened his hand, but kept his fighting stance.

"I suppose that's what you talked about in front of her uncle and everyone."

"After you and your squeaky cello disappeared, Miriam walked with me to...to...the Tiergarten and back."

"Herr Rathenau would never let her walk with you or anyone else unchaperoned. Not at night—"

Erich gave a derisive snort and leaned back haughtily against the wall. "That's what *you* think. Go ahead, ask her! We went for a walk and—"

"She didn't tell you those things, about the cabarets," Sol said, but in a softer tone.

"Well, something like that." Erich took a bent cigarette from his pocket. "Want to go outside with me and smoke this?" He straightened the cigarette, then dabbed saliva on the paper to help hold it together where it had torn.

"You said we wouldn't take any more. Remember, you were the one who got sick—"

"I took them for Miriam." Erich pulled several more cigarettes from his pockets, most of them damaged.

"Her parents let her *smoke?*"

"They're dead, remember? She lives with her uncle." He thought about the way Miriam had looked, dancing in the lamplight. Funny how he wanted to tell Sol about that and didn't want to, both at the same time. He rolled one of the cigarettes between his fingers and remembered how she had taken his hand, *that* one, and kissed it. "Boy, I sure would like to do things to her."

"What things?"

"You know. Things."

"She wouldn't even let someone like you hold her hand."

"Bet she already kissed me."

"Liar!"

Erich felt his face redden. He shoved Sol against the wall. Sol swung wildly, managing a glancing blow off Erich's temple before Erich surged in with body punches.

"Be quiet, children!" Sol's father called out. "Look who has stopped outside. Herr Rathenau himself."

The boys dropped their guard and started into the shop, but Sol's father shooed them back into the alcove. Sol peeked around the curtain. "To see him twice in two days," he said in awe.

"Did he come in the limousine or the convertible?" Erich tried to see over Sol's shoulder. "Is Miriam with him? Maybe she suggested he come so she could see me," he whispered excitedly. His heart pounded at the possibility of being with Miriam again.

"Stop breathing down my neck." Sol shifted slightly so they could both have a clear view of the door.

The bell above the shop door jangled. With a theatrical wave of his hand, Herr Freund ushered in the Foreign Minister. Rathenau entered—alone. He wore a gray suit and maroon cravat and carried a walking stick under his arm. A huge diamond twinkled in its knob.

"How nice to see you again, Herr Freund."

The statesman surveyed the shop, breathing deeply as though savoring the rich aroma of tobacco that permeated the air.

Herr Freund slipped behind the counter and quickly removed the dice cups. "How might I serve you, Herr Rathenau?"

Now that the counter was between them, his tone was comfortable. Erich understood that feeling of putting something tangible between himself and someone to whom he felt in some way inferior; he had often wished he could do it with his Freikorps-Youth leader. He recognized the defensive gesture that allowed clerk and customer to maintain their separate worlds across the barrier of Meerschaum pipes and open cigar boxes and glass.

"A couple of cigars, to begin with," Rathenau said. "I'm to accompany my mother to the Schauspielhaus tonight. A troupe from Frankfurt is attempting *Faust*...mediocre talent, I'm told, but exuberant. Give me something light but full-bodied. Perhaps it'll help me forget that I'm allowing myself to sit through yet another butchering of Goethe."

Erich watched Herr Freund select two fine Havanas. Herr Rathenau paid for them with a banknote, then indicated he would take another, for immediate use.

"Perhaps you would honor me by accepting one of these." Reaching under the glass, Herr Freund produced a single cigar. He twirled it in his fingers, breathed in its aroma, and placed it on a small velvet pad, which he passed to the Foreign Minister.

"Something new?" Herr Rathenau asked.

"I have named a cigar for my son and a gold-tipped cigarillo for my daughter. We were about to name one for my partner's son."

"About time," Erich whispered, surprised.

"With your permission, however," Herr Freund said, "we should like to name this latest…a Rathenau."

Furious at having lost out to the Foreign Minister, Erich watched Herr Freund clip the cigar and light it. "Too early in the day to soak the tip in cognac," the tobacconist said, tossing the end in a trash basket and handing Rathenau the cigar.

I hope you choke on it, Erich thought, as the Foreign Minister moistened his lips with his tongue and rotated the cigar in his mouth, relishing it as one might a fine brandy.

"Excellent—and I am deeply touched by your tribute." Herr Rathenau raised his brows in appreciation, patted Jacob on the shoulder and blew a stream of smoke toward the ceiling's ceramic friezes. "You have proven yourself to be a seller of smokes without equal. And now, as to my main reason for stopping by—"

Herr Freund's smile remained fixed. He leaned forward, hands on the glass, shirt sleeves rolled up, the glow from the overhead lamps shining dully on the bald spot where his hairline receded.

"As I implied," Rathenau said, "I did not come simply for cigars. I came to see the boy."

"I was right." Erich poked Sol playfully in the ribs. "Miriam must have asked him to come."

"Is that you, Solomon, hiding back there?" Rathenau asked. "Come on out."

The boys exchanged startled glances.

"Go on!" Erich shoved his friend a little too hard and Sol practically fell into the shop.

"That was some performance you gave last night," the Foreign Minister said.

"I know I was awful, sir."

Erich secretly applauded Sol's honesty. Apparently Herr Freund felt otherwise, because his face tightened.

"Well, you're no virtuoso, but Miri liked your Haydn. Judging by your degree of discomfort with performing, however—" Rathenau smiled and put an arm around Solomon's shoulders— "I rather suspect you might be persuaded to give up playing in public."

Seeing them side by side, Erich was struck with how diminutive the man was; Rathenau had been seated at the party, and his stature and bearing had lent him an illusion of height.

"Sir?" Sol frowned, his face a study in puzzlement.

The statesman released him and laughed out loud. "Just teasing, young man. You did a fine job, under trying conditions. It is not easy to follow an act like my Miriam's."

He glanced curiously toward the curtain.

"Ah, young Weisser!" Rathenau looked directly at Erich and chuckled. "Took a fancy to my young lady, did you not?"

Erich had been holding the edge of the curtain and peeking around it. Feeling as if he had been reprimanded for staying suspiciously long in the bathroom, he jerked his head back behind the curtain. He would not go out there now, he decided, even if they tried to drag him out.

Then he heard Rathenau say, "I have taken a liking to your Solomon, as has my niece," and he was filled with such hurt that he stepped back against the wall as though someone had pushed him. His face burned and his heart thudded ferociously.

"With your permission, Herr Freund, I would like your son to join me for lunch today at the Adlon." The Foreign Minister's voice dropped toward the end of the sentence. "I have no son of my own, and probably never will have. I was impressed by his effort last night and I wish to reward him—"

Pretend Sol's a dog, Erich told himself. Send him a message. *Get him to invite me. Don't go without me.*

"You *liked* my performance?" Sol sounded amazed.

"Sol—" Jacob Freund said.

Erich crawled forward and, parting the curtain just enough to peek out, saw Rathenau hold up a hand in a gesture of forbearance. "Quite all right, my friend. The boy is naturally confused."

The Foreign Minister reached out and touched Sol's cheek. Erich put his hand against his own face.

"I shall explain myself further at luncheon, young man," Rathenau said, "unless, of course, you have other plans. Or perhaps you'd simply rather not come."

"Oh, no...I mean yes...I'd love to come, but—"

"But?" Herr Freund sounded dumbfounded.

"Herr Foreign Minister," Sol said, almost too softly to be heard, "...could...do you think...could my friend, Erich, come with us?"

The Foreign Minister eyed Sol's father, who returned the look without a sign of emotion. There it was, Erich thought. What Papa called the attitudinal interchange between classes. Herr Freund, the impassive merchant; Rathenau, his statesman's gaze bespeaking loftier aspirations and ideals than the sale of cigars, even to customers of wealth and power.

"Solomon will be honored to go with you, Herr

Rathenau," Herr Freund said, his expressionless voice and face masking what Erich was sure must be a racing pulse. He remembered what he had heard the night he'd awakened and his mother was crying and his father was shouting, *That Jew is humble-ambitious, I tell you. Humble-ambitious!*

"What time should we have him ready?" Sol's father asked.

Have *them* ready, Erich corrected. Surely Rathenau would include him in the luncheon, now that Sol had asked—

"We have established that it is all right with you, Herr Freund," the Foreign Minister said. "Now let us hear from the boy."

Not *boys*. Erich felt his heart plummet and he chided himself for ever having admired the Foreign Minister.

"I am...honored," Sol mumbled. His hand trembled as he pushed his glasses back up onto the bridge of his nose.

Ask him again, Erich begged mentally.

"Good. I shall call for you at—" Rathenau opened his watch— "shall we say twelve?"

Father and son nodded in unison. Herr Freund walked around the counter and opened the door for Rathenau. Sol looked back, grimaced, and followed the two men into the street.

Erich crept along behind the counter for a better look. The statesman's chauffeur, a massive, homely man, leaned comfortably against the limousine. When he heard the bell above the door, he straightened up. He smoothed back his hair, which hung to his collar, slicked it beneath his cap, and held open the car door. Rathenau ducked inside and slid open the glass panel that separated the front seat from the back. Then he leaned against the plush, fawn-colored leather upholstery, gloved hands resting on the head of his walking stick, and his horseless carriage rolled away.

Thinks he's a king but he is just a little man with too much money and power, Erich thought. Like Papa says they all are.

"You see?" No longer impassive, Sol's father gripped his son by the arms. "All that practicing paid off. I told you it would!"

"He can't truly want me to play for him again, can he?"

"Who knows what he wants? Just that he *wants* is what's important." He put an arm across Solomon's shoulders. "You're a good boy, Solomon Freund, the best, but you listen to me. I know your intentions are good, but if Herr Rathenau wanted Erich to go with you, he would have said as much without your prompting." He patted Sol on the rump as if to give him a running start across the street to the apartment. "Go! Get ready!"

Sol glanced into the shop and shrugged his shoulders. His body said, *I tried.* "Must I take my cello, Papa?"

"Questions, always so many questions. No, my son. No cello." Herr Freund took out the long black key attached to a silver chain dangling from his belt loop, and shut the door.

In disbelief, Erich listened to the key rasp in the lock.

"Papa, you're locking Erich in!"

There was a second metallic scraping, and Jacob pulled open the door. Erich waited until Herr Freund had stepped back before he exited the shop. Keeping his gaze on the merchant, he eased around him as if around a large cat.

"I'm sorry, my boy. It seems we forgot you in all the excitement." Jacob smiled.

"Just forget you forgot!" Hands in pockets, Erich backed several steps up the street before turning and stalking away.

"Erich?" Solomon called tentatively.

Erich kept walking. No use going home, he thought. Papa would be mulling over his racing forms, downing sherry like beer to compensate for not having enough money to go to Mariendorf and bet on the trotters. Once he heard Rathenau had chosen to take Sol to lunch instead of Erich, he would start complaining again, and yelling, and his mother would cry. Why did they always have to be so predictable?

He headed toward the Tiergarten, remembering how Miriam had smiled and put her arm through his when they had heard the barrel-organ man playing "Glowworm." She had kissed him—sort of—and he had kissed her back—almost.

Well, he would show them.

There would be no almosts anymore.

Chapter twelve

"Hello, Konnie." Miriam smiled at her uncle's chauffeur. "Thanks for coming to get me. Where's my uncle?"

"He and that young man are still at the Adlon, Fräulein—"

"*Miriam*, please! Which young man?"

"Young Herr Freund, Fräulein Rathenau." The chauffeur opened the rear door of the limousine.

Trying to cure the Germans of their excessive formality was an exercise in futility, Miriam thought, throwing her tennis racquet onto the back seat. But she was not about to stop trying—not until someone could give her a satisfying explanation of why people who had known each other for most of their lives still called each other Frau and Herr.

"Thanks again for the lesson, Vladimir." She waved to her tennis instructor, who was standing halfway between the court and the curb, staring at her. "See you on Wednesday. Don't forget to bring some of *Mashenka* for me to read next time."

Ignoring Konnie's disapproving look and the open door, she got into the front seat of the limousine.

"My uncle took Solomon Freund to the Adlon for lunch?" She thought about the doe-eyed boy with the cello. He had never come back to the party, so she had not been able to tell him how she had felt about the Haydn. "Did he take the other boy, too? His friend—Erich?"

The chauffeur shook his head and started the car. "Home, Fräulein?" He glanced sidelong at the tennis dress she had brought back from America.

"I think not," she said impulsively. "Where are you picking up Uncle Walther after his walk?"

"At young Herr Freund's home."

"Then that's where we'll go. I'll wait there with you."

The chauffeur gave her another disapproving look. "Do you not wish to change?"

"No, Konnie. Thank you. This will do perfectly well."

Uncle Walther would not exactly approve of her being seen in public like this, she thought, but she was not breaking any laws. Besides, he was enough of a renegade himself that he generally forgave her those kinds of trespasses. He tried to be stern, but the indulgent twinkle in his eyes betrayed his pride in her independent spirit.

As they made their way into the city, Miriam thought about the two boys—Erich and Solomon. Romantically, they were much too young for her, of course, but they were the most interesting boys she had met since her return to Berlin. She was used to young men like

Vladimir falling all over her; it was flattering, but dull. There were lots of Russians in the ballet company in New York. They were attractive, but so serious about themselves. Vlad was no different, except that he was a writer, or wanted to be, instead of a dancer.

They were rounding a corner several blocks from Friedrich Ebert Strasse when Miriam spotted Erich waiting to cross the street.

"Stop the car!" She rolled down the window. "Erich! Erich Weisser! Come over here."

Erich looked up, squinted in her direction, and blushed.

"Here!" she called out again. "We'll give you a lift home."

She pushed open the door and beckoned. He darted across to the car and slid in beside her.

"We're going to pick up my uncle," she said. "Why didn't you go with them?" Oh Lord, she thought, seeing the expression on Erich's face. "Next time we'll all go," she added, hoping to alleviate some of the embarrassment she had caused. Konnie pulled up in front of the tobacco shop. "We could wait for them at your place," she said to Erich. "Didn't you tell me you lived above the Freunds?"

"Yes, but...but..." Erich stopped stammering, and looked angry as he took a breath. "My parents aren't home."

Miriam started to ask why that mattered. This is Berlin, she reminded herself. Here, parents expected children to be little Victorians, even if they themselves were anything but. "Okay. Then let's wait in the car."

"That's our shop over there, remember?" Erich pointed at the cigar shop.

Perfect, Miriam thought. She had forgotten about that. Now she could buy her uncle some of his favorite tobacco as a surprise. "Let's wait in there, then," she said.

"The lights are out."

"So?"

"Herr Freund hasn't come back yet. It's locked up." He stopped, as if he'd had an idea. "Come."

"Shall I wait here, Fräulein Rathenau?" Konnie asked.

"Whatever you like, Konnie." She thought about it. "Why don't you come back in, say, half an hour. They should be back by then."

She and Erich got out of the car and headed toward the shop. When they were at the door, he pulled out a key chain from his hip pocket and opened the oblong leather pouch attached to it.

"Don't you have a key?" Miriam asked.

Erich took out a pick and shook his head. "Have to pick the lock," he mumbled.

"Why do you carry lock picks?"

He shrugged. "Just because."

Like in the movies, Miriam thought, enjoying herself until it occurred to her that someone might think they were breaking into the shop—which they were, in a manner of speaking. "Hurry up!" She pictured her uncle's face if he arrived and found them being questioned by the police.

"It's open." Erich pushed at the door, and the bell above it jangled. "Quick—inside." He let the door close behind them.

"It's too dark in here. Put on a light, will you?"

Erich hesitated.

"Come on. I want to buy some tobacco for my uncle."

The boy walked across the store and turned on a single light near a red velvet curtain. She followed him and pulled the curtain aside. It led to a stairway, going down.

"Have you ever smoked?" Erich asked, from behind the counter.

Miriam shook her head. He reached under the counter, pulled out a cigarette, lit it and handed it to her. She drew on it and started to cough. Laughing, he took it from her.

"That is not funny," she said, though she could not help but laugh, too. "Let me try again." She took a second draw. Her head started to spin; she felt dizzy, like when she had tried champagne for the first time. The taste in her mouth was dry and musty. "Tastes like old shoes," she said. "See."

Leaning toward him, she kissed him on the lips. He stood there with such a shocked expression on his face that she could not resist. Putting her arms around him, she kissed him again.

A bell jangled and the shop was flooded with light.

"What do you think you're doing!"

Miriam whirled around to see Herr Weisser striding toward them.

"Smoking, kissing, breaking into the shop! What kind of a girl are you?"

Jacob Freund came in behind his partner. "Calm down, Friedrich. Please."

Herr Weisser turned to face him. "Calm down? Look

at her! Acting like a streetwalker, and you tell me to calm down. I told my wife last night—already you were making eyes at my boy—these rich Jews, I told her. They're not to be trusted!"

"Friedrich! Control yourself!" Herr Freund, obviously mortified by his partner's outburst, took off his glasses and began to clean them.

"I'm sorry, Herr Weisser." Miriam spoke slowly, struggling to mask her anger. She was bristling at the insults.

"Sorry? That's a thirteen-year-old boy and you say you're sorry?"

Miriam glanced over at Erich. He was standing against the shelves, his face red and angry. "Papa, we were—"

"I can see what you were doing!" his father bellowed. "You! Fancy lady! Sit down!" He turned to glare at his son. "You! Go home and wait for me!"

Erich did not move.

Warily Miriam made her way to the small round table that held an ebony-and-ivory chess set, and sat down on one of two identical spindle-backed chairs. While she waited for her uncle, there was nothing she could do but sit and listen to Herr Weisser carry on about her corrupting his precious son. The whole thing was ridiculous! Erich was nice, but he was hardly an angel who needed this kind of protection.

If only Uncle would get here. He would set things to rights. She was always happy to see him, but never more than she would be this time. Clearly, she was in trouble, but since the most reprehensible thing she had done was not discourage Erich from breaking into his own shop, she would be forgiven. Well, maybe she *had* encouraged him just a little....

Feeling far less grown-up than she had when she'd arrived, she decided that when her uncle came, she would allow herself to be led away without a glance in the Freunds' direction. She would find another time to talk to Sol about his music. In fact, she would not even meet his gaze or smile, lest he or his father think her coquettish—though why it mattered she had no idea.

Chapter Thirteen

Sol looked around the dining room of the Adlon Men's Club. He should have tried harder to have his friend included, he thought, but he would make up for it; he would remember every detail, from the Foreign Minister's custom-tailored dress-suit and broad crimson sash, to the room itself, elegantly set, Spartan, crowded with the rich and powerful. He was proud, and more than a little astonished, at having been included in this milieu, but the rigidity—the lack of *Gemütlichkeit*—troubled him. Surrounded by the quiet buzz of intense conversation between men whose faces he recognized from *Der Weltspiegel* and the Movietone News, he felt small and embarrassed. A dose of the cabaret's magic—women and flowers and music—might lend a more festive air to the room, he thought. Everyone seemed so serious!

"The Idle Inn is more fun," Rathenau said, apparently reading the expression on Sol's face. "I prefer the Biergarten and would rather break bread with common men, but there is much unofficial business of State transacted here on Sundays."

At a table next to them, a man raised his glass of drinking water. "To your good health, gentlemen." He and the others at his table gargled their water and spat it into their finger bowls.

Sol mumbled something about never before having realized the bowls' proper purpose, and Rathenau laughed. "An end-of-the-meal fashion established by the Kaiser," he whispered. "I wouldn't suggest you do it elsewhere. Your hosts might not understand."

During the course of their meal, a variety of people had stopped at the table. Rathenau introduced him to each one. Earlier, walking toward the dining room, he had cautioned Sol to give more attention to listening than to eating. "Disregard anti-Semitic slurs," he had said. "Hear what they're saying *behind* the bigotry. Don't overlook a single nuance or inflection...and don't forget a word you hear."

Forget! As long as he lived, he would remember this day. These were men who could open doors for him— and for Erich—with a word or a wave of the hand. Not that it was all that important for him; he was going to be a scholar—study, teach maybe. But Erich...he was going to be "something big!" Anyway, that's what he said. With the right education, the right clothes, the right connections, you could do anything, Papa said, and these were surely the right connections—here in this room.

"Come along, Sol." The Foreign Minister led him into the lobby of the hotel. "Bear with me. I have some business to conduct as we leave. Then we'll take a *Spaziergang*—a stroll. Konnie will pick me up at your flat."

Sol followed him across the lounge toward two men seated in wing chairs, smoking and reading newspapers. A third man, dressed in the blue and gold of an officer's uniform, sat reading in the corner, his back to them and his boots on a hassock.

"I tell you it's a disgrace," one of the men said as they approached.

The other, blond, with a Tartar mustache that only partially concealed a scar along the edge of his mouth, looked up and nodded. Rathenau extended his hand. "Good to see you again, Auwi."

The second man, a rotund fellow with steel-gray eyes and the downturned mouth of a carp, leaped to his feet and shook hands with the Foreign Minister.

"Glad you're here, George." Rathenau looked at Sol. "Solomon Freund, I'd like you to meet George Viereck, literary executor for the Kaiser, and," he nodded toward the seated man, "the Kaiser's son, Prinz August Wilhelm. 'Auwi' to his friends."

The prince raised a desultory hand in greeting. Viereck pumped Solomon's hand so heartily that Sol found himself backing up.

"I think you'll recognize this lazy old soldier over here," Rathenau said.

A pasty, doggy-cheeked face sporting a drooping white mustache peered out from around the side of his chair.

Solomon swallowed thickly.

Field Marshal von Hindenburg!

Von Hindenburg cast a rheumy eye at Sol, cleared his throat, and reopened the weekend edition of the *Börsen Zeitung*. "Protégé, Herr Minister?" he asked. "Send him out on the balcony to wave to the masses like Jackie Coogan. You're his countryman, George. Is the Coogan boy really so talented, or is our city simply in love with youth for youth's sake?"

"I'm afraid neither Prinz Wilhelm nor the Feldmarschall is in a very good mood." Viereck's German was edged with an American accent. "The price of newspapers has gone up again. I remember when a single mark bought a quart of Fauwenhauser."

"Third time this week," the prince said sourly. "All this babbling and squabbling, inflation out of control—" he slapped the paper—"revolutionaries and reactionaries running amok, foreigners and Jews and postwar profiteers stealing the country from under us!"

Stung by the racial slur, Sol looked to Rathenau for guidance. The Foreign Minister flashed him a look that said *stay calm*.

"We Germans were like the woman in the Aladdin story, too quick to give away the old lamp." Von Hindenburg cleared his throat huskily and adjusted his purple sash. Four starfish-shaped medals gleamed upon a chest once more massive than his belly.

"The Kaiser's greatest wish is to return and march with the workers against the government," Viereck said.

The American looked from Solomon to von Hindenburg, who drew his bushy brows together in an exaggerated frown. "Can the boy be trusted?" the general asked in a rough voice. "He has the features of a Jew."

You have the jowls of a bloodhound, Sol thought, stiffening.

"He *is* a Jew. Therefore I trust him as I do my own judgment," Rathenau said. "Fully."

"You think too highly of Jews, Herr Foreign Minister," von Hindenburg said.

"Perhaps not highly enough," Rathenau replied in an even tone.

Solomon lowered his gaze. For a while he had felt invisible; now he was certain everyone in the room was staring at him. He pretended to examine one of the massive tapestries hanging on the wall.

For all the times Sol had walked past the Adlon, this was the first time he had been inside. The outside was simple, a plain building with long wrought-iron windows, but the inside—tapestries and floor-to-ceiling shelves filled with leather-bound books, crimson curtains, walls wainscoted in mahogany and vaulted ceilings buttressed by elaborate plaster trellises. Words like *putsch* and *purge* and *anarchy* seemed to float in the air and he would not have been surprised to find the Kaiser walking across the candelabra-lit lounge.

"The Kaiser cannot regain the crown, he knows that," he heard the prince say. "He seeks only *Heldentod*, the hero's death he was previously denied."

So the Kaiser had desired *Heldentod* after all! Sol could hardly wait to tell Erich. Other boys at school had claimed the Kaiser was a coward. At the expense of several black eyes and split lips, Sol and Erich had insisted otherwise.

"Our beloved Wilhelm shall have his wish," von

Hindenburg said. "I shall serve as scapegoat for our military humiliations and the sheep shall flock to someone—perhaps Walther here—who will lead Germany, if not to higher heights, then at least to solidarity."

He snapped his fingers and a waiter appeared with a tray of brandy snifters and a decanter. "Let us drink to solidarity," von Hindenburg said.

The four men drank, and Sol was filled with awe at how calmly and quickly history could be rechanneled.

Within moments he was out on the street, following Rathenau, who moved silently and at an energetic pace.

Sol's notions of a *Spaziergang* underwent a dramatic change. His father's penchant was for leisurely constitutionals along well-worn paths, conversing as he walked or pausing at benches to rest and argue a particular point, while Rathenau hiked wordlessly along Wilhelmstrasse, as if allowing the city's penury and seething anger to be his mouthpiece.

His senses opened by the Adlon luncheon, Sol took in everything with a tourist's unease: the farmers and fishmongers near the Ministry of Justice, hawking wilted wildflowers, lettuce, and oily, overpriced herring; the air, filled with grit and the stench of exhaust; the buildings' gray austerity. The streets seemed more littered with garbage and more a-sprawl with drunks and other dispossessed than he recalled: *Schieber*—foreign blackmarketeers—worked every street corner; political saviors wearing red cockades or black armbands stood on principles and soap crates, embracing immutable ideals Sol was sure they would be willing to discard for a meal or a few hundred marks; scurrying urchins poked and pleaded, offering shoeshines, sisters, the wisdom of white powders, the serenity of a syringe.

There were women, too, posing as ladies while promising to raise skirts but not prices, offering heavenly communions to be consummated in the privacy of the nearest alley.

"What this nation needs is a generation of *reasonable* Nationalists—Gentiles *and* Jews—willing to work together for God and good government...the dream of a true democracy," Rathenau said. He slapped his walking stick against his palm. He was walking so fast that Solomon had to run lightly to keep pace with him. "Europe has a history of vesting absolute power in one individual. I intend to position myself to block that sort of thing from happening again."

He halted. Putting his hands on Sol's shoulders, he looked down into the boy's eyes. "As I watched your performance last night, you reminded me so much of myself," he said. "Struggling. Forced to play solo. You are the new generation, Solomon. With my help you may not have to accept, as I had to, that, in Germany, Jews will always be second-class citizens."

As suddenly as he had taken hold of Sol, he let go. "Constant vigilance is exhausting, Solomon," he said in a tired voice. "There are times I want to lie down and pull Berlin's sidewalks over me."

Sol looked down at his feet. How many weary men's spirits lay beneath the city? Perhaps theirs were the voices he heard, he thought, wondering fleetingly what the Foreign Minister might say about the voices and sounds in the sewer.

"Back in '18, I decided to retire," the Foreign Minister said softly, moving on. "I've a summer house in Bavaria—"

"Papa showed me pictures of it in *Der Weltspiegel*," Sol said.

"I intended to live there, away from all this. Fortunately for Germany—though unfortunately for me, since it thwarted my retirement plans—I decided to have the bedrooms repapered. One afternoon, the paper hanger and I talked as he worked. After listening to him, I realized that, with people like him around, my role in our country's history remained incomplete."

They rounded the corner at the Reichschancellery and headed down Friedrich Ebert Strasse. The cigar store was half a block away.

"The man proposed that Germany depopulate the African island of Madagascar and repopulate it with European Jews," Rathenau went on. "'The solution to the Jewish problem,' he said, 'is to pen them like wild dogs, tame them, and use what assets and abilities they possess for the good of humanity.'"

Until now, Sol had done what he did when his parents spoke Yiddish, a language he only partially understood: he had allowed the conversation to flow around him like a piece of music he had never heard before. Usually, if he relaxed into it that way, the pieces became a cohesive whole. However, what the Foreign Minister was saying now made no sense at all.

"He wanted to send the Jews to Madagascar? He must have been crazy!"

"I thought so too, and had him removed from the premises," the Foreign Minister said. "Shortly after that,

I heard that he'd entered politics, and now Bavaria's National Socialists support his ideas—"

Shouting interrupted him. Sol stared in the direction of the voices. Down the block, Erich was backing out of the shop.

CHAPTER FOURTEEN

"You may be my son, but your actions are those of an imbecile!" Herr Weisser yelled. He was standing in the doorway of the shop, shaking his fist at Erich.

"Leave me alone, Papa!"

Erich turned, dashed across the street without any regard for traffic, and disappeared into the apartment house.

Herr Weisser, his face red with rage, fell silent. Apparently, Sol thought, he had run out of effective yet moderate epithets to hurl at his son.

"Maybe we should detour through Leipzigerplatz before going inside," Rathenau said.

Solomon shook his head. Once Friedrich and Erich started arguing, it would take longer than a stroll through the plaza for their tempers to cool. "Erich probably tried to sneak another dog into the apartment," he said, wondering why Herr Weisser had gone back into the shop instead of following his son.

"That much trouble over a dog?"

"Herr Weisser has agreed to let Erich keep a small dog in the apartment, but Erich says the little ones are toys. It's worse since he's joined the Freikorps-Youth—"

Sol stopped and, with a sick feeling, glanced up at Rathenau. During the waning months of the war, the Foreign Minister had financed a Freikorps unit, a movement that had begun before the war with Wandervögel—birds of passage—boys and girls who enjoyed outdoor activities. Some of those young men had been part of Rathenau's corps, but the years of fighting had hardened their idealism into hatred. In Sol's opinion, the postwar Freikorps-Youth was a step further down. A big step. Many of the boys were homeless ruffians, easily influenced; and the leaders, Jew-haters.

Judging by the set look on his face, the Foreign Minister had heard all right—and taken note. Sol practiced the truth in his head: *It just slipped out. I didn't mean to kill your chances with Miriam.* At least he had not told Herr Rathenau that his friend talked to dogs. This was bad enough, but that would really have done it!

"Anyway, they fight about dogs," he said weakly as they entered the shop.

"Calm down, Friedrich, for God's sake," his papa was saying. "Why make a national tragedy out of it? They're just children."

They? Sol thought, wondering what Papa meant. Then he saw Miriam seated in the corner, her hands demurely folded on the table. He could see her face clearly now.

She was even more beautiful than he had thought at first, and younger, nearer to fifteen than seventeen. Her eyes were a startling violet, and though her chignon was almost black, her skin had the bone-china delicacy that usually went with auburn hair.

"Miriam! What's going on? What are you doing here?" Rathenau looked from her to Herr Weisser, who was glaring at her as if she had two heads.

Jumping up, she ran over to him and threw her arms around his waist. "They're making such a fuss, Uncle Walther!" The action pulled up her tennis skirt; Sol tried not to stare too hard at her tanned legs.

"Fuss? Smoking, kissing!" Friedrich spun around toward her uncle. "Is that what they taught your niece in America?"

"I asked Konnie to bring me along when he told me you wanted him to pick you up here," Miriam said. "I wanted to surprise you. Erich was here, and we talked—"

"Talked?" Friedrich looked flushed. "You two broke into our shop!"

"Erich was showing me his lock picks," Miriam said.

"Showing *off*, you mean, and you encouraged him! And what did you two do once you were in?" Friedrich pointed at her. "For shame!"

Rathenau took hold of Weisser's hand and, looking less than amused, drew down the man's arm. "Such a small matter, Herr Weisser. Don't upset yourself so. We should all remember that when the trivial becomes important, the important becomes trivial. Why don't we go to your parlor, have coffee and a cigar, and talk this out like gentlemen."

"Talk! That's all you Jews are good at."

Sol saw Papa pale as he stepped in front of Herr Weisser and silenced his partner with an ominous glare. Rathenau's face hardened, and his knuckles tightened around his walking stick as if he wanted to thrash Friedrich Weisser. Taking Miriam by the arm, he said softly, "I guess this is a family matter after all. Come, child."

"At least let me call a taxi for you." Sol's father did not take his gaze off Weisser.

"My chauffeur will be here momentarily." Rathenau reached out and shook Sol's father's hand. "Things will work out. We'll get together...another day."

"So! He's gone!" Jacob Freund said to his partner after Rathenau stepped outside. "Shame on you, Friedrich! They say he may become Germany's president, and you treat him like dirt. What the children did was foolish, but—"

"You're an imbecile yourself if you think such behavior trivial. If you had seen them, behaving like that in my shop!"

"Our shop, Friedrich," Jacob said.

Sol watched his father carefully. His voice was gentle, yet it clearly indicated that Herr Weisser had overstepped both business and personal propriety. The business, begun by his father a dozen years before the war, involved a seventy-thirty split between the two men. Herr Weisser had been a bicycling *hamster*—an impoverished peddler who went out to the countryside each morning for produce to hawk—before Papa took him into the business, first as *Shabbas* help, and permanently when Papa had volunteered to fight for his country and needed someone to run the shop.

"Why don't we do as Herr Rathenau suggested? Let's go home—your home if you prefer. We'll drink a good strong cup of coffee. Talk."

"For all the good it will do," Friedrich said, but he began locking up the store.

In the apartment's parlor, Friedrich told his wife what had happened, and the argument was renewed. Sol, to his surprise, was not sent out of the room. He sat quietly listening to the two men: his own father, rational and positive, trying to make his friend see that he had overreacted; Friedrich, his voice raised, maligning the Rathenau family at every opportunity.

The two men had reached an impasse when Recha and Sol's mother, apparently hearing the commotion, came upstairs from the Freund flat. Mama wiped her hands on her apron. "What is the matter?" Her house dress smelled of baked bread. Her golden hair was pulled back in a bun and perspiration traced a path through a white splotch of flour on her temple. "I heard shouting." The lines around her eyes deepened with concern as she looked from her son to her husband. When Jacob started to explain the situation, Recha interrupted.

"What's so bad about kissing? It's in all the movies!"

Her father placed his hand against the small of her back and propelled her into the kitchen. "And stay there," he said.

"Forever?" the child wailed.

Jacob smiled fondly and swung his daughter off her feet. His breath came out in a huff, the way it did when he lifted a heavy crate; he set her down awkwardly, looking at her as if he realized for the first time that this spindly-limbed young lady was no longer a toddler.

"You think you're twenty again, Papa!" Mama said.

Both men chuckled and Solomon relaxed. For once he was glad he had a sister. Thanks to her, the tension seemed broken. Now Papa will take out his snuff box, Sol thought affectionately.

His father did not disappoint him. Pinching a little snuff between thumb and index finger, he sniffed it up and sneezed loudly several times. He blew his nose on a large white handkerchief, leaving a residue of brown snuff-stain.

"Time to take care of my son." Herr Weisser stood up and opened his hand to indicate a spanking.

"Take it easy on him, will you?" Sol's papa said, the hint of a smile on his face. "He didn't do anything any healthy boy doesn't want to do."

"Maybe you'd better come along, Jacob," Herr Weisser said, "or I'm likely to lose my temper all over again."

They are just like Erich and me, Sol thought as the two men delegated their anger to that crevice they reserved for such breaks in friendship and went together to look for Erich. After checking his bedroom, they tried the library.

Erich was there, rummaging through the drawers of his father's massive mahogany desk, strewing papers all over the hand-polished parquet floor. A vase of meticulously arranged white gladioli teetered atop the desk. Erich made no effort to keep it from falling and it crashed to the floor.

"Clean that up! Now!" his father ordered.

"C'mon, I'll help you." Sol bent and began to gather up the broken porcelain from amid the water and flowers.

Erich glared down at Sol, then continued rummaging. His eyes shone with such fury that Sol stepped backward and bumped into Friedrich Weisser.

"*Mein Gott!*" Erich's father said in a tone of utter disbelief. "He's after my revolver."

"And when I find it I'll use it."

Losing all semblance of control, Friedrich Weisser hurtled forward and pushed Erich away from the desk. "Just who did you hope to shoot?" He spoke so quietly he could hardly be heard. "Me, your mother, our friends? Yourself?"

Erich steadied himself. "I hate you," he said in the same quiet voice. He held up his injured hand as if to slap his father. "You hear me, I—"

He shuddered, a slight tremor, and then blinked in surprise. Sol realized his friend had suffered another of the lightning seizures. He held his breath, but as most often happened, the slight seizure came and went so swiftly as to be almost indiscernible.

"Now you listen to me!" Erich's father took his son by the lapels. "If you ever—"

With his good hand, Erich peeled his father's fingers off his shirt. Sol watched Friedrich Weisser stand unmoving as Erich reached behind himself and, still holding up the injured hand like an icon, opened the door. For a moment, they just stood there as if posing for some ill-conceived photograph.

"*Hamster,*" Erich said in a quiet, ugly tone. He turned and left the room. One door slammed as he left the apartment; another as he left the building.

His father started after him, but Jacob Freund gently restrained his friend. "Let him be. He'll be back."

Friedrich Weisser sat down heavily in one of the library chairs. Suddenly he looked to Sol like a very old man. "He'll never return. Not really. In body, perhaps, but never as my son."

CHAPTER FIFTEEN

As dawn approached, Sol lay awake listening for the opening and shutting of doors and for the creaking of the apartment house's worn wooden stairs. If only I had been able to talk Rathenau into taking Erich along to the Adlon or had refused to go without Erich, he thought. Maybe none of the trouble would have happened. And mentioning the Freikorps-Youth to Rathenau! He felt guilty about that too, even if Erich did not know of the betrayal.

He had to find Erich and make him come home.

There were only two places Erich could have gone—the Freikorps camp or the sewer. Looking for him at the camp would be foolish and dangerous, especially at night; on the other hand, the last thing Sol wanted to do was go to their hideout, where the voices waited.

Still, anything was better than just lying in bed feeling bad.

He rose, dressed quickly, and crept into the kitchen. The key to the shop was in its usual place, hanging from a hook on the wall. He put it in his pocket. Erich could pick his way in through the cabaret, but Sol could not. The shop was his only hope. Once inside, he would go down to the basement and call to Erich through the tobacco-shop grate. Then Erich could let him in through the nightclub by opening the door from the inside. As soon as this crisis was over, he would ask his friend to teach him his lock-picking secrets. That would please Erich...make him feel superior.

Feeling much better, he poured himself a glass of milk and ate a piece of his mother's marble cake before wrapping up a slice for Erich, along with some cheese and liverwurst and two pieces of bread. Holding the package in one hand and his shoes in the other, he turned to leave.

"Going on a picnic?" his father asked from the shadows.

Sol started to put the package down on the counter.

"I won't keep you from sneaking food to him, nor will I say a word to Herr Weisser. But if you do this thing, you do so against my wishes. Whether or not you believe it, helping that boy defy his papa may not be in his best interests. Herr Weisser is not always right, we both know that. He is a difficult man. But Erich has to learn that he's not yet grown up—"

"But, Papa—"

"No arguments, Sol. Do what you must. However, if you go, I shall put you over my knee when you come home and spank you until my arm aches too much for me to lift it."

JANET BERLINER AND GEORGE GUTHRIDGE

The emotionlessness of his father's voice bespoke his sincerity. This is all Erich's fault, Sol told himself. He gets out of line, and I am damned if I do and damned if I don't.

He hesitated. Then, trembling, he crept outside quietly, wanting to run but knowing the noise would upset Papa all the more.

Sol's plan to get into the sewer worked perfectly. Erich was there, heard him at once, and let him in through the cabaret. In their hideaway, a single candle was burnt down almost to its holder. It was too dark to see for sure, but judging by the sound of his friend's voice, he had been crying. He was wearing his uniform.

"Go home, Erich," Sol said. "Your papa will forgive you."

Erich seated himself cross-legged on the flooring crates, his hands sagged in his lap. "He'll forgive me, all right. He always does. But who needs forgiveness? I'm going to live in the camp. They'll let me stay there permanently if I promise to care for the dogs."

"Dogs can't take the place of family."

"For me they can."

Solomon handed the food package to Erich, who immediately devoured the cake.

"He just stood there looking at me," Erich said after a time. He put the cheese and meats in one of the knapsacks the boys kept among their other things in the hideout. "Never came after me or really tried to stop me from leaving. Some papa *he* is!" He wiped a tear from his cheek and glanced at Solomon as though daring his friend to comment on his crying. "Well, I know where I'm not wanted. Some of the other boys are already living at the campsite, even though we're only supposed to use it for meetings."

"Those are boys without families."

"And some who don't want families. They're the ones I want to be with." He whirled the knapsack around to his back and slipped his arms through the straps. "Come with me, Sol. You'll love it there."

"Don't be dumb! Everyone knows how your leaders feel about Jews."

Erich waved his hand airily. "That's just talk. The real toughs have joined a new unit, the Storm Troopers or something, and won't have anything to do with us."

"Forget it."

"*Your* loss." Erich picked up the candle and, apparently unconcerned that he was leaving his friend in darkness, hoisted himself onto the two-by-twelve and struggled up through the drain. He looked down at Solomon from outside the sewer; the candle cast shards of light across his face, and to Sol's surprise there was hurt in his eyes. Then he was gone.

Sol leaned against the damp wall and felt the darkness suffuse him. Exiting the sewer required only a grope and a quick climb, but the events of the past twenty-four hours had sapped his energy. He closed his eyes, painfully remembering the hope for his future—God and good government—that had fluttered in his imagination like a small bright bird as Rathenau ushered him along Wilhelmstrasse. Now the Foreign Minister and his niece were gone from him, probably forever. And the Weissers...would things ever be the same between the two families?

And what about Erich? Had he lost his best friend, too?

Oh God, let me die. A woman's voice. *I did not know...I did not know.*

Sol lurched away from the wall, flailing his arms in search of the two-by-twelve. He clutched at the plank, too distraught to scramble up, and peered around desperately in the dark. "You did not know *what?*" His words emerged as a strained croak.

My mother dug ginger roots with her bare hands.

An old man's voice, and a woman's, a different one, heavy with accent. *Looks like sweetbreads, eh Margabrook? Hungry enough to eat it?*

Lice, the old man said quietly. *Lice. Let the dead dream their dreams in peace.*

"Who *are* you!" Sol yelled in frustration, his voice resounding through the sewer. As it died away, the infant shrieked at him from the sewer's far reaches, followed by laughter and a low growling.

Snarling and snapping, something moved toward him.

A chill crept up his back and turned into a trickle of sweat. Spurred by terror, he fought to get up on the plank, kicking wildly in an effort to boost himself. His feet found the side of the sewer but failed to gain purchase on the slick bricks.

The breathing drew closer.

He gained the plank. Below him the breathing resonated strong and regular as a bellows.

His hands beat at the darkness. "Get away from me!"

Gripping the plank he frantically arched his back, straining to reach the drain. Somehow he found the power to stand. Balancing precariously he slid his hands up along the slime of the wall toward the edge of the hole and pulled himself through with an ease and strength he did not know he possessed. Then he slammed down the grate and pushed his sweat-soaked hair away from his forehead.

The creature was caged. He was safe…but from what? Would he ever understand?

What is the price of five sparrows, Solomon?

"Erich?" Sol whispered.

Laughter answered him—Erich's laughter.

The sound flooded the subbasement with a horror far more terrifying in its familiarity than whatever unknown thing lurked beneath the grate. In some deep-down part of him that made no sense, he knew with absolute certainty that the laughter was Erich's—and that it was not human.

C HAPTER SIXTEEN

A ginger cat meandered from the shadows and into the amber light the street lamp cast on the cracked sidewalk. Arching its back as if trying to gain warmth from the lamplight, the cat cocked its head slightly and waited as though expecting to be petted.

After glancing around to assure himself that no one would witness his avoiding the animal, Erich crossed the street and did not look back to see if the cat were still watching. Much as he loved dogs, he mistrusted cats. He had never been able to reconcile his pleasure in their sleekness and independence with their lack of loyalty.

After pulling up his shirt collar against the unexpectedly damp wind that caught him as he left the lee of the buildings, he rubbed his neck, trying to work out his exhaustion and tension. He glanced at his watch. Half past six. He had been walking for over an hour. If only he had taken Hawk, his bicycle, he would be in his camp bunk by now, dreaming of roller-skating with Miriam in the Grünewald or of sitting with her in the Schauspielhaus, watching her while she watched Rudolph Valentino play *The Sheik*—though he could not understand why she thought his effeminate looks so wonderful. As far as he was concerned, only dog and horror movies were worth seeing.

Except with Miriam.

So what, he thought, if he'd only seen her twice! He knew what he wanted, and he would take her anywhere...not that he had much chance of ever seeing her again after Papa's outburst. If only the Foreign Minister had taken *him* to luncheon too, none of this mess would have happened! What made Solomon so special? Like Papa said: Jews of a feather...

Still, it was not Solomon's fault, so he should not be angry at his friend—especially since Sol had come down to the sewer, at night yet, to make sure he was all right. Rathenau and Papa, they were the ones who had caused the problem. A rich fool and a stupid *hamster*. No wonder Herr Freund treated Papa like an underling.

He clamped his lips together and clenched his fists, fighting to harden himself against the squirrely feeling that always formed after a fight with his father. Go home, Erich, it said. Forget what your father did and take your punishment like a man. You're smart and tough even if he isn't. You will find a way to fix things with Miriam.

The next realization followed just as inevitably. His father would not punish him. Too many hours had elapsed. The time for yelling was over; by now Papa was bound to be sleeping off a sherry sulk. Awakened, he would listen silently as Erich stammered an apology, then with a sluggish wave of his hand send him to his bedroom. After an hour or two he would come in to say he understood. And would accept. And forgive.

Who did he think he was—God?

Anger rose in Erich again, like a pot of frustration boiling over a stove whose flame would not go out. If he tried to remove the pot, his fingers would burn; if he did not, it would boil over. Again.

Abruptly, he cut through an alley toward Lutherstrasse. He would walk past the rectory and see if a light was on. Not knock or anything. But maybe Father Dahns would be outside watering the tulips before morning Mass. He would know what to do. After all, was not that what *real* Fathers were for—to fix things?

Once Mass began he could slip down the back stairs and nap for an hour among the pews stored in the basement. He knew the building well, catechism classes having been a mix of piety and hide-and-seek while Father Dahns—elderly, always smiling—alternately scolded and blessed.

Erich had loved the Mass, with its colors and mysticism, but had stopped attending two years ago. How could he confess that he adored the pageantry more than God, if indeed there were a God? After Papa's shouting, Mama's tears, and Father Dahns' questioning, amid the smiles, about Herr Weisser's own absence from church, there had come Papa's mute, angry acquiescence...and, for Erich, Sundays in the stockroom.

No. On second thought, he had better not talk to

Father Dahns; it was just too complicated. Besides, he was *not* going back, no matter what Father Dahns said, not even if Papa found him and begged or beat him.

He felt in his pocket and discovered a few coins, enough to take a tram to Wannsee and the Youth camp. If only he had enough to go really far away, someplace where Papa would never find him. Munich, maybe—the camp leaders called it Heaven. Or maybe hike and camp all over Germany, as the Wandervögel had before the war.

I am as much to blame as anyone, he thought, stumbling along and blinking bleary eyes at the neon lights of the El Dorado nightclub. *Always trying to be the big shot.*

In the half-light of the overcast morning, he could see people lounging near the infamous club, smoking and laughing, waiting for the doors to open. Inside, it was said, men danced with men and kissed each other right in the open and, in darkened corners, rubbed each other's penises. Why would men do such things? Nah, it was nonsense—rumors concocted to draw people away from the Tauentzienstrasse, where women with whips and laced-up boots turned good German men into sex slaves. Like in that movie he had sneaked into— *Goddess, Whore, and Woman.* Not even Sol knew he had seen it.

Well, maybe not actually seen it, but almost. The usher had found him soon after the opening credits, so he had not really seen much and, truth to tell, he had not been sorry to be thrown out. Ugh! No wonder the papers called the film "criminal, sensational, erotic, sadistic." Erotic was one thing. He liked that word—

liked how it made him feel warm inside. But the sadistic stuff—did human beings honestly do those things?

Erich avoided the figures outside the El Dorado as if they were alley cats. Afraid to turn his back on them, he moved in a wide semicircle, fighting an urge to run as some of them looked his way and smirked. Clear of them, he swiveled and, fear chilling his exposed back, started to hurry away.

"Want a lesson, *Schatzie?*" A blowzy blonde leaned out of the shadows. She sucked deeply on a silver cigarette holder as long as a reed and blew a stream of smoke his way. "What do you say, baby-face? I'll make bacon and eggs for breakfast." Apparently mistaking his shock and curiosity for interest, she held out a languorous arm, gloved in elbow-length white lace.

Erich shook his head and, knapsack slapping against his back, dashed down one alley and rounded a corner. Bacon and eggs sounded awfully good, but thanks to Solomon he was not starving. Slowing, he licked the vestiges of Frau Freund's double chocolate icing from his fingers. That damn Solomon! Getting mad at him was easy; staying mad was impossible. He was always so *nice*.

He looked around to get his bearings, then tried another alley. It proved to be a dead-end littered with garbage and peopled by rats. Maybe he should take a tram back to the flat and forget the whole thing like Papa would—or at least he could pretend to. He ran back to the main street and found he had circled back to the alley corner, near the prostitute. He turned in another direction in the alleys' maze.

When he saw the blinking of the El Dorado neon

toward the end of the next alley, he congratulated himself on how cleverly he had circumnavigated the woman. He could see three figures swathed in shadow near the nightclub's back door, but could think of no way to avoid them. With renewed bravado he decided to walk by and pretend not to notice them or what they were doing—whatever that turned out to be.

Whistling softly, he plunged his hands into his pockets and started forward. He had taken no more than a few steps when a man called to him.

"Over here. Join us—there's always room for one more."

Gorge rising in panic, Erich stopped in his tracks. He stared in the direction of the voice. Otto Hempel was slurring his words slightly. Like Papa, when he's had too much to drink, Erich thought. Nonetheless, there was no mistaking the voice—or the silver hair.

Run, he told himself. *Get away.*

But the same combination of fascination and horror he had experienced in the movie theater kept his feet planted as firmly as if he had taken root on Lutherstrasse.

"A shy one, huh? Rather just watch, would you?" The Youth-group leader laughed softly. "Well, that's all right too. But why not move closer? I'd like to see your face."

Leaning against the building, Hempel placed one hand against the back of the head of a blond youth kneeling in front of him. His other hand held what appeared to be a riding crop. A uniform jacket lay crumpled on the sidewalk, beside his feet. Near the jacket, head lowered and bare to the waist, was a second boy about Erich's age.

Raising his hand high in the air, Hempel whipped

down hard on the youth's bare shoulder. The boy whimpered but did not cry out.

"Don't!" Erich's shout emerged as a gargled whisper through the bile in his throat. Finally able to move, he started toward the youth and held out his hand to help him to his feet.

The boy shook him off. "Get away!" He stared up at Erich, his eyes filled with hatred. "Find your own. This one's ours!"

"More! Beg for more." Hempel's voice was husky.

"More!"

Even in the half-light, Erich could see thick red welts forming where the crop had bitten into the boy's skin, crisscrossing each other as again and again the crop came down. Then Hempel groaned loudly and, tossing the whip aside, pressed down on the blond head with both hands. He moved against the boy's head with short, purposeful jabs.

Crawling forward, the second youth joined his friend and knelt at Hempel's feet.

Feeling sicker than he ever had in his life, Erich turned and ran blindly down Lutherstrasse. Where he was going did not matter—home, Munich, the camp—as long as he put distance between himself and what he had just seen.

CHAPTER SEVENTEEN

"Solomon. Wake up."

"It can't be time," Sol groaned. He had tossed and turned until well beyond daylight, hopelessly trying to make sense of Erich's overreaction and of the horrible voices and sounds in the sewer. He felt as if he had only just closed his eyes. "Erich hasn't—"

He started to say that Erich had not banged on the floor upstairs the way he did every morning so they could walk to the *Gymnasium* together. Then he remembered it was Saturday—*Shabbas*—the day Erich went to school without him. He had slept right through his friend's morning noises.

"Must I go to synagogue?" Sol asked, knowing full well what the answer would be, especially so close to his bar mitzvah. "I hate missing school."

"Hate is not a word to be used so lightly," his father said. "Besides, there are schools and there are schools.

At times one becomes more important than the other. If we allowed you to go to school on *Shabbas*, it would make trouble for those Jewish children whose parents forbid it." He opened the curtains and stared out the window. "Already it's too late for us to get to the morning study group. You were sleeping so soundly, your mother and I decided not to wake you. Now get a move on. I intend to be there in time for services. These days, fewer and fewer people come to *shul*—they will need me to make a *minyan* for morning services."

"Are Mama and Recha coming?"

"Mama has a headache. Recha must stay with her."

Pushing aside his eiderdown, Sol swung his legs over the side of the bed. It gave him a sense of pride to think that once he had been bar mitzvahed, he could help make up the *minyan*—the ten men needed before a service could be conducted. For now, though, he counted only as the son of Jacob Freund.

Picking up Sol's glasses, which lay lenses-down on the night stand, Jacob breathed on them and rubbed them vigorously with the edge of Sol's sheet. "Still angry with me about that spanking I gave you last weekend?" He handed Sol the glasses.

Sol put a hand on his behind.

Jacob Freund smiled sadly. "Some lessons can only be learned when pressure is brought to bear. You will have to make many more...painful, shall we say...decisions in your life. Teaching you cause and effect is part of my job."

"But—"

His papa silenced him with a wave of the hand. "But? There are no *buts*. We both did what we had to do—

you felt you had to help your friend, I felt you were doing yourself and his family an injustice by encouraging the estrangement between Erich and his papa. Now get dressed. It will do us good to sit together under the eyes of God."

As he was getting ready, Sol replayed the events of the week. His being with Herr Rathenau. Erich threatening his papa. The monster snapping at his heels in the sewer and the inhuman laughter that, somehow, incomprehensibly, was Erich's. Except for his luncheon with the Foreign Minister, the events seemed less like reality than the ghoulish, neo-Gothic movies playing all over Berlin: *Dr. Caligari*—and *The Golem,* which had Judaic implications.

Erich had been acting very peculiarly the whole week. His moodiness was nothing new, nor was his quick temper, but at least he had shared things before. This week, he had been uncommunicative, refusing to talk about where he had gone after he left the sewer, not answering when Sol asked why he had not gone to live at the camp after all. He had not even talked about Miriam and, if that were not strange enough, he had stayed in his room listening to music, and reading. *Erich, reading!*

Half an hour later, Sol and his father were on their way to the Zoo Station to take the S-Bahn to the Grünewald—a concession to the late hour, since they usually obeyed the Sabbath law and walked all the way. Even from the station, it was a fair walk to the synagogue, which lay nestled among the oaks and chestnut trees that proliferated in the lush suburb. Berlin's most affluent citizens, including Walther

Rathenau, had villas there, and Erich's camp was only a couple of kilometers away, a short rowboat ride across the Wannsee.

What if Erich had played truant from school, as he often did, and they came across him strutting down the road in his uniform?

The idea was enough to make Sol genuinely anxious to get to *shul*. Anything was better than the possibility of having to explain Erich's uniform to Papa. Even if he would soon be considered a man in the eyes of God, the contemplation of such a thing sent his stomach going into the kind of loop it did on the roller coaster at Luna Park. Perhaps if he gave himself up to the sense of peace that pervaded the synagogue, God would see fit to send him some rationale for the events of the past week.

"We should hurry, Papa, or we'll be late."

His father smiled and increased his pace. Minutes later they were in the foyer of the synagogue, greeting the beadle at the door and donning their *yarmulkes*. Skullcaps in place, they slipped into their assigned seats near the *bimah*, the pulpit.

Sol craned his neck and looked upstairs where the women sat, just in case Miriam had come to services. There were rarely women at morning services, even on Saturdays. They came mostly on Friday nights and holidays, when services were as much a social as a religious event. As Papa had often explained, even an Orthodox temple like this was not designed simply for prayer; it was a gathering place for Jews, a center of safety where they could exchange ideas—a meeting place. While the men did their socializing on the steps of the temple, in the community room, and on the grounds, many of the women—restricted from the acts of ritual in the synagogue, though no less dedicated to God—were not quite as disciplined. Like most boys, until he had begun his bar mitzvah studies Sol had prayed upstairs with his mother and sister. He did not quite understand why the men and women were separated, but he had rather liked it up there in the balcony, where he could watch the sunlight on the stained-glass roof of the tiny *shul* and look down proudly on the congregation of men wearing hand-embroidered skullcaps and wrapped in *tallis*, silk shawls that covered the shoulders of their *Shabbas* suits. They bent over prayer books and sang in deep and varied voices to their God and the God of their fathers. While the men repeated the ancient words that gave them such extraordinary comfort, he would listen as the women quietly gossiped, commented on each other's hats, decried the behavior of their children, and defended themselves against the shushes of the more devout women who had come to pray.

When Sol was sure Miriam was not there, he opened his prayer book. The Hebrew letters swam around on the page as if defying him to set them in place. He had the feeling someone was staring at him, and it was all he could do not to swivel around and look up again.

Deciding that he might as well practice his Hebrew, he concentrated on the Service. As always, once he gave himself over to it, he enjoyed the songs and the familiarity of the prayers. Even the sermon did not bore him, and by half past ten, having wished the rabbi and various members of the congregation a good Sabbath, he was almost sorry to be going home.

"Aren't we staying for the *Oneg Shabbat?*" he asked, referring to the bread and wine served after Sabbath Services.

"Not today," Jacob said. "We have been indoors enough. It's such beautiful weather. We shall walk home through the Tiergarten."

The day may have been beautiful in his father's prayer-misted eyes; in truth it was typically overcast. Even so, Sol enjoyed walking, especially in the Tiergarten when the smell of oncoming rain heightened the scent of the trees and masked the city's noxious odors. He liked to watch men in their double-breasted suits move arm-in-arm with their fashionable ladies toward the restaurants that dotted the Tiergarten's western edge. Sometimes he made bets with himself about which of them would end up at The Cigar Box, just beyond.

Surrounded by city and smoke, Berliners considered the two-hundred-hectare park their Eden, a notion the boys shared. They loved the arboretum and zoo, the restaurants and lake and open fields. There was plenty of room for playing ball, for roller-skating and riding bicycles. On lazier days they filled their pockets with acorns and chestnuts or simply watched the passengers riding past in open-topped, double-decker buses that rang their way from Potsdamer Platz to Pariser Platz and the Brandenburg Gate. Sometimes they lay near the lake on a palette of daisies and pansies and watched the young lovers who drifted by in rowboats, walked hand-in-hand along the narrow pathways, or monopolized benches that prostitutes considered their private domain.

Sol felt good strolling with his father in

companionable silence up the Konigsallee, each in his own way enjoying the rare opportunity of unhurried time together. Perhaps when they reached the Tiergarten, he would broach the subject of Erich's unfathomable anger. Perhaps even confide in Papa about the sewer.

Jacob Freund slowed to indulge in a pinch of snuff. "Our city is all business and energy," he said. "Men must have cigars to consummate business deals, and women cigarettes to contemplate how to spend the money their husbands make. On weekends they smoke to assure themselves the past week has been successful and that next week shall be even more successful. It is a good arrangement, an excellent legacy for you someday, Solomon, despite these inflationary times. For Erich, too."

He smiled. "You know how his father came to be with me? I advertised for help on Saturdays. He was hired to be our *Shabbas* goy, our Sabbath Gentile, as Mama called him. By the time I was inducted, he knew the business…I thought running it while I was away would stabilize him. Six years, it has been…."

Sol had heard the story many times. He nodded and mumbled once in a while as if he were listening, and returned to thinking about the events of the past week. He was pleased to be forgiven for the fuss he had made about playing the cello. As for the spanking, Papa had told him that was a matter of a lesson to be learned rather than punishment. They had not talked much about Rathenau or the luncheon—

What about Rathenau? Sol asked himself, as they passed the small local police station. Would there be more luncheons? Would the statesman keep his promise to make him a member-in-training of a generation of German Jews committed "to God and good government"? Or had Erich—and Miriam—ruined that?

"See that man? Chances are, even he buys a cigar now and then." Jacob pointed at a house being constructed across the street, next to the trolley stop. A bricklayer in coveralls lifted his peaked cap and grinned down at two women in nurses' uniforms who had stopped beneath his scaffolding.

"How goes it, Helene?" the workman shouted, balancing precariously.

The shorter of the two women smiled and waved. "Fine, Krischbin!" She had her hands cupped near her mouth to be heard above the late-morning traffic. "Still slapping up bricks, I see. You must like it up there."

"Who's your friend with the big blue eyes?"

The women grinned at each other. The second woman laughed and straightened her gray skirt. "Fräulein Steubenrauch," she called out. "Judith."

"Steubenrauch, huh! Related to the general?"

The women nodded and Krischbin looked impressed. "I did a job for him once. Liked him well enough. But his son was—" The man touched his temple as if to indicate derangement. "Fancied himself a revolutionary. Kept talking to me about joining his organization and helping to rid the Fatherland of—"

The woman's face soured. "Hans is just a boy."

"He has a mean mouth," the man said. "You should—"

A Daimler Benz neared, drowning out his words.

Sol pulled at his father's sleeve. "In the car, Papa—it's Herr Rathenau!"

"And why not? His house is practically around the

corner from *shul*. For shame he is never seen in synagogue when he lives so close. It might do the girl good, too, to be taken there once in a while."

Sol imagined Miriam dancing the cancan on her way to services, making partners of the birch trees, their trunks encased in silver leotards. As the car cruised past them, he waved, but the Foreign Minister was not looking his way.

"Do you think he will ever bring Miriam to see us again, Papa?"

A second convertible, this one with the top down and carrying three young men, closed on Rathenau's car as it slowed for the S-curve.

"Maybe someday. For now, he'll probably seclude her at his estate or send her to his sister in Switzerland. A word in the wrong ear, and Berlin will buzz with talk of Jewish immorality. Herr Rathenau can ill afford that kind of—"

Screeching tires interrupted him. The second car was overtaking Rathenau's, forcing it to the side of the road. The Foreign Minister, looking angered, shook his walking stick. They're in for it now, Sol thought, staring in disbelief at the rudeness of the rowdy occupants of the other car.

One of the youths—all three of whom were wearing leather jackets and caps—leaned toward Rathenau's car. Probably to apologize, Sol thought, looking at the young man's healthy, open face and reassuring smile.

"No!" Fräulein Steubenrauch screamed.

Tucking a machine pistol in his armpit to steady it, the young man fired point-blank at the statesman, who threw back his arms and collapsed.

"*Um Gottes Willen.*" Jacob knocked Solomon to the sidewalk and landed on top of him. "*Don't move!*"

From beneath his father, Sol blinked up at a crazy-tilting, slow-motion world. He could see the workman gesturing frantically at the nurses as he flattened himself on the swaying scaffolding.

Another of the leather-coated men stood upright. Clinging to the top of the windshield, he threw an egg-shaped object. It bounced on the tonneau and fell from the roof of the enclosed rear compartment of Rathenau's car into the street, where it lay spinning.

As the larger car started to roar away onto Wallotstrasse, the man tossed a second grenade, arm swinging with a follow-through.

The bomb went through Rathenau's open window and landed in the back seat. Konrad, screaming for help, tacked crazily to the left and pulled up on the tramlines near the entrance to Erdener Strasse.

"Herr Rathenau!" Sol yelled.

An explosion erupted. Rathenau's car seemed to rise and jump forward. The body in the back tossed upward like one of Recha's rag dolls, and Sol heard himself screaming.

Shrieking, Helene left her friend and ran toward Rathenau's car. She climbed in and bent over the Foreign Minister. Sol imagined him slumped, gazing toward the gray sky, mouth open, face covered with blood.

Konrad mashed gears and sent the Daimler squealing in reverse. He jammed the gears again, did a screeching U-turn onto the wrong side of the street, and raced away in the direction of the police station.

"They've killed him, Papa!"

Jacob Freund rolled off his son and sat on hands and knees, watching in shock as the workman climbed from his scaffolding and helped Fräulein Steubenrauch to her feet. As Sol started to stand, Jacob grabbed him by the lapels and pulled Sol's face close to his own, which was chalk-white.

"I wish you long life." His words were the ones Jews use to cover that moment of shock when death reminds you that you are not immortal.

"I wish you long life too, Papa!" Sol desperately wanted to cry, but no tears came. "Herr Rathenau, Papa! Wasn't he a good man?"

Shaking with fury, Jacob held Sol's cheeks, fingernails digging into the skin. "There is nothing Rathenau can do for us anymore," he said in a hoarse whisper, "but there *is* one thing you can do for him. Remember this day. Remember that we Jews can never be safe from our enemies. And may God help you, Solomon Freund, if you ever forget!"

Sobbing, Sol struggled to free himself. He watched Fräulein Steubenrauch stumble across the tram tracks and stagger in a daze down the street. Seeing the unexploded grenade lying on the pavement like a *dreidel*, he jerked from his father's grasp and ran toward her, waving frantically. "Get back!"

The world roared.

Instinctively he threw himself against the curb, sobbing with fear and sorrow as bits of metal and dirt rained against the back of his jacket.

Then silence filled the morning as if a storm had abruptly stopped. Summoning his courage he turned his head and saw the woman sprawled, twisting and squirming, on the pavement.

"Please don't be dead." He crawled toward her.

She momentarily lifted herself with her arms, blinking as though she were waking. Her nurse's uniform was shredded, her face and shoulders splotched with blood.

"I convinced myself they wouldn't do it," her lips told Sol. "I could have...have...warned Herr Rathenau, but I was afraid to get involved. I was afraid...." She laid her cheek against the pavement as if it were a goose-down pillow, and sighed.

Whimpering, Sol picked up one of the cartridge cases scattered along the street. "Don't be...dead." He held it out to her between forefinger and thumb, like an offering.

She looked up at him, her cobalt-blue eyes shining with tears. He felt himself swimming inside them, drawn into her dying. Filled with terror, he felt something rise from her and fight to enter his body as she shuddered, sighed, and lay still. He began to shake.

"There was nothing either of us could do," his father said, coming up behind Sol. Stooping, he took the woman's pulse. Then, releasing her wrist, he held Sol in his arms. When Sol's sobs had quieted, Jacob shrugged off the jacket of his *Shabbas* suit and draped it over her. He glanced around anxiously as police-car klaxons rang through the Grünewald.

"This is no place for a Jew to be found." He took Sol's hand and led him away. "May God rest her soul."

"Something happened to me, Papa!" Sol was sobbing. "I could feel—"

A fog enveloped his mind. In a world that seemed a

dream, he was aware of a taxi, its door yawning. The glass that separated passenger from driver seemed to hold an image of Walther Rathenau, composed and elegant and gracious as they threaded their way toward the Adlon; and superimposed upon that was a vision of the statesman, slumped over and covered with blood. When they stopped on Friedrich Ebert Strasse, he recognized the shop and the need to vomit.

"Have you heard the news?" Friedrich Weisser asked as they entered the cigar store.

"We saw it all," Jacob said.

"Saw it! My word!" Friedrich wiped his hands on his apron, his eyes sparkling with envy. "Is it possible? They say the chauffeur miraculously wasn't hurt by the grenade."

"There were two grenades."

"Two! Nothing about *that* on the radio."

Sol's mother came hurrying across the street, her shawl fluttering. "Jacob! Solomon! I've been so worried!"

"We're fine, Ella. Sol's dazed. But fine."

"We must close the shop," Friedrich Weisser said. "The radio said people are already entering the streets to demonstrate against the murder. There could be looting."

"Yes. Close the shop," Jacob said. "Who is demonstrating?"

"Workers from the factories. They say they'll be marching four deep within the hour—"

"We must join them."

Ella Freund touched her husband's arm. "But there could be danger. They will never miss us if we mourn him here, at home."

Janet Berliner and George Guthridge

"We shall join them nevertheless," Jacob said. "All of us."

His wife turned away. "You men are all the same. If Walther Rathenau, may he rest in peace, had listened to his mother, he would be alive. They say she did everything she could to stop him from becoming Foreign Minister. She knew his life would be in danger."

Sol heard the conversation but could not respond to it. Once in the apartment, he came out of his stupor. He felt strange. Angry. Sad. He knew something had happened, something more than the obvious tragedy, but he did not know what. He was grateful when his mother suggested they do something normal, like wash up and eat lunch, yet he felt guilty that he was hungry.

"It's nearly one," she said. "Who knows when we'll get home?"

Apparently sensing his son's discomfort, Jacob looked across the table at Sol. "Life must go on," he told Solomon. "Eat your soup."

Sol did so, and was washing the bowl when he heard Herr Weisser yelling. Please, no more trouble, he thought, opening the front door. Erich stood in the main foyer, in uniform. He *wants* his papa to get angry, Sol thought, remembering what Erich had said about his father. What he cannot stand is his papa's weakness. Why can't Herr Weisser see that?

"So! Now you're wearing your defiance," Herr Weisser said. "Go to your room and change. I'll give you," Friedrich glanced at his watch, "two minutes."

Erich climbed to the next landing and looked down over the banister. His voice sounded choked with anger, though whether at himself or at his father, Sol could not tell. "I'm not going anywhere. Especially not with you."

Visibly controlling his temper, Friedrich went up the stairs and, bending before his son, straightened the boy's Freikorps tie. "They've shot Herr Rathenau. There's a demonstration. We do business in this city. We cannot afford not to pay our respects...all of us."

Erich pulled away and went up farther. "He's dead— that's all that matters to me. *Rathenau, old Walther, shall have a timely halter!*" he sang, insolently and off-key, staring at Sol, who had seen the German youth song printed in the *Social Democrat.*

Please don't sing the rest, Erich, Sol begged silently, remembering the last lines: *Shoot down Walther Rathenau...The Goddamned swine of a Jewish sow.*

"Shoot—" Erich began.

Something's boiling over in him, Sol thought. Something that's been brewing all week.

Face reddening, Friedrich started after the boy, but Frau Weisser gently caught her husband by the wrist and slightly, darkly, shook her head. Sol heard Erich race up the remaining stairs, unlock the apartment, and slam the door behind himself.

"It's not my place to interfere between parents and son, but we're all involved." Jacob climbed a step and reached out a hand to his friends. "We will always be involved with one another. What the boy has done is despicable. You must make him come with us. Can't you see he's crying out for you to be strong?"

"You knew about this uniform he wears?" Herr Weisser asked Solomon, raising his hand.

Sol backed away, sure he was going to be struck. "He told me not to tell."

"You knew, yet said nothing!" Then a look of vapid acceptance came over Friedrich. "You are not to blame, Solomon." He shook his head sadly. "It is that *boy* up there. I keep telling myself—" he was speaking to Jacob now— "it is because of the seizures, but we cannot blame everything on those. I cannot remember when Erich was not rebellious. My papa used to tell me, 'Life is not always cause and effect, despite what your so-called science claims.' I should have listened to his advice. I should have understood." He took his wife's hand. "We go now, Mama. The boy can do as he wishes. He always has."

Without waiting for Erich, the rest of them went down the stairs, out the main door and into the June sun, which had broken through the clouds. Before long, they were part of a spontaneous, giant procession snaking silently up Unter den Linden toward the Reichstag. Already, people said, Rathenau was being brought there to lie in state.

Gone were the ladies in expensive hats and the riders who used the grassy sides of the boulevard to exercise themselves and their horses, gone the men in top hats and the children and toy poodles.

The workers owned the boulevard. They marched, faces set and in silence, alongside street-corner hooligans, politicians, and prostitutes. Like an orderly lynch mob, they moved steadily forward, four and then six abreast as people joined from every alley and side street.

Above the crowd, the black-red-gold banners of the Republic waved in the breeze alongside the red banners of socialism. Politics were set aside for the first time in over a decade as Berlin mourned a statesman who had begun to set into motion his personal dream of a better Germany through negotiation.

"He was so much the aristocrat," Friedrich Weisser said, his mouth close to Jacob's ear. In order to talk to his partner, he had to lean over Solomon, who marched between the two men. "I never realized he had such a following among the working class."

"In a year, they will claim he was purely a man of the people." Jacob Freund was staring straight ahead. "They will even conveniently forget he was a Jew."

For the first time in his life, Sol felt his father's bitterness as his own. "In a year," Sol said, "they will blame his murder on the Jews."

Chapter Eighteen

"It's been some time since your bar mitzvah, Sol," Beadle Cohen said. "I have missed you. Will you be returning for advanced Judaic studies?"

Sol rubbed his temples, hoping to ease his headache. Bar mitzvah boys went two ways: some swore they would never read another word of Hebrew or Judaica in their lives; others, suddenly filled with sentiment, expressed the intention of becoming rabbis or Hebrew scholars and never doing anything else. Unsure of how he felt, he had devoted what little time he had—when not studying or working for Papa—to reading and rereading his growing library of books on Jewish mysticism.

He had come to no conclusions, except to decide that, for the time being, he fell somewhere between the cracks.

As a bar mitzvah gift, the beadle, already responsible for the library of mystical books in Sol's room, had given him the *Book of Formation* and the first book of the Lurianic Kabbalah. Both were inscribed with his usual message: "When you are ready, you will understand."

Thus far, all Sol understood was that Luria believed Jews were born with a consciousness of their heritage— a sort of untapped well of accumulated experience and knowledge.

"Beadle Cohen, I need your guidance. I know I want to continue learning," he said, "but I don't really want to be part of a set traditional program."

As always, the beadle got straight to the point. "You don't look well. Is there something I can do to help you?"

Sol paced around the beadle's study—wondering where and how to begin—suppressing the urge to shout, scream, throw something across the room. He was moody and depressed most of the time, struggling with unaccountable angers, convinced he was being haunted by the soul of the woman who had practically died in his arms, and fighting blinding headaches. The voices came more and more, repeating words and phrases that made no sense.

"I have nightmares," he said slowly. "I see Erich hanging from the grating. I hear...sounds. Strange, ugly laughter that is Erich's, but isn't human."

Except for the bar mitzvah, which Erich had attended despite the pressure of his Freikorps-Youth friends, Sol had seen little of his friend since Rathenau's death. He knew that the Weissers had finally given Erich permission to belong to the group, and he had watched Erich's uniformed comings and goings, but they had not done anything together. They had not even gone to the hideout, which was just as well. He was still trying to escape his memories of the assassination and of Erich's ugly behavior that day.

"I keep thinking Rathenau's assassins are after me...."

"Tillessen, von Salomon, and the Techow brothers are in prison," the beadle said.

Sol knew that. And Kern and Fischer, the ringleaders of what had proved to be a conspiracy, had been tracked down, too. One was shot to death; the other committed suicide. Yet in his nightly imaginings, they came to his window, holding knives and grenades, looking for the boy-witness.

"I get headaches," he said. "I hear voices...one woman cries out *'Oh God, let me die. I did not know...I did not know.'* Another talks of *sweetbreads* to someone called Margabrook who speaks to her of lice and the dreams of dead men."

Haltingly he told the beadle about the sounds in the sewer, and about the feeling that something had entered him, taken possession of him as he had looked into the eyes of the dying woman.

The beadle listened without interruption. "Ever see flashes of light?" he asked when Sol fell silent.

Sol nodded. "Right before the headaches come. The doctor says it's part of them."

"That is one possibility. There are others. You have read *The Book of Formation?*"

Again Sol nodded. Terrified, searching for answers, he had read and reread it. The more he came to understand, the more afraid he became.

"Solomon ben Luria was a mystic and a prophet," the

beadle said. "He knew the past and had visions of the future. They were always presaged by brilliant flashes of light."

"I see nothing. I just hear voices, over and over—"

"Give it time, Sol."

"Are you saying—"

"God has the answers. The only help I can offer is to suggest possibilities."

"For example?"

"Are you sure you want to hear this, Solomon?" The beadle looked extremely serious. When Sol nodded, the beadle sighed in resignation and said, "All right, then. I'll tell you what I think. I have known you for a long time, Sol, and I do not say this lightly. I believe it is entirely possible that, like Ben Luria, you are a visionary. I also believe you have a dybbuk in you, and that it is muddying your abilities. When…if…the dybbuk leaves you, everything will become clear."

"I don't want any…any *thing* in me," Sol said, then mentally backed away, embarrassed even to countenance such an outrageous possibility. Like most Jewish boys, he had heard of dybbuks—vaguely—some kind of soul that was unable to transmigrate to a higher world because the person had sinned against humanity.

"I just think I'm going crazy," he said. "Am I? Tell me…*please!*"

"Sometimes," the beadle said, "dybbuks seek refuge in the bodies of living persons, causing instability, speaking foreign words through their mouths."

"You're saying that *that's* what is wrong with me?" Sol asked, dazed.

"Perhaps."

"Well, get rid of it! It's affecting my schoolwork. It's affecting my whole life! My parents are worried—and I don't blame them. I can't talk to them about something like... How could I possibly tell them!" Exasperated, he put his head in his hands.

The beadle waited for Sol to calm down. "Sometimes a rabbi can exorcise a dybbuk," he said at last. "But that is not always the right answer. You are strong, Solomon. For those who are strong, a dybbuk can open doors into worlds that other men cannot enter. Eventually it will depart as it came—unbidden—and then you will understand its message. Go home and think about it."

Leaving the question of his studies unanswered, Sol went home. That night, lying in bed, he wished he had opened himself up to the beadle sooner. He had almost forgotten how much he treasured their discussions. The man was the only person he knew who was not afraid to acknowledge the difference between rhetoric and original thought. He really listened, debated each point, gave of his knowledge, yet left the conclusions open so that Sol never felt like a young know-nothing fool when he expressed his views.

It was amazing, Sol thought, how quickly life could change. Bedtime had once been the best part of his day. In bed, it had no longer mattered that when he took off his glasses he could not see things in sharp focus. He had liked the way his lace curtains clothed the night sky in crisscross patterns and the way the moon looked dressed in lace. He had even made up stories about moon men and about beautiful princesses held captive in lunar craters.

But, as with so many other things in his life, the death

of Walther Rathenau had altered all that. Reality had conspired to draw aside the lace curtains in his life. These days, after his parents made sure he was in bed and closed the door, his inclination was to reach for his glasses; as he watched the clouds chase each other across the moon, his head was filled with thoughts of the Adlon luncheon and of assassins who lusted after blood and power, instead of Hessian princes who fought moon men with swords bejeweled with stars. More often than not, he fell asleep with his glasses on, even on nights like this when he could see the full moon with clarity. Ringed with dark clouds, it was set in a night filled with questions. Why did God allow assassins? Why am I a Jew first and a German second? Falling asleep was no longer an easy drifting, but a time for doubts and fear—and headaches—

He felt a sharp stab of pain in his left temple. Groaning, he pressed his knuckles into the pain. There was another stab of pain and a flash of light which dissolved into pinpoints floating in the night like fireflies. A cobalt-blue glow superimposed itself over the darkness and he huddled, terrified, under his eiderdown.

Don't think about it, Margabrook. Just drink the tea, he heard a woman say, her voice familiar.

Best you get rid of it now, Peta, a man said. Sol knew the voice well. *If you don't acknowledge the soldiers' twisted idea of a joke, who knows what they will put in the teapot the next time.*

Then the lights...and the headache...were gone. All that was left was the blue glow and, emerging out of it—

—*a paraffin lamp casts a lavender shadow across a rude*

table in the center of a one-room wooden shack. Snow blows through gaps in the wall-boards. Beyond a single small window, curled edges of snowdrifts mass like breaking waves. Smoke veils the ceiling. A man in a ragged army overcoat and woolen scarf huddles close to a brazier's red coals. Frostbite has scabbed and pockmarked his dark sunken cheeks. His eyes are dull, his hands wrapped in bloodstained gauze. An emaciated woman wearing an old blanket, an ancient carbine slung across her back, steps from the shadows in the corner and leans over him. Carefully she unwinds the gauze from one of his hands. The fingers are gangrenous stumps.

Eyeing the old man angrily, the woman uses the edge of her blanket as a pot holder and removes the cast-iron teapot from the brazier's grate. She raises the lid of the teapot and looks inside.

Her face hardens.

"You've seen worse," the old man mutters. Lifting the edge of his coat, he unsheathes and hands her the bayonet that was strapped to his leg. "Pick out the thing and save the tea."

She has started to pour the contents of the teapot into the snow through a large crack between two of the unplaned floorboards. Apparently deciding the old man is right, she takes the knife and clanks it around inside the pot.

"What a waste." She pulls out a steaming thumb, stuck through with the knife. "Looks like sweetbreads, eh Margabrook?" She swipes the knife against the brazier. The thumb slides off the blade and onto the floor; she pokes at it like a child worrying a snail.

"Doesn't matter what it looks like," the old man says. "Don't even think about putting it in your mouth. Between us, we get enough food to stay alive."

"So what."

"You'll hate yourself."

"The only thing worth hating is hunger." The woman reinserts the bayonet and turns the thumb over to scrutinize it. "You Nazis! *Your* mandate is hatred. *Mine* is survival."

"Nazi? No! But I *am* German, and proud of it." He lowers his voice. "I joined the Nazis because, like you, I thought survival was everything. I have learned. It is what survives in *here* that counts." He thumps his chest with a gauze-wrapped fist. "Retain what little dignity the world still accords you, Peta. Forget what the others out there have become and leave that thing alone."

"You don't know what hunger is," she says. "When you had nothing to eat, you fed on idealism. I've had none of that with which to fill my belly or heart."

Unbuttoning his coat, the old man takes out a tin cup and holds it up. The woman fills it and her own cup from the teapot, gulps down her tea, and pours herself a second cup.

"What I'd give for fresh goat's milk," he says, touching palsied fingers to his lips as if complimenting the chef. "You city dwellers know nothing of such delicacies. My mother milked the goats every morning—"

An explosion rattles the shack and snow billows through the cracks. The old man shakes his head sadly and returns to his tea, ignoring the yellow-and-red starbursts that bruise what sky can be seen through the window. "Again the steppes test us," he says, putting down his cup.

The woman unslings the carbine and checks the bolt, dry-firing the weapon three times. "Here, put on your *Kopfschützer*, old man." She hands him a balaclava. Having pulled one over her own head, she helps him up. "Make sure there's enough paper stuffed inside or your ears will fall off from the cold, like Hansie's did."

On crippled feet he hobbles to the door and waits for her to open it. A gust of wind pulls it from her hand and slams it against the outer wall of the hut.

Facing them is a long gentle slope ending in what appears to be a frozen lake shining like a silver platter beneath thick low clouds. Except for clumps of rushes, feathery with ice and sticking up here and there at windblown angles, the area seems without vegetation— a white treeless waste. Along the edge of the lake, white-clad infantry move like phantoms before a line of tanks. Bursts of smoke from the armored vehicles are followed seconds later by the sharp crack of firing and sprays of snow farther up the hill.

At the crest of the hill, behind a breastwork of what looks like ice-covered logs, a group of men crank howitzer barrels into position. Others pull white canvas tarpaulins off mortars and machine guns. From that distance, the men and machinery look like a collection of animated pewter miniatures.

"I've had goat's milk." As she surveys the battle scene, the woman speaks as if their conversation has never been interrupted. "I have eaten and drunk almost anything you can name."

"Your family was wealthy?"

Through knee-deep snow they crunch uphill toward the gunnery. From all over the hill, people like them emerge from huts and, like disconnected threads, move toward the battlement.

"Nonpracticing Jews and Party members like us managed some luxuries," she says. "Unfortunately, Papa had reservations about the Party and talked too much. Someone informed on him. They convened a Kolhosp court and accused us of being exploiters of the poor—*Kurkuls*. My parents were sent to help dig the Baltic Sea-White Sea Canal, or so we children were told."

Her expression softens as she speaks of her parents. Now it hardens again. "They disappeared. The Komsomol sent my brothers and me to a collective and assigned us to the worst of the subunits—the crocodiles."

The man nods, saying nothing.

"They said we who gobbled the bread of the Soviets had to meet harvest quotas. We were villagers and townspeople competing against farmers and even they could not meet the quota, because whenever they did, it was raised."

She halts in front of a pair of boots sticking out of a snowdrift. "These will keep the chilblains away from my toes." She tugs at them. "Come on. Help me."

The old man bends to help. They both pull, but nothing budges.

"If we failed to meet the quota, we were put on the *chorna doshka*, the blacklist." Gasping, she lets loose of the boots. "Our rations were halved. Not until the Soviet is satisfied! they'd tell us. Nurse the fields.

Nurture them. Fill up on the conscience of the collective!"

"Bastards," the old man says. "I was much luckier than you. I grew up in the Oberharz, in Hahenklee, right next door to Paul Lincke's house. Once he even walked to Goslar with us, to watch the figures dance around the old town Glockenspiel. He said they should be dancing to *his* music. Often my friends and I watched the cable car carry tourists around Bad Lauterberg or watched them eat cake in the cafés. Before going home, we dug in the garbage for leftovers. When the tourists stopped coming, we roasted crickets and field mice and picked gooseberries and wild mushrooms. We thought ourselves kings—except for those who died because they could not tell toadstools from *Steinpilze.*"

"They say seven hundred thousand have died in the Ukraine," the woman says. "God only knows how many of those starved to death! We thought it a blessing when you Nazis came to liberate our village. We thought you'd put us in ghettos and leave us alone."

She looks up; the howitzers are returning fire. "Lend me your ax," she says.

The old man ignores her demand. "When this war started, I was too old to enlist. Like an idiot, I pulled strings and became a soldier for the Reich! I was assigned to an extermination center in eastern Poland. Would you believe I thought I'd be killing lice? *Lice!*"

"You're an old fool, Margabrook."

"Daily there came new truckloads of Jews. They were asked for volunteers who could operate heavy equipment. The endloaders were assigned to dig graves.

Each hour we shot so many people we had to soak our rifle barrels in cold water to cool them." He snorted sarcastically. "The Jews dying by the hundreds, and we worried about rust! At twilight, when the graves were filled and covered, our Untersturmführer made the endloader operators lie on the mounds, heads together and feet outward like daisy petals. Then he shot them in the stomach and watched them bleed to death. A flower of death to commemorate man's capacity for evil."

"I suppose that is why you won't carry a carbine, even here at the Front?"

"There are no real Fronts. This is a world without Fronts. Only backstabbing and lies…lies," he repeats softly.

"You're right, old man. Now give me your ax or I will take it from you."

He touches her arm and points at the breastworks. "Let the dead dream their dreams in peace. Look at them. A wall of dead soldiers masquerading as logs to protect their living comrades in a treeless land."

He steps closer to the battlement. The woman follows.

"Don't give in…as I did." He stares at the frozen bodies. Icy limbs protrude in impossibly contorted positions. Faces are molded into snow-covered masks.

The woman shrugs. "Stalin starves people, Hitler shoots them, we use them as logs. What's the difference?" When he doesn't answer, she turns back toward the boots. "The hatchet, please, old man. I am younger and stronger than you are, and I intend to survive. I want those boots. When the rest of you run out of paper to wrap your feet in, mine will be warm."

He hands her the hatchet. "Three days now the clouds

have held." Knee-deep in snow, the old man looks up at the sky. A worker next to him grabs hold of a corpse and flops it down as if it is a sandbag. The old man glances at it, then at a row of fresh bodies. The setting sun—its palette congealed blood and military uniforms—decorates the dead with ribbons of russet and gold.

With the woman's first determined swing, one of the soldier's legs cracks like a large dry stick—

Sol sat upright. His heart was pounding madly, but his headache was gone. So were the blue glow and the voices. All that remained was the stillness of midnight.

He recalled that the beadle had spoken of visions. Could this...he shook his head and lay down again. A nightmare, he decided. He had fallen asleep while trying to analyze the voices, and his night-mind, encroaching upon his wakeful efforts, had created faces, bodies, a story to match some of the voices: the woman's, talking of sweetbreads; the old man, Margabrook, speaking of lice and saying, "Let the dead dream their dreams in peace."

He shuddered, remembering the boiled thumb.

Think about something else.

Miriam.

He looked over at the framed photograph Erich had given him as his bar mitzvah gift, wrapped in a square of mauve silk. He still had not figured out how Erich acquired the photograph of Miriam, but he was glad he had it. He smiled, remembering how she had winked at him during the most serious moment of his bar mitzvah speech. Later, just before he intoned the blessing over the long *Challah*, the slightly sweet, plaited bread that looked like a woman's shining braid, she had pushed her way through to him and kissed his cheek. He had felt so benign about everybody that day, as if writing his speech and thanking them all for their love had been a tonic. Take one spoonful morning and night for three days and the world will look better.

He snuggled into his pillow. If he could just figure out how to feel that way every day, he thought.

C HAPTER NINETEEN

Camouflaged with the green-and-brown facial pastes the Youth leaders had given them, Erich and some of the other boys from the group hid behind a hedge and spied on the last of the day's Wannsee picnickers. Night had long since fallen. Moonlight lay upon the lake, and still the people lingered, gathering their foodstuffs, folding blankets, and slipping into their clothes.

It was the boys' assignment to watch and report, though for what reason Erich could not figure out. There was all too much about the Youth group that he could not understand these days, though nothing as much as the experience near Lutherstrasse, which had spoiled things for him more than anyone would ever understand. Anyone, that is, except Solomon, who was the one person he could never tell about it. No more than he could ever again convince himself that Rittmeister Otto Hempel was his ideal.

Worst of all was what seeing the Rittmeister that night had done to his relationship with the other boys at the camp. He had never really been close to them, but he'd never felt completely felt estranged, either. Now he found it harder and harder to relate to them at all. Except for the stuff about the Jews, his belief in the original ideas of the Wandervögel remained unshaken. For that reason, he shut his mouth when they talked of the perfection of their hero, Otto Hempel, and when they downgraded Erich because of his friendship with Solomon—though with all his faults, Sol was a prince compared with these boys.

"I'm hungry," one of the younger boys said, staring in the direction of the nearest picnic basket. "You'd think they'd throw some of that food away."

"I'll check the garbage cans," a second boy said.

Erich put a restraining hand on his arm. "They're not supposed to see us. You're a soldier. You can go without food till later."

"We've been crawling around for hours just watching. It's boring. Aren't we supposed to do something to the people?"

The whine in the boy's voice was beginning to irritate Erich. He would have said something, but one of the older boys got in first. "Quit whining, kid. Good question, though. Anyone know why we're here?"

"We're doing what we were told to do. That's enough," someone answered.

"Says who?"

Another boy joined them in the underbrush. His eyes, accented by the ragged lines of paste, gleamed in the moonlight. "Come and look," he said. "They're dressing at the naked beach!"

Not naked beach, nudist beach, you idiot, Erich thought. He glanced through the woods toward the whitewashed fence that demarcated the nudist beach from the family picnic area. "Why would you want to watch people putting their clothes *on?*"

"When the women have their skirts but not their tops on, it makes their…" the boy cupped his hands over his chest, "stand out."

Though he had no interest in seeing unclothed people, Erich understood the boy's fascination. He had spied through and over the fence dozens of times. Everyone he knew had, even Solomon. The first times had been exciting, but the truth was that he found little erotic about assorted naked women lounging around, displaying their lumps and sags, or men with their penises flopping around like cooked noodles. What he did like was watching the women dress. That made his heart beat wildly in his throat. When a woman was naked, his interest waned within moments, but when she dressed herself, the result was just the opposite. He wondered if the other boys felt that way, but feared to ask, lest they laugh at him for being abnormal.

"They're hard, aren't they?" one of the boys asked.

"Titties?" The boy's friend sounded incredulous. "They're soft. Like pillows."

"They bleed, you know," one of the boys added. "Girls bleed. Women, too."

"Once a month," Erich said, feeling obliged to contribute. "Down here." He patted his crotch, proud to dispel the belief he knew some boys had—that the bleeding happened at the breasts, the reason for brassieres.

The possibility of the female phenomenon was debated, but Erich was not listening. A bitch's keening had floated toward him from their camp across the lake. Grace's voice. Crying in pain, her pregnancy bothering her again. He did not look around, as he once would have, to see if the other boys had heard her too. He had accepted long ago that he was attuned to the canine mind in a way that no one else was. He could feel not only the animals' thoughts, but their emotions. If he mentioned any of that to the other boys, all they would do was laugh at him, like the time he had asked, as circumspectly as possible, about the sexual habits of the Rittmeister, who was most of the boys' favorite leader.

Probably does it to *lots* of women, the boys agreed.

What about with …boys? Erich had asked.

Maybe you want to put a straw up your penis or a stick up your butt and let him watch, they had said, laughing uproariously. Maybe you want to kiss his wiener or put *that* in your butt!

Erich had flown in with his fists, but the others ganged up against him. He had grabbed a burning log and started swinging, and they had backed off. No one had challenged him since, but the laughter continued to haunt…and hurt. He could not abide being laughed at in the first place, but *again*, by the same boys, especially when he knew he was right…that was unthinkable. As for putting a straw up one's penis, supposedly the ultimate in sexual satisfaction, he could no more imagine himself like that than he could imagine willingly tolerating their derision.

Grace's mental cry for help came again, less urgent now but equally disquieting. She was a beautiful shepherd, or *shepherdess*, as he preferred to say. He spent as much time as possible with her, often to the detriment of learning woodsman skills or practicing his javelin throwing, at which he had become adept. Whenever the leaders began deprecating the Jews, or praising the contributions of the Storm Troopers or the National Socialists, he would sit stroking her, staring into the campfire and listening to her voice, her inner being. Or he would put his head against her silky coat, pretending to look for fleas and concentrating on her so hard that he heard the minds of her unborn pups.

"Let's find some food or go see the naked people," the smallest boy said, careful to eliminate the whine from his voice.

After minor discussion about whether they should leave their present posts, the boys set off, spreading out among the trees as they had been taught. Erich looked back once at the traditional picnickers departing the park, envious of family outings that were pleasant, fun, concluded without the battles that inevitably took place when he and his parents spent any time together. Then he moved forward with the others.

When the boys reached the fence, they found the nudist area empty. They gathered to decide whether to raid the garbage cans, as was customary, or simply to return to camp.

Then, drifting out from the edge of the lake came a woman's laughter, musical, tinkling. A young man and woman ran from the shadows, a gray French poodle prancing alongside them on a leash. The man put his arms around the woman's waist and pulled her off the ground, twirling once as, her arms around his neck, he kissed her, the dog struggling to keep up with the choreography.

Back on her feet, the woman tied the end of the leash to a sun-umbrella post, pulled off her sweater, and unhooked her brassiere. The man stripped off his shirt and trousers and placed them neatly in a pile next to her tumble of clothing. The moonlight bathed his white back and buttocks. Sitting down, she shed her white shorts and reached up as if to tug on his penis. He dodged her hand, laughed, and pulled her to her feet.

"I know him," the oldest boy said. "His name's Stein. A stinking crop-crippled Jew."

Erich cringed at the boy's use of one of the Rittmeister's favorite phrases. With a sense of impending disaster, he watched the couple race hand-in-hand toward the beach and plunge into the water, leaving the dog to yip sadly at having been left alone.

"Just look at them," the same boy said. "Dirtying our lake. If only the Rittmeister were here. Bet he'd teach them a thing or two!"

The boys looked at one another expectantly. The sudden quiet chilled Erich. "Let's steal their clothes," he said, to alleviate the tension and prevent some worse idea from taking form.

He grabbed hold of the fence, pulled himself over, and stood on the other side for a moment, wondering if this was such a good idea. Before the other boys had a chance to huddle and decide on a more dangerous plan, he snatched up the clothes and sprinted into the trees. He tossed the things among the branches—the boyfriend would have a scratchy climb among rough bark and needles, but could retrieve everything—and, feeling the brassiere's satin lining, turned to watch the others coming toward him, ready to show them his trophy.

They were fanned out amid the shadows. The poodle increased its yipping, warning its owners instead of begging to be let loose, but the couple was too busy splashing each other and kissing to hear the change of tone in his bark.

The youngest boy seized the leash and tugged the poodle after him. The dog, its legs splayed, tried desperately to pull away. Another boy ran over, holding a garbage can lid like a shield, and slammed it down against the animal. The dog squealed and collapsed, its legs kicking. Fear and pain raced up Erich's neck and down to his ankles.

"Hey there!" the man yelled as he came tearing toward them from the water. "Stop that!"

The smaller of the two boys grabbed the poodle by the tail and pulled it beneath the trees. The one with the lid slammed it down again. Erich and the poodle shrieked simultaneously with the pain of the impact. For a moment Erich felt too dazed to react. Then he stumbled toward the animal and its attacker, aware in his peripheral vision that two of the other boys were hurling rocks at the man, who was running naked from the lake. Through stunned senses, he saw him halt, arms raised against the stones, while the woman huddled in the water, trying to cover herself.

He was almost at the poodle's side when one of the boys yanked another garbage lid from its can and held it up, blocking Erich's way. "We all know how you feel about Jews!" the boy said. "Are you with them or with us?"

Erich pushed against the lid, but his strength, like the poodle's, had ebbed. He felt defenseless against the boy and his two rock-throwing friends who had raced over to join the fight.

"He's a Jew dog, Erich!" one of them yelled.

Another boy spat on the ground. "A *French* Jew dog!"

A rock bounced off a tree trunk as the man returned the rock-barrage, but the boys had lost interest in him and were concentrating on Erich and the dog. One held the dog's collar, another the hind legs, while a third continued to beat down with the lid.

"Cut the damn mutt's legs off!" someone shouted. "That's what the Rittmeister would do!"

A jackknife blade snapped open, glinting in the moonlight, and the boy with the knife knelt over the poodle. Though the boy had his back to him, Erich could see the blood-hunger in his eyes.

I'm seeing through the dog's eyes! Erich thought.

Knowing that the action was not going to increase his popularity with the other boys, yet having to defend the dog—and thus himself—he picked up one of the lids that had been dropped nearby. Lunging, he pushed it against the face of the boy with the knife, so startling him that he dropped the weapon. Erich tried to get it, but he was too late. Someone picked it up and slashed down at the dog. The poodle howled, and pain sliced through Erich, sending him reeling.

"Again!" the boy at the collar said. The dog twisted savagely. "Cut him again, Albert!"

The knife slashed down and Erich collapsed to his

knees. *Bite!* his mind cried out to the dog. *Bite, for all you're worth.*

Something warm filled his mouth.

"It bit my hand!" one of the boys wailed. "The son of a bitch bit me!"

The others abandoned their attack on Erich and turned to look. One of them stepped forward and kicked at the dog with his hiking boot. Erich felt the kick in his ribs. Just as he thought he would faint from the pain, two cars pulled up. A party of loud merrymakers exited the cars, heading their way. The pounding stopped. He staggered to his feet and stumbled toward the fence. Knowing he was too weak to climb, he sat down in the grass and fought to catch his breath as he watched the last of the boys scatter, hooting, into the deeper shadows. The man and woman were kneeling over the dog, she shrieking.

Sobbing with equal parts of pain and shame, Erich crawled to the lake. He washed the taste of blood from his mouth and, using handfuls of sand as soap, cleansed the paint from his skin. He was ready to leave when he felt another dog call to him, this time from across the lake.

"Grace," he whispered.

She too was in pain, though not from death but from birth. He must go to her. The problem was, if she were in desperate straits, he would need help, and he would sooner die than ask the leaders—or certainly the other boys—for anything tonight.

Which left only Solomon.

Chapter Twenty

Something clunked against the window frame.

Sol was immediately wide awake and terrified. He pulled the edge of his eiderdown close to his throat and waited for a face to appear, plastered against the pane and framed by the night—Rathenau's, perhaps, a bloodstained Reichsbanner handkerchief covering his shattered jaw as he demanded to be led to the sewer where the dead lived.

Moving as little as possible, Sol crept his fingers along the night table in search of the lamp. Not that he really wanted to flood the room with light and turn himself into an icon, unable to see out while the night saw in.

"Solomon!" A loud hoarse whisper.

Erich.

Shaking, Sol threw off the covers and padded to the window. Cupping his hands against the sides of his face to reduce the glare of moonlight, he squinted toward the scrawny blue-spruce hedge that demarcated the lot of the apartment building from the sidewalk. Erich crouched near the hedge corner where they had played in the days before they had found their sewer hideout.

Wondering fleetingly what had become of the toys they'd had then—his war ambulances, specially ordered from Planck's in Frankfurt; Erich's hand-carved hook-and-ladder; the miniature human figures he and Erich fought over—Sol opened the window and thrust out his head.

Erich waved furiously. "Come down!" He went over and shut the apartment building door—evidently he had just come from within—then jumped over the hedge and grabbed up his bicycle, which was lying on the sidewalk. Mounting, he motioned again for Sol to join him.

"What is it? Tell me!" Sol cursed under his breath. He sensed trouble. Erich seemed to be less and less the boy with whom he had grown up. Everything might have been so different if he had come along to the Adlon, Sol thought sadly and with a renewed pang of guilt at not having tried harder to persuade Rathenau to include Erich in the invitation.

"We're still blood brothers, aren't we?" Erich raised his wrist in the old gesture. "Come down. It's important!"

Sol pulled himself into his trousers, a corded sweater, and a pair of old shoes. He put on his cap and took a rucksack from the crowded shelf that held his schoolbooks and his pewter Hessian soldiers. Tucking his jacket under his arm, he poked his head into the hall and stared at his parents' door.

No, he decided, returning to the window; if his parents

heard him, this adventure would be over before it started. He was tired of kowtowing to Erich's demands, yet he felt flattered when his friend insisted on including him in his unlikely adventures.

The sill was wide and he was able to balance in a squat while he shut the window behind him. Tossing down the rucksack and jacket, he launched himself two meters to the ground and landed briefly on his feet before his knees gave out and he tumbled onto the dirt.

"Hurry!" Erich stood with one leg in the hedge, urging Sol forward. "It's Grace. She's about to have her pups—and there's no one to help her. I heard her crying. Something's gone wrong."

"You *heard* her? All the way from Wannsee?"

"You have to help, *Spatz. Please*, Sol."

"You want me to go with you to Wannsee? To the *camp?*"

"I don't really understand the Jew-hating and the awful things they say, honestly I don't."

"If you don't understand, why parrot them?"

"I'm going to change things, Sol!" Erich's voice was tense. "When I'm a leader I won't let them do those things. Our group used to be different. We weren't like those others who do things—"

"Things?"

Sol had heard about those "things"—the initiation rites, like the older ones peeing on the younger ones to delineate authority; like demanding that they give up loyalty to everything but the group.

"Come on! *Please!*" Erich trundled the bike onto the street and, one foot on the curb for support, kept it steady.

Sol mounted the handlebars. Erich's bike was a secondhand Machnow Herr Weisser picked up at an auction over on Muhldamm. Erich had painted the bike red and black, the new colors of his Freikorps unit. Sol had no bike of his own. His mother felt they were too dangerous in a city.

Erich shoved away from the curb. The bike wobbled as he fought to balance it and Sol.

They passed the open square of Potsdamer Platz and wound through the Kurfurstendamm's more squalid section, where soap-streaked windows, spiderwebbed with shadows, were made lurid by the moonlight. Dilapidated marquees announced burlesque shows. Handwritten signs pasted on shop windows advertised going-out-of-business sales. Butcher shops boasted of specials on high-quality meat—Grade A cats and dogs, more than likely, Sol was sure. Homeless huddled in doorways or lay curled on the pavement. Whores with black, slicked-down *windstoss*—pixy-cut—haircuts and throats heavy with Charleston beads leaned against *Litfass-Saulen*, adding their bodies to the peeling advertisements pasted around the thick, two-meter posts. The women exchanged gossip and cigarettes with homosexuals sporting sheepskin jackets, striped sailors' shirts, and tan dungarees.

Life in the city was unkind, Sol thought, yet at that moment he felt far less frightened by the loiterers than by the friend he had known most of his life. Lately he hardly knew Erich at all.

"Queers! I hate them." Erich picked up speed. "They should all be shot."

With seemingly superhuman balance he steered the

bike with the palm of his crushed hand and, reaching under Sol's left arm, held an object before Sol's nose. His thumb was hooked through the trigger guard of Herr Weisser's pistol. The weapon looked very large and very silver beneath the street lamp.

Sol swallowed in fear. "You stole it?"

"No. I wrote my beloved papa a letter," Erich said, his head down as he pedaled, "explaining that I thought I should inherit it a little early!" He straightened and, thrusting out his lower lip, blew a breath up over his sweaty face.

"You make me sick when you talk like that." Sol looked at his friend in disgust. "Good thing you can't fire it."

"The hell I can't."

"I thought your papa said he had taken out the firing pin, after…" Sol did not feel like finishing.

"I made a new firing pin on the metal lathe at school…out of a Groschen nail. *And* I've got bullets.…"

"What were you really angry about that night?" Sol asked. "We've never talked about it."

"Papa, mostly. He's so…*weak*. And Miriam…that whole thing was so unfair. Rathenau not inviting me, I mean. It makes me mad, sometimes. It's like you people have a special club and there's no way in—"

"You people?" Sol felt his stomach forming another knot.

"Don't get mad at me," Erich said. "I just mean that it's as if you have this club and the rules are that you help each other—like we do at camp. It's a club, too—"

A club where you help each other to hate better, Sol thought, glancing uneasily at the people they passed.

Judging by his friend's anxiety to get through this part of town as fast as possible, Erich's bragging about roaming Berlin's alleys after midnight was doubtless just that—bragging. Like saying he had slipped a hand beneath the tie-strings of Ursula Müller's underwear. His evenings out probably consisted of nothing more than beer, song, and knockwurst around a Freikorps campfire.

"Slow down!" Sol shouted as the handlebar nut rammed into him.

Erich pedaled faster. They rode on in silence through the city, past an abandoned Bolle Wagen, the milk cart's giant ladle and pails of milk and buttermilk gone with the nag that had once pulled it daily to Sol's neighborhood. According to the *Tageblatt*, when the nag collapsed, hungry Berliners fought its owner and each other for the horse meat and the warm, protein-rich blood.

At last they entered Zehlendorf and headed toward the Grünewald. Three-and-a-half kilometers long and fifty meters wide, the Kurfurstendamm stretched from Kaiser Wilhelm-Gedachtnis Kirche all the way to Koenigsallee. At its eastern end were some of Berlin's most elegant shops; at its western end stood the graceful suburban homes of Zehlendorf. In between was the city's sordid section.

Sol felt a stab of resentment and loss. Although many Jewish businessmen and industrialists lived in the two suburbs, this was a world he would never inhabit. Among the shadowy lushness of oaks and chestnut trees, slender white-stemmed birches stood guard, shining silver, like armored lords before the moon. Except for the occasional Audi or Model T puttering past them, or the prestigious Buick that swerved to avoid their unexpected presence, the streets were deserted. Twice, flashlights lanced toward the road—probably watchmen determining what creaky machine would dare disturb the sleep of their employers.

He imagined being married to Miriam, living in a villa and surveying the tree-lined avenue from behind a tall window. Erich could be Otto von Bismarck, a royal guest with a taste for fine wines and rare books. The three of them would be out riding near Jagdschloss Grünewald, their headquarters for the hunt.

But such imaginings served only to deepen his sense of loss. The time had come, he thought, to accept the fact that the door Walther Rathenau briefly cracked open was forever shut.

CHAPTER TWENTY-ONE

By the time Erich steered into Wannsee Park and dumped the bike, his chest felt tight with the effort of pedaling, and his breath was coming in short harsh huffs. He looked around uneasily, in case the other boys were still on this side of the lake, saw that the picnic area was empty, and sprinted across the sand to the edge of the Wannsee.

Beside the small dock was the beach for swimmers and, beneath the trees, an open-air restaurant with signs that listed rules for picnickers. The largest one read: "Families May Brew Their Own Coffee Here."

"See those willows?" Erich whispered when Sol joined him. He pointed across the lake. "That's where we're going."

"I know—" Sol did not sound happy. "What was that ride? 'Joy in Hardship' lesson one?"

His Youth camp's motto was "Strength through joy in

nature." Sol consistently called it "joy in hardship." Before the war, the cluster of Spartan three-sided huts had been an apolitical Wandervögel camp for children who liked nature, hiking and singing around a campfire. Now the Freikorps ran it.

Erich squinted toward the willows. Shouldn't have dragged Sol into this, he thought, praying that none of the really tough guys had decided to spend the night at the camp. Even if some of the boys had decided to go home, there were always two or three who had run away from their families and had nowhere else to go, and at least one leader who stayed to guard the camp. If he and Sol were caught hanging around, it would simply be a question of who was in the most trouble—Sol, or himself for bringing Sol there.

Crouching, Erich crept along the beach. "We'll have to row across." He pointed toward a rowboat beached at the fence that enclosed Wannsee Park. "But first swear you'll never tell anyone about tonight. If you do, I'll turn you into a vampire, just like—*blaah!*" He jumped on Sol, teeth bared and fingers curved like claws. "Just like Nosferatu!"

"Idiot!" Sol shoved him away. "I won't tell. What's the big secret, anyway?"

"Shake on it." Erich clasped Sol's hand in the Wandervögel handshake. He felt a momentary resistance and stared deeply into his friend's eyes. Then Sol grinned and Erich felt his grip harden. "I better never find out you broke your word," he said.

They pushed the boat onto the moon-dappled water. As Erich rowed, Sol clutched the oarlocks to help keep them from creaking. "We should have wrapped the oars in silk," he whispered, apparently beginning to get caught up in the adventure. "That's what Hessian spies—"

Erich put a finger to his lips and glanced over at a sleeping fisherman whose canoe bobbed gently in the water. Watching people fish sure wasn't interesting, as it used to be. Not since Berlin banned the used of grenades.

When they reached the other side they tied the boat to a branch and crept into the foliage, wilder and denser on this side of the lake and still wet from the previous evening's rain. By the time Erich parted the last set of branches and peered into one of the huts, he was as damp as if he had been walking in a drizzle.

"Do you see her?" he whispered, examining the tiered bunks inside, three on each side. A few of them held sleeping figures.

"I see *them!*"

"Shsh!" Erich clamped a hand over Sol's mouth and pointed toward a young sentry who sat, hunched over and asleep, beside a blackened fire pit.

Sol sputtered and backed away. "I didn't think anyone would be here," he whispered. "I should go home."

"Alone? Out there?" Erich started crawling through the undergrowth. He felt Sol's hand on his shoulder, holding him back.

"We're crawling around some woods in the dark, looking for a pregnant mutt—"

"Don't call her that!"

"We're in danger of being beaten up by your buddies

and our families are probably worried sick," Sol said, ignoring him. "But that's okay because we're here to see your favorite dog."

"Please, Sol," Erich said. "She's the top of the Thuringia strain, the camp mascot, *and* pregnant. I asked for one of her puppies but they said no because they'd taken her all the way to Holland, to Doorn, to mate her."

"They mated her with one of the *Kaiser's* dogs?"

"Not just *one* of the Kaiser's dogs—last year's German Grand Champion. Remember that Movietone segment about the Sieger Dog Show? Remember Harras von der Juch? That's the sire."

"If she is so valuable, how come one of your leaders didn't stay around to take care of her?"

"They're stupid, that's why."

Sol could not fail to be impressed, Erich thought as he started crawling again. In front of him, twigs crackled softly as he moved ahead. Grace, mated to Harras, the offspring of Etzel von Oeringen, son of Nores of the *Kriminalpoletzei!* Then again, what did Sol know? *He* couldn't commune with dogs or rattle off their family lines as if they were his own.

Well, Sol *did* know Etzel, but everyone knew the dog that had been taken to America and became the star of the Strongheart movies, each of which Erich had seen close to a dozen times. He was saving for another movie marathon when the new German shepherd film came to Berlin, the one starring Rin Tin Tin, a dog bred in the trenches during the war.

"Why did we come here?" Sol asked. "I mean, *really?*"

"I *told* you. I heard her calling. Also, I want one of

her pups," Erich answered truthfully. "If we're there when she gives birth, they'll never know."

"What if they catch us stealing?" Sol sounded scared.

"They'll scream at me, discipline me—threaten to cut my nuts off and feed them to the squirrels." He looked at Sol. "With you they might not just threaten."

"Because I'm Jewish?" Sol narrowed his eyes in anger.

"Because you're not Freikorps."

Sol backed away but Erich grabbed him. "Just kidding." He knew his voice lacked conviction. "That's where Grace is supposed to be." He pointed to a tiny hut whose front was covered with chicken wire. "But I know she's not there. She...escaped. When that kid watching her fell asleep."

"Maybe she's resigned from the Freikorps," Sol said.

"I'll find her." Erich led Sol behind the other huts and along the far side of the camp until they reached the biggest hut. The outside of its rear wall looked like the heavily decorated chest of a general; nearly a hundred sports medallions hung alongside four javelins. Beneath them, sheltered from the weather by an overhang, were shelves cluttered with badminton rackets and nets, soccer balls, shot-puts, medicine balls, and an array of black track shoes.

"That's mine." Erich pointed at the longest javelin. It was white, with two red stripes taped near the center. The chrome tip was honed to a gleaming point. "Isn't she a beauty?"

"Yes, but where's the *dog*?"

Feeling more than a little hurt by Sol's quick dismissal of his javelin, Erich concentrated. Suddenly he bounded away from the hut and toward an enormous weeping willow on the west side of the camp, its canopy so full it touched the ground. He waited for Sol to catch up before he held the branches apart.

He was shocked at what he saw.

Though Grace could not have chosen a more pastoral sanctuary, she looked anything but the consort of a German champion. She raised her head to see who had intruded upon her. Then, as if the action had completely enervated her, she laid her head back down on the ground. Her head appeared abnormally extended, her ribs were prominent, her abdomen sagged. Moonlight, seeping through the willow, mottled her coat, which looked gray and lifeless. In the lee of her belly, their eyes closed to slits, their tiny paws curled and vulnerable, lay two pink hairless pups, covered with bloody mucous and forest duff.

A third pup lay to one side, swaddled in a bluish membrane and still attached to its mother.

Feebly Grace wriggled her mouth closer to the umbilical cord so that she could chew through it. As she moved her head her throat spasmed. She gagged and jerked in what was obviously terrible pain.

"Erich?"

"She's going to die." Erich felt a lump in his throat, and tears were right near the surface.

Again the dog picked up her head. This time she held it rigid; her eyes bulged, her throat convulsed. A stream of bloody vomit gushed from her mouth. Her head slumped and she lay staring, through sad dark eyes, at the willow trunk.

Erich wanted to rush to Grace, stroke her, comfort her;

at the same time, he was afraid to touch her—afraid, and nauseated. She used to be so beautiful. He pictured Miriam lying there, pregnant and...ugly. When they were married he would tell her, *no children!*

"For God's sake, Erich, what is *that?*"

Sol clutched Erich's shoulder and pointed at a distended sac that lay on the dog's hind side. Pink and quivering and slicked with blood, the sac looked like an oversized fleshy larva—an oval reddish mass stippled with spongy-looking knobs.

Shaking, Erich knelt to examine the sac. Grace looked at him, and shivered.

"What's happened to her?" Sol whispered.

"I think this came out of her." Erich pulled a face.

"Ugh! What *is* it?"

"I don't know," Erich said slowly, "I have this feeling...I think...she wants us to put it back in."

"No!" Sol's face was ashen. "We'll kill her. We don't know anything about that stuff."

Carefully, Erich lifted the membrane-covered pup and pulled off the film. His stomach clenched and he had to breathe deeply to keep from throwing up. "We should go for help, but we can't. If I bring back a leader and he finds out you're a Jew, we're both in *bad* trouble—"

"And if the others find out about Grace being here, you'll never get a puppy," Sol said, a cynical tone in his voice.

Erich gently set the whelp next to its mother. "Remember what I told you about some of the camps?" He paused, wanting Sol's full attention. "There's no guessing what they would do to you."

Sol huddled next to Grace. "So what do we do now?"

"We'll need hot water, clean towels—like in the films." Erich rose to his feet. "Here, guard yourself with this." Acting a lot more casual than he felt, he threw his father's gun on the ground near Sol's feet. "I won't be long."

He hurried through the tall grass. Behind him he could hear Sol speaking to Grace in the soothing tones his parents used when he was ill. What, he wondered, had really made the leaders bring hatred into the camp?

What was so bad about Jews, anyway?

Take Sol—he'd never had a problem with Sol being a Jew. But then Sol was different. He was just...Sol. *Spatz*. A sparrow.

The leaders had said that Germans should follow Martin Luther's suggestion. Seize all Jewish property and send the Jews to mines and quarries and logging camps.

Now there was a stupid idea. The Jews *he* knew weren't exactly the most *physical* people in the world.

Dismissing the subject, as he usually did, he crept around the camp looking for things he needed or might need. He found a pot and poured in water from the drinking barrel, letting the liquid run over his hand so it would not ting against the metal and wake someone up. The top bunk of the empty hut nearest the willow turned out to be strewn with bedcovers and camping gear—some crybaby who'd had second thoughts about staying the night, Erich figured. He flung two blankets and a couple of dirty towels over his shoulder; he got lucky and found a flashlight, which he put in his hip pocket together with a sewing kit and a fishing leader. Then he sprinted back to the willow.

"Couldn't get *hot* water. This'll have to work." He tried

to sound confident. This birthing business was awfully complicated. C'mon, Grace, he begged silently. *Tell me what to do.*

"What are we going to do?" Sol asked, echoing Erich's plea to the dog.

Erich hoped Grace would commune with him, but— nothing. "She's too weak. We'll have to decide as we go. If only I could remember what the Rittmeister wrote about whelping!"

They spread one blanket on the ground, maneuvered the animals onto it, and covered them with the other. Grace did not resist. There was a dead weight and a rank wet odor to her, and her skin felt clammy and coarse.

"She's feverish," Erich said. "Feel her nose—it's hot and dry." He drew the blankets around her, forming a cocoon for the pups. "Hold her still!" He folded part of a blanket forward to expose her hindquarters. "This is going to hurt her."

Sol cradled the dog's head in his lap and leaned over to brace the torso with his hands. Erich turned on the flashlight and wedged it in the crook of the willow. It cast a weak circle of light over the dog.

Kneeling beside Grace, Erich plunged his hands and then a towel into the water pot. "Don't even breathe, Solomon." He began to clean the sac. "Just hold her."

The dog's eyes were filled with apprehension and pain; she was shivering slightly, but she did not struggle.

"I've got her," Sol said.

"I know. I know. We have to be careful. I think it's her uter-in." He felt sick as he softly put his fingers on the 'thing.'

Think about something else. He glanced at Sol, whose

face was set in a stoic expression. Bet he's thinking about something he read in a book. That's his answer to everything.

As gently as he could, Erich continued to work. He pictured his own bookshelf at home. Though he pretended he never read—mostly to annoy Sol—he owned many books about dogs and uniforms and Imperial history. He could quote passages verbatim from lots of them. His favorite was *The German Shepherd Dog in Word and Picture* by Rittmeister Max von Stephanitz, the "father" of the German shepherd. Through controlled breeding, he had produced a master-breed based on efficiency *and* beauty. According to him, the German shepherd was not a means to an end but an end in itself.

"You got her, Sol?" Erich tentatively patted the uterin with the dry towel. Why had none of his books taught him what to do in a situation like this? With the back of his wrist he wiped away the sweat that beaded his forehead. "Here goes. It can't be that different from stuffing a chicken. I've seen my mother do that plenty of times."

Taking a deep breath he began to ease the organ inside. It had come out of her, so it had to fit back in, but it seemed too big—awkward and shapeless, like a pile of raw sweetbreads.

"Steady," Sol told him.

"I'm doing the best I can!"

"Sorry."

Sol stroked the dog, as if hoping to relax her tense muscles.

"That's my lady." Erich tried to keep his voice quiet

and gentle but the dog stirred beneath his touch. "Oh God." He lowered his head and examined the part of the organ that remained in his hands, though he had no idea what he was looking for. "I must have done something wrong."

"Careful!"

Raising his gaze but not his head, Erich glared at Sol. "I *am* being careful. Just hold her! If something goes wrong it's *your* fault."

"My fault?" Sol glared back, then looked away.

Watch yourself, Erich thought. All you need now is for Sol to leave.

Whining deep in her throat, the dog shivered, trembled, and began to whimper.

"There." Erich sat back and wiped his forehead again with a blood-covered hand. "I think it's in." He took the large needle and a loop of transparent leader from his breast pocket. "This was the thickest stuff I could find." He held up and scrutinized the loop before threading the needle.

"What's that for?"

"To sew her up, stupid."

"You'll kill her."

"Just hold her and keep quiet. If I don't sew her up, the…the…*thing*—it might come out again."

Sol bent his head. "*Baruch ato adonai…*" he whispered, gripping wads of her shoulder muscle in his hands. "Blessed art Thou, O Lord our God, King of the Universe, who knows and does good things—"

"*Now* what are you jabbering about!"

"A prayer. For the dog."

Erich adjusted the flashlight so the beam was truer,

hunkered down behind the dog, and began to work the needle. "You people have prayers for dogs?" He hoped Sol's God would hear even if Grace were not Jewish.

The animal's breathing became raspy and ragged. Growling, she tried to bring her head around and scrunch her backside away from the pain. She fought to rise as Sol held her down. "Papa says there are prayers for everything," Sol said, "but it's okay to make them up, too, long as you don't *ask* for things—just give praise and thanks, and believe."

"Finished." Erich exhaled loudly, arched his back and stretched. Maybe a little more praying wouldn't hurt, he thought, too embarrassed to say as much. He washed his hands. "Let's clean the pups." Folding aside a blanket corner, he picked up the tiny mewling creature he'd handled earlier and scratched it gently behind the ear. Grace lay unmoving, her head in Solomon's lap. Erich reached over and stroked her muzzle. "You're okay now," he said. "Uncle Erich saved you."

"I helped." Sol maneuvered his elbow so Erich would have trouble petting the dog. "I did a lot!"

"In an emergency, *Spatz*—" Erich pushed Sol's arm aside—"you're about as useful as a blind man on a battlefield."

Sol looked darkly petulant. "You always do that," he said in an injured voice. "Insult me. Take all the credit when things go right and blame me when they don't."

Erich set down the pup and lurched to his feet. He clenched his fists. Sol was right, he thought, feeling foolish. He lowered his guard and put a hand on Sol's shoulder. "Just kidding. You know I didn't mean it."

"Yes, you did. Go ahead—you might as well hit me."

Erich looked down at his mangled hand. Despite it, he was an expert boxer; his friend never stood a chance against him in a fistfight. Yet when it came to words, Sol was the expert. He was like a conscience, Erich thought. Too quick with questions, too accurate and truthful with analyses. No wonder the other boys at school avoided him.

"You said it yourself, remember?" Sol jerked his head up angrily. "You said, 'She's going to die'!"

Furiously, frustrated beyond words, Erich punched down, hitting his friend with such force that Sol was slammed against the tree.

Grace's head, abruptly released from the protection of Sol's lap, bounced lightly and lay still. Sol rolled over, groaning as he clutched his temple and his glasses.

"Goddamn four-eyes!" Erich hopped around, his knuckles pressed against his lips.

"Feeling better now?" Sol muttered, taking off his spectacles and squinting at them in the weak light. They were bent but intact. He straightened the wire rims a little and put them on again.

Erich blew on his knuckles and fought the pain. If only Sol would lose his temper! That damn self-control of his was the most annoying thing of all. "You think you're a man because you've had a bar mitzvah! Hell, you haven't even undressed a girl, let alone—"

"Neither have you."

"Well, I could have. Ursula Müller wanted me to."

"She'd let anyone."

"Not a Jew, she wouldn't!"

Sol rose, apparently ready to resume the fight regardless of the inevitable outcome.

Though he was angry with himself for his outburst, Erich flexed his muscles. Then something wet and warm soaked his ankle. He looked down, horrified, to see Grace spasm. Her eyes were wide with terror. Blood gushed from her mouth and over his shoes.

"We've got to try to help her!" Erich collapsed over the dog, his arms around her neck. "Sol, please!"

"Take back what you said."

"Go to hell."

"I'll go, all right—back home." Sol stepped away and parted the branches.

"You know I didn't mean it," Erich said quickly.

Sol hesitated and Erich knew his friend would stay. Funny how you could love someone, need him, and be infuriated by him at the same time.

"Try pouring water down her throat," Solomon said. "It might help break the fever."

The thought was logical enough but Erich did not want logic; he wanted a miracle. Again and again he begged her to live. He cuddled and covered her; he poured water across his hands and patted her nose. When she did not respond, he reached inside the blanket and drew out the other two puppies.

"If she notices them she'll want to live," he said.

Standing in the moonlight, he toweled the tiny heads. Then his hands opened and he let the puppies fall, one at a time, onto the blanket.

"They're dead, Solomon!"

Sol touched the pups and nodded, saying nothing. A strangling sound from Grace pulled Erich to his knees beside her.

"They're just pups, don't you see?" He lifted a dead

whelp by the scruff of its neck. "You can have more! Look, there's another one here." He ransacked the folds of the blanket and drew out the live pup. "We're here, girl. Me and the pup."

Sobbing, he rubbed Grace's nose with her pup. Sol placed a consoling hand on his friend's shoulder.

Erich shook it off. "Don't touch me! Don't touch the dog, either, or—"

He spotted the gun, still lying where he had thrown it. Without thinking about what he was doing, or why he was doing it, he grabbed hold of the pistol and pointed it at Sol.

His friend backed away, arms up, face constricted with fear.

What am I doing? Erich stared in disbelief at the pistol, wondering how the thing could possibly have gotten into his hands. There was a dull pressure at the base of his skull, then an electric charge that made him arch his back involuntarily. He rose up onto his toes as the thin, hot sensation ran the length of his spine, split in two, surged to his heels—and raced up again. He jerked involuntarily, groping for something to hold on to, but the force was too great and darkness spilled over him like paint.

He staggered forward, stumbled, tried to keep himself from falling into the blackness that was pulling him down into some bottomless abyss.

The choice was not his to make.

He felt the gun drop from his hand; felt the darkness envelop him; felt, rather than heard, himself scream.

CHAPTER TWENTY-TWO

Erich's scream hit Sol in the solar plexus with the force of a fist. He scrambled to his feet. All he could think of was that the pistol must have gone off accidentally. But then why hadn't he heard a shot?

He grabbed the flashlight from its perch in the willow and shone it directly at Erich. His friend had fallen onto the blanket; his fingers clutched at the air and his head lurched from side to side.

Trying not to panic, Sol recalled the only other time he had seen Erich having a full-blown seizure—after the accident in the sewer. His usual lightning seizures were over before anyone could fully react. A trembling or a simple spasm. A split-second rigidity. A gasp, during which, Erich said, he felt as if he were falling off a cliff—into darkness.

But this...

Sol sighed with relief as Erich stopped convulsing and

opened his eyes. Turning awkwardly onto his side, Erich wrapped his arms around Grace's neck and pulled her head into his lap. "I...I loved you s-so much," he stammered, his voice broken, high-pitched. "We were a *t-team*." He kissed her muzzle, neck, ear.

Grace gave a guttural sound, like a deep-throated purring. Erich released her head. She slipped onto the ground like a heavy sack and lay staring at him, her legs moving against the dirt as if she knew her destiny and wanted to crawl away from it.

Erich stared blankly up into the branches. Without moving his body, he patted the blanket. "Men don't l-let their friends s-suffer." He stopped. His hand ceased moving. Balling the fingers of both hands into fists, he turned onto his side and began to sob. He stroked the dog as he wept.

Suddenly he swayed to his feet.

The action drew Sol out of the strange inertia he had been feeling and he darted forward, hoping to grab Erich and keep him from falling again. Erich easily shoved him away. Then he pushed between the branches and disappeared among the moonlit grasses and alders.

Now what? Sol thought, his heart thudding. There was no telling what Erich might do next. So what alternatives did that leave him? He could find his way home, but if something happened to Erich, he would never forgive himself. Besides, leaving meant taking the boat, which would infuriate Erich and possibly antagonize him permanently. He could not risk finding a camp leader, but many doctors lived in the Grünewald.

Wondering briefly why Erich's scream had not brought someone crashing through the trees from the campsite, he turned his attention to Grace. Even given Erich's emotional state, he was right about one thing: the dog needed to be released from her misery. At least he had not tried to shoot the dog. Gunfire would surely have brought trouble.

Sol checked the surviving pup. Asleep. Every now and again it quivered violently, as if the memory of its birth-throes intruded on its dreams. How sweet and small and defenseless it looked. He stroked it gently with the side of his finger.

Feeling powerless to change whatever course of events Erich was putting into motion, he looked around for something useful to do. He would bury the two dead puppies, he decided. He moved outside the umbrella of the willow and, using his hands and the heel of his shoe, fashioned a shallow grave beside a patch of wild strawberries. He placed the puppies inside, covered them with soil, and matted it down. Feeling the need for ceremony, he bent and smelled a flower whose center was white as snow and whose edges were tinged with red. He plucked it, and a second one, and laid them both on top of the grave. Bowing his head, he began a few words of prayer.

"What do you think you're doing!" Naked to the waist, Erich sprang toward Sol through the grass, his javelin raised overhead.

Terrified, Sol backed away and dashed wildly past the willow. Behind him, an animal's scream shattered the night. He stopped running and listened, but already the screaming had ended. All he could hear was his own pulse thundering in his ears.

JANET BERLINER AND GEORGE GUTHRIDGE

He trudged back to the willow and carefully, quietly, parted the branches.

The scene made him gag.

Erich had rammed the javelin through Grace's left eye. Blood and something black oozed from the socket as the dog twisted and jerked against the shaft, which Erich held firmly, leaning his weight against it. "I love you," he said. "I love you."

Except for the small sound of her haunches thudding against the earth as she struggled to free herself, Grace made no noise. Her mouth opened and closed.

She slumped, shuddered, and lay still. As blood drained from her mouth, Sol thought of the Kabbalistic belief that animals, too, had souls.

In the silence, a cricket chirped.

Erich tugged the javelin from the wound. It made a sucking sound. He dropped it, clutched his head, and fell to his knees, eyes open wide.

This was no lightning seizure, Sol thought, panicking. Either his friend was having a grand mal seizure or this was his grotesque idea of a joke.

"Erich?"

His friend did not respond. Instead he began to shake as if with uncontrolled fury. His lips were pulled back, his teeth exposed. With each exhalation, his nostrils opened and closed like overworked valves. Then he toppled forward and lay jerking.

Have to do *something!* Block the mouth open if Erich ever has a bad attack, Papa had said. Otherwise he might bite his tongue in two. But block it with what?

He reached for the javelin, but the bloody tip made

him retch. Seeing a stick close to the willow trunk, he leaned forward to pick it up.

The stick proved to be a root, stuck firmly in the ground.

He pulled at a willow branch. It bent resiliently. Frustrated, he returned to yanking at the root; it ran from the ground like a cable being unearthed. In desperation he lowered his head and gnawed at the wood. Something syrupy sweet oozed into his mouth, but he could not rip through the sinewy pulp.

Angrily thrusting aside the root, he reached for the javelin—and spotted the pistol. Though he had never touched a revolver before, he unloaded it easily and rolled Erich over. His friend was bathed in sweat, twitching. Saliva drooled from his mouth.

The barrel proved to be too short to fit neatly between Erich's lips, so Sol crammed the chamber in. He took a deep breath to calm himself, then with the edge of the blanket toweled Erich's face.

Suddenly Erich gripped Sol's shirt as if for support and arched his torso into a taut bow. His eyes rolled up until only the whites showed. Releasing Sol, he stretched out his arms and emitted a choking snarl. The gun fell from his lips. He reached upward with rigid fingers, muttered a stream of unintelligible syllables, and sagged in Solomon's arms.

Slowly he opened his eyes. "There was a jungle." His voice rasped and he licked his lips as though his mouth were parched. "A clearing in a jungle. And overhead, a moon. It was...melting." His tone was in some way accusatory but he did not resist when Sol eased him onto the ground and covered him with the stained blanket.

"You were there, Solomon. I saw you." Erich's face was pale and he seemed sleepy and disoriented. "I saw you." He was shivering.

Sol sat back, feeling flushed and wondering if it was his turn to faint. His head exploded with light and it ached so badly he could hardly see through the blue glow—

—an arm dangles from the battlement of bodies, its wrist blue and icy, its black hair frozen and stiff. Thousands of bodies—thousands of dead soldiers—are the bricks and mortar in a breastworks five bodies thick.

The woman, Peta, crouches beside the breastworks, her carbine poked through an aiming hole at white-clad infantry ascending the hill. Some of them are crossing the slope laterally at a crouch, some are crawling, others stoop to fire at her position.

She pops off several rounds. Down the hill, a soldier clutches his head and topples. She sits on her haunches and watches the old man labor to drag yet another body toward her.

"I could use a bowl of semolina soup." He lets the body drop.

"Phfui! Food for pigs!" She positions the body, readying it to be hoisted to a worker on the higher tier. "No matter how much you sift semolina, it's like eating sand."

Above them, the worker grabs hold of the corpse and flops it down like a sandbag.

"Three days now the clouds have held," the old man says. "One more hour and we will have survived another day. Maybe your God does hold you Jews in special favor."

"You think Jehovah is maintaining our cloud cover?" Laughing, the woman rams a cleaning patch down the barrel of her carbine and reloads the magazine. "Perhaps we could get Him to send in a few yaks or Siberian ponies!" She stares down the hill. "Here come more people they don't care about. Look at them. Penal troops this time, I think. Surely no one believes they're real soldiers!"

The old man peers through the aiming hole.

"Dissidents," he says. "Children of White Russians and probably a lot of Jews like you, who never knew what it was to be Jewish until... Senseless! Germans shooting Russians, Russians shooting Russians, Jews shooting Jews, and in the end it's the winter that will kill us all." He looks along the line of people working behind the barricade. "What are you doing here, Peta, shooting at your own kind!"

"Thank our revered Russian traitor, General Vlasov. That bastard saved Moscow, then switched sides. He's over at the hut—waiting to inspect his *troops!*" She turns her head and spits into the snow. "When he defected, he promised the Ukrainian Jews the return of their families and a homeland in Madagascar. If we fought for Hitler at the Russian Front, he said, the German forces would be free to finish taking London."

She tightens her jaw and fires three times. No one falls. Behind them, mortars begin to pop; far down the hill small fountains of snow and the roar of explosions confirm the shells.

The old man plugs his ears with his fingers. "You believed him?" he shouts.

She says no more until the firing has lessened. Pulling his hands from his head, she shouts, "I chose to believe!"

"Like you chose—" He stops in midsentence and stares down at her boots.

"I might have liked that soldier had he lived," she says softly. "But he didn't, and I will. Go back to the hut." Her blanket is flapping wildly in the wind. She tightens it around herself. "Warm your old bones at the brazier, Margabrook. Just don't throw out the meat I left to thaw in the hut. I don't want it to refreeze."

The old man recoils in horror. "God help us both."

He reaches out his hand. The woman seems to know what he wants. She reloads the rifle and hands it to him, then she follows him toward the hut. A man wearing the uniform and medals of a general stands in the doorway.

Margabrook falls to his knees in the snow.

"They will kill you, old man," the woman says, but she does not stop him when he lifts the rifle.

The shrieks of incoming shells muffle the rest of her words and sound of her carbine as it is fired again and again. The man in the doorway clutches his belly. He takes several steps into the snow, staggers, falls.

Margabrook drops the rifle. He is crying. The tears freeze instantly on his eyelashes.

"My eyes!" he screams—

"You'll tell no one!" Erich demanded, sitting up, his voice strong again.

Startled, Sol looked up. His headache had gone, along with the flashes of light and the eerie blue glow. "I...I think I just had a vision, Erich." He remembered what the beadle had said about Solomon ben Luria. "There was this—"

"The hell with your visions! I'm talking about Grace and about me. You'll tell no one what happened. Ever! Or that I cried and acted...weird!"

Gripping the javelin, he staggered to his feet and pointed the tip at Sol's chest.

"Whatever pleases you," Sol said. "Just put that thing down."

"Promise you won't tell!"

"Promise."

"Damn right, or you'll be one dead bar mitzvah boy." Eyes wild, Erich squatted and, still threatening Sol with the javelin, found the pistol.

"Look—you had a seizure. You're not yourself. Leave the gun alone. You might shoot yourself...or me."

A look of dismay gripped Erich's features as he checked the revolver. "The bullets! You stole them."

"I didn't steal them. I—"

"I never thought you'd do something like that!" Erich thrust the spear close to Sol's throat—and pulled back, eyes narrowed.

With a sick, sinking feeling, Solomon retrieved the cartridges from among the forest duff and handed them to Erich. There were soft clicks as Erich inserted the rounds.

"I *saw* you in that jungle clearing." With each word, Erich shook the pistol barrel as though scolding a child. "While I was having the seizure-thing. I *saw* you as clearly as I'm seeing you now!" He motioned with the pistol. "Come here, *bar* mitzvah *boy*."

Erich stuck the javelin in the ground and, keeping the

pistol pointed toward Solomon, stooped and rubbed his damaged hand in Grace's blood.

"Here!" he commanded.

Sol stepped forward fearfully. "You're acting crazy. I'm your friend, remember?"

Erich smeared blood all over Sol's cheeks. "That's why I'm doing this." He looked Sol straight in the eye. "I know you didn't *mean* to cause the...seizures, or make me see what I did."

Sol pulled away from Erich. He wasn't afraid anymore, just angry at himself for having submitted so readily to his earlier fear. "Cause them? How could *I* cause them? I'm not God!"

"It's because of you and your ghosts," Erich said angrily. "I saw a jungle and heard a baby crying. There was a kind of scroll and big rocks...like gravestones."

Sol wiped his cheek with the back of his hand and looked at the streak of blood he had wiped off. With his tongue he tasted a salty tear as it reached the corner of his mouth. Something was terribly wrong with his friend, but what?

"Something was snarling," Erich said. "I couldn't see what it was. But I could see you. You were there, watching." He leaned closer to Sol and squinted, an artist admiring his work. "We're on the warpath now. Just like in the movies. Whatever it was, we'll fight it. *Together*. But no more seizures. You got that? Now—your specs." He took the glasses off Sol's face and smeared them with the dog's blood. "There, I've cleansed *them* too."

He handed them back and Sol put them on. He squinched up his nose, forcing the glasses down enough so he could see a little, albeit poorly. The world was a blur of light and shadow. Vaguely he saw Erich stoop and, bloodying his fingers again, make circles on his own cheeks and forehead.

"Now help me bury Grace," Erich said, "and if you know what's good for you, you'll keep your crazy visions to yourself."

Grace was big and the ground was hard. Digging a shallow grave for the puppies with his hands was one thing; this was another. Erich, on his hands and knees scraping at the ground with the pistol handle, apparently came to the same conclusion. After a few minutes, he stood up.

"Let's just cover her." He piled the bloodied blankets and one of the towels on top of the dead dog.

Gratefully Sol stood up. Soon all traces of the dog were buried beneath a dense pile of undergrowth, topped off by some branches and twigs that Erich found a few feet away.

"I think I should say a prayer," Sol said softly, pushing his anger and confusion aside.

"Why?" Erich wrapped the live puppy in the remaining towel and put it in Sol's rucksack. He slipped his arms through the rucksack straps. "Dead is dead."

CHAPTER TWENTY-THREE

Erich could not remember ever having felt so tired and thirsty, not even after long hikes with a heavy pack or running multiple wind sprints in preparation for his first javelin competition, near Oranienburg. Had he suffered a grand mal seizure? Did it affect everyone like this—first a sense of enormous strength, as though he could conquer the world, then debilitating fatigue?

The closest he had come to the aftermath of this seizure was the way he had felt after wandering around the city that night before someone had the good sense to shoot that power monger, His Highness Herr Rathenau.

He glanced over at Sol—stumbling half-blind toward the boat, tripping over rocks and limbs—and felt bad. Funny how he could think things like that when Sol was not around, and feel no hint of conscience. Never mind conscience; when he was with the other Freikorps boys, thoughts like that gave him status.

Happy to wait for Solomon to catch up, he untied the boat, dropped in the javelin and climbed in. He had not meant to hurt Sol physically or emotionally, he thought, so why had he done it? Because Sol made it so easy for him? *I blame Sol every time something happens that I cannot control, because Sol always forgives.* One day he would go too far; Sol would declare him a fool and move on and there would be no apologizing, no understanding.

Erich sighed and shook his head. "Rinse off your glasses and get in," he said when Sol was within earshot.

Sol peered at him over his smeared spectacles and took hold of the boat's gunwale.

"Go on—rinse them," Erich said.

"I don't know if I want to." Sol climbed into the boat. "It's a pleasure not to have to see your ugly face." He swished his glasses in the water, dried them off on his shirt and tried to adjust them. They ended up even more lopsided than before.

"Take off your war paint too, if you want," Erich said. "I'm leaving *mine* on."

Solomon leaned over the boat to wet his face, sat up without washing, and squinted curiously at Erich through the dripping lenses.

"Here." Erich pushed the oar handles toward him.

"Me? Row?"

Erich nodded. "You row well."

Sol positioned himself on the middle seat, his back to Erich. "You were crazy back there, you know," he said over his shoulder.

Erich slipped off the rucksack, put it in his lap and

lay back, head on the bow as he gazed at the moon. Sol did row well, he thought, pushing the memory of the seizure away. The boat moved straight and true, leaving a wake in the moon's reflection.

When they neared the other shore, Erich put a hand on Sol's shoulder. "It was because of the seizure," he said. "Shake?"

They gripped hands and gazed into one another's eyes, but Erich remained unsatisfied. He grabbed Sol's arm and rubbed his wrist against Sol's. "We're brothers in blood now."

"We've been blood brothers for ages, remember?"

Erich stood up. Despite the boat's sudden rocking, he jumped deftly into the lake, holding the rucksack above his head. The cold thigh-high water refreshed him. He felt a new surge of energy and heaved the javelin toward the sandy beach. "Now," he said, sloshing toward the shore, "we're also brothers in blood."

While Solomon nosed the boat to the dock and tied up, Erich found the spear, jogged over to the bike and waited impatiently for his friend to cross the beach. Deciding Sol was fine and he had done enough penance, he hopped onto Hawk. Yelling, "Race you back home!" he took off with such power that the front tire lifted off the ground. The seizure and Grace's death seemed like a bad dream. He was feeling good again.

Whooping loudly he hoisted the javelin like a spear.

"Wait for me!" Sol shouted.

Erich glanced back. Laughing, he rode in circles around the oaks and birches—then pedaled off into the shadows.

"Damn you, Erich!" Sol yelled. "Where are you!"

Erich walked the bike out from behind the foliage. Remounting with a kind of insolent ease, he leaned over the handlebars and thrust his face directly in front of Sol's. "Start running. We're brothers all the way now. That means *you* have to get in shape, like *me*." He lifted a foot onto the higher pedal as if to ram the bike into Sol, who backstepped rapidly, turned, and made for the street.

"Are you or are you not going to give me a ride home!" he demanded as Erich rapidly caught up with him.

"Home?" Spear lifted, Erich let out a loud war-whoop, like the ones in Wild West films.

Glowering, Solomon trudged off toward the Kurfurstendamm. "Some friend you are."

"*Some friend you are,*" Erich mimicked, making another whirlwind circle. Then he steered down the street and returned at high speed, skidding to a halt at Sol's feet. "*I* don't want to go home yet!"

His friend kept walking resolutely, not looking back even when Erich nosed the front wheel up behind him. "Don't go," Erich said.

"Why not? You can manage fine without me!"

"I'll let you ride the bike home if you'll stay around a little longer." Erich made his voice sound low and contrite.

Sol turned and smiled as if in disbelief.

The reaction did not surprise Erich in the least; he knew he guarded his possessions somewhat too jealously. "Honest—you can ride Hawk all the way back," he said.

"We really should go home, Erich. I'm tired, you've been…ill and," Sol glanced at the rucksack, "that puppy's probably dying of hunger."

Oh Lord, Erich thought. He had forgotten all about the puppy. He had an idea. They were not more than minutes away from the Rathenau estate. Miriam and her grandmother were living there. This was as good a time as any to sneak in. The old lady would be fast asleep. He would give Miriam the puppy and...

Sol mounted the bike. "We'll do whatever you want for a little while longer and then go home, okay? Get on."

"I'll run." Erich glanced at his biceps with satisfaction. "That way!" He pointed in the direction of the estate.

"Bet we're headed to Miriam Rathenau's," Sol said.

"Very good, Solomon." Javelin in hand, Erich glided along with the fluid ease of a warrior. "Only took you a year and a century to figure that out."

He fell silent and looked back over his shoulder. Sol was frowning, as if trying to solve an obtuse mathematical problem.

"Erich, what really happened that night before Herr Rathenau...when you ran away?"

Erich did not answer. He was not ready to talk to Solomon or anyone else about that night.

"Mind your own business." Erich clenched his fist. "I told you. I slept at the camp and went to see Miriam the next day to get the photograph for your bar mitzvah present." And she let me in for all of ten minutes, Erich thought angrily, keeping that information to himself.

"She won't let you in this time," Sol said. "Not covered in dirt and blood."

Erich looked down at his chest and arms, flexed his muscles, and lifted his blood-smeared face in a statuesque pose. "I guess some water wouldn't hurt," he said reluctantly. "Their dogs will go nuts if we try to get in while I'm painted up like this."

"*Guard* dogs?"

"Don't worry, I'll take care of them." *Better than I took care of Grace*, he told himself angrily.

The boys were almost upon the estate when they spotted a pump. They took turns at the handle, using Erich's shirt as a washcloth.

"Did you scrub behind your ears, Solomon?" Erich said in a maternal falsetto, stuffing the shirt under a hedge. "No sense keeping this. Let's go."

The Rathenau house was constructed of limestone and surrounded by a tall stone wall. Square turrets latticed with ivied trellises were surmounted by mock parapets scalloped with friezes. Ornate cornices shadowed many of the narrow leaded windows, and moonlight glinted off the circular stained glass set above the front portico. A golden flagpole rose over the roof.

"That's Miriam's room." Erich stuck his arm through the side gate's iron grating and pointed toward the far turret. There, beyond a trellised balcony, white curtains draped French windows.

"You're something, Erich! You wouldn't walk in Rathenau's honor, yet you have the nerve to come here."

"Why should I care about her uncle? I didn't even like him."

"You didn't even know him."

"What difference does it make!" Erich took hold of the grate and peered through as if between the bars of a cell. "Tonight's the night, Fräulein Rathenau."

"Not while I—"

"Relax! I just meant I'm going to promise to take her to Luna Park."

There was loud barking and growling as two sleek shadows raced across the grounds and lunged at the gate.

"Down, Princess." Erich kept his voice silky as the Doberman and the Russian wolfhound snapped and snarled and thrust their muzzles between the bars. "Down, Piccadilly."

"Piccadilly?" Sol's tone was a mix of terror and disbelief.

"Something to do with your pal the Rat's hatred of England." Erich knew his disrespect would aggravate Solomon. "There's a circus or something over there by that name." He reached out and, closing his eyes and tensing, let his hand slowly descend between the bars. "Easy, girls."

The dogs quieted and Erich stroked the terrible heads, wishing with all his heart he were petting a living, breathing Grace. "We can go in now." He wondered how long it would take for him to stop feeling queasy about what had happened at the camp.

"You're sure?"

"Course I'm sure." He was already climbing the gate.

"I could wait here for you—"

"*Please*, Solomon."

Looking forlorn, Solomon began to climb. He crossed the iron spearheads that rose from the gate top and dropped to the turf at Erich's urging. The dogs circled and sniffed him.

"Lead on, Princess," Erich whispered. "Let's go."

Together, he and the dogs raced across the lawn

toward the west-end turret. He started up the ivy- and rose-laced trellis. "We go hand-over-hand along the eave, then drop to her balcony," he said to Solomon. "It's not much of a drop. If you stretch, you'll be able to touch the balcony rail with your toes."

"How do we get back down?"

"With difficulty. Or else sneak through the house."

"You're insane."

"So is the world—or that's what my dear papa keeps telling me." Erich dropped quietly as he could onto the balcony's hexagonal tiles.

"I'll stay here," Sol said from the trellis. "Who's in the house besides Miriam?"

"Her grandmother." Erich squatted beside the French doors and tried to peer in through the curtains, which were too sheer to block the view completely. "Some other relatives, too. I don't know who. They were there when I was here before. I think they came in from all over Europe after the Rat kicked it."

"He was *assassinated*. And please don't call him that!"

"I keep telling you—dead is dead! Anyhow, there's also a whole platoon of maids and valets and gardeners."

He rapped lightly on the door. The sound seemed to shimmer in the air like something tangible.

"I'm going back!" Sol said.

"Stay...please!" Heart pounding in his ears, Erich pressed his face against the door's edge. A small night lamp stood on a vanity neatly arrayed with silver-handled brushes. Moonlight swam in the vanity mirror. He could see the corner of a bed with a pink coverlet. He rapped on the door again, a little louder.

"Maybe they've gone away," Sol whispered.

Erich had about decided the same thing when a light blazed and Miriam emerged, looking as if she had thrown off the bedcovers in the middle of a dream. Her face shone like ivory, an effect intensified by the edging of cream-colored lace around the neck and sleeves of her peignoir and by the tumble of long dark hair that framed her face and shoulders. He caught sight of the silhouette of her breasts.

If only he were older...richer...taller—

If only he were Jewish.

Frightened by the intensity of his feelings, he twisted his head to look for Sol. The action sent him off-balance, and he grabbed the balcony rail.

"Something wrong?" Sol asked. "Another seizure?"

Erich twisted his head around to answer, but Sol shook his head and held a finger to his lips. Then he ducked behind the corner and Erich turned back to see Miriam staring at him through the glass door.

CHAPTER TWENTY-FOUR

"Who's there?" Miriam called out, more curious than afraid.

She pulled on a pink robe, framed along the collar and cuffs with vanilla fur, and walked toward the balcony door. With the light on in the room, she could barely make out a dark shape outside the door; she could see a circle of moisture where his nose, or perhaps his mouth, had been pressed up against the glass.

Quickly she doubled back and switched off the light she had turned on when the rapping at her door had wakened her.

"Erich?"

She stifled her laughter for fear of hurting his feelings. Before going to bed she had drawn aside the thin, gauze curtain that usually covered the door and separated her from the moonlight. Oma called it a privacy curtain and insisted it should be kept drawn, which had always seemed ludicrous to Miriam. Her room was, after all, not in the middle of a traffic pattern. Every now and then her fantasies included a handsome beau climbing the trellis to her balcony, a Scarlet Pimpernel in a red velvet jacket, lace at his neck and a plumed hat set jauntily on his head—not this bare-chested hopeful Romeo-with-a-rucksack who stood out there now.

"What on earth are you doing here in the middle of the night!" She opened the door and looked past him, down at the trellis. "Where's Sol?"

Erich shrugged. "Not here."

Miriam frowned. There were little lies and big lies, and times when both were necessary. What she could not abide was a *wasted* lie. A pointless one. Someone else had been out there, and who else but Sol would consent to come out with Erich at this time of night?

Boldly, though awkwardly, Erich leaned toward her as though to kiss her on the lips. Miriam pushed him away. "You know you shouldn't be here. You especially shouldn't be here doing *that*."

"You liked it at the shop."

"Maybe I did like it," she said honestly. "Just don't do it." She had liked it all right, but not enough to be the booty in a bet, which was probably what this was all about. Still, she had to admit she was enjoying the idea that Erich—and Sol—had braved the dogs and the trellis to get to her.

"How did you get past the dogs? I thought I heard them barking. And why aren't you wearing a shirt?"

"I can handle dogs." Erich took a step backward and looked over the rail as if to see the animals below.

"You're lucky they didn't attack you! Well, now that you're here and in one piece, you want to tell me why?"

Erich grinned, and she felt foolish. Talk about giving someone a—what did they call it in America?—a straight line.

"Brought you a present," Erich said.

"My birthday's not till the end of September."

"It's an unbirthday present."

Removing the rucksack from his shoulders, he reached inside and took out a tiny puppy. He held it by the nape of the neck, its legs dangling.

A stuffed dog—from Erich? She might have expected that from Sol, but not Erich. A snake, an alligator, a live dog maybe, but not— She reached for it.

"Here!" she said. "No! Take it away!"

At the point of tears, she thrust it back at him. This was no stuffed dog; it was living, breathing. Like Susie—

"What's the matter? I haven't done anything wrong."

"I'm sorry," Miriam whispered. "It's just that my parents were taking my English sheepdog to the veterinarian when they were—" She took a sharp breath. "Well, you know."

But he did not know, she was aware. Not about the fire or her fears. How could she explain to this too-young boy that she wanted a dog more than anything else in the world, yet was terrified that owning one would cause her to lose someone she loved?

Erich kissed the puppy on the nose. "*Her* mother's dead, too. T-take her…go on. Please." A sense of worried begging shone in Erich's eyes.

A rustling from the trellis provided Miriam with the

distraction she needed. She stepped toward it and was about to say something more about Sol when the guard dogs growled.

"They're just jealous," Erich said, too quickly. He waved a hand near the trellis as if shooing away a fly.

Signaling his friend, Miriam thought. Hope the dogs don't tear Sol apart. "Those dogs *are* jealous." She decided not to mention Sol again. Sooner or later, she would find out what was going on.

"She needs to be fed," Erich said.

"Who? Oh, you mean the puppy." Miriam reached out tentatively and stroked the dog; it was soft—and warm. "Look at your tiny paws." She wished she had the courage to hold it.

"She's going to be a beauty," Erich said. "I bet you and I love dogs more than anyone else in Berlin."

Miriam steeled her resolve. Carefully, as if the animal were made of eggshells, she took the dog from Erich. "You're right, I do love them, but—" Frustrated with herself, she sighed deeply. "I can't accept the gift, Erich. I just…can't."

"Sure you can."

"No!"

She handed the puppy back to him. He kissed it on the nose again and rewrapped it with the towel. She watched him place it in the corner of the balcony and did not retreat when he stepped forward and took her awkwardly in his arms. For a moment, not wanting to think about the puppy, she gave in to his boyish embrace, then pushed him away.

"Stop it. If anyone sees us—"

"No one will see."

She felt a mixture of agitation and pleasure as he put his arms around her again. "Please, Erich. Don't." He kissed her throat insistently. "This is stupid." She tried to ignore the warmth creeping through her. "We're asking for trouble."

She pulled roughly away and did her best to glare at him.

"I'm sorry." His bravado was gone and he sounded on the verge of tears.

He is just a boy on the edge of manhood, Miriam thought. And she did like him—a lot. Well, maybe she didn't *like* him all that much—he was too mixed up and too…Aryan. What she liked was the person he *could* become, if he discarded the arrogant set of his shoulders—if the slight hardness around his mouth when he was refused disappeared—

If! Ifs didn't count, she knew that. Like the "if" at work right now: *if* he didn't give her that warm feeling when he looked at her, when he touched her, she would have sent him away at once. In fact, she would have had nothing to do with him in the first place.

Relenting, though only slightly, she placed his arm around her shoulder and kissed him on the cheek. He was barely taller than she as she leaned into him. Barely taller, Gentile, too young…but still, *if*—

She felt his arm tighten around her. Oh, hell! She stared up at the moon. What did it matter; she was not exactly going to marry him!

Turning to face Erich, she closed her eyes and let herself enjoy their first real kiss. Just one, she told herself, and then she would go back to bed.

Chapter Twenty-five

The rose vines irritated Sol's cheek, and his forehead itched. The dogs panted, circled, whined, rose on hind legs to paw the ivy. Moonlight and silence veiled the balcony.

Around the corner from the balcony, he went farther down the trellis. The wolfhound growled and the Doberman climbed onto the latticework in bright, angry anticipation. Sol cursed softly.

Above him, Miriam gave a small sigh.

Definitely not his idea of a good time. Erich was up there playing Romeo, while he was playing—what? Monkey?

Carefully he maneuvered closer to the corner and peeked around. Miriam's head was cocked flirtatiously to one side while Erich held her. Earlier, his heart had skipped a beat when she had insisted that he, Sol, was here too. Now he could feel his heart turn inside-out with a quite different emotion. What was it? Anger?

He knew what Papa would call it. Jealousy.

Fighting tears, he dropped from the trellis. The dogs, apparently sensing that he had discarded his fear of them, left him alone. They continued to whine and stare up at the balcony.

Grateful for that, at least, Sol charged through the gardens and climbed the gate. He picked up the bike, shivered with fury and slammed it down. Never again did he want to touch anything belonging to Erich Weisser.

If it weren't for Papa, he told himself, there wouldn't be any Erich Weisser hanging around the store, tormenting people, treating Miriam Rathenau as if she belonged to him. The Weissers would still be hawking vegetables and speaking *Plattdeutsch*.

He chided himself for being so small-minded. Yet as he began to walk, all he could think of was how to get back at Erich for everything—but especially for dragging him out to the estate and then dismissing him with that imperious wave of his. He felt stupid for having fallen for Erich's friendship routine one more time, so stupid that even the Grünewald's mansions and chateaus, set among manicured gardens and neatly trimmed trees, seemed to mock him with their mien of regal repose.

Leaving the Grünewald, he found himself outside the Goethe *Gymnasium*, at the corner of Westfalische and Eisenzahn. The streets were empty, as were his pockets. No way to take a taxi or tram, and by the time he walked home, Papa would be awake.

Then he remembered. The money in his shoe! His

mother had put it there. For emergencies, she had said, God forbid you should ever need it.

Sitting on the curb, he removed his shoe and worked the lining of the instep free. There, protected by a bit of chamois, was the ten-mark note that had initially given his arch a callus.

He retied his shoe and, with a feeling of slow, suffocating desperation, unfolded the money. Even if he could get home before Papa arose, he would have to try to stay awake all day under his teacher's scrutiny. Worse, Erich would be in school. Sleep or no, Erich would go to school just so he could brag about what he had done with Miriam. A knot of admirers had surrounded him all morning after he told everyone that Ursula Müller had offered to drop her drawers for him.

Liar!

And I was right there among them, eager as the others, wanting to believe him.

Curling his fingers around the money, he made a decision. He was probably the only student at Goethe who had never skipped a class. As Erich would say, there was a first time for everything. Assuming Papa was not wise to the fact that he had been out almost all night, he would pretend to go to school—only never arrive.

A bus turned onto Eisenzahn Strasse. Rising to board it, he wondered if he shouldn't avoid going home altogether. No, that would worry his parents too much. Being caught playing hooky might earn him a paddling. He could handle that. He could not handle the pain of deliberately hurting Mama and Papa.

A few hours later, having catnapped at home, Sol trundled off to school—with his mother's blessing and without Erich, who "will be a little late for school today," as Frau Weisser had come down to inform Sol.

Avoiding the usual route, Sol made his way into the center of the city. He had decided to spend the day at Luna Park, but it did not open this early. While he stood among the crowds of the Tauenzien Strasse, yawning and bleary-eyed, his attention was caught by one of the KadeWe's window displays—a window devoted to Käthe Kruse dolls. The window dresser had seated them like an audience around a life-sized model of Grog, Berlin's most famous clown.

"*Schö-ö-ön*—beautiful," Sol thought he heard the department-store dummy say, although its mouth did not move.

"*Schö-ö-on,*" he repeated, completing the famous circus routine. Snapping his mouth shut and feeling foolish, he looked around. Too little sleep, he thought, excusing himself. As if it were not bad enough to hear voices in an abandoned sewer, now he was hearing a clown mannequin talk! The live Grog only left Circus Busch at Christmas to work department stores and other places where crowds gathered.

"*Schö-ö-ön.*" With slow marionette motion the mannequin lifted a hand in an awkward greeting, its mouth fixed in a rictus-grin.

Sol stood staring at the colorful marble eyes, ignoring the hoi polloi on their way to coffee, cake, and gossip at Kranzler's, and forcing them to walk around him. Was it Grog? A mechanical man? He might have stood there all day, had a man with an umbrella not bumped into him and shouted at him, breaking the spell.

Feeling a sudden need to get away, he turned and ran past the counter at Aschinger's where he had intended to stop for a bowl of their inexpensive pea soup and sausage, which would have held him until he got to the sour-pickle barrel at Luna Park.

"*Das ist die Berliner Luft...*" A barrel-organ man—the oldest one Solomon had ever seen—played outside Kranzler's. Sol slowed down to listen and to watch the animal perched on a stool beside the hurdy-gurdy. Black and white, with jade-green eyes, the tethered animal looked like a cross between a large monkey and a teddy bear.

The man played on, head lolled to one side as if his neck were broken. He was toothless, and a great bib of creased wrinkled flesh hung below his chin. But his music was beautiful. A Paul Lincke medley filtered through the air and Solomon swayed, mesmerized—

The man's eyes popped open, revealing milky unseeing pupils.

"*Lieber Leierkasten Mann, sieh mich nicht so traurig an,*" Sol said. "Dear barrel-organ man, don't look at me so mournfully."

The animal reached down and closed the man's eyelids. Wondering why German children had a verse for everything, Sol stretched to offer the animal a Groschen.

The animal emitted a weird wail that sounded like someone sliding a hand up and down the scale of a saxophone, and snatched the coin. Sol lurched back in pain, clutching his hand. He looked at his palm, then at the animal in frightened disbelief. A gouge brimming with blood ran the length of his lifeline.

"Gotcha, did he, boy?" The blind man laughed. "He does that with people he doesn't like."

The animal leaped onto the old man's back and curled across his shoulders, looking like a fluffy winter wrap.

"What *is* it!" Half in horror, half in fascination, Sol held his palm to his lips. He had a feeling he had seen something like the animal before. But where?

"It's an indri," the hurdy-gurdy man said. "A type of lemur. The name means—'behold!'" His head lolled to the other side and he began cackling. "A Frenchie went into the jungles of Madagascar looking for the cynocephalus—a mythical dog-headed boy. When the natives pointed out one of these little fellows, they shouted, 'Indri! Indri!' to get the man's attention. So that's how it got its name." He hawked deep in his throat and spat a brown stream of tobacco juice onto the street—and onto Solomon's shoes.

"Are you a dog-headed boy, Solomon?" the old man asked as Sol backed away in terror.

"You *know* me?"

"I know everyone who's anyone in Berlin—even if *you* don't know who you are."

Shaking his head against what *had* to be a nightmare, Sol turned and began running toward the Zoo Station. Behind him, the indri caterwauled and the old man shouted, "Well, are you a dog-headed boy? Is that what your dreams say?" and cackled insanely.

Boarding an open-topped bus and too afraid to look back, Solomon followed a long-legged prostitute in a short skirt and leather boots up the stairs and to the front seat. She placed her whip across her knees and patted the seat beside her.

"Don't worry," she said. "I like 'em young, but it's been a hard night. I couldn't lift my whip even if you begged me."

Embarrassed and upset, Sol looked around the bus. The seat next to the woman was the only empty one left. He sat down and examined his hand. It was stinging, but already the bleeding had begun to stop. He would probably get blood poisoning and die, he thought, sitting up stiff and straight and trying not to think too clearly—for fear something might make sense and he would discover he was not dreaming.

While he watched the city pass in a blur, the woman next to him drifted into sleep, her head against his shoulder. The bus bounced them both around as it negotiated the three-and-a-half kilometers to Halensee at the upper end of the Ku'damm. The journey seemed interminable; Sol could hardly wait to see the Halensee Bridge.

Directly below that lay Luna Park.

"Hallensee! Luna Park!"

Sol disengaged himself from the sleeping woman and disembarked. "*Achtung...Achtung! Hier spricht Berlin!* ...Attention!...attention! This is Berlin speaking!" Alfred Braun's voice boomed through the loudspeakers of the Funkturm. The radio tower was Berlin's tallest building and loomed high over the city, the bridge and the park.

"Luna Park!" yelled the main-gate barker, using a megaphone so his voice would carry from the amusement park below the bridge. Anxiety rippled through Sol; was today, he wondered, one of those during which people could take off their clothes in the Park?

At least the barker was clothed, so probably this was a regular day after all.

"Open seven days a week! Ride the carousel and the Ferris wheel! Risk your lives on the roller coaster! Win prizes!"

"*Achtung!*"

"Luna Park! Open seven days—"

"*Achtung!*"

Blinking and slack-muscled from sleeplessness, Sol staggered down the hill to the Park. The barker's hand emerged as if disembodied and took one of the notes Sol had changed—when? Last night? Sol couldn't recall.

"*Luftballons. Nur ein Sechser.*" Inside the gate, a man holding a rainbow of balloons in a deformed, white-fleshed hand gripped Sol's arm. "Balloons. Only five pfennig."

Sol shook loose and ran into the Park. When he stared back over his shoulder he saw the man was wearing a white glove and grinning like a clown.

Trying to clean his glasses, Sol staggered among the booths.

"Wheel of Fortune. Three turns, three winners."

"*Glühwürmchen, Glühwürmchen…*"

The song drew Sol away from the booths to the carousel. Around and around it whirled while the song played over and over, a giant music box without a stopping mechanism. He thought he saw a dark-haired girl in a cream-colored peignoir on the other side, sitting on a white horse and reaching for the brass ring that dangled from a rope amid the galloping circle of wooden steeds.

But the carousel was empty, its animals riderless.

He rubbed his eyes. Whatever had possessed him to skip school!

"Berg und Tal Bahn!" a barker shrieked, offering Sol a roller coaster ride.

"Three turns, three winners!" another called from the closest booth. "Win an ostrich feather for Mama!"

The roller coaster went up and down and the carousel kept turning around and his head spun and the ground tilted—

"A stuffed doggie for your Fräulein. Every time a winner!"

"Three turns, three—"

"Visit the Panoptikum, the Hall of Mirrors. See yourself as you really are!"

Yes, Sol thought. Yes! That was what he wanted, what he needed—to see himself as he really was. He paid and stumbled through the door. The mirrors leered and wavered, but it was dark inside, and cool. If he could just lie down for a while. Here, where the carousel was muted.

He sagged in a corner, his back against a mirror and, sighing, let his eyes close.

"Up! Out! What do you think this is, a hotel?"

A huge hand held fast to Sol's lapels and a bearded barker in a pinstriped coat pulled him to his feet. His glasses slipped off his nose and he struggled to rescue them. When he looked up, the man grinned at him and dissolved. Images appeared in a convex mirror, tall as the Funkturm. A goatee, the white flesh of a deformed hand, Erich and Miriam—arms around each other, pointing and laughing—

"Glühwürmchen…"

Sol could hear the strains of the carousel's calliope, pulling him back outside, away from the laughing images in the mirror. He glanced at the door, wondering how he was going to find the strength to get out of here and make his way home. He looked back at the mirror, afraid he might see a manifestation of the dybbuk.

A thin convex version of himself stared back at him. Nothing but a jealous and tired thirteen-year-old who was more than ready to go home.

CHAPTER TWENTY-SIX

OCTOBER 1924

Miriam surveyed the disarray of her room. Her navy-blue private school uniform lay crumpled on the floor. Her suitcases, half-packed, stood beside the door. Makeup was strewn all over her vanity.

"Here, Killi," she said, close to tears. Obediently, the shepherd came over and nuzzled her. "You'll like being with Vlad," she told the dog, more for her own sake than for the animal's. How she'd battled Erich about calling a female dog Achilles, she thought. The name, he'd insisted, had come to him out of the moonlight, so even if this was a bitch, no other name would do. Sad as she felt, she could not help but smile at the memory of Erich's appearance on her balcony that night with the puppy, his fumbling attempts at caresses, his pride in saying *bitch*, as if it made him older and taller to say it out loud in her presence.

That night was really the beginning of their friendship.

Why was it she found beginnings so easy and endings so difficult, she wondered. She picked up her journal from the top of her suitcase. There were so many memories.

She stopped herself, calling upon her pragmatic streak. There was much to be done before the train left for Paris; she could not allow sentiment to distract her, at least not until she picked up the boys en route to the train station.

Mentally she ticked off her list. Finish packing. Hand Killi over to Vlad, who had agreed to make things easier for her by meeting her at the cigar shop—

Dammit, what did Sol and Erich expect her to do now that she had graduated from school—hang around until they grew up too? Her choices were clear enough. Go back to America, enroll at the University here in Berlin, or do what she was doing—join a dance company and start trying to earn her own living.

Not that she had ever wanted for anything, not even last year during the worst of inflation, when an egg cost eight hundred marks and even middle-class Jews like Sol were forever having to stand in long Gentile-first lines for milk and other staples. She wished her grandmother could live forever, but the truth was that even if Oma died she would not lack for money. Perhaps with her funds, she could assure that Sol would never again have to stand in lines. The estate would be hers, and Oma's jewelry and money—and the trust fund in Switzerland. Oma was there right now, making sure everything was in order before joining her in Paris.

Eventually it would all be hers, but that wasn't the same as earning it herself. Besides, she loved performing, and she had a right to her own life. Time to leave; time to get on with it.

Good intentions notwithstanding, she sat down on the bed and opened her journal, a gift from Sol for her sixteenth birthday. It bulged with mementos. Ticket stubs. A dark curl she had kept from the day she'd had her hair bobbed. Photographs: Vladimir holding a tennis racket, his eyes telling her he'd had a different game in mind for a long time; Oma, her arms filled with freshly cut roses, her shoulders bent with the weight of her sorrow for her sons—

And the boys. Always the boys—alone, together, she and Erich, she and Sol, the three of them—

The boys would be men when she came back. If she came back.

She leafed through the pages, stopping here and there as a word, a sentence, a pressed flower triggered memories of the last two years. Sol, his nose buried in a book; Erich in his ridiculous uniform. Erich and Sol under a tree in the park, picnicking on Braunschweiger and Pickart bread and arguing about Adolph Hitler's jail sentence for his part in the Munich Beer Hall Putsch—

She opened the journal at random.

Wedged between two pages was a letter from Sol, written to her the day after he had talked to her. In it, he spoke about his fears for the Jews, about his dream of spending his life studying and interpreting the mystics in ways everyone could understand, and about his visions...*I remember the day Erich hurt his hand*, he wrote. *We were taking him to the hospital in a taxi. I was exhausted, and terribly upset. I thought I had fallen asleep in the car and dreamed about standing in line for hour after hour to buy two bottles of milk for Mama. In the dream, the milk cost a fistful of money; in the dream, Jews had to stay at the back of the line until all non-Jews had been served. And then, as we all know, it happened. Really happened. I wonder how many other things I have "dreamed" in that way will turn out to be visions of the future. Not too many, I hope, for few of my dreams are pleasant.*

On the same page, and on half a dozen of the following ones, she had pasted photographs of the three of them at Luna Park. She read the captions. *Erich protecting me on the roller coaster. Erich being romantic on the Ferris wheel. Me, hugging the music box Sol won—after a lot of trying—at the pfennig-toss.* How jealous Erich had been over that!

She took the music box off her vanity and placed it next to her handbag. She was leaving enough behind; she could surely afford to take a few things for no reason other than sentiment. The memory made her smile, and she opened the lid and listened to "Glowworm."

So sweet, those boys. She closed the music box.

Again she opened the journal but this time there was nothing random about her choice of page. She ran her finger along an electric-blue peacock feather. Pulling it off the page, she attached it with a hat pin to the soft felt cloche she had picked for the journey—the same one she had worn on the ferry to Pfaueninsel—Peacock Island—that Saturday....

She and Erich had gone to the island alone, leaving Sol to his renewed studies with the beadle. She had probably learned more about Erich that day than before or since, she thought as she picked up her journal and skimmed what she had written. They had talked about Sol's visions and about Erich's views of the world and the Great War. At first, listening to him, she had thought him against war, but she had slowly come to realize that he imagined himself as a member of the German nobility, willing to sacrifice himself for his king or his lady and doing battle for both to prove his heroism. What had surprised her was his clear perception of his own shortcomings—his need to control others and the temper that would not allow him to live up to his conception of what he would like himself to be.

And what he could be! Miriam thought. A pressed lilac blossom fell from the journal and fluttered onto the bed, wafer thin and diaphanous—like the dress she had worn in celebration of free-love advocate Isadora Duncan and her marriage to the Russian poet, Sergei Esenin. She had packed the dress. She would wear it on some stage somewhere, when she needed to be close to Sol and Erich.

She riffled through the pages and found her description of the day she had worn the dress. The limousine ride to Wiesbaden, the three of them,

Achilles, and the ever-obliging Konnie. A picnic in the park…

Erich stood stiffly upright and held the rough army blanket to one side like a toreador's cape. Sol grinned, put down the picnic basket and took out his harmonica, which he kept wrapped in one of his father's Reichsbanner handkerchiefs.

"Play the 'Toreador's Song,'" Miriam said, positioning herself.

Sol played—badly—but that didn't matter. It was drizzling slightly—that didn't matter either. Miriam could feel the rhythm through the thin strains of the harmonica. She stamped her feet, swirled, charged the cape again and again. At her side, watching them, was a small statue of Pan. She danced around him, paying tribute to Isadora, her free-flowing movements inspired by Sol and Erich, and by the music of friendship. Erich watched, forgetting to move the blanket and lusting after her body. She liked that. Most of all she liked the way Sol watched her, loving her being.

"I'm starving." Erich threw the blanket on the ground and reached for the picnic basket.

But Sol played on and she danced just for him. When the song was over, he shook the harmonica and put it back in his pocket. Smiling, he walked over to a blooming lilac, plucked a flower, and presented it to her.

"The star must have flowers," he said.

Not to be outdone, Erich pulled off a whole branch. Soon they were plucking the blossoms and throwing them at each other, tumbling around on the blanket like puppies.

Later, emptying out the picnic basket, she found blossoms among the crumbs....

How carefully she had orchestrated that day—and others too. Like the time she had arranged to meet the boys in front of the Siegessäule for an on-site debate about the stupidity of putting up a *victory* monument after a defeat. Or the time the three of them had pedaled all the way to the Grünewald, she and Sol together on a borrowed bicycle-made-for-two, to visit the estate of a close friend of her family.

They had entered the estate through wine vaults so enormous that they pedaled through the rooms. In the vaults they used the bikes for a jousting tournament, Erich proclaiming himself Tannhäuser and Miriam the Lady Venus. Sol astonished himself by winning and Erich astonished her by laughing in appreciation of his friend's skill. What fun they'd had among the dusty bottles, playing hide-and-seek in the darkened cellar...until Sol's ghosts came. She remembered his face, pinched and drawn, as he turned away from Erich's attempts to cajole him back into the spirit of the game.

Beginning to feel maudlin she snapped the journal shut, but not before she allowed herself a final memory—

She flipped to her last journal entry.

Wedged into the page, not yet pasted in, was a photo of Erich and Sol taken at the estate less than a month ago. The three of them had been sitting holding hands amid the dying roses of an Indian summer day. As dusk turned the sky pink she had told them of her decision to leave Berlin. First one and then the other, unembarrassed by the other's presence, swore to wait for her.

"I can't marry both of you," she had said.

"Ja, but would you if you could?" Erich had asked.

"I would."

He had plucked three long grasses and wound one around her ring finger and another around his own. The third one he handed to Sol. "Now, say 'I do!' and the three of us will be joined forever."

Sol, his eyes dark and intense, looked at her and then at Erich. Tossing aside the strand of grass, he had released her hand and walked away to stand by himself. She had wanted to go to him and comfort him, but Erich had held her back with a look that almost frightened her...and the moment passed—

"Almost time to leave, Fräulein Rathenau," Konrad called from downstairs. "May I collect your suitcases?"

Panicked, Miriam looked at her watch. "Give me another fifteen minutes, Konnie."

She threw the rest of her things in the cases and slipped into her clothes. In fifteen minutes, exactly, Konrad was back.

"I...I will miss you, Fräulein Rathenau." His usually implacable face wore a saddened expression.

Impulsively, Miriam hugged him. "And I, you, Konnie. Will you be here when I return?"

His face scarlet, Konrad nodded. "Your grandmother has been kind enough to give me a retainer. I shall stay here and take care of things as...best I can. I am not so young anymore and it would have been difficult...."

He stopped, as if embarrassed by his sudden garrulousness. He picked up the smallest of her cases and tucked it under his arm, lifted the other two as if they weighed nothing, and left the room. Achilles followed him to the door, then stopped and turned around as if waiting for her to come. She picked up her handbag, hat, and gloves, and glanced around one more time. Swallowing hard, she left the room and went quickly down the stairs and out the front door.

"Shall I wait right here?" Konrad asked when they drove up to the shop.

Miriam got out of the car and nodded. Taking Achilles by the leash, she tethered her to a pole outside the shop.

Sol sat at the table, the *Book of Formation* open in front of him. When he saw her, he simply stared.

"You look beautiful, Miriam." Jacob Freund stepped from behind the counter. "You will doubtless turn Paris on its ear."

Miriam had already said her farewells to him and to Sol's mother and sister. She had said less fond farewells to Erich's parents, who had long since forgiven her—or so they said—for "corrupting" their son. Despite their forgiveness, there had never been any love lost among the three of them.

"Where's Erich?" she asked. "We don't have much time. As soon as Vlad gets here I have to go."

"Why don't I tell him to hurry?" Herr Freund said.

"Thank you, Herr Freund," Miriam said.

"There is one condition," Jacob Freund said seriously. He opened his arms and smiled. "An extra hug for an old man, if you please."

"That's easy." Miriam was happy to oblige. She liked Sol's mother and sister, but her fondness for them did not equal the way she felt about Jacob. She really did love him, she thought, enjoying the smell of tobacco and Aqua Velva as he put his arms around her.

"Hey—come back with that!"

Miriam and Jacob whirled around to see Sol give chase to a little boy in uniform. Sol did not get very far, for he bumped head-on into Vladimir, who had stooped to pet Achilles.

"Thieves!" Jacob muttered. "There are more of those these days than customers." He glanced over at the table. "If my son does not start paying more attention, there will soon be no more pieces left." He walked over to the ivory chess set. "The ivory queen is missing!" He shrugged. "Ah well! The ebony one has been gone for months."

"I'm sorry, Papa." Sol limped back into the store.

"Today I forgive you," Jacob Freund said. "You have reason to be distracted. Tomorrow, you will not be as easily forgiven. Leave your books at home, Solomon. There will be plenty of time for you to read those things when you are older. Ah, here's Erich at last."

Miriam looked up to see Erich crossing the street. Please, Erich, she prayed. No more fuss about Achilles. They had already argued enough. First Erich had said he wanted to take the dog to the camp. Sol reminded him that the animal could not be kenneled there, since Erich had stolen it from the camp in the first place—a fact Miriam had not known. A compromise was reached; come the new year, Vlad would move onto the estate to act as caretaker—and to finish writing his novel. The dog would belong to Erich but would remain at the estate, where he could visit her any time he pleased.

"Erich! Hurry—there's not much time!" Miriam called out from the doorway.

Erich stopped in midstreet. He lifted his hand in a tentative wave and, ignoring the traffic, turned around and rushed back into the apartment building.

"What now?" Sol said.

"Maybe we had better go and find out or I'll miss my train." By now they were all gathered on the sidewalk and she was, once again, precariously close to tears. "Vlad, go. Please." She raised herself up on her toes, kissed him quickly on the cheek, and dropped to her haunches next to Achilles. "Don't forget me, Killi." She hugged the dog.

Quickly, without looking back, she crossed the street, Sol close behind her. They ran into the building, up the stairs, and into the Weisser flat.

"I was going to put it on for you, but...I've changed my mind." Erich stood at the window of his room, his back to them. His uniform was laid out on his bed. Miriam sat down heavily and stared at it. "You hate it—don't you!" He did not turn around.

"I hate what it stands for," Miriam said quietly.

"I'm going to change all that." Erich's voice was deadly calm. "You wait and see if I don't." He looked back out the window. "I'm not going to spend my life in that cigar shop, waiting on people who think they're better than I am." His face hardened. "Go now—both of you!"

"Erich—"

He turned to face her. "You'll come home, Miriam." His voice was still calm, and surprisingly soft. "I will be here."

"Will you write?"

"I'll—try. I'm not much good at that."

She wanted to kiss him one more time, but she did not. "I may never come back." Her voice was almost a whisper.

"You'll be back." Erich was looking at Sol. "One day, Miri, you'll have to make a choice—"

"Perhaps I will choose someone else," she said.

He smiled, though the smile did not reach his eyes. "I don't think so," he said quietly. "It will always be the three of us, tied together...." He let his voice trail off and turned back to the window. "You'd better go."

When they were in the limo, Miriam took Sol's hand. They had not spoken since leaving Erich's room.

"Perhaps I should not come to the station either," Sol said.

Miriam tightened her grip on his hand. We have never embraced, you and I, she thought, hearing the echo of Erich's words. *One day, Miri, you'll have to make a choice...the three of us.*

"Will you miss me, Sol?"

"Would I miss my right arm if they cut it off?"

"Will *you* write?"

"Do you want me to?"

She laughed softly. "Would I miss my right arm if they cut it off?"

With a sureness that surprised her, he put his arms around her and kissed her. She returned his kiss, tentatively at first, then with a warmth that shocked her.

"I've never said this before because I didn't want you to laugh at me." He sat back against the leather, but did not release her from his embrace. "But now…I love you, Miri. I always will."

She leaned against him, filled with a sense of wonder at how right this felt.

"*Always*," she said softly, "sounds like a very long time."

PART II

"I HAVE AND KNOW NO OTHER BLOOD

THAN GERMAN, NO OTHER VOICE, NO OTHER

PEOPLE THAN GERMAN. BANISH ME FROM

GERMAN SOIL, I WILL REMAIN GERMAN,

AND NOTHING CHANGES.... MY PEOPLE

AND EACH OF MY FRIENDS HAVE THE RIGHT

AND THE DUTY TO CORRECT ME, SHOULD

THEY FIND ME INADEQUATE."

—WALTHER RATHENAU

FOREIGN MINISTER 1922,

LETTER JANUARY 23, 1916.

Chapter Twenty-Seven

Sol looked from the profusion of geraniums bordering the patio of the Tiergarten café to the trees beyond. Already it was September. The trees were almost bare and the earth was a carpet of leaves and acorns. To him it seemed only yesterday that the scent of May lilacs hung in the air.

"Beautiful, isn't it!" He looked across the table at Erich and wondered what had happened to the years.

"The Führer loves nature, doesn't he, girls?" Erich leaned down and petted his two German shepherds. Achilles, lying like a bunched blanket against his legs, lifted her head and gave a contented *ruuff*. Taurus, the younger dog, sitting with ears perked, appeared not to respond to the affection except to shake her head, dog tag clicking, after Erich was through.

"He's probably much too busy at the Reichstag to make time for oaks and elms." Sol was hard-pressed to keep the edge of sarcasm out of his voice.

"He'll be here," Erich said.

"I'm not waiting much longer."

Erich pounded the metal table with his fist. "Dammit, Solomon, he'll *be* here!"

"*Schlemiel!*" Sol grabbed hold of the tankards of beer. "You wouldn't want to stain your precious uniform, would you?"

Erich's face reddened. He gripped the table edge as if he were about to vault it like a gymnastics horse. "I've warned you not to speak Yiddish in public," he whispered, glancing at the threesome who had just arrived and stood waiting to be seated. "Even one word is dangerous!" He lowered his voice still further. "You're pushing your luck, Solomon."

Sol looked at the threesome—an elegantly dressed couple and a tall silver-haired man in a blue serge suit who stood behind them, a hard feral smile on his face. He kept one hand possessively on the woman's shoulder and the other on the man's while he surveyed the Biergarten.

"Who's the one with the silver hair?" Sol asked. "Anybody important?"

"Important, no. Dangerous, yes!" Erich whispered. "That's Otto Hempel. He's only an Untersturmführer, but he's SS. I don't have the power to protect you from people like that even if I do outrank him." Erich clutched Sol's wrist. "Watch out. *Please.*"

"I'll hold my tongue if you hold your temper." Sol pulled his hand away. "Maybe you should befriend Hempel. You serve the same king, after all."

Erich ignored Sol's mocking tone. "The only people he wants to get close to, other than the High Command, are boys—bent over with their pants down. Goddamned queers are worse than whores." His voice was laced with disgust. "I hate immoral people!"

He glowered and sipped his beer. Sol watched Achilles wolf down a bockwurst that had rolled off the table during Erich's outburst. Taurus took no notice. Like Erich and me, Sol thought. Erich, so quick to seize any opportunity that he claims will help our families weather the Nazi storm, while I wait and watch.

Deciding to give the Chancellor ten more minutes, he listened to the threesome's conversation.

"They're all the same." The woman was addressing the shorter man. "Take that French philosopher, Bergson, and that renegade Jew—whatshisname?—the one who emigrated recently?" She tossed the tail of her narrow boa angrily around her neck.

"Einstein?" The man sounded bored.

"Right. The one who said you can bend light or something? I mean, who cares? Only a Jew would be interested in such foolishness. So what do the other Jews do? Give him a chair at the university. Does he stay there? No! Takes off for North America. To tell them our secrets, no doubt. *Our* secrets. *German* secrets."

"Eavesdropping again, Solomon?" Erich asked. "I think you look upon it as sport—though from the sounds of it, you'd be better off not listening."

"Same old argument," Sol said impatiently. "Always

the Jews. We've conspired with the Communists to create *Kultur-Bolshevismus*. We're trying to rot Germany's moral fiber by corrupting its scientific and artistic institutions. Such absurdity would almost be funny if so many people didn't take it seriously."

He gave a sad smile as the woman started in on the architect Walter Gropius and the Bauhaus Movement.

"Just don't listen," Erich said. "Don't be a masochist."

"How can I help but listen?"

"All that glass and concrete," the woman said. "The building has no character. Much like you, my darling!" She removed a shoe and, balancing on one foot, dumped out a stone. "As for your wonderful ideas! Let's go for a walk, he says. It might improve your temperament! Ridiculous! Walking is for Jews and peasants. Besides, there's nothing wrong with my temperament that a good *man* couldn't cure!"

"What can it matter to you how something's built?" the shorter man asked in an even tone, as if the intimation that his manhood left something to be desired was unworthy of his attention.

"It matters because it's decadent!" The woman held onto her anger like a cat with a bird in its mouth. "Like those vulgar American skyscrapers. You can't tell the front from the back."

"Cubism and the concept of the multisided universe are simply reflections of the times."

"Nonsense! Your fancy theories reflect nothing but radicals and Jews, wanting to change everything. Like the roof of that monstrosity—the Bauhaus! It's flat, for God's sake! A flat roof in the Fatherland! It's un-Christian! Un-German!"

"Not to mention impractical, since it's likely to collapse under the first snow," the SS man added.

"That's right. *You* tell him, Otto," she said to the second lieutenant. "If Franz won't listen to reason, maybe *you* can make him understand."

"Perhaps you should calm yourself, Helga, before you bring on another migraine," Hempel said. "As for me, I do my best not to think." He raised his hand and snapped his fingers for a waitress. "It muddies the emotions."

The waitress, a girl of no more than seventeen, offered a choice of tables, one within view of Erich and Sol, the other in a prime spot around the corner and overlooking the lake with its weeping willows, swans, and blanket-wrapped boaters. The woman, appearing to seethe from her companion's treatment of her, indicated a preference for the table closer to Sol and Erich. Seating herself in Erich's line of vision, she arched an eyebrow, smiled, and draped her calf-length skirt so her ankles were seen to best advantage.

Sol looked from her to Erich and tried to assess him through her eyes. The young first lieutenant did look handsome in his uniform. Were it not for the mutilated hand, he would appear the perfect Aryan, as if he had stepped from one of the State-financed propaganda films at the Marmorhaus. The ribbons above his breast pocket added just the right touch of color, even though they represented completion of Abwehr military-security instruction and not gallantry in action. The neat mustache that graced his lip had surely stirred the heart of many a Fräulein on the parade field and at sports rallies in the Oranienburg grain fields.

"Ever have a woman like that?" Erich picked up his beer, toasted his admirer, and drank deeply.

Sol shook his head. "Have you?"

"She's no beer-and-bockwurst lay, I'll tell you that. You might try it some time. Do you good."

"Me?" Sol laughed.

"Why not? You're good-looking enough, in a Semitic kind of way. Lots of misguided women go for the dark brooding type. You can't spend the rest of your life moping after Miriam." He paused and his eyes darkened. "Have you heard from her lately?"

Sol shook his head. "I did write and tell her about the estate, but that was three months ago. Maybe more. Perhaps she never received the letter."

"Or perhaps she just doesn't care anymore. How long has it been since you heard from her—at least three years."

"We've both had birthday cards."

Erich laughed. "I'm sure Vladimir has too. She has a new life, Solomon. Face it. Do yourself a favor and get yourself one of those." He nodded in the direction of his admirer. "How old do you think she is? Forty? Forty-five?"

Sol shrugged, knowing that whatever he said would give Erich the opportunity for some acidic reply. When it came to Sol's shyness, Erich seemed unforgiving. As for his comments about Miriam, Erich's philandering was no indication that he had forgotten her, Sol thought. Different people used different ways to protect themselves; for Sol it was isolation, for Erich, just the opposite. That didn't mean a thing.

The woman leaned back, gave her order to the waitress, and made a limp-wristed motion with her hand. "Send the Gypsy to read our tea leaves. I wish to see if life has any excitement in store for me."

"I'm afraid she's unavailable, Fräulein," the girl said apologetically. "She says there is too much wind upon the water today for her power to be effective."

"Ridiculous!" The woman darted her gaze across the lake. "Not so much as a breeze. You bring her out here!"

"I'm sorry," the girl replied. She lowered her voice. "You know how stubborn the lesser peoples can be, Fräulein."

The waitress departed for the kitchen. With a defeated sigh, the woman sat back on the white wicker chair. Glancing toward Erich, she pushed at her auburn hair, then shook her fashionable center-parting back in place. Her gaze roamed from his eyes to his ribbons and down his shirt buttons; she recrossed her legs, pointing a slim foot in his direction, her red patent-leather shoe as covert an invitation as a lighthouse beacon. "If the Gypsy is unavailable, perhaps *he* could read my tea leaves," she said in a voice just loud enough to make certain Erich heard.

Franz took her hand and pressed it to his lips. "You are a wicked creature. Such a taste for soldiers."

The taller man leaned over and quietly said something to the woman. She stiffened. When she looked back at Erich, her eyes had narrowed.

"A well-preserved forty, I'd say," Erich whispered. "They're best about that age…no games, and they work hard at it."

"Seems your SS friend has changed her mind."

"She knows what she likes." Erich settled back confidently. "She'll come around."

Other than dogs, Sol thought, the only two things that seemed to arouse his friend were conquests and contacts. The right ones. Erich's Reichsakademie studies had been but a means to an end, like his interest in mathematics and physics—derived from recognition of his excellence, not from fascination with the subjects themselves.

"Such women excite me." Erich's voice was suddenly husky. "They know everyone who's anyone, and ultimately they talk. The SA Storm Troopers can keep their barrel-chested wives and simple-minded whores. I'll stick with the cream. By the time I leave here, I'll have her key and telephone number."

"Doubtless you'll use both."

"Shsh!" Erich's brows drew together and a look of concentration entered his eyes. He set down his beer and turned toward the graveled path that serpentined through the woods. "Did you hear that?"

"Hear what?"

"Them! Him! I told you he'd come."

Sol listened for the crunch of boots on gravel. He could hear nothing, but then Erich frequently sensed sounds and movement before others did. After his Freikorps unit became part of the Hitler Youth, his superior woodsman skills had earned him a two-week intensive camp in the Black Forest. He was an excellent tracker, as good and sometimes even better than the dogs he worked with so closely and loved so much; they too had senses beyond human ken.

Erich gripped Sol's wrist. "I've never seen him up close before. My God, this is a day, Solomon!"

Solomon. These days it was always "Solomon," as if Erich were deliberately distancing himself from the old days. Just as Herr Weisser had become "sir" to Erich ever since their big blow-up after Rathenau's murder. No hint of disrespect, only a coldness, as if Erich were no longer an integral part of the Weisser household or of the cigar shop, with its Jewish co-owners. Yet he insisted that he had come to hate the Hitler Youth and was bent on moving up in the Party proper precisely *for* the sake of family and friends.

There was a missing puzzle piece somewhere, Sol thought. He could feel his friend's sincerity when he said things like that. And yet—

"Can you hear him? I told you he'd come!"

Jittery as a first-day kindergartner, Erich smoothed his hair, straightened his tie, picked lint from his lapels.

Sol saw the SS man sit up even straighter than before and turn his head toward the trees. Now Sol heard voices, one resonating louder than the rest, demanding attention with the deep throaty insistence of a cello. He listened, torn between curiosity—he had never seen the Chancellor at close range like this—and the strong urge to run.

CHAPTER TWENTY-EIGHT

Sol watched Hitler and three paunchy Storm Troopers saunter into the open. A white terrier pranced at the Chancellor's side. While Achilles simply looked from the terrier to Hitler and lifted her brows with lazy disdain, Taurus emitted a low growl. The little dog immediately cowered behind its master's legs. Almost imperceptibly, Hitler glanced down. He shifted his gaze to the tables and looked around with the air of a man who had arrived at a popular restaurant to find his regularly reserved table taken. Then he stared over the heads of the café customers, out across the lake, as though absorbed in a vision only he could discern.

"Führer, *wir folgen Dir!*" The woman, Helga, shouted words lifted from a popular election poster: "Führer. We follow you!"

The Chancellor bowed slightly to acknowledge her adoration.

"Mitt Gottes Willen," Erich added softly. Rising to his feet, he clicked his heels and saluted Helga's small compact hero. "With God's will."

Hitler and his entourage lifted their arms in an answering stiff-armed salute, which induced most of the customers to shout *"Heil!"* and raise their arms in return.

The Chancellor was the last to lower his arm. Rumor had it that he took special pride in maintaining the salute for lengthy periods in front of female admirers, as if doing so proved his virility. He had apparently issued a standing challenge to any Storm Trooper who believed he could hold the salute longer than his Führer.

Grateful to the few who merely gestured in desultory fashion, Sol kept his arm lowered. Hitler looked his way. Fortunately, the Chancellor's attention was not on him, but on Erich's dogs. After looking with disgust at Achilles, Hitler fixed his gaze on Taurus.

"A beautiful dog. A fine, proud bearing. Good lineage?" He moved toward their table.

"The best, mein Führer," Erich replied. "Descended from the German grand champion."

"In animals, as in people, breeding is everything." Hitler's gaze roamed the audience. When he was sure he had their attention, he lifted his finger like a schoolmaster and said, "Genetic purity creates strength of character." As if it were being scolded, the terrier backed under the nearest table. "Your animal's name?"

"Achilles. And this—"

"I was not referring to the old one, Herr Oberleutnant."

"—is Taurus. Achilles' offspring."

Sol saw anger flare in Erich's eyes.

"Taurus!" Hitler patted Taurus on the head; she did not respond to the display of affection. "Born in May?"

"The fourteenth."

"And your name?"

"Weisser." Again Erich lifted himself into military bearing. An odd expression crossed his features. "Erich Alois Weisser. I had my name legally changed to honor your father."

The bastard doesn't miss a move, Sol thought, stunned by his friend's audacity. There was a certain appeal in Erich's lying to someone who told so many lies, but why this particular lie? Why work this hard at impressing a man he purported to despise?

What had happened to Erich's unwillingness to compromise that had caused them so much pain when they were boys?

He had finagled his way into the Reichsakademie despite his hand and come back from his training camp in the Black Forest full of tales of the people he had met there—men in counterespionage whose mere hints about the training center in Oranienburg had been enough to convince him not to ask too many questions. He was, he had told Sol many times, thankful to be in the security division, where he could acquire power and correct abuses without inflicting pain. As for his being taken with the Nazi Party, he insisted he saw its potential for bringing Germany out of the Depression and, like everyone else, desperately wanted to see an end to that, as well as to repression. Recently, he had managed to get a promotion and to maneuver his Abwehr canine unit into headquarters security. *I'm not guarding Goebbels, I've penned him,* he had said when the orders came through. *I intend to use him before he uses us.*

To Sol it sounded too easy; all too terribly familiar.

"Weisser." The Führer mulled the word like a fine cognac. "A good German name. A good German dog. I shall remember you."

"Maybe I was not born too late after all," Erich said, as the Chancellor patted him on the shoulder and stepped away. He looked as if he'd been touched by a god and rendered immortal.

Examining the newly appointed Chancellor as objectively as he could, Sol tried to see what it was about him that commanded such worship. He looked nothing if not ordinary in his oft-photographed, belted trench coat: a nose too large for his face; eyes, blue and clear and seemingly without guile or, more accurately, without expression at all.

A Storm Trooper pulled up a chair for Hitler and the Chancellor sat down. "You must all read Schopenhauer," he told his entourage as if continuing a lecture cut short by his emergence from the woods. "Detailed knowledge of his philosophy must be required of all Germans. My dear Schopenhauer teaches us that although all forms of life are bound together by misery and misfortune, we higher forms must struggle against, and separate ourselves from, the lower." His hands fluttered as he spoke, not with the careful theatrics with which he endowed his Reichstag-balcony speeches but, Sol thought, like the wings of an injured bird. "His books, with their affirmation of the strength and triumph of the will, kept me going"—another flutter of the hands—"no, kept me *alive*, during those terrible days in the trenches, when we dined on rats and died from typhus and influenza and were up to our knees in mud."

Again he lifted the index finger. "Yes! Everyone will read Schopenhauer."

He patted the terrier and looked at the three Brownshirts. They stood at parade rest, watching the woods as though they expected trouble from that quarter. "You may leave," he told them. He waved in the direction of the woods. "Anywhere I go in our beloved Fatherland, I'm among friends."

The men looked startled but did as they were told. At once, Hitler called over the waitress.

"Bring me apple-peel tea and the Gypsy."

She looked nervously in Helga's direction before obeying.

"I told you he would be here today to consult the Gypsy," Erich said, a little sheepishly.

"It's all so..." Sol searched for the right word. "Absurd."

"Like your voices and your visions, Solomon? Perhaps you and he should both attend the Psychoanalytic Institute. I hear Freud's old students are paying people to come for analysis."

What entitles you to be a judge of sanity, you and your dog fixation, Sol thought, glaring at his friend. Saying you feel *married* to your canine unit. Sorrowing openly over Rin Tin Tin when he died in Jean Harlow's arms. If that weren't something for Freud! As for his own voices and visions, and the dybbuk he had believed in so fully, that was over...the stuff of childhood. According to his readings and to the beadle, the practical necessities of adult life had stunted his development as a mystic, forcing the dybbuk into inactivity; he preferred a less complex answer.

The waitress trundled out a serving cart, its wheels creaking across the flagstones and interrupting Sol's introspection. Lemon cakes glittery with colored sugar and edged with frosting graced a large cut-glass plate; a porcelain teapot wobbled precariously, threatening to knock down two china cups nestled on a stack of cake plates and saucers.

"The Gypsy will be out momentarily, mein Führer." The waitress placed a cup and saucer and the teapot on Hitler's table.

He took hold of her hand, looked at it, and smiled. "They told me young girls were painting swastikas on their fingernails." The girl smiled back at him proudly.

"Find out why that Gypsy bitch is keeping me waiting." He dropped eight sugar cubes into his tea with a fine waiter's precision. "Tell her I have a good mind to—"

"A good mind to what?"

The Gypsy's voice was soft and sweet, not so much lacking in respect as filled with a surprising familiarity. She wore a simple, long black knitted dress, cut low in the front to reveal enormous breasts. Her feet were bare. The scalloped edge of a red lace shawl framed a mass of curly black hair and draped her ample shoulders, lending her broad-hipped and overweight body the voluptuous innocence of a Rubens model. She looked at Hitler with dark eyes that hinted of humor, sensuality, and a depth of understanding. Sol felt drawn to her.

"He often consults her in private," Erich whispered.

"When he has a specific and immediate problem, he comes here."

"How did you know he would be here today?"

"A contact—"

"Sit!" The Chancellor pointed toward the chair beside him.

The woman glanced sidelong at the chair and, with the barest hint of disdain, took Hitler's cup.

"She doesn't seem to be treating him with reverence," Sol said.

"He makes no secret of the fact that he hates Gypsies almost as much as Jews." Erich's whisper was tense.

Apparently Hitler also found the Gypsy lacking in servility. Lifting the teapot he thrust it toward her face. "*This* is indicative of the life of Adolph Hitler. Not some little teacup." He slapped the teacup from her hands, sending it crashing to the flagstones. She knelt to pick up the shards.

"My apologies, Herr Chancellor." Her tone mocked him. "By all means, swirl the leaves in the teapot."

Using both hands, he swirled it around. Then, red in the face, he poured the remaining tea onto the flagstones. The Gypsy started as the hot tea splashed her, but she took the pot from his outstretched hand. Tipping it slightly, she examined its interior from this angle and that.

"Well?"

Motioning him forward, the woman placed her lips near his ear and murmured words unintelligible to anyone but the Chancellor.

He lurched upright and, rigid with rage, grabbed the

ends of her shawl. "How dare you!" He crossed the corners of the shawl as if choking her would force her words back down her throat. "My Reich shall live a millennium!" Face fiery red and jugular engorged, he released her.

Coughing, the Gypsy started to rise. At once, the silver-haired second lieutenant glided from his table and seized her from behind, his forearms across the front and back of her neck in a choke hold. As he forced her head up, she gagged in pain. Looking down into her fear-filled eyes, he blew her a kiss.

"Gypsies and the Jews, they are one and the same," Helga said loudly. "They give us nothing and take all we have in return."

Hitler's eyes were shut, his face drawn tight with wrath as he raised a fist above the table. Sol waited for the hand to bang down, sealing the Gypsy's fate; but the Chancellor unclenched his fist and, fingers quivering with fury, pressed his palm against the table. "Let her go. And I thank you for your trouble."

"No trouble." Hempel released her. "I live to serve."

Hitler peered down at the Gypsy, his eyes little more than slits. "We shall begin again."

He looked up in the direction of the waitress, who hurried indoors. She emerged almost at once, carrying a fresh pot of tea. The Chancellor took it from her. "This time," he said, "no mistakes. Speak the truth, and in specifics."

Slowly and deliberately he tilted the teapot and poured the searing hot tea onto the flagstones directly beneath the Gypsy's dress, scalding her bare feet and ankles. She screamed in pain and backed away—into the arms of Otto Hempel. Without a moment's hesitation, he yanked her into an empty chair and gripped her arms so she could not clutch at her scalded flesh.

The onlookers gasped and Sol felt his stomach clench. Achilles gained her feet and Taurus moved up under Erich's arm. An angry sound began in Taurus' throat. Erich, his face scarlet, did not seem to sense the danger. Sol tugged at his friend's shirt. Erich glanced at him and patted Taurus, who immediately quieted.

Absorbed by the drama, the audience pressed closer. Several of them rose from their chairs, apparently more eager than afraid, more participant than spectator.

The Führer held up a hand and smiled reassuringly.

Like a master magician, he looked down at the woman through eyes that seemed capable of mesmerizing stone. "Think *past* the pain," he told her. "Be German, not Gypsy. Love your land and your Führer so much that human frailty ceases to exist." He held the teapot, slightly tipped, over the woman's lap. "Concentrate."

Hitler tipped the teapot further. The woman stopped moaning and set her face hard.

"You will see your way to the truth? Remember there is always more tea."

The Gypsy nodded. "No more lies," she said hoarsely.

He swiveled the pot around and handed it to her. Eyes bright with tears, she examined the contents. Her face went vapid. She looked from the teapot to the Führer, her chin trembling, her eyes filled with terror. When she spoke, her words were incoherent.

"Tell me!"

The woman's breathing became raw and rapid. She peered back into the teapot, squinted up at Hitler and, quivering, shook her head. "Mein Führer..." Her voice trailed off.

"Say it!" Hempel put his arms across her throat and tilted up her head. She nodded and he released her, shoving down her shoulders in his disgust.

"I saw...power." She was bent over. Gasping. "Your power." Sobs punctuated her words. "Two...Berlins. One here...in the east. One...in the west."

"A Berlin in the Americas!" Hitler's eyes gleamed. He waved off Hempel when the Gypsy, shaking her head and attempting to stand, sagged to the flagstones. "And why should it be otherwise?" the Führer asked his audience. "Did English religious fanatics carve a nation from that wilderness? No! *German* brains and *German* backs! A Berlin in each hemisphere. It is," he formed a fist, "our destiny! A world made whole by German blood!"

Helga's feverish applause broke the ensuing silence, and soon the other watchers joined in. Everyone except Solomon and Erich, who sat with one hand on the head of each dog, staring blankly toward his Führer.

Papa was right, Sol thought. The Chancellor was deranged and dangerous not only because of his delusions, but because he believed the myth he had created.

Helga believed it. So, it seemed, did Erich. More dangerous yet, Hitler placed people in the power structure who believed it, too. Goebbels was a perfect example, which, of course, was why Hitler had elevated him to Gauleiter of Berlin. He had been nothing but a scrawny government clerk and failed novelist with a penchant for pornography shops and sleazy cabarets; now he was making speeches from the Reichstag steps. Sol himself had heard the man call the Rathenau assassination a blessing, had seen someone walk from the crowd and slap the Gauleiter's face with a black glove, shouting, "It isn't for garbage like you that we murdered him!"

Since then the assassins had been granted sainthood in the Nazi hagiography.

Only the Jews and the Gypsies remained sinners.

Sol touched Erich's sleeve, but his friend shrugged off the hand. "The man's nothing but a bully," Sol whispered.

Here was a man who, within four months of taking power, had managed to eradicate virtually every vestige of democracy in Germany, including the Nationalist Party that had supported his candidacy. In less than a year, Hitler had gone from losing an election by six million votes to gaining over fifty percent of the Reichstag seats. Bully or no, it would be nothing short of insanity to take him on alone. One did not, after all, use stones to fight tanks. Not unless one happened to be David.

"It makes me sick to see him act that way," Erich said bitterly. "But as long as Germans demand a scapegoat for the war and the Depression, as long as the SA and SS hold the reins of power, Hitler must play the brute."

Solomon dabbed beer from his lips and set the wadded napkin on the table. "Are you so sure it's an act?"

Erich sadly shook his head. "God, I hope so."

The emotion in Erich's eyes told of a need to talk

things out, but this was hardly the place. "I have to get back to the shop," Sol said. "You coming? We've seen almost nothing of you since you moved into your flat."

"I...I can't." Erich's lips tightened. "That damn Goebbels stepped up the time schedule for the headquarters' move. The estate's still being renovated. We moved Goebbels' office furniture yesterday. Tonight I move in the dogs."

He paused, as if he had just thought of something. "Listen, Sol. I'm not giving up my flat, but I won't be able to use it much now that Goebbels has stepped up security. It's yours if you want to—"

"Use it for assignations? Thanks anyway," Sol said. In a way, he envied Erich being out on his own. There was no way he could leave; his parents needed him too much.

"It's incredible, the tensions I'm under, Solomon," Erich said. "Hurry up and wait, hurry up and wait. We don't even have kennels. There are no documents to guard, no personnel...*nothing!* Why must we start before we're really prepared?"

He put a hand on Sol's forearm. The momentary look of need in his eyes caused Sol a passing moment of guilt at his constant examinations of Erich's motives.

"I asked you here because I needed to have a drink with someone *real*. And to relax, just for a minute." Erich downed his beer and raised his hand to signal the waitress. "Let's have another."

"I'm sorry, truly I am," Sol said quietly, "but the urge to throw something at that man—preferably my fist, for all the good it would do—is just too strong."

Sol felt very conspicuous, and very Jewish. What was

he doing here? It was Friday afternoon, and *Shabbas* would soon begin. His place was at home with his family. He stood up. "I have to leave."

"*Wir folgen Dir! Wir folgen Dir!*"

The cry rang out, punctuated by cheers as the SS man, noticing the Gypsy trying to crawl away, used his shoe to push her past the fence. The Chancellor's terrier growled and scampered over to tug at the hem of her dress.

"Careful with her." Hitler grinned. "I may need her again...in a millennium."

For as long as the Chancellor needed her, the Gypsy was safe from everything except his tantrums—and not for a moment longer. Would it be the same with the Jews, Sol wondered, or would hatred ultimately prove to be stronger than Hitler's need for what Walther Rathenau had called Jewish assets and abilities? The phrase was Rathenau's, the delusion Hitler's.

The Gypsy pulled herself away from the terrier and rose laboriously to her feet. As she limped toward the woods, a pianist in the main part of the restaurant struck up a *Lady Moon* medley from the recent Paul Lincke revival. Sol felt ashamed and embarrassed. He had desperately wanted to go to her aid earlier, but to do so would have been both foolish and dangerous.

As if a performance were over and the postshow party had begun, the milieu abruptly changed to cocktails and light laughter. Hitler sauntered among the crowd, making casual conversation and shaking hands. The terrier bounded from table to table, for scraps fed by people eager to please anything the Führer loved.

Without another word to Erich, who sat in the midst

of the festivities unemotional as a corpse, Sol slipped away from the Biergarten. Taking the long way around Hitler, he headed for the trees to find the Gypsy and offer her what help he could. He had hardly gone beyond the first line of trees when he came upon her. She lay beneath an oak, sobbing, her head on a pile of leaves. Her dress was pulled up to her knee; he could see angry red patches on her calf.

Sol stooped and placed a consoling hand on her shoulder. "Those are ugly burns," he said. "You need medical attention."

Sitting up, she peeled a leaf from her cheek and looked at him through narrowed eyes. The tree's branches cast fingers of shadow across the blotches where her mascara had run. "I can help myself." Pulling down her dress, she turned her head and stared toward the Biergarten.

Sol followed her gaze and saw Erich approaching at a run, the dogs at his heels.

"What do *you* want with me?" she asked when he was near enough to hear her.

"I wish to get you medical assistance." Erich stooped as if to examine her.

She batted his hand away and, wincing, covered her legs with her skirt. "What you *wish* is to convince yourself that your beloved Hitler didn't hurt me."

"I didn't come here to be insulted," Erich said testily.

"I didn't invite you to come." She spat on the ground. "Leave! Go back to your idealism!"

Visibly fighting for self-control, Erich looked at his watch. "The dogs and I are due at the barracks in twenty minutes. Do you or don't you want my help?"

"No."

JANET BERLINER AND GEORGE GUTHRIDGE

"Then that's how it will be." Erich shook Sol's hand with a kind of military stiffness. "Tell Recha and your parents I said hello. I hope your father feels better." He nodded toward the woman. "If he decides she needs help, I'll pay the bill."

Hand raised in farewell, he walked into the woods.

"I have perturbed your friend, Solomon," the Gypsy said.

A shock ran through Sol as the Gypsy spoke his name. Then he laughed at himself. How easily the simple was overlooked! She had obviously heard Erich call him by name.

He squatted beside her.

She squinted as she peered into his face. The scrutiny made him uncomfortable. "I know you, Solomon Freund," she said. "I am a dancer in the dwelling place of dreams."

She looked down at her leg, which had already begun to blister. Removing her shawl, she wrapped it loosely around the burn. Closing her eyes, she began to rock, as if to relieve the pain.

Sol bent closer.

Her eyes snapped open. "You will not escape your dreams, Solomon."

"It is one thing for you to know my name. But you seem to know all about me." Sol backed against the oak.

"Over the years, my sleep spoke." She lifted a painted brow. "My dreams divulged. You're older, stronger now, Solomon." Her voice was soft, vibrant, and when she reached out with trembling fingers and touched Sol's cheeks, her eyes were moist, though whether with joy or grief he wasn't sure. "When your visions return, respect them. Even fear them. But listen to them, Sol. Listen. And learn."

He was stunned by her words and the extent of her emotion.

"Listen and learn," she said again. Removing the shawl from her leg and grunting in agony, she managed to stand. When he moved to steady her, she pushed him away. "Leave me now," she told him. "I have to go back alone."

"Go back? To the Biergarten? That's crazy!"

"Do not concern yourself with me, little sparrow," she said softly. "There are paths we each must walk. Mine lies in that direction, yours..."

"Could we—"

"Meet again? I think not." Head down, she limped off.

Sol let her go. The truth was, he was afraid of hearing anything more of what she had to say. Hands balled into fists in his pockets, he made his way through the Tiergarten, his route a palette of memories splashed on a canvas of autumn leaves, his mind an amusement park where the thin strains of a calliope echoed the pianist's lively rendition of Lincke's melodies. *Shine little glowworm*, it mocked. Shine on this fool who for a decade has thought himself free of the voices, believing them sealed in the sewer, left behind except in memory when Kaverne closed after Rathenau's murder. *Glow and glimmer* on the nightmares that will not, after all, die childhood's natural, gradual death.

Still shaken by the afternoon's events and by the Gypsy's knowledge of him, he reached the Zoological Gardens, near the Bahnhof Zoo Station.

In a gazebo decorated with lights, a woodwind quintet was playing Schubert for passersby. Sparrows twittered in the trees; grebes, with dusk approaching, called a warning from the ponds. Men and women in trench coats strolled arm-in-arm toward Lochau, the intimate café as famous in its own way as Kranzler's for its coffee-cake conversations. In the Hansaviertel—where the rich frittered away their days—wealth, fame, and love always seemed possible, as though the wealthy could mold hope into reality out of the gray air. How often he and Erich and Miriam had wandered here, talking of the future and of a prewar past that, of the three, only she clearly remembered. How often they had hiked and bicycled to the Reichstag! How often he had watched Miriam stare wistfully at the Siegessäule and say that the lady with the golden wreath, her arm lifted high over the city, made her long for New York.

A train hooted its way into the Zoo Station as Sol trudged through the gate that separated the gardens from the street. He stood for a moment to watch with growing loneliness as people detrained—men with satchels, women lugging hatboxes and children, all of them with somewhere to go and circumnavigating him as they might a pole or a tree.

"Solomon? Sol?"

Miriam's voice sang out his name, its cadence lilting above the street noise. Sol dipped inward for its source, into the well of visions in the sewer and nightmares in his bed, certain that now he was dreaming in the streets.

CHAPTER TWENTY-NINE

"Need help with your suitcase, pretty lady?"

Miriam shook her head at the overweight, overcoated man. He had sat in the seat across from her all the way from Paris, and again during the journey from Frankfurt, where she had changed trains for the last part of the trip home. Though he had stared fixedly at her ankles, he had made no previous attempt to talk to her. Her suitcase was heavy and she was tempted to let him help her as far as the taxi rank and worry about getting rid of him later. Not that she could afford a taxi, but what the hell.

Apparently sensing her hesitation, the man stepped closer. The look of delighted anticipation in his eyes quickly changed her mind, and she shook her head again. "Thank you, I can manage," she said politely but firmly.

He made no effort to hide his disappointment.

For the thousandth time Miriam wondered why she hadn't contacted Sol or Erich. They had never been far from the periphery of her consciousness in the nine years she'd been away. She had written to Erich a couple of times and he had always responded, but through Sol. Eventually, she gave up the effort except for a birthday card once a year which he dutifully reciprocated, never so much as adding anything but his name.

Sol was a different story. They corresponded regularly at first. His letters had been a great source of pleasure and comfort for her, especially after her grandmother died. Through him she learned that Erich had given up his veterinarian apprenticeship in favor of an appointment to the Reichsakademie. As of Sol's last letter three years ago, Erich was hopelessly devoted to dogs; making progress in the Abwehr; and conquering attractive, influential women. At the time, Sol was enrolled at the Language Institute, studying the Talmud and the Kabbalah, and helping in the tobacco shop. In deference to practicality, he was also studying bookkeeping and accounting.

When she sold the last of her grandmother's jewelry and her life began to sour, she stopped writing to Sol. Running through the money so fast was her own fault, she thought. Somehow she'd convinced herself that the well was bottomless.

There followed three years of silence, then she'd received the letter that had brought her back here. She dug it out of her handbag and read the beginning again:

Meine Liebe Miriam,

It has been so long—so very long—since I last heard from you. When half a dozen of my letters went unanswered, I at first worried that perhaps something terrible might have happened to you. Finally, I decided that you were simply too busy with your new and glamorous life and that the best thing I could do was send you warm thoughts, keep loving you, and pray that someday our lives would once again intertwine.

Now, I have heard news that I feel I must impart to you. Forgive me, I hate to be the bearer of bad tidings, but someone had to tell you—*they* are gaining more power every day, if not every minute. Some time ago, Erich told me that it was the good Dr. Goebbels' intention to conscript your home and use it as his headquarters—mostly, I fear, because it is far enough away from Wallotstrasse and the ever-vigilant SS that his bedroom activities with every willing star-struck blonde in Berlin will be overlooked.

Whatever the reason, I begged Erich to intercede on your behalf, as I did last year when—as I wrote and told you—I found out that the most valuable of the paintings and furniture in the house were appropriated. Whether or not Erich could have done anything to help without significant injury to himself is something I cannot judge. I do know that by early October the move into your estate will be well underway—if not completed....

Miriam folded up the letter and put it in her bag. She knew its contents by heart. The letter had taken more than three months to find her; three days later she had booked her ticket home.

Standing alone on the steps of the station, she asked herself why she had really stopped writing to Sol—and answered herself in the same way she had done for three years. In Erich's case, it was annoyance; in Sol's, she had found herself unable to reply. She wanted the ink of her adolescence to blur...wanted her future to be a tabula rasa. The past, which held the pain of youth's broken promises, needed to be relegated to the past.

She laughed at herself.

Those were fine thoughts, or at least pragmatic, but the truth was she wanted to see Sol *and* Erich. Wanted? No, longed! Dammit, she missed them both. Loved them both. Her love for Erich, she had long since decided, was perverse. When she thought of him, she felt aroused; loving him was stupid but exciting, like walking by a river during an electric storm. Worse yet, he made her dislike herself.

Sol?

Sol was mist and rainbows and the smell of Frau Freund's *latkes*.

Thinking about those made her remember her hollow stomach, growling with hunger. She hadn't eaten anything more nourishing than a sweet roll in days.

She inhaled deeply, but the smell around her was hardly that of potato pancakes; as usual, Berlin's sidewalks were splotched with dog droppings. Still, it was Berlin. Whatever else that meant, she was home.

Dropping her suitcase at her side, she massaged her

shoulder and congratulated herself for having had the good sense to leave the rest of her things to another ex-member of her troupe. She leaned sideways to pick up the case again and noticed a young man across the street. He was standing motionless in the path of the other passengers, who had crossed over and were moving around him as if he were a tree that had taken root in the sidewalk.

Come on, Miriam, don't be an idiot, she told herself, aware of her pounding heart. Nevertheless, she squinted to see more clearly in the encroaching dusk.

"Solomon! Sol Fr—!" She stopped. It was too much to ask of the Fates and, besides, *Freund* was too Jewish a name to yell.

The young man turned his head in her direction but did not react. Embarrassed, she changed her gesture into a wave and smiled as if she had recognized someone behind him. She was beginning to feel like an absolute idiot. Such happy coincidences were the stuff of dreams.

Then again, she'd made a fool of herself before, she thought as he took one step, and another, until he was running toward her.

"My God, it *is* you!" Sol grinned widely as he dodged a car.

"Who did you think it was? A ghost?"

She opened her arms and he embraced her, lifting her up and whirling her around.

"Miriam Rathenau at your service, sir." She laughed and held onto her hat.

"You look wonderful." He let go and stepped back to admire her.

And you *feel* wonderful, she thought. "What do you

think?" She executed a pirouette. "Is Berlin ready for my return?"

"If the city's not, I am."

She smiled at his open appreciation. The worse she felt, the more carefully she dressed, as if looking good worked some inner magic that forced her to take a more optimistic view of her life. She had put on a stylish calf-length tweed skirt and matching jacket. Her legs were stockinged in black silk, and a white silk blouse and cloche cap completed the outfit. Aside from a tall feather, the cap resembled a Pilgrim's bonnet and would have looked very proper had she not turned the edge up saucily on one side.

"Can it really be you?" Sol made no attempt to hide his pleasure. "You were a girl when you left Berlin."

"I'm twenty-six, Sol."

"Well, you look seventeen, at most."

"I'd *love* to believe you, darling, but you need to have your eyes checked."

For an instant she sensed a change in Sol, as if she had said something tactless. Then he said quickly, "I feel like I should spout poetry or say something philosophical to mark the occasion."

"You could give me a kiss for starters." She smiled. "And maybe carry a disgustingly heavy suitcase?" She folded her arms around his neck and stood on her toes.

To her surprise, his lips tasted of beer; his kiss was warm, but that of a brother. He was a man now, not the tentative boy she had left behind; tall and handsome, with that kind of brooding intensity in his eyes that many women found irresistible. Was there someone else in his life, some other woman—a wife? She glanced at his left hand.

The extent of her relief at seeing a ringless finger shocked her.

"You've come home…for good?" he asked.

"For good or bad. Depends on your point of view." She linked her arm through his and he lifted her case with the other. "In answer to the question in your eyes, my Sol, yes, I received your letter. I got it a few days ago." She stopped. There would be time for all that, and for asking about Erich. "Could we be serious later?" she asked.

Sol looked relieved. "Been in Paris all this time…I mean, since your last letter?"

"Paris, Amsterdam, Zurich…everywhere." She waved as if to include the universe in her experience.

Sol looked at her slim waist. "Aren't world travelers supposed to get fat from sampling all sorts of delicacies?"

"Me, fat? Never! Matter of fact, you could take me to your parents for a *Shabbas* meal. It will be my first in…too long."

She laughed and nuzzled her head against his shoulder. Clutching the post of a street lamp, she swung around it at a tilt.

"It's so good to be back, Sol! So good to be with someone I know." She looked toward the Brandenburg Gate. "We share so many memories."

"Mother and Recha were sure you had become the toast of Europe. When we stopped hearing from you, we decided you had gone to Hollywood and married Errol Flynn or someone. We kept expecting to see you on the

Movietone News, wearing furs and posing for photographers."

"Why an American?" She pouted coyly and once again tucked her arm through his. "Why not Willy Fritsch? I'm sure I could have dazzled him into a trip down the aisle. But I've simply been too busy to take time off to marry a star!" More seriously, she added, "Actually, for the past three years I've been with a dance company from Stuttgart."

"The Stuttgart Ballet?"

"I wish. You see before you the star of that traveling talent showcase, *La Varieté Nouvelle*." Star ballerina of third-rate theaters, she thought as she bowed grandly to hide her unease. "Danced excerpts from every great ballet on Europe's worst stages, for a lot of applause and little else. Did a bit of everything. Lehar. Lincke. *Giselle*, the Sugar Plum Fairy, you name it."

"Even so, Recha's such a balletomane I swear she gets programs from Siberia. We should have seen your name *somewhere*."

"I used a stage name." Again Miriam waved her hand in the broad gesture that encompassed fate and the universe. "Every time I handed someone a portfolio of my American performances, they looked duly impressed—and slammed the door in my face. Eventually I realized that people were afraid my name would attract Nazi attention. All I had to do at *Nouvelle* was audition, so I became Mimi de Rau. Like it?"

"*Mimi, you make me sad and dreamy*," he sang softly.

"Chevalier you're not." Miriam laughed with delight. "I am *très Parisienne, n'est pas*? So verree Frrench." She rolled her 'rrs' and tried to look like a seductress.

"So, has the company come to perform in Berlin, Fräulein de Rau?" Sol asked as they reached the apartment house.

"Hardly!" She gazed up at the barred windows. "We made the mistake of performing in Munich. The Chamber of Culture shut us down." She frowned at the Minister of Propaganda's latest lunacy: a few weeks before, Goebbels had formed the Chamber *to protect the public from non-Aryan influences in the arts*.

"The company's director was Jewish?"

"No, but they decided he was because of his nose. Next they'll be *measuring* everyone's noses."

Though Sol laughed as he held open the door, he did not sound amused. He had doubtless heard the rumors that the nose-caliper test was a reality in some places and that circumcision examinations were a possible next step. "Failure to fit accepted parameters" and "Jewish tendencies" had become familiar catchphrases.

"If you don't have work here, why did you come back?"

Miriam reached in her purse. After some digging, she produced a large latchkey. "I came across the keys to Uncle Walther's house the day we were notified the company was being disbanded, which was also the day your letter found me. The front door key fell off the ring and into my hand. I took it as an omen."

"Think of it this way—you would rattle around like a ghost if you lived in that mansion...alone."

"Good old Solomon—always finding something positive, even in evil. If I could afford to live there, I could also afford servants, Solomon." She kissed an index finger and pressed it to his lips, then turned her

JANET BERLINER AND GEORGE GUTHRIDGE

palms up in mock despair. "But that's all moot, isn't it. I'm penniless. Can you love a Poor Little Match Girl?"

"You're not bitter about the estate?" Sol sounded shocked.

"Bitter? No. Furious! But later, Sol, please."

"Just one question. Didn't your grandmother leave you anything?"

"Everything she had left, which was mostly jewelry. Didn't take me long to spend it. You know me—used to the good life!"

"What about your trust fund?"

"Gone. After Oma's death, I found out inflation had eaten up most of her fortune. The Nazis took what was left. She and I lived on the trust. I couldn't deny her anything, Sol. She was old, and used to a certain way of life. I just figured, when it was gone, it was gone. I probably should have sold the estate years ago but, to cut a long story short, Princess Miriam 'Mimi de Rau' Rathenau has been paying for her own bread and butter—and precious little jam."

Sol put down the suitcase and gave her a hug. "I can't promise you butter, but you are always welcome to whatever bread we have."

She kissed his cheek. He reddened slightly. After fishing in his pockets for the key, he opened the front door.

"*Mutti*? Recha? You'll never guess who's here!"

No one answered. Sol peered into the music and sitting rooms. "They must still be in the food lines."

"Hello?" Miriam called. "Herr Freund?"

Sol sent Miriam a cautionary look and signaled her

into the library. The room had two tall narrow windows. The one nearest the door was trimmed in Dutch curtains and spilled light onto a table cluttered with papers. The other was covered by a shade.

Seated near a corner, facing the darkened window and slowly rocking back and forth, was Jacob Freund.

"Oh my God!" Miriam thought of Jacob Freund as she had remembered him. Gentle. Dapper. Resolute.

This couldn't be the same man.

Jacob stared straight ahead, face set as though sculpted. Though not yet sixty he looked eighty. His cheeks were sunken, his cheekbones protruded. He stared toward the window shade through eyes that, clouded with film, seemed distended from their sockets. His hair was white and butchered; liver spots mottled his scalp. His right hand lay motionless on the blanket across his lap. His left forearm was on the rocker's arm. A silk ribbon dangled from his left hand, which hung as if it had no bones; attached to the ribbon, moving like a pendulum with each slight twitch of his hand, was an Iron Cross.

Try as she would, Miriam could not stem the tears. "Is he always...like this?"

"It comes and goes." Solomon put his hands on the old man's shoulders. "Miriam Rathenau's here, Papa."

The chair continued its rhythm. Sol motioned Miriam aside.

"His eyes... Is he *blind*, Sol?"

"He has chosen to be blind."

She looked at Sol in horror. He gripped her arms as if he wanted, needed to hold her. "Accept it," he said. "I have." He stared at the carpet. "At least I think I have."

They waited helplessly for a response or any sign of recognition from Sol's father. When none came, Sol guided Miriam into the kitchen. He poured them each a buttermilk.

Miriam turned and stood in the archway, staring at the old man.

"Seems like everything is a rare treat these days." Sol handed her the beverage. "It's hard to buy anything, what with 'We do not serve Jews' signs going up everywhere. At first it was only, 'Don't buy from Jews'...."

"What do you mean 'chosen'?" Miriam kept her eyes on Jacob as she drank. "How can he have *chosen* to be blind?"

"His eyesight's been failing for years but he can still see—with glasses. However, he refuses to get another pair. He says there's nothing left he wants to see."

"Then he's not completely—"

"Not yet." Sol's voice faltered. "He broke his glasses the day von Hindenburg appointed Hitler as Chancellor."

Nine months ago, Miriam thought. Some people give birth to sweet-smelling babies; we Germans bear tyrants.

"That evening," Sol said, "Papa placed his glasses under the chair and rocked back, crushing them. Since then his condition has worsened rapidly—"

"What's the prognosis?"

"The last doctor who came said it was acute depression, complicated by what we've known for some time. He has *retinitis pigmentosa*. Basically, a splash of melanin on the back of the retina." He struggled to finish. "I'm afraid it's degenerative."

"There must be something…other doctors…."

"There's nothing we can do. It's getting harder and harder to find a doctor willing to come to a Jewish household."

"There must be Jewish doctors."

Sol shook his head. "Most have left the country. The rest have to employ constant watchfulness to preserve their own safety, for all our sakes."

"He just sits and rocks?"

"Sometimes he putters around the house, but he doesn't go to the shop anymore. I've taken over for him. Mother helps with the books. I'm a linguist, not an accountant, despite all those classes."

"You're a student, Sol. It's all you should ever have to do."

Sol wiped off her buttermilk mustache and she chuckled despite herself. They eased into the table's corner-bench and deliberately talked of pleasant things—sunsets in the Alps, where she had learned to ski; and of how she had performed an excerpt from *The Dying Swan* in a rainstorm on a Rhine tourist barge. As they washed and put away the glasses, she asked him to come with her to the villa.

"Why torture yourself?"

"I want to see what dust has gathered and what insults the sparrows have deposited. We'll be back before dark, in time to celebrate *Shabbas*," she told him. "Promise."

Still, he hesitated. "Why not wait until tomorrow? You'll be more rested."

"What is it, Sol? What's really bothering you? We both know they have taken what's mine. I've had to face that. There is something else. Isn't there."

"Miri." Sol took her hand. "When we—Erich and I— heard about this, we talked about it. He was very upset. He said he would do what he could to stop it, but he doesn't have that kind of power."

"Erich…"

"We have to talk about him. He's there, Miri. At the estate. In charge of guarding it for Goebbels—"

"No!" She hadn't meant to shout but the word rang out like an alarm. She lowered her voice. "Why Erich? Explain it to me."

"He'll have to do that himself. I just wanted you to know. We could bump into him—"

Miriam glanced in Jacob Freund's direction. "Let's go. Now!"

Outside, they stood hand-in-hand as Solomon flagged a taxi. "I need to find work," Miriam said as they slid inside. "A cabaret, anything, it doesn't matter."

Sol gave directions to the driver. She leaned close to the window and looked across the street at the cabaret's faded awning. "If only Oma had not closed Kaverne."

If only, she thought, wondering if her life would always be filled with those two words.

Suddenly all she wanted was for this day to end. Her emotional bucket was filled to overflowing; she envied the taxi driver his isolation, closed off from them by a glass partition and separated from the outside by glass and metal. It had all been too much. The news about the house, the company disbanding, the long train rides back to a hate-filled city that had once been home. Seeing Sol was wonderful, but Jacob… When she'd insisted on going to the villa *now*, she'd failed to realize how tired she was. She wasn't at all sure she could handle anything more; under the circumstances, she was especially not sure she could handle seeing Erich again.

She glanced at Solomon, grateful that he understood her need for silence. With any luck, Erich wouldn't be at the estate—

Luck hasn't exactly been your middle name of late, she reminded herself. Her only hope of making it through this day was to set aside her feelings. There would be time enough to examine those. For now, the best thing she could do was to act and react, and leave the thinking—and the feeling—for tomorrow.

C HAPTER THIRTY

The cab rounded the last S-curve before the estate. Heart racing, Miriam waited for the villa to come into view. Even had the place still been hers, she reminded herself, she could not afford to park so much as a dog in the driveway. It took wealth to maintain an estate, not just income—all of which was moot, since she had neither. Her uncle had kept the place immaculate. The lawn was always manicured, the chestnut that shaded the west chimney pruned, the ivy that covered the gate and guardwall-ironwork trimmed. There never seemed to be an end to the work that needed to be done. The east wall regrouted, the trim of the front-door canopy touched up. Always something.

The cab stopped and she stepped out. While Solomon paid the driver, she walked over to the east gate and gripped the bars, inhaling the richness of newly mown grass. The place was even more beautiful than she remembered. There was so much to the villa she had taken for granted. Red-and-black brickwork graced each corner and set off the entryways. The wrought-iron grills over the windows nicely contrasted with the limestone. The black, red, and gold cobblestones in the crescent-shaped driveway had been chosen to match the colors of the Weimar Republic.

She remembered the wording of Uncle's will. *Meine Vorfahren und ich selbst haben sich von deutschem Boden und deutschem Geistgenärt*...my forefathers and I myself have nourished ourselves from German earth and spirit...*should death of inheritee occur before liquidation of my estate, the grounds and buildings shall revert to the German people, to serve as a showplace for art and artifacts by Germans of Jewish descent....*

On the roof, a man in a carpenter's apron hoisted a flag from the flagpole on the southeastern turret. The cloth unfurled in the breeze.

Red, with a white circle and a black swastika.

"Take that down!" Shaking the gate, she thrust an arm between the bars. "You hear me, you bastard? Take it down!"

She dug into her handbag for the keys to the estate and tried each of them in the lock. None worked.

"Stop it, Miri." Sol took hold of her arm. "They are not going to fit. You can be sure they've changed all the locks." He pointed toward two workmen opening the western gate for an army truck. "If someone sees you, we could be turned in."

"Turned in? This is *my* home!"

"This *was* your home!"

Furious, Miriam shrugged off his hand and hurled the

keys through the bars of the gate. They clinked as they landed.

Covering her mouth with her hand, she watched a tar sprayer enter the other gate and move along the driveway, suffusing the air with stench. A yellow steamroller with a puffing exhaust followed, its driver waving frantically and shouting invectives at the workmen as if he were in charge of smoothing out the broad boulevard of the Unter den Linden during rush hour.

"I won't believe Erich is a part of this!"

Sol's dark eyes held an answering reflection of her own hatred and helplessness. She put her arms around his neck and laid her head against his chest. This time, when he held her close, she could feel his love for her. She breathed in the smell of him. Please don't let go of me, she thought. Outside of myself, you are all I have left.

The stuttering of an engine right behind her made her turn her head. A motorcyclist in leather helmet and goggles crested the hill and roared past. The rider, bent low for aerodynamics, seemed almost part of the machine.

He glanced sideways toward her and did a double-take, changed his balance, and throttled down. The engine screamed in protest. Jamming down a boot, he swung the machine in a shrieking U-turn, bumped over the curb and skidded to a halt in a cloud of dust.

Sol pulled Miriam back against the gate.

Gunning the engine, the rider raised his goggles.

"Erich! Are you crazy?" Sol shouted. "You almost killed us!"

Miriam said nothing. Her heart was pounding as much from the rush of adrenaline as from her first sight of Erich in nine years. For a moment she forgot about the house, the Nazis—the real world—and stared at this man who, together with Sol, had occupied so many of her thoughts. Except for the area the goggles had protected, his face was grimed with dirt and exhaust. Still, she'd have recognized him anywhere. He never really had looked like a boy, she thought. More like a miniature man waiting to catch up with himself.

"So! The prodigal has returned, and more beautiful than ever."

He smiled, obviously pleased with the drama of his entrance. Turning off the cycle, he put down the kickstand and draped an arm across the handlebars. His body seemed charged with the power of his machine, the supple muscularity of his torso evident even in his leather jacket. Like a confident warrior on a steed, Miriam thought, glancing at Sol. He looked jealous, and angry with himself. Damn Hitler and all his barbarians! Damn *you*, Erich, for the weakness at the back of my knees.

Deliberately she put aside who he had been and looked at what he had become—at his army motorcycle and the swastika on his sleeve. "How dare you take my house!"

"Me?" He seemed taken aback.

She glared at him. "You and yours!"

With the back of his hand, Erich wiped sweat and dirt from his face. "*They* took your house while you were cavorting around Europe. You should have sold the estate years ago!"

Should have? Who was he to tell her that! Her grief

over Oma's death, and her desire to keep the villa in the family despite the downturns in her finances and career, had made her procrastinate, but that did not excuse these Nazi thieves. "Why didn't you stop them?" Miriam asked quietly.

"I tried." Erich looked uncomfortable. "I confronted Goebbels."

His brows were pulled down, his need to rationalize clear. Though she could not think of a single thing to justify his association with these madmen, Miriam held herself in check. Let him bury himself with his own words, she thought, over her weak-kneed reaction to seeing him again.

"I looked into the situation myself." Erich's face wore an expression of deep concern but she believed none of it. "I demanded to see papers. Almost lost my commission because of it, but I saw them." He slapped the cycle to make his point. "I even went to an attorney. It was all there in the new laws, spelled out in their usual mumbo-jumbo—their right to appropriate whatever they wanted for the good of the Fatherland. I had to apologize—*officially* apologize," his voice rose, "to that goddamn cripple. He's been watching me like an alley cat ever since."

"It all boils down to one thing, Miri," Sol said wearily. "Empty Jewish houses don't stay empty very long."

"I wish them dead. Every last one of them." Miriam felt like a bomb, ready to explode. Grief, love, her initial delight at being in Berlin, even her feelings for Solomon—gone, all of it. There was room for nothing but anger.

"I'll keep trying, Miriam. Anything's possible, I

suppose, even with the Nazis." Erich lowered his voice as he said the word. "They control the courts, but they are not above the law of the jungle. Goebbels is under fire for his earlier Bolshevik writings. He may be more approachable now." He lifted her hand and, looking into her eyes, brought her fingers to his lips. "How about formulating our battle plan over dinner? There's a new Italian place. They serve exquisite eggplant parmigiana, the wine cellar's superb, the violist plays a wonderful Albinoni sonata...."

"When?" She was toying with him, looking for a way to pierce his arrogance.

He pulled back his jacket wristband and looked at his watch. "Would an hour from now be too soon?"

"No, Erich. It can't be too soon." She forced herself to smile at him and to ignore Sol's obvious discomfort.

"I can't make it any sooner. I'm sorry, my love."

"Good. An hour, then, and I'll have my house back."

His smile dissipated. "Really, Miriam! This isn't a game—"

"Of course it isn't a goddamn game!" She was half-shouting, hysteria driving her.

Erich glanced anxiously across the villa grounds. The tar sprayer and steamroller had stopped and the men were looking in his direction. "Control yourself." His tone was low and anxious. "This is hardly the place for—"

"For *them!*" She shook her fist at the workmen.

Sol placed his hands on her shoulders and drew her away. "You'll get it all back."

Erich gripped the handlebars, put his machine in neutral, and walked it clear of the gate. "My idealist friend! Your little universe in perfect harmony!" He put down the kickstand. "You really do believe all of the wrongs of the world will be redressed."

He stopped, as if he sensed something beyond the hill. After a moment she heard dogs barking and gears grinding, and an army deuce-and-a-half crested the rise and came grumbling toward them. Sticking out of rubber-rimmed portholes in the truck's canvas canopy were several yelping German shepherds.

Erich took a key from his pocket and stepped up to the gate. "I have to see to the dogs," he said over his shoulder, nearly shouting to be heard above the din of the animals and the engine. "Look, I gained a certain advantage with the Führer today. Maybe I can go to him about the house."

"Sure," Miriam said sourly, her anger renewed by seeing him with a key that fit. "He'll break a leg for a Jew."

"You never know." Erich unlocked the gate and swung the left side wide. He returned to unlatch the foot bolt of the right half and push it open. "The Chancellor sees benefits where his underlings see obstacles."

Like a huge lumbering animal oblivious to anything in its path, the truck closed in on them, huffing and spitting exhaust as it pulled toward the gate. Sol pulled Miriam out of the way. Erich signaled and the truck snorted and rolled into the drive, making its way toward the azalea garden. She watched forlornly as it plowed across the lawn, its tires pulling up long divots.

"As long as Hitler holds the reins of power but weaklings like Himmler and Goebbels and Röhm are in the harnesses, the country's running on feeble legs…the Führer knows that," Erich said.

"The Führer apparently knows everything," she replied, debating walking onto the estate while the gates were open.

Before she had made up her mind, Erich shut them. When he reached out between the bars as if to touch her shoulder, she made no attempt to draw closer to him. She felt nothing, nothing at all.

"I'll be back when I've shown the trainers where to bed down the dogs."

He turned and ran after the truck. It rumbled down the hill separating the front lawn from the gardens; he rushed down the stairs between the marble lions and past the rose beds.

"Do you know him?" Miriam asked. "Know him at all?"

"Erich Alois Weisser!" Sol's voice was laced with disgust.

"Alois?"

"Hitler's father's name. That's what he meant by 'advantage with the Führer'! He told his precious leader he had already changed it. Now he'll have to find a way to pre-date the documents."

The tar sprayer started up with a growl. The steamroller's engine rumbled and the machines resumed their steady pace toward the east gate. The truck, it seemed, had needed to enter before the tar was laid down. Schedules had overlapped in a rare display of inefficiency. Whole minutes had been wasted, Miriam thought bitterly. Erich should inform the Führer so he could have those responsible shot.

"Erich Alois Weisser," Miriam said. "Why not!" Ultimately, she thought, environment and background won out against rebellion, especially here in Germany.

"He's always wanted to be some other person, to have lived in some other time. Why keep his surname? He's never been his father's son."

"Don't torture yourself like this. Let's leave."

"No. Pamper my masochism." Crossing her arms, she continued staring at the villa.

The tar sprayer neared the gate, and the driver, a huge man with a concave, rubicund face, climbed from the cab. "You can see it when we're finished," he said, shooing them away as if they were stray animals or waifs. "I know you're curious, but off with you now. We don't want anyone holding us up or getting injured."

She ignored him. "You were there, weren't you?" she asked Sol. "The night Erich gave me the dog."

"I left when you and Erich—"

"Why didn't you stay...why were you there at all?"

Sol took off his glasses and cleaned them with his handkerchief. "I don't know, Miri," he said slowly. "I always found it hard to say no to Erich." He put his arm around her. "As for why I left—I guess I couldn't imagine why you'd want me there."

She mustered up a smile. "Will you ever know your own worth?"

He laughed gently. "*I* knew. The question in my mind was, did *you*? Now we really must leave. Erich's right about one thing. It is dangerous, our being here."

You were so right, Uncle Walther, she thought, remembering what he had said the evening after Friedrich Weisser's ridiculous overreaction to finding her kissing Erich. *Keep your eye on young Solomon Freund. You may not think so now, but I tell you his spirit is much like your own. He will not be defeated easily.*

"You're not afraid, are you?" she asked.

"Yes. And if you're not, you should be. Erich thinks I'm oblivious to the real world, and in a way he's right. But I am not stupid. There are times when fear is the only expedient means of self-preservation."

She could feel tears very near the surface. How could a day be so tender yet so terrible?

"I'm ready to leave," she said. "But I'll be back—shaking the gate and shouting until Goebbels himself has to deal with me."

CHAPTER THIRTY-ONE

"Miriam! Here's someone you might remember," Erich called out, returning to the gate with Killi at his heels.

He saw Sol steer Miriam to the crest of the hill. She shook him off and they looked around and stood unmoving for a moment. Then they turned their backs and disappeared over the rise.

"Come back. Please." Erich grasped the bars of the gate and let Achilles' leash slip from his wrist. Wearing a red cape with a swastika emblazoned on it, the shepherd wandered up the driveway.

"She doesn't l-love us anymore, K-Killi!"

He had asked Sol to write and tell Miriam that he had taken Achilles; she had not even asked about the dog. He had imagined her running back to the gate, stooping, opening her arms—to the dog, and to him for looking after Achilles so well. Instead...

He eyed the dog, which was circling around a

scattering of keys someone had dropped on the driveway—sniffing and whining, growling, backing away.

It's so easy for them to blame everything on the Nazis, he thought. Because they're Jews...

In midthought he mentally castigated himself. Now he was beginning to sound like Goebbels! But Solomon and Miriam—! "They don't understand," he said under his breath, to Achilles. He and the dogs were in *military* security. Abwehr—not something foul, like the Gestapo. Didn't his friends know that? Couldn't they see the difference?

He and the shepherds *had* to wear the trappings. That simple. "Only a j-job," he said. He did not believe the Party line. He hated anti-Semites. They reminded him of...Papa.

In nearly a dozen years he hadn't used that word.

Tired of Achilles acting like a foolish pup over a bunch of keys, he silently commanded her to return. She did so instantly, crawling forward on her belly to allow him to stroke her huge smooth head. But he found, for once, that he could not enjoy the dog. He kept imagining what his friends were saying about him. Miriam, in that hysterical anger only women seemed capable of, telling Solomon, "He wears their uniform, he represents them!"

Solomon, in that quiet voice of his, the one that meant business, replying, "He claims he can use them, but he is fooling himself. They are the ones with the power. They are using *him!*"

He felt blood rush to his face. As though he truly had heard their words, he seized his sleeve, pinching the Nazi insignia between his fingers, ready to tear it off. His eyes moistened from the fury of his frustration. "One day you'll thank God you have a friend on the inside!"

Feeling enormous fatigue he sat down next to Achilles. He was sorry about the house, he really was. On the other hand, he had worked so hard for Miriam! Well, maybe not exactly for Miriam, but she had always been in his mind. For *her* he had worked to get himself and the canine unit into the center of things, where no one could dislodge them—where he could do some *good*. For people like the beadle, too.

He slapped the leash against his palm, remembering with a sad inner smile the Christmas Day Beadle Cohen had come around again, to present him with the leash behind the apartment building.

If only Goebbels and his goddamn greed had not interfered! Then Miriam might have appreciated his efforts, or at least feigned interest. He wanted her to see how his unit worked together, dog and trainer in a wonderfully transcendent Gestalt. The team was at a point where neither verbal commands nor hand signals were necessary. By the time the trainer issued a command, the dog was underway. Almost impossible to believe, and yet, through love and discipline, he had achieved it. Even the two misfits at the estate, the affenpinscher and Hempel's wolfhound, were good dogs. Or could be with the right training.

No one could deny the achievement. Not even Goebbels or Himmler. Once the dogs were absolutely ready, he would wangle an audience with the Führer. Hitler would have to be impressed—man and animal thinking as one. Then maybe the High Command would be more amenable to the plight of Miriam...Weisser.

He snorted. Taking himself seriously again! What could he be thinking? Did he need her so much? Or just want her.

Achilles growled, up again, nervous, looking through the gate, toward the hill. He tied her leash around a bar and stepped outside, admitting to himself that he wished his friends would return. But he heard—and sensed—nothing from beyond the rise.

Maybe it was for the best that they not come back, at least for now, he decided. Killi was not young anymore and she tended to get jealous of anyone who had his attention. Miri might not understand that, even though the dog wouldn't attack without provocation.

None of the dogs would hurt a fly—except on command.

C HAPTER THIRTY-TWO

If he could not do this, the years of believing in his psychic connection with dogs were a farce. He was a farce. *Give me this*, Erich said to himself as if in prayer. *A birthday present. For Bull and Grace. For the years of feeling their pain as they died.*

Muffled in protective gear and standing at "six-o'clock" on the field of attack, he watched the twelve shepherds. They sat in a tight circle, facing outward, eyes bright with excitement as they waited for the attack command.

Peering between the wires of the facial shield, he did a final visual check of the other trainers. They stood at varying intervals from the dogs, each man covered with thick padding and a mask. Feet braced, each stood ready to absorb the lunge of seventy-five pounds of canine fury; each was one position to the left on the clock from where his animal would attack—close to the dog once the attack began, yet not the dog's prey.

Only Corporal Krayller was with his own dog.

Krayller was a huge man, yet Erich knew he was almost certainly having difficulty controlling the tiny, feisty affenpinscher. The two of them were in the center of the circle, the hub of the wheel of dogs, where they would remain throughout the exercise. Once the attack commenced, Krayller's terrier would assume a role perfectly suited to its size and temperament; for now, however, it was forced to remain absolutely still.

For this particular maneuver, which Erich called Zodiac, the field of battle was broken into a clock, each of the twelve shepherds securing the position respective to its name. Thus, Aquarius was responsible for attacking the one o'clock position, Taurus the five o'clock, Pisces the nine. The central position, however, required persistence rather than power—a dog agile and quick-tempered enough to keep its eyes on everything and capable of issuing a warning if the enemy compromised the circular perimeter. And so the affenpinscher.

Never before, Erich thought, had he asked—expected—so much of his dogs or of his trainers. *The attack command is to be mental and given from a considerable distance.* He was not even sure it was possible, especially since the dogs' attention would be divided between target and trainer, though the maneuver had proved successful when the dogs received visual, not mental, commands.

Since the beginning of the month he had also begun incorporating a new tactic into the strategy, one calculated to approximate a surprise attack. Regardless of how far from the hub each aggressor was, the dogs were to hit all twelve targets at the same time. They would have to function as the perfect team he believed them to be, as aware of each other's timing as they were of their masters' wishes.

Get the exercise right, he thought, and you will all get the day off tomorrow, and maybe a second day as well. Maybe the Party felt Christmas was symbolic of the Christian yoke that had held down the Fatherland's true potential for too long, but that philosophy had not yet been accepted by the masses.

The trainers looked at him. Waiting. He took a deep breath, let it out slowly. Concentrated. The white light filled his mind. When he could see nothing else, he thought of the eyes of the shepherd.

He nodded.

Zodiac!

The shepherds moved out, slinking among the dead flower gardens, crawling across the snow-crusted lawn. Keeping down, silent, lethal. Hardly a breath in the frosty air.

Soundlessly, simultaneously the animals seized the targets. Going first for hands that held sticks or pistols, then for the crotch. The men went down under the onslaught but the dogs continued the attack, tearing at the padding. Not so much as a growl—the only sounds those of the targets, beating muffled arms against the dogs.

In the real world of trained dogs and defense, the bite would be so painful that an unprotected target would be nearly paralyzed, Erich knew. He held one hand instinctively over his groin, as thankful for the padding as he was for the dogs' performance.

Again he took a deep breath, let it out slowly. Nodded. Return!

Twelve shepherds backed off twelve fallen men, the dogs creeping backward, ever watchful of their assailants, like a film run in reverse.

Heart pounding with happiness, Erich picked himself up. Nodded. Concentrated—

City!

Seemingly the friendless, loneliest strays in the world, the dogs meandered back toward their targets. Some of the shepherds lay down, head between forepaws, others sat up and begged, others held out a paw—ready to shake. Some whimpered, some panted.

None growled.

Twelve tails wagged, ticking like metronomes.

Twelve men reached to pet an animal, feed it, shoo it away.

And were attacked, as silently as before. The dogs' pent-up fury kindled in their eyes and the froth of their mouths as they tore at the crotch—then at the throat.

Return!

Again benign, but watchful. Ever...watchful.

Center.

The dogs slowly retreated a few steps and eyed their adversaries carefully. Looking back now and again to make sure they were not being followed, they padded back to the terrier and resumed their initial position in the closely knit circle.

"Got it!" Erich cried. "Yes! Yes! Perfect!"

Trainers' caps and shouts of joy soared as the men ran

to congratulate their charges, who stayed where they were. Unlike their masters, Erich thought proudly, they were obeying the fact that no orders to break ranks had been given.

Someone applauded from the part of the driveway that slanted down to the garage beneath the villa. Erich turned to see Hempel smiling approvingly.

"Bravo, Herr Rittmeister!"

Only twelve more days with the bastard! The transfer Hempel had requested was confirmed. Twelve days until Epiphany.

Erich smiled at the irony. What a grand gift for himself—and for his men, who hated the first lieutenant almost as much as Erich did—to have Hempel leave on the anniversary of the day that celebrated the coming of the Wise Men to the Christ child. SS Lieutenant Otto Hempel—soon to be Captain Hempel, commander of one of Himmler's units that rounded up dissidents and other undesirables.

As far as Erich was concerned, Herr War Hero Hempel could command the licking of the Führer's feces.

Ignoring the first lieutenant, Erich went over to Taurus. Apparently aware of how well she and the other dogs had done, she was panting with pride and wagging her tail—no deception this time. Erich knelt beside her, hugging her and stroking her broad, thickly muscled back.

Her ears perked up, the wagging ceased and she looked over Erich's shoulder. Her vigilance was not necessary to tell him that Hempel had walked around the retaining wall and was crossing the lawn. The hairs on the back of his neck warned him as much.

"Simply superb." Hempel stuck his cigarette back in his mouth and, bending, extended a hand.

Erich took no notice of the hand except to avert his head from Hempel's brandy-breath. "Drinking again, Obersturmführer?"

Compensating for Erich's lack of response, Hempel patted the head of the enormous gray-and-white wolfhound leashed at his side, as if that were what he had intended to do all along. Erich disliked the dog, not because he disliked the breed—a lithe, silken-coated cross between an Arabian greyhound and a Russian collie—but because of Hempel.

"Yes, really superb," Hempel said. "All except that stinking affenpinscher."

"His name's Grog," Erich said. "They all have names. I would think you'd know that by now." He rose and began leading Taurus to the dog-runs. "Good job!" he called to the other trainers. "Street security tomorrow and Wednesday."

They grinned. "Street security" meant keeping their homes free of foreign insurgents—except, maybe, St. Nicholas. Only those unlucky enough to have pulled guard duty would be required to come to the estate during the next two days.

"Grog," Hempel said. "Fits him well, unfortunately. A clown at the center of the zodiac. I tell you, he simply has no presence." He thrust out the leash he was holding, forcing the wolfhound forward as though against its will. "Wagner is perfect for that post."

The dog, long and lean, bred for speed rather than vigilance, looked up at Erich with doleful eyes.

"Wagner is SS," Hempel said, "and the SS are destined to be at the center of everything."

Always the same argument. The terrier was not what really concerned Hempel. It was just that he—The Great Otto Hempel—had no part in the production. How many times, Erich wondered, had he almost told Hempel that he *knew?* Knew that the same sophomoric antagonism he had displayed these past two years on the estate had put him on a collision course with his superiors after Ypres?...and that the only war wound he had suffered was an emotional one, when his predilection for young recruits—for very young recruits—had surfaced and he had been drummed from the service?

So what if Hempel had helped quell the Communist insurrection in Berlin! His new commission had come not from service to the Fatherland but from service to Goebbels, as lackey.

Erich chained Taurus to her dog-run and brought her food and fresh water. He took no overt notice of Hempel, who nonetheless continued to follow him around, mumbling about the affenpinscher. Erich reminded himself that this was not the time to have it out with Hempel.

Right now, his duty was to his dogs and to his men. Darkness was descending, and he knew they wanted to get home. He had them form ranks, thanked them for a good day's work and announced, "For their efforts, each dog shall receive a bonus of one extra pound of meat! Dis-*missed!* Tell your families I said...hello."

The men laughed at his oblique Christmas reference.

Slipping out of their protective gear, they ran to pet their dogs a last time and headed down to their lockers.

Then all but Ferman were gone. He had drawn Christmas Eve duty. Resolutely the little man—whom Erich had nicknamed "Fermi" after the Italian physicist because of his high forehead and dark hair—came out of the garage and trudged toward the guard house at the east gate, helmet on and Karabiner 90 slung over his shoulder.

Erich thought of Hawk, lying abandoned in the garage. On impulse, he decided to exercise Achilles. He would ride Hawk, he thought—he rarely rode the bicycle anymore, even though he had repainted and modified it to look like an adult's bike. A romp with his old friend would be fun.

The dog had the first kennel, the one nearest the house. He unhooked her from her chain and attached one of the long leashes for running that hung like equine tack over a railing at the end of the kennel. The dog licked his face and snuggled into him. He put his arms around her. He loved the feel of her, the warmth and fur and muscle, and he loved giving her what she seemed to desire most—affection and the freedom to run.

Sensing a presence behind him, he looked up. Hempel stood next to the elm, smoking, looking at the sky.

"I'm taking Achilles," Erich said. "She needs a good run."

Immediately he was annoyed at himself for explaining his actions to a subordinate officer, especially when it was Hempel.

Hempel drew on his cigarette. The end glowed briefly

brighter. "A good limp-along might be more accurate," he said.

Erich rose to his feet, stiff with anger. "Your attitude is intolerable!"

Hempel ground out his cigarette, took a bottle from the crook of the tree and drank from it. "My apologies, Herr Rittmeister. The comment was inexcusable." He patted the wolfhound. "Sometimes my anxiety to embrace my true destiny makes me careless toward anything that is old, that represents the past. We are the first of the new world, are we not? And yet one cannot forget..." His voice became bitter, and he stopped talking.

The admission startled Erich. Tensing, he stood, expecting trouble, but Hempel just looped the wolfhound's leash around the rail and, straightening, extended his right hand as he offered Erich the bottle with the left. "We should bury the hatchet. We serve the same master, after all."

Against his better judgment, Erich shook hands. A chill seized him; the hand was strong but cold as stone.

"A toast," Hempel said.

Erich took the bottle. "To the Führer," he said brusquely, and handed the bottle back to Hempel.

The lieutenant drained what was left. "To the SS! The soul of the Fatherland." He flipped the empty into the hedge. "I remember that first Christmas after the war, when I joined the Freikorps and we fought to keep Berlin from falling to the Bolsheviks. How black things were!" His facial muscles tightened. "Now nothing can keep us down. Nothing!" Eyes gleaming, he looked at Erich.

"Hitler and Himmler and others of vision have shown us the German phoenix can rise from the ashes and become supreme."

Erich itched to get away. Even Hempel's contempt was more palatable than standing here listening to platitudes about the Fatherland's greatness and the wonderful men who were leading her to world supremacy.

"Four days ago, at the SS Yuletide bonfire, I saw the future," Hempel continued. "Reichsführer Himmler himself invited me to Wewelsburg."

Erich tried not to show surprise. Wewelsburg was the SS high temple—a moldering, Westphalia clifftop castle recently overhauled by detention-camp inmates. It was there, seated with his SS knights at an Arthurian round table, that Himmler held court. If Hempel had received a personal invitation to attend the Solstice celebration there, the climax of the Nazi calendar, he had more prestige in the SS hierarchy than Erich had realized.

"Anyone who has seen it must believe in our cause! We sang and the flames created by the burning pages of all those books filled the darkness." Hempel looked up into the night. "And I knew I had a soul." His voice cracked from the intensity of his emotion. "They say we sense the primitive when we gaze into flames—that we claim the past. I did not see the past, I saw the future. I saw our destiny. We will burn the world clean of impurities. It was as if the flames were calling to me."

Achilles began to growl but Erich barely noticed. Hempel's sense of certainty was so crystalline that he felt drawn, not to the man but to the dream. He looked for the Christmas star. No matter how much he hated Hempel and everything he stood for, he understood the man's desire. The difference between them was a matter of choice, and degree.

Hempel shook his head in amazement. "When I looked beyond the flames, I saw the Reichsführer, fire glinting in his glasses, and I knew. He smiled at me and I knew I was...blessed."

"So your loyalty, your commitment, is to Himmler rather than Goebbels?"

"Allow me to tell you about commitment, Herr Rittmeister." Hempel's feral smile returned. "The bonfire burned through the night. We stood there, without coats, at parade rest, from midnight until dawn. No one ordered us to. It was simply *right*. There were a hundred and forty-four of us—all personally selected by the Reichsführer for the ceremony—and not a man moved, even when it began to sleet, until the sun broke through the clouds. I felt...purified. Redeemed."

He pulled out and lit another cigarette.

"Then Reichsführer Himmler said he had something to show me. He looked at me as if I had been transformed—which indeed I had—and led me inside, up to the Supreme Leaders' Hall. Not a word from him once we were inside the castle. Not a word."

Hempel shook his head in wonder. "I've seen a thousand castle rooms, but nothing that compares to that one in Wewelsburg. Circular, with windows that made the dawn-light look almost mystical. The swastika chiseled into the vaulted ceiling." He arched his hand to show Erich.

"Around the wall were twelve pedestals, each with an urn. I'd heard they existed, and now I was in their presence!" He sounded breathless with the wonder of it. "They are there to hold, as each man dies, the incinerated coat of arms of Himmler's twelve most trustworthy knights."

Gently he took hold of Erich's shoulders. "I shall achieve that immortality. With your help."

As gently as they had been placed, Erich removed the hands.

"My help?"

"You and your dogs. They're special. We both know that. The canine equivalent of what we Germans shall be in a generation. One people. One mind. One soul." He made a fist, then said in a husky voice, "But they're not SS. They never will be as long as you are in charge of them."

As if she understood the words, Achilles' growling became more pronounced; Erich's once benign mood became a growing fury that twisted in him like a rope. There would, he thought, be no pleasant bicycle ride tonight.

Chapter Thirty-Three

Damning himself for wanting Miriam's approval—even after his success with the dogs—Erich shouldered his way toward her dressing room. People not associated with the show normally were not allowed backstage, but he came to see her at least twice a week and was used to making his way relatively unnoticed between the performers and props crowded in the cabaret's stage wings. His presence usually aroused nothing more than an occasional leer.

Tonight, however, he was carrying a pineapple, its aroma unmistakable even in the wine- and sweat-filled air. He could probably buy any chorine for the price of one slice of the coveted fruit, he thought bitterly. Certainly the fruit gained him attention, such as might have been given a Yank overtly carrying nylons. If anything, his gift was even more appealing here, where desire was the stock-in-trade. The cabaret's name was, after all, Ananas: *Pineapple*.

A long-legged chorus girl dressed in little more than feathers and flesh emerged from the storeroom that served as the main dressing room. Eyeing him, his uniform with its new captain's bars, and the pineapple with open and equal admiration, the girl bent to smell the fruit.

"Which tastes better, you or the pineapple?" She tickled him under the chin and laughed when he batted her hand away. "Wish you were waiting for me, Poopsie." She wiggled her bottom. "That one won't give you ice in winter, you know."

She was pretty enough, but he couldn't manage a smile; the woman disappeared in a flurry of dyed ostrich feathers.

He could see Miriam's dressing room from where he stood. Though she knew he was coming, the door was closed. The paint had peeled where a star once marked it, leaving only two faded points. Everything in the club was tawdry and cheap. Everything, he told himself, except that goddamn Miriam. Which was doubtless why he continued to make an idiot of himself, bringing testimonials of love—and despair—to heap at her feet.

Striding to the door, he raised his hand to knock, decided the hell with that and turned the handle.

Miriam sat before a cracked mirror framed with tiny, flame-shaped lightbulbs. Some cast a pink glow; other filaments glared from plain glass. The mirror was decorated with faded sienna photos, bits of ribbon, ragged feathers and splashes of makeup.

"Know how to knock?" she asked Erich's reflection.

She picked up her mascara, spat in it and mixed it

vigorously with the small brush she used to apply it to her lashes. As she leaned forward to put on a layer of eye shadow with the tip of a finger, one of the narrow rhinestone straps that held up her dress slid down her shoulder. The dress was little more than a silk slip, black and flimsy, an illusion as thin as stardom's hope. Erich had to stifle the urge to unzip the back and slide his hands beneath her arms and over her breasts—to make love to her, now, at once, on the grimy carpet if need be.

"What do you want?" she asked brusquely, without turning.

"I came to warn you."

"About yourself?"

She stood and, placing each foot in turn on the chair, adjusted the seams of her black lace stockings. Her dress was slit up to her thigh on one side, and he could see the edge of black lace panties.

"Say what you have to say, then leave me alone." She slipped into silver shoes and straightened the dress against her hips. "I'm tired of you bothering me, and I'm just plain tired—period. I'm here until four in the morning and up at ten to help in the shop. I eat on the run, take the trolley here to dance for the animals...I have no time for what you want. Nor," she looked right at him, "would I take the time if I had it."

"You don't have to live with the Freunds or work in the shop." He set the pineapple on the vanity. "I've offered to get you a place of your own."

As always, she ignored his offer to take care of her. Lifting the pineapple by its green topknot, she thrust it back into his hands. "Why don't you try this on one of the other girls? They may be stupid enough to confuse exotic with erotic."

Her tone was cold and uncompromising. In the two years since her return to Berlin, she had yet to give him one gentle look, one pleasant word. She had been, at best, polite until he had told her finally that he could do nothing about her estate. Surely she knew he had tried his best. He had broached the subject with those few individuals he knew who dared speak frankly to the Führer. Professor Gerdy Troost, widow of Hitler's favorite architect. The Harvard-educated eccentric Ernst Hanfstaengel, who had drawn and published, with Hitler's consent, caricatures criticizing the Führer. Leni Riefenstahl, the actress turned filmmaker.

Of the three, only Fräulein Riefenstahl had agreed to look into the matter. She had met him over a cognac to inform him quietly, "You pursue this, and your Miriam Rathenau could lose a lot more than her estate, and so could you. Goebbels would rather have that house than all his harlots."

Clearly Leni was right, Erich thought. The house was not the issue, not anymore. The danger to Miriam, and to Solomon and his family, was growing more evident by the day. Somehow he had to take care of them, but how? He could try to help them get out of the country, but that would ensure his losing Miriam. Not that he had ever really found her again since her return to Berlin.

Damn little Jewess! Who was she anyway? Nothing but a saucy ex-debutante who thought herself better than everyone else. Which was probably why he wanted her—because she considered herself inaccessible. Jews were so stubborn! And foolish!

What if she or the Freunds did something stupid and were arrested? Only God, if indeed He existed, could withstand an SS interrogation. Even if talking meant implicating him—and just knowing him was enough to do that—he would want them to save themselves. Add to that his reputation as an officer, an Abwehr member no less, who had criticized the Reich and who openly worshipped the niece of the man who exemplified everything the Reich detested....

No matter what he did, Erich thought, he could only lose.

Feeling awkward and angry, he continued to hold the pineapple on his open palm. "Tomorrow is Christmas, Miriam. If you don't want this, give it to...to someone." He was thinking of the Freunds and his parents but was unwilling to mention them by name.

"Tomorrow is Christmas! That's what you crawled in here to tell me? Wonderful. I'll mark my calendar and make sure there's room at the inn."

He lowered the pineapple. If any other woman dared treat him like this, he'd give her a boot in the backside and send her out the nearest door. "You must be careful, Miriam."

"What are you, my protector? I'm told you beat up one of Himmler's cronies after the show the other night because he made a comment about me. Sounds like you should be the one to be warned. Your dear friends may not appreciate your solicitude."

"I am not concerned with what—"

Someone rapped twice on the door, stopping him from

adding more lies to the ones he had already told himself. He had been about to tell her that he didn't care what others in the Party thought of him—that, unlike them, he could never be a racist. He alone among his classmates in the Bavarian camp and in the Berlin-Tegel classrooms was different. Was Solomon not his friend? He knew most of the others in the Party were not fit fodder for pigs, but that would change as the Führer rose above his petty need for scapegoats.

"Duty calls." She lifted an index finger. "In the future, if you want to talk to me come to the shop. You do remember where it is, don't you?"

"You know I don't go there."

"More shame on you, Oberleutnant Weisser." She spoke with such venom, he recoiled as if from a snake bite. Then, frowning at his uniform, she corrected herself. "Forgive me. I see it is Rittmeister Weisser. That little choreography of your name-change paid off, did it?"

"This warning isn't something to shrug off, or laugh at." He put a hand on her forearm as she opened the door.

Her glance at his hand contained only contempt.

He let go of her, feeling ashamed. Why was it that the lower he seemed in her eyes, the more he wanted her? "The cabaret scene's under fire by the National Socialists. There could be trouble. Real trouble."

"You're telling me nothing new."

Her gaze strayed to the pineapple and, for an instant, she looked hungry. Women! Why couldn't she be like the rest, capable of love at any time as long as there was some price tag attached?

"Don't you know that we're part of the Jewish conspiracy to pervert the purity of Germany's young men?" she asked. "Their strength and virtue might become so drained they could no longer lift blackjacks and billy clubs against old women and rabbis. We must not corrupt you boys with elegance such as this." She gestured toward the dirt-encrusted pipes that crisscrossed the room. "We must save ourselves for true-hearts like Herr Himmler, and pray that Goebbels—the darling—will honor us with a visit."

"They wouldn't come here."

"Oh? Göring already has. Twice. Our manager led everyone in a standing ovation. I wonder if that fool even entertained the possibility that Henri was mocking him! I wouldn't be at all surprised if Goebbels showed up too. He does hate to be outdone. Wouldn't it be wonderful if he got a hard-on watching Rathenau's niece strut her little butt!"

"Stop it!" Furious beyond caution, he gripped her arms. "You have to leave this place. It's dangerous, immoral, not for you."

"Where else can a dancer with Jewish blood find work these days?" She jerked free of his hold. "As your mistress? While you're earning your keep playing footsie with the Nazis, I could take in laundry, and while you're entertaining the officers' wives, I could earn pin money in one of those cabarets where they have sex onstage. Would that turn you on?"

To taunt him, she took a wide-legged stance and placed her hands on her hips. *"Zieh dich aus, Petronella, zieh dich aus,"* she sang. "Get undressed, Petronella, get undressed." She had Trude Hersterberg, the most famous of the stars who satirized Berlin's penchant for nudity, down pat.

Erich's head pounded. It frightened him, this side of her.

"I could fornicate with one of your shepherds onstage. Now that would be unique! Pisces and a Jew going at it while you Nazis applaud and Goebbels stomps his clubfoot!"

Stunned by her outburst, he let go of her. Without another word she walked from the room, not with the saucy hip-swing some of the other performers affected, but with the grace he remembered from long ago. At the end of the hall, where a red curtain hung in an archway whose plaster was badly chipped, she turned and blew him a kiss. "Happy birthday, Erich."

He stood in the dimly lit passage, damning her again— and himself for allowing her to stir him so. Only he seemed to bring out this side of her. It was as if she were punishing him for not having been born a Jew or for not being foolish or philosophical enough to scrape off his foreskin and cover his head with it like a caul, seeing only what his culture wanted him to see...thinking its hooded thoughts.

He could feel the anger rising in him, as it always did after yet another defeat at Miriam's hands. The time had come to stop treating her like the princess she pretended to be. Why should he have to feel like this whenever she rejected him? He wasn't a leper, unclean and unworthy. His approach had been wrong, that was all. She was always pushing him toward the edge. Tormenting him. Pushing him to be more insistent. He could see her now, fighting him and fucking him with equal abandon.

Sometimes he stood outside the cigar shop, watching her with Solomon and envying their ease with one another as they arranged cases and swept the floor and waited on people. With Solomon, the Freunds, sometimes even with his own parents, she laughed freely, her spirit one of dogged optimism. She was also like that with those customers who could no longer afford real Havanas or Cubans and bought cigars made of cabbage leaves soaked in a solution of nicotine.

He had seen Solomon walk her to the trolley, watched them exchange smiles as she boarded. Their umbrella of shared warmth made him feel small and cold, an uncovered child curled up asleep on a drafty floor.

Not that he was jealous of Solomon, he assured himself—even given the probability that Solomon and Miriam were sharing a bed.

After all, he did not lack women. On the contrary; the wealthier and more powerful their husbands were, the more the wives seemed to want him. Because it pleased him to do so, he made them beg for what they wanted. Lately, however, the more they writhed and moaned, the more he loathed them, and himself. He slept little, and usually alone, falling asleep to dream of Solomon's hand on Miriam's pubis, his mouth on her breasts.

"You shouldn't be back here now." A balding, thickly sweatered dwarf lifted a broom like a quarterstaff and shook it at him. "It's show time."

Erich shoved the pineapple into the dwarf's arms and

pushed past him into the nightclub. The place was crowded, a-throb with a four-four beat. Faded, water-stained green-and-white awnings sagged from black poles; a pink, plaster Venus de Milo wearing a maroon brassiere decorated the bar. Men in ratty suits and overalls, some cradling bar girls in short leather skirts and silk stockings, lounged beside tables covered with green-and-white tablecloths. The air was heavy with smoke and stank of sweat.

Onstage, a clown wearing a green-and-red shirt, baggy pants, and a wolf's mask which sported a bulbous nose, boasted of his days as a waiter at Luna Park. "There I was on Naked Days, in my formal attire," he said, eyeing the derrière feathers of a blond-wigged Red Riding Hood who came prancing onstage, "while Berlin's best families romped nude around me."

As if determined to make up for lost time, he took hold of the blonde, knelt beside her, and began working his nose under her feathers and into her ample posterior. Wide-eyed, the girl jumped forward with a startled "Oooh!" The audience screamed its approval, cheering and whistling and stomping in time to the music.

Appearing to gather her resolve, Red Riding Hood turned and confronted the beast with her only weapon. She opened her cape, and wriggled. A St. Nicholas beard covered her pubis, and her red brassiere, studded with jingling bells, had holes that revealed blinking green nipples. The drooling wolf's pants burst open and a prosthetic penis the length of a broomstick sprang up, a Christmas bow tied behind the knob.

Daintily she tugged at the ribbon, and a banner unfurled under his wolfhood. It read: *"Sieg Heil."*

The crowd roared and the curtains closed. Knowing Werner Fink, on loan from Katakombe on Bellevuestrasse while that club was being revamped, would be on next, the audience grew silent. They had come to see the infamous *conférencier* half in the hopes that they would be there on the inevitable night of his arrest, for why and how he had survived this long remained a mystery.

Fink stepped out between the curtains and threaded toward a table. The spotlight followed him. He was a pasty-faced man with heavily mascaraed eyes and hair slicked with black shoe polish.

Standing there in his black shirt and tie and too-small black jacket, he surveyed the audience.

"We were closed yesterday, and if we are too open today, tomorrow we may be closed again."

Laughter followed Fink's famous opening lines; several men in the audience raised their mugs and shouted, *"Prosit!"* Erich, who liked Fink, wondered if the man had avoided arrest precisely because he was so outrageous. It might be useful to keep that in mind.

The *conférencier* made his way to center stage. "No, I'm not Jewish." He placed a white-gloved hand to his forehead. "I only *look* intelligent."

The drummer hit the cymbal. Mugs were lowered and the laughter became more restrained. A man in the uniform of the SS, seated at a table to the far left of the stage, stood up, his face a study in disgust. He clicked his heels, saluted smartly, and strode out of the nightclub. Erich quickly took the man's chair.

Fink stared out over the stage lights. Cupping his hands like a megaphone, he asked, "CAN YOU HEAR

ME ALL RIGHT? ANYONE OUT THERE WHO'S NOT HARD OF THINKING?"

Erich was close enough to the stage to smell the sweat of the performers and to see the spray of saliva that emerged from Fink's mouth as he continued his diatribe. However, the awning overhead was ripped and hung annoyingly in his face, disturbing his vision. He slapped it aside.

"Just tear it down." The swarthy man seated at the table placed the elbow of his grimy leather jacket on the table and revolved his black cigar with his tongue, chewing rather than smoking it. Picking a clump of sodden tobacco off his lip, he frowned and wiped his hand on his grease-spotted white shirt. Coarse black hair poked out of an old workman's cap, and a two-day growth of beard completed the picture of a man of the masses.

In the subdued applause that followed, the man said, "The name's Brecht. Bertolt Brecht."

Before Erich could give his name, Fink's rapid-fire delivery filled the room. "I love black shirts." He opened his jacket and puffed out his chest. "Brown ones, too. I salute them!" Raising his hand in the Nazi salute, he looked from his hand to the floor and back again, and said, "That's how deep we're in the shit."

While Fink bowed to polite applause, a dancer who doubled as a waitress sauntered over to Erich's table. He ordered Berliner Weisse mit Schuss, champagne-beer with a shot of raspberry syrup. When she brought the glasses she bent and placed a napkin on his thigh, giving him ample view of her cleavage. He knew he was expected to slip folded money between her breasts. He glanced away. She gave him a hard smile, swiped at the table with a bar rag and walked off.

"I can tell you from personal experience," Brecht said, "that one has more honey in her pants than a Bremen beehive."

"Not interested."

"*Chacun à son goût*—to each his own." Brecht sipped his white beer. "Me, I come for the sequins and sex. There's no art to the shows anymore, except for Fink, and I hear he's hanging on by his fingernails." He eyed Erich's uniform suspiciously. "I suppose you're another of those who has come to write him up so he can be punished by the keepers of order."

Is that what he looked like to Brecht? A keeper of order? How laughable! His dogs...*they* were the *real* keepers of order, capable equally of killing upon demand and loving without reservation.

"Just here for the main attraction," he told Brecht.

Brecht shook his head. "Now there is wasted talent."

Erich had heard of Brecht, some poet or playwright who hung around cabarets like a pig around a corncrib. People of such so-called occupations were worthless; as waffle-brained as Solomon, except that they had the bad taste to air their souls in public.

"In case you haven't heard, I'm not to be called a *conférencier* anymore," Fink went on. "The government says I'm an *Ansager* because that *other* word is too French. So many changes! Government, language, the newspaper on the bottom of my bird cage, my face if I'm not careful. Change everywhere except in my pocket! Only one thing never changes—the beauty of our very own Mimi de Rau!"

As he backed into the wings, the curtains swung open. Reclining on an ottoman and haloed in red light was "Mimi," kohl-eyed and wearing a spangling headdress roped with fake jewels. From her ears hung brass baubles. Erich recognized them even if the rest of the audience did not. They were matching *dreidels*, like the ones the Freund and Weisser children had spun each Chanukah until the world went mad.

"*Sei lieb zu mir,*" she sang, her voice sultry while her earrings told the world in her own small way that life had spun her around once too often. "*Komm nicht wie ein Dieb zu mir....*"

Erich could feel the crowd's pulse quicken as people responded to her version of "Mean to Me," the popular Dietrich song. "Be kind to me. Don't come like a thief to me...."

"Time was when a talent like that would have embraced the audience. Now she merely entrances them," Brecht said.

"Go to hell."

"Already have. It rang with the tramp of jackboots, so I have returned here to Limbo, where the entertainment's better. Take the lady on stage, for example. There's a Christmas treat. Voice like an angel, body waiting to be unwrapped."

Knocking over the beer, Erich grabbed Brecht's throat so fast that it appeared the playwright's cigar must shoot from his mouth. For an instant the men stared at each other, Erich with his mangled hand raised to slap the playwright, Brecht with his eyes bulging.

Brecht took the cigar from between his lips. "Meant no insult, friend." Despite its being unlit, he thumped the cigar on the ashtray as if to dislodge imaginary ash.

Erich released him. Embarrassed, he stared at the table. The man was not out of line. "Look, I'm—"

"Sorry? Don't be." Brecht rubbed his neck. "The Fatherland has too much to be sorry for already."

"*Sei lieb...zu ...mir.*"

Miriam's song, plaintive and sensual, floated to its conclusion amid a burst of applause.

She rose slowly and drifted forward, arms outstretched as though to embrace a lover. Erich looked around the audience with cynical detachment. Strange how the only time she did not stir him was when she was performing. The red stage lights were intended to make her look wanton, but the effect was both illusion and delusion, for her demeanor made it apparent she was untouchable. That knowledge seemed to inflame most spectators, yet the more the other men wanted her the less enticing he found her. It was only when he and she were alone, or when he was alone and she was alive in his fantasies, that he could not control his childhood desire of wanting her to love him. Not just screw him. Love him.

CHAPTER THIRTY-FOUR

Miriam stood quietly at the microphone, waiting for the applause to die down. She had one more song to do before a big production number that did not include her. During her first two songs, she habitually took little notice of the audience, viewing them as heads of cabbages, featureless and brainless. By now, individuals began to take form. The regulars, there to pinch the bottoms of the waitresses and to drink as much as they could in as little time as possible. Goebbels' spies, probably playing with themselves in the dark under the tables. Bertolt Brecht, always at the same table, always with the same laconic expression.

She looked over at Brecht, and winked. He winked back. It was their private nightly tradition, an acknowledgment that they admired each other's work and talents.

Erich, sitting tonight at Brecht's table, turned red. So

he had noticed the exchange, she thought. Good. Maybe that would finally keep him away from her. How much more overt did she have to become before he'd give up the challenge of getting her into bed?

She took hold of the microphone and faced Brecht.

"This song is my tribute to you, Bertolt." She smiled at the playwright. The orchestra began the overture from *Threepenny Opera* and segued neatly into *Mack the Knife*.

Listen to the words, Erich, she thought, and began to sing.

At the end of the song, the curtains swung shut, draping around her. When they reopened, she stepped onto the stage apron and descended the stairs that led to the floor. She had to mingle with the patrons at least once each night; part of her job. It helped when Brecht was there. She simply headed for his table and had a drink with him.

"Going to drink with your Jew-lover friend?" One of three boys seated at the table next to Brecht's took hold of her arm as she tried to walk past. His tone was friendly, conversational, but his free hand was tapping the beat of the music on a pistol lying on the table. "I'm talking about that one there. The Rittmeister." He nodded toward Erich. "C'mon, *Judsche*. Try some real men. It'll make you feel like a German."

Miriam looked at Erich, sensing his body tighten with coiled fury. Hadn't he once boasted to her about his Oriental fighting lessons? Said he took them and guerrilla tactics from Otto Braun himself, who had, as Li Te, fought alongside Mao throughout the Long March. Well, use what you learned, dammit!

The youth stared coldly at Erich, his hatred apparent.

"You have run with the wrong pack too long, Weisser."

"Who sent you here?" Erich's voice was deadly calm, barely audible beneath the music.

"Never mind who sent us!" another said. "We'll fuck 'The Star' after you do. Three at once! Cork all three holes at the same time!"

"Do what you want with the whores." Erich still sounded reasonable, rational. "No one touches Miss de Rau."

"Shoot the Jew-lover, Klaus," his buddy said. "Who cares who he is!"

But the boy holstered his pistol. "We've done our job. Let's go." He spat on the floor and stood up. "If you love the Fatherland," he said, "you'll stay away from this pigsty in the future...or we'll burn it down around you."

"Like you did the Reichstag?" Brecht was seemingly beyond caring what the boys might do next.

"That was the Communists."

"Jews."

"Foreigners."

Shaking, as angry as she was afraid, Miriam watched the boys go out the door, a Machiavellian chorus of avenging angels. Whatever it was that had happened to German society that February night the Hollander, van der Lubbe, torched the congressional building, she was certain it would take a cataclysm to assuage it.

"Jewmongers!" one of the boys screamed before following his friends into the street.

He flipped a wine bottle over his shoulder. The sound of smashing glass coincided with the crash of the cabaret door as it slammed shut behind him.

Stooping awkwardly in her tight dress, Miriam picked

up a champagne glass and a bottle from one of the front tables. Leaning across Brecht's table, she said to Erich, "You brought them here. They came for *you*. The rest of us were only diversions." She filled the glass.

"They would have come anyway. I warned you."

She glanced up at the stage. Oblivious to the drama on the floor, a circle of ersatz Ziegfield girls in scarlet ostrich feathers strutted around the stage. Forming a crescent, they opened their feathers to reveal g-strings and tasseled nipples.

"Yes, perhaps they would have come," she said, staring at Erich. "But not tonight."

Turning from him she lifted her glass as if it were a chalice.

The girls took their final bow. The music stopped. The applause quieted.

"I had a friend once," she told the audience. "Today was his birthday. I wish to sing his favorite Christmas carol."

Erich grabbed her arm. "Haven't you had enough for one night? You could be arrested for blasphemy."

"This has nothing to do with you," she said. "Erich *Joachim* Weisser was my friend. I'm singing this for him."

Twisting from his grasp, she raised her head. "*Stille Nacht*," she sang. "*Heilige Nacht….*"

As her voice filled the room she prayed—that someday God would replace bullets and broken glass with love.

Chapter Thirty-five

Erich pushed money at the taxi driver and stepped out into the wind. Alois. Joachim. *Names*. Didn't *she* use a stage name? Was she so imperceptive that she didn't realize his being in the Party was as much an act as hers? Women! Not one of them worth the price of a pineapple.

He looked up at the bedroom Goebbels occupied when he was too "busy" to go home to his wife and family. Surely on Christmas Eve...

The light was on. Above the villa shone an icy star, as if to remind Erich that Adolph Hitler, the twentieth-century Messiah, had ordered him to keep an eye on the Gauleiter, who remained suspect in the Chancellor's eyes. The way Goebbels behaved, like probably sending those youths to Ananas, made it hard to believe the man was educated. It was as if the osteomyelitic inflammation of the bone marrow that had caused his foot to be deformed had also attacked his brain, wiping out any semblance of normal behavior.

Even now, the Gauleiter had probably passed out with his head between some prostitute's legs.

To hell with him, and Hitler—and women. Erich pulled his collar up against the wind and followed the path around to the dogs. Only they were worth anything. He could hear them as he approached, barking and howling at the moonless sky, as restless as he.

He shook the chain-link fence he'd had erected along the west end to separate the sloped, circular dog-runs from the rest of the grounds, and the dogs came charging. When they reached the ends of their chains, they were jerked from their feet, only to circle and charge again. Their ferocity sent a welcome chill up his spine.

"Password!" The bolt of a carbine rammed home and an overcoated helmeted soldier with the broad shoulders of a Greco-Roman wrestler hustled from the shadows; the affenpinscher yipped and ran in such circles at the end of its leash that it became entangled and had to roll over to extricate itself.

"*Tannenbaum,*" Erich said. "And Merry Christmas, Oberschütze."

"Oh, it's you, sir." Krayller lowered the 98 from his shoulder and grinned down at his monkey terrier's antics. The dog was barely bigger than its master's hamhock-sized hand; he loved it like a father might an infant. "Merry Christmas."

Putting the rifle butt against the ground, Krayller stooped to pet the dog, which rolled over to have its belly tickled. "I'll let you in, sir."

"I thought Holten-Pflug had drawn the midnight shift."

"Well, their new baby and all—"

"You're quite the altruist, Johann."

As Erich walked through the gate, he smiled at Krayller's affection for the little dog.

"What's the meaning of all the commotion?" Hempel strode toward them, a bottle in one hand, in the other a Mann—connected to his holster by a black braid. Though he was clearly inebriated, the alcohol seemed to have tightened rather than loosened his rigidity. He did not stop walking until his nose almost touched Erich's.

"Have we disturbed the Gauleiter's...holy night?" Erich asked, not backing up.

"Don't be impudent."

Hempel raised the gun. Erich brushed it aside nonchalantly. Touching Krayller's shoulder, he sent the lance-corporal back to his post. With a flourish he probably would not have exhibited had Hempel not been present, the corporal clicked his heels together and, saluting, bellowed "Heil Hitler!" loud enough to be heard in the upstairs bedrooms if not throughout the rest of the Grünewald.

"Someday his impudence will get him shot." Hempel reholstered his gun. "The way he mollycoddles that excuse for a dog! It's unmanly." He paused, then added in a low voice, "Like a man who would rather fuck than fight for his country when she is at war."

"Like Doktor Goebbels, Herr Obersturmführer?" Erich glanced again at the bedroom light, wondering if by some quirk he would have to defend Goebbels in order to put down Hempel. "And is the nation at war?"

Hempel's smile did not waver. "I'm referring to you, Herr Rittmeister. The Fatherland will always be at war, if not from without then from within." His gaze flickered with contempt, but perhaps sensing Erich's clenched fist, he took a step back. "I mean nothing derogatory, Herr Rittmeister. It's just that we've much in common, you and the Oberschütze and I—bachelors who are married, as the best of German men should be, to ideals rather than to wives or to our mothers. I hate to see any man prostitute his possibilities. I'd as soon see Krayller dead...nothing personal against him, you understand."

"As you said," Erich glared up into his adversary's face, "our country is at risk, from within and without. You are to be commended for helping Herr Goebbels in his efforts *within*—" Erich pointed toward the villa. "But just as you do whatever you must, it is the duty of myself and my men, and whatever dogs we feel best belong in the unit, to keep these grounds patrolled. That is what you need to understand. As far as I'm concerned, that is all you need to understand."

He waited for Hempel to back off, but the man did not move. "Anything else we need to agree to tonight?" Erich asked.

"All we have ever asked is that you keep the dogs quiet when we are," again the smile, "in conference."

"You're speaking for Herr Goebbels?"

"I have always spoken for Herr Goebbels." Hands in pockets, Hempel walked over to the scarecrow elm, where he had an undisturbed view of the Gauleiter's window.

Always his insistence about his closeness to Goebbels, Erich thought as he strode toward the kennels. Well, bad as Goebbels was, at least he was man enough to prefer women over boys. Greeting him, the shepherds yelped with delight and tugged at their chains. He wanted to pet Achilles, but instead he unhooked and leashed up Taurus. Killi reminded him too much of Miriam and her stubborn rage. What would he have done if those youths had raped her? What could he have done?

Involuntarily he remembered an experience he had tried to bury. One Easter, while motorcycling down for field training in Bavaria, he had witnessed the aftermath of a rape—the people of a village walking past a naked woman sitting on a wagon tongue in an alley, crying. No one went to her aid; they simply averted their eyes. A Jew, obviously. *And I did nothing either*, he thought, just roared away, speeding deep into the Black Forest, the wind—surely it was the wind—making his eyes water.

She could have been Miriam...*could have been Miriam*... That night, as he camped alone beneath the stars, those words echoed in his head like a song. He kept asking himself why he had done nothing. By morning he had neither answers nor sleep. When the sleepless nights continued during the bivouac, he requested a pass to attend the Passion Play at Oberammergau. Maybe Father Dahns had been right all along. Perhaps religion did hold answers or, if not, then at least clues to the secrets.

As Christ was nailed to the cross, an elderly woman behind him whispered, "Mein Hitler," and the response, increasingly louder, quickly serpentined through the audience.

Soon each character in the play had a German counterpart. Even Bethlehem, which the audience took to be Berlin. Mutterings and murmurs and lisped whispers hovered about him like prayers breathed by dark angels. He left after the first curtain call, when the rest of the audience rose in ovation.

Was Miriam blind to everything beyond the stage lights? Was that why she insisted on putting herself in danger, like staying in that damn cabaret and singing, of all things, a Christmas carol?

"The shepherds do need a responsible leader, Herr Rittmeister," Hempel said, coming forward. "Human as well as canine. Nothing personal, you understand, but they lack proper orientation. As you do. You've run with the wrong pack too long."

Erich saw in Hempel's eyes the same haughty disdain for others he had witnessed in the youth at Ananas.

You have run with the wrong pack too long—

"*You* sent those animals to the club! Not Goebbels." Erich felt the rope of his gut twist tighter. "They were your *boys!*"

"And why not? You *must* learn—"

Erich's fury exploded. *Get him, Taurus. Tear the son of a bitch to pieces.*

Taurus lunged for the lieutenant. For an instant, Erich hesitated—just long enough for Hempel to know the attack was no accident. Then he grabbed her collar and tugged her away.

The lieutenant lay on the ground, shaking. His wolfhound whined and licked his face.

Erich stared down in horror. He had allowed—instructed—Taurus to attack an officer. He should stoop and help the man. Apologize.

He could not bring himself to commit such hypocrisy. Instead, after mentally commanding Taurus to sit, he leaned over just enough to remove the Mann from Hempel's holster. The braid on the handle felt slick and soft. Looking more closely he realized it was human hair. Nauseated, he unhooked the braid and pitched it and the pistol into the hedge.

The lieutenant groaned and opened his eyes. As he sat up, he gave Erich a perverse, suave smile.

"How kind of you, Herr Rittmeister, and how crass of me. I forgot it was your birthday and did not buy you a gift. And here you are giving me such a priceless one." He fingered blood-rimmed teeth marks on the back of his hand. "I do believe you have given me incentive for doing anything I wish to you and your brood."

Fist clenched, Erich stood over him. "The hell I have."

"Something's already in the works, Herr Rittmeister. When the dogs are fully trained, I will have them." His smile broadened. "But not now. Not yet."

"Stick to buggering boys." Fuming, Erich strode down the section of drive that ran to the garage, Taurus trotting alongside. She has tasted blood, Erich thought. The worst thing that could happen to a guard dog. Would that make her too emotionally unstable for duty? If so, he would cover for her; that was what partners were for.

He opened one of the garage doors and switched on the light. The place was dank and smelled of oil. Two rows of vehicles, civilian cars and military jeeps and cycles, faced one another beneath the bare bulb. The cars that were still Konrad's responsibility, Rathenau's limousine and the Daimler, were parked on each side of Goebbels' SSK Mercedes Benz. Beside the limo hulked the Gauleiter's pride, a Minerva Landaulet imported from Belgium. Next to the Daimler an empty parking space awaited the prize Goebbels wanted: a Sears, from the American catalogue.

Erich had never touched the Daimler. Now, running a gloved hand across the smooth curve of its fender, he thought of Miriam, sheathed in black silk, singing before the floodlights. He banged his fist down. Why must she always demean him! Why did he keep pushing? He should not even be associating with her, or with Solomon—especially after tonight's episode at Ananas. Any fool could see their ties were a danger to him, and to them...more so, now that he and Hempel had declared open warfare.

He cursed himself for allowing Hempel to goad him like that. If Hempel filed charges—not that he could prove anything—things could get messy. The man's past was an open secret; his own could as easily become one. Any of his Abwehr superiors could insist he cut all ties with his impure past. Burying it could literally mean burying Miriam and the Freunds.

He shuddered.

Trading his overcoat for a flight jacket and the leather helmet he kept in one of the lockers along the east wall, he climbed onto his cycle. He kick-started it with such force that he almost toppled the machine, and raced the engine without regard for Goebbels' comfort. He roared out of the door and up the incline, waving at Krayller to open the gate.

With Taurus loping next to him, Erich wound his motorcycle through the Grünewald and past the Tiergarten. He had gone through Potsdamer Platz and was cruising up Friedrich Ebert Strasse, throttled down and coasting in neutral, by the time he acknowledged to himself he wasn't running from something as much as to something: he wanted to go home.

He slowed to a halt in front of the cigar shop. It looked dark and forlorn, and the lights of *Das Ostleute Haus* bathed him in blue. Snow had begun to fall. He gripped his lapels together against the cold and stared at the elongated reflections the street lamps cast as the pavement gave itself over to white. Across the street, the curb and the ragged blue-spruce hedge seemed like a line someone had drawn in the powder, daring him to cross. But he was not ready—yet.

A woman in a fur coat stepped around the corner and into the blue light. For a split second it seemed as if one of the furrier's mannequins had come alive. Then he saw the whip and the high-heeled boots so capable of trampling across a man's conscience. The fury and nervous near-exhaustion he had thought he had shed on the Ku'damm returned to suffocate him.

"Evening, soldier." The woman lifted her gaze seductively.

Taurus, panting from the run, went rigid and bared her teeth. No sound. Her affect was one of silent, mean cunning.

The woman backed away. "Some animal you've got there." Fear in her voice.

He switched off the engine but held onto the handlebars as he strained to see into the Freund-Weisser apartments.

Twirling her whip, the woman circled Taurus and stepped saucily toward Erich. "Want to be my slave? Or perhaps I should be yours? I don't mind pain if the money's right."

"How much are you willing to pay?" Erich asked in an offhand tone, not looking at her.

"Pay?" She laughed and tried a new approach. "Don't want to be alone on Christmas Eve, do you, Sugar Plum?"

"That's exactly what I do want."

Still gripping the cycle, he stared into the darkness, imagining Miriam kissing Solomon's fingers, easing his hand down over her breast and belly to her thighs, she sliding her fingers down his chest. Damn her! Those three in the alley behind the El Dorado had gloried in whoredom, yet even in his mind's eye he could not force Miriam to compromise herself.

"What's wrong, honey? Cat got your tongue?"

She took a feather from her coat and drew it across the nape of his neck. Giggling, she slipped a hand in his coat, reaching for his crotch. He debated having her get on her knees to service him—power-prayer, he called it—but pulled away.

He wanted to wish his mother a Merry Christmas and maybe drink a schnapps with his father. He could stand the old man for that long. Except Miriam might hear him upstairs and think he had come around because of her, he thought, knowing full well that he was making excuses and that Miriam could not possibly distinguish his footsteps from those of any stranger.

"Prefer boys?" the prostitute asked.

"Bitch!"

Letting go of the cycle, Erich backhanded her as hard as he could. The machine fell with a crash. Dropping the whip, the woman put her fingers tentatively against her cheek. Erich slapped her again. Hard. As she stumbled and landed on her knees, Taurus leapt. She sank her teeth into the wrist, just above her the glove. When the whore's flesh broke against her canines, Taurus quietly hunkered down. Belly tensed and shoulder muscles rippling, she swallowed and bit deeper.

Blood ran down the whore's arm and she screamed, her face contorted with terror, her acne-scarred cheeks as death-white as rotted carp flesh. An electric tingling rolled down Erich's spine. He stiffened. The street lamp took on the form of a lopsided moon, and a feeling that he was surrounded by greenery and gloom suffused him. He felt hot, sweaty. Then, just as abruptly, he was cold again, looking down on the whore and thinking how ludicrous women really were.

For all their power, life rendered them as helpless as men.

CHAPTER THIRTY-SIX

Berlin was alive with lights.

The New Year, the Führer had assured everyone, would ring in greater times for the New Order, and so the Reich was beribboned and pulsing with music and laughter.

Solomon waited outside Ananas for Miriam to finish her performance. Around him, couples clung to one another as they reeled along the pavement, many with half-finished bottles of champagne in hand. He tried to feel their joy, but he could not see or feel beyond their swastika armbands—their emblems of hope and the coming happiness. He kept to the shadows, estranged from the crowds yet part of them—like a man dining alone in a fine restaurant, aware of the quality food but unable to enjoy it because he had no one with whom to share the meal.

He wished Miriam would hurry. Since the Christmas Eve incident on Friedrich Ebert Strasse, he had walked her home every night rather than having her take the trolley. According to the papers, an overcoated, enormous-nosed Jew had attacked one Gisela Haas while she was out collecting money for the poor. *Der Stürmer*, the most viciously and openly anti-Semitic of the papers, compared her wounds to those inflicted by Peter Stumpf, the self-confessed werewolf convicted of lycanthropy in Cologne in 1598 and flayed alive on All Hallows Eve. It was suggested that perhaps the Jew was seeking a virgin's menstrual blood for another satanic rite to be perpetrated against the Holy Child.

Such nonsense! Not that the truth was relevant; only the danger to Miriam was. The heritage of the family who owned the cigar shop was no secret, nor was hers. Audiences at Ananas knew she was Jewish. Fink, now the cabaret's manager, did what he could to defuse the jeers and shield her from the bottles that were occasionally thrown while she performed, but it was up to Solomon to keep her safe. If she walked in the streets unescorted, it was just a matter of time before something happened to her.

Miriam emerged at last, slipping furtively through the cabaret's service entrance. She held her coat close, like protective armor, and smiled at the sight of him.

"How do you always manage to look happy?" Sol bent and kissed her, wondering for the thousandth time what miracle had finally brought her to him.

"Shouldn't I be? The past is gone. Buried. No sense dwelling on its ugliness." She looped her arm through his.

"You have a God-given talent for optimism." The way

her eyes reflected the holiday lights overhead enchanted him.

Right before Chanukah, a week before Christmas Eve, she had come to his bedroom with the ease and familiarity of a wife. Her attitude was perfect, for had she been hesitant, he might have kept his distance, and had she been too bold, he would have been overly concerned with his performance. He had consummated the sexual act only once before, with a prostitute Erich goaded him into buying. It had been a dismal failure, too ephemeral to constitute reality, and he had continued to think of himself as a virgin.

With Miriam, lovemaking was a glorious event. Like children holding hands at the ocean's edge, they laughed and splashed and leaped over waves, daring each other to go together into deeper and deeper water, and he did not even care that his parents and Recha might hear them.

Nodding and smiling at passersby like any Gentile couple, they walked home along Leipziger Strasse, past Wertheim's. Like the KadeWe's square-block delicatessen, perhaps the world's largest, Wertheim's was for all practical purposes off-limits to Jews. The Depression had again brought scarcity to the Fatherland, so Aryans—real Germans—were to be fed and clothed first.

Thank God people still found money for tobacco, Sol thought, seeing the crowd that milled outside Die Zigarrenkiste. "Looks like Herr Weisser was right," he said. "He insisted business would be good tonight, so we should turn up the lights and stay open late. 'What good is a holiday brandy without a fine cigar.'"

Miriam laughed at his imitation of Herr Weisser. "See, you worry needlessly about leaving him to handle the shop."

Sol hugged her, slipping his hands inside her coat so he could hold her more tightly.

She was right; he worried too much. Like his father, he feared things might not be done correctly unless he did them himself. He needed to rely more not only on Miriam and Herr Weisser but also on his mother and Frau Weisser. On Papa too, perhaps. Lately there were days when Papa's melancholia—he laughed at himself for his use of the illness' archaic name, as though that romanticized it and thus lessened its reality—released its grip. At those times, Jacob was able and willing to help with small tasks. Since Christmas Eve, when Miriam came home from Ananas so distraught and Sol held her through the night as she cried, Jacob kept the curtains and window open when he rocked. He wanted, he said, to hear all the horror outside, and did not seem to mind the chill that seized the room.

Sol checked his watch as they neared the crowd. Three in the morning. "Herr Weisser has extended his midnight special. He enjoys spreading happiness on nights like this."

"I think the general idea is for the customers to do the spreading...of their money."

Sol laughed but his laughter died in the air. Grabbing Miriam's hand, he rushed forward. Something was very wrong. The crowd was static, gawking. Nobody was going inside the shop, no one coming out, and the door of the shop was open, its glass shattered.

"I don't care who they are, people ought not to be

treated like that," said a hefty woman on the crowd's outskirts.

"Nonsense, Luise." The skinny man beside her was on tiptoes, straining to see. "They've been cheating people for years. Don't you listen to what the Führer says?"

The man swore at Sol as he and Miriam shoved past and entered the shop. "All his fault," someone said.

"No. He was a nice man. I liked him."

"Money-sucking Jews. We should rid Germany of the lot of them."

The inside of the shop was a shambles. Display cases lay overturned and broken on top of merchandise that would never again be salable. Herr Weisser, his face red and swollen and splotched with darkening bruises, lay amid strewn money and broken glass. His head was on his wife's lap. Leaning against the upside-down cash register, she wept and stroked his cheek.

Friedrich lifted a hand when he saw Solomon, then his head lolled and his hand fell to the floor.

"Fred offered them money. They wouldn't take it," Inge Weisser said. "They said it was tainted. Jew money. Can you believe, they called him a Jew? They beat him, kicked him. Four of them held his arms and legs and two others...two others...oh God! They dropped the cash register on him." She put her head in her hands. "It's his ribs. I think one has punctured a lung."

"A Jew, they called me!" Friedrich Weisser wheezed and then caught his breath. "Me! A Jew!"

"If I had only been here," Inge Weisser told Sol. "I would have told them the truth, that they had the wrong—"

As if realizing what she was saying, and to whom, Frau

Weisser covered her mouth with her hand. She is determined to blame this on us, Sol thought angrily as two burly men carrying a makeshift stretcher shouldered their way into the shop.

"I've been here before," one of them said, glancing around. "People like these never learn." He shook his head. "Waste of our time, if you ask me."

"What are we supposed to do? Leave the old man to die? He could be your father."

They knelt and eased Friedrich Weisser onto the stretcher. He whimpered. "Cover me with cheese and charge admission," he said through compressed lips.

His bitter humor made Sol wince. Weissenberg, the Weimar-Berlin healer considered by many to be a saint, had claimed he could resurrect the recent dead by applying cheese curds to a body. When cheese and corpse began to stink and the police stepped in, he ranted that his impending miracle had been circumvented by police interference.

"Anyone else hurt?" Sol asked Frau Weisser.

She shook her head. "Your mother was here when they came, but she's safe."

"Mama? Where is she!"

"At the apartment. She got away." There was a biting edge to Inge's voice. "Left my Friedrich to those animals!"

"I'll go and find her," Miriam said softly, touching Sol's arm as if to quiet his nerves.

Sol followed the stretcher out the door. Inge clung to her husband's hand.

"I'm sorry, Freddie. You said we should insist they send her away, but I wouldn't listen," she said. "That Miriam and her cabaret dancing! First we lost Erich because of her, now they came to finish what they started at the nightclub on Christmas Eve!"

"Did they mention me, Frau Weisser?" Miriam's voice was tight.

After a moment's hesitation, Inge Weisser shook her head. "Not exactly, but…but you may be sure they were after you!"

Miriam's shoulders sagged, and she looked very pale.

"Please, Frau Weisser," Sol said. "I know how upset you are, but watch what you're saying."

"I am watching! I'm watching my Friedrich here! Where were you when the Brownshirts arrived? Out on your nightly stroll!"

Sol leaned over Friedrich. "I'll find a way to get in touch with Erich—"

"No!" Herr Weisser's voice was amazingly strong. "I don't want to see him." He stopped and closed his eyes before he went on. "He did not come. Not even for Christmas…or for his birthday."

Sol patted the man's meaty hand. "I must check on Mama, then I'll come to the infirmary. You'll be all right."

"He'll be fine. We'll all be fine, won't we, Solomon-the-Wise! Especially your papa over there!" Frau Weisser spat on the street. "My Friedrich might die, but Jacob Freund will be fine!"

Solomon looked sadly at the woman he had known most of his life, realizing he did not know her at all.

CHAPTER THIRTY-SEVEN

Miriam put her arms around Sol's waist and her cheek against his back. She leaned against him for a moment, warming him, then took his hand and led him to the apartment like a child.

They found his parents and sister in the library. His mother stood in the corner, body pressed against the wall as if only it stood between her and collapse. Her left cheek was badly bruised. Recha, dressed in a white pleated floor-length gown, sat with her head tilted against the rocker back, staring at the ceiling. Her father stood behind the chair, gripping its scroll tops and staring blankly out the window toward the store front.

"Thank God you're all right, Mama," Solomon said.

"They called me a whore, Sol. Me! A whore!" His mother twisted a blond curl around and around her finger. Her voice was soft. Toneless. She was not crying. "They said any Gentile who was in partnership with Jews certainly copulated with them. As God is my witness, I didn't deny our—Him—but I didn't argue with them either. I wanted to live, Solly. For you and Papa and Recha."

"Anti-Semitic garbage talk." Jacob's chin was stubbornly lifted, his voice stronger than Solomon had heard it in years.

"They thought I was Frau Weisser and that Friedrich was Jacob. One of them hit me, then they told me to get out." She was twisting her hair with both hands now.

"I just sat here," Jacob said. "What kind of man would do that while his wife and best friend—"

"I'll have it cut." Ella Freund pulled her curls down in front of her eyes. "And dyed. What do you think, Sol? Recha? Miri? How would I look with black hair?" She posed like a little girl pleading forgiveness for some silly infraction of family rules.

Recha rose from the rocking chair and faced her mother. "You will look beautiful, *Mutti,*" she said quietly.

"She's right," Miriam added. Hoping her voice had not betrayed her concern, she kissed Ella Freund's cheek. The woman smiled, her face strangely calm. She had the look of a piece of fragile porcelain, as if she could shatter from the slightest touch.

Sol looked gratefully at Miriam. She could see her own fear mirrored in his face.

"I sat and rocked!" Jacob lashed out at the chair with his foot. In his near-blindness he missed and kicked again, knocking the chair on its side. Kicking at it a third time, he splintered two spindles.

Recha put her arms around him. He twisted, then allowed his body to slacken. "They'll be back," he said.

"What then? Shall I sit and smile while they rape my wife and daughter and plunder my shop whenever they choose? Or should I sell them pencils so they can write their names on our souls."

"I could take money from the till and go to Fenzik's," Sol's mother said. "He cuts hair so well."

"There could be a thousand tills, Ellie." Jacob Freund spoke in a measured tone. "You still could not go there. Fenzik's has been off-limits to us for a year. Jew hair, eyes, flesh. We have become Jewish shadows."

Recha kept her arms around her father. "You'll see, Papa. After the holidays, things will calm down."

Miriam silently applauded Recha's optimism as she watched Jacob Freund gently push his daughter away and shuffle toward the hall. His footsteps faded, stopped, returned. He was right, she thought. They had all become Jewish shadows, true children of the light.

"Pack!"

He dropped two battered suitcases at his wife's feet.

"Pack?" she asked. "Are we going to Mainz for a vacation?"

"You're leaving. You and Recha. Getting out. That's the least I can do for you."

He turned and plodded back toward the bedroom. Ella hurried after him. "I'll cut it myself, Jacob. And dye it too. Black as the Queen of Sheba's I'll make it."

"Pack!"

"Will you go too, Papa?" Solomon asked.

Jacob stood in the archway, one hand against the wall. "I've gone too many kilometers in that rocker to run now. Recha and *Mutti* will go to Amsterdam tonight, to your Aunt Hertl's." He glanced at Miriam. "She should go too."

"If Solomon stays, I stay." Miriam looked quickly at Sol. She was too involved with him even to think of leaving. No matter what.

"I'm staying too," Recha said. She picked up an ermine cape that lay on the desk and draped it around herself as if it could protect her from what was happening.

Waltzing up to Recha, Frau Freund whirled her around. "You too, my sweet," she sang, as if at a party. "We'll cut and dye your hair as well. Then Papa won't send us away!"

"Neither of you will touch your hair," Jacob said. "These days it is a blessing to look like *goyim*. It will help on your trip."

"Ernst says that with my looks, if I legally change my name and move in with him, no one need know," Recha said.

"That you are Jewish?" Jacob was picking up the rocker. Now he lifted it off the floor and set it down, face rigid with rage. "My daughter would deny her heritage so easily?"

Recha backed up. "I have no intention of denying anything, Papa, not in the long run. But Ernst says I'm destined to become a star. A star, Papa! He's the best in the business. He should know."

"He knows what is in a father's heart? He knows what is in the mind of God, who made you one of His Chosen People?" He raised his arm as if to strike her. Sol stepped between them, ready to take the blow.

"Please, Papa," Recha said.

The arm Jacob had raised faltered, and he lowered it. Recha picked up her cape and fondled it, as if it were a living thing. "I wish I did not love you so much," Jacob said, gripping the chair. "Do this thing for me, Recha." He closed his eyes as if in prayer. "Take your mother to her sister, to safety. For almost three years I have sat here, thinking myself half-blind and sick because the world is blind and sick. But it is my beloved wife who is not well. I have made her that way, too dependent on hope. Take her to your aunt, then do whatever you must."

Recha had been so proud when her agent gave her the ermine, Miriam thought, remembering the day, a few months ago, when the girl signed the contract to pose for Mercedes advertisements. The golden-haired sylph who had sniffled her way through the evening at Kaverne, so in awe of Miriam, had blossomed into a beauty. Her bootpolish-brown eyes had attracted the producer of UFA films and landed her a bit part in *The Blue Angel*. Her parts since then were small but important, as she put it. She had begun to be noticed. Miriam remembered Recha's confidence about an affair with a rich playboy associated with the film industry. He smoked opium and could make love only if the lights were on; he believed the dark brought out the devil in a woman. Rachel Roland, as Recha called herself, was all grown up, and entitled to make her own choices.

Or was she? Wasn't it her duty to go with her mother, who appeared to be on the verge of some kind of breakdown?

Recha trembled and looked at the floor. Sol started to move to her, but she lifted her hands and moved away from him, as if she were so filled with despair and the knowledge of separation that she wanted no one to touch her. "I love you, Papa."

"I know you do."

He gazed at her quietly, then lowered himself to his knees and drew back the ancient Oriental rug. Using the fingers of one hand to feel the nubs of the numbers while he worked the dial with the other, he opened the safe he had recessed into the floor. He removed several bundles of paper. Lifting out a tray, he reached farther down and took out a wad of currency and a leather pouch.

"Here are your birth certificates, what money and jewels we have left, and a few odds and ends of sentimental value." He held them out, waiting for someone to take them.

Recha did so. "The final audition for the *Lady Moon* revival is this weekend, Papa. It's a major role. Ernst will kill me...."

"Would you rather the Nazis killed you...and your mother?"

"I'll have Ernst talk the studio into a late call," Recha said after a lengthy silence. "I'll take Mama to *Tante* Hertl. But I'm coming back when she's settled. Life is dangerous, Papa, but I intend to live it as fully as I can. The mistakes I make will be my own."

"Even if they are fatal ones?"

"Especially those."

The comment brought silence. They packed in silence, closed the apartment door silently behind themselves, walked somberly to the station. New Year's Eve was not a popular night for travel. On one hand, it meant seats might be available; on the other, it meant the Freunds would be conspicuous. Recha was elected to purchase the tickets while the rest waited near the train, which was huffing steam by the time they arrived.

Relatively few people boarded the gray-brown Amsterdam-bound train. Miriam stood with Sol and his parents, terrified that Recha would have difficulty buying tickets. She heaved a sigh of relief when she saw the young woman run toward them along the platform, waving two tickets.

"No trouble," she called out breathlessly. "The clerk recognized me. He was too busy trying to get my autograph and make a date with me to look at our passports."

Jacob caught her in his arms and held her close. "It might not be quite so easy at the border," he said. "Remember—none of what you're carrying is as valuable as life itself."

She patted her coat. The lining hid a false pocket which held the family jewels. She had been instructed to use them for her mother's needs, and for bribes if necessary. In the coat were her great-grandmother's pearl brooch, her mother's diamond rings, her grandmother's tourmaline that she considered her own.

"The tourmaline goes last, Papa."

"Maybe nothing will have to go." Jacob put his arm around his wife's shoulders and kissed her. The train hooted. "*Mutti* is in your hands, and she is our most precious jewel," he said softly.

"I don't understand why I have to go all the way to Amsterdam to have my hair cut and dyed," Ella Freund whispered. "You are sending us away, Jacob. Why are you sending us away?"

"Papa and Sol will come to Amsterdam in a week or so," Miriam said. "Me, too." She tried to look cheerful as she helped Sol's mother on board. Not that Ella would notice, she thought, fighting tears. The rational, practical person who had been the strength of her family had been displaced by a stranger...an elderly, pathetic victim of the times.

"Promise you'll come?" Ella Freund leaned precariously from the top step.

"Promise," Jacob Freund answered.

"No tears, now," Recha said, her eyes brimming.

"No tears," Sol said.

Miriam's head was against his shoulder and she held tightly to his hand in an effort to control her emotions. The engineer sent a last steam blast echoing through the station, and the train began to move. Miriam and Sol walked alongside the cars, together with other people likewise in motion, offering good-byes and good wishes.

"Be happy," Miriam called. "Remember, life's a passing dream, not—"

"Not a dress rehearsal!" Recha said.

Within seconds, all that remained were those left behind and a series of disembodied arms and hands waving as the train chugged away. Miriam and Sol watched until it was lost in the collage of Berlin buildings, while Jacob stared across the track as if the train were still there. He seemed startled when Solomon put an arm across his shoulders to steer him from the depot.

Back at the apartment, Jacob wandered into the library while Miriam went into the kitchen to make coffee. The place was strewn with possessions left over from the heat of packing. After she and Sol sat quietly together for a while, they set about folding and putting away the clothes. Among a heap of Recha's lingerie they discovered a packet of family photographs. The top one was a picture of Sol beside his cello.

Were we ever really that young? Miriam wondered, watching him snap the packet shut and remembering again the party at the cabaret—the night she had first seen Solomon.

When everything had been tidied up, she and Sol went to the library to return the photographs to the safe. They had reached the archway before either of them saw Sol's father.

Jacob Freund sat in his rocker. His Iron Cross dangled from his hand and he stared at the wall. He wore his *tallis* and *yarmulke*. Both the prayer shawl and skullcap looked sadly out of place.

"Papa?" Sol sounded like a little boy.

Jacob curled his fingers around the medal and, putting it in his vest pocket, took out his gold watch and held it up for Solomon to see. "I've prayed for your mother and sister's safe journey. The time for prayer is over. Be a good boy and get my spare glasses from the accessories box in the shop cellar. I'm so blind without them I cannot even see the hour hand! The whole world is a blur."

He smiled but there was something dark about his face, as though his skin were underlain with shadow.

"I'm on my way, Papa."

"On second thought, let the three of us go together."

Miriam took Jacob's one arm and Sol the other. They helped him make his way slowly out of the building and across the street. A bit of glass fell from the broken door as Sol opened it and turned on the lights.

A cold calm lay inside; even the air seemed brittle.

They let go of Jacob and he walked around the shop, moving as if through a house unused for decades and filled with memories that could shatter like crystal if anything were disturbed. The cash register lay on its side like a wounded animal. He stooped, but did not touch it.

"Stay with your papa," Miriam told Solomon. "I know where to find his glasses."

She had never been downstairs alone. It seemed to yawn open as she drew aside the curtain and started down. The flooring that once had separated the basement and cellar had been removed decades if not centuries ago. In the small weak light, the storeroom seemed narrow and abnormally deep.

She descended softly, the wood quietly creaking. Reaching the bottom stairs, she stretched to the shelving rather than take the final step, and felt through the accessories box until she located the glasses. Her forehead was damp as she started backward up the stairs.

Nothing to be afraid of, she told herself. Even Sol doesn't hear voices down here anymore. Still, she found herself listening for the wail of an infant and for a woman crying, "*Oh God, let me die!*"

A steady drip-drip-drip resounded through the cellar, drawing her attention toward the sewer. Her throat tightened and her hands shook violently. A cold sweat seized her as she watched cellar-seep as dark as blood serpentine toward the grate.

She lurched up the stairs and tore aside the curtain that separated her from the shop.

A skinny figure stood there, motionless.

"Papa?"

Jacob's face held the solemnity of *Yiskor*, the prayers for the dead that Jews repeated every *Shabbas* in synagogue. "So much to be done. We must have the shop running smoothly by the time Friedrich returns." Jacob took his glasses from her.

"Why don't we all go to Amsterdam. There are other shops—in countries where we need not fear for our lives."

"This time the Nazi rabble came in the night," Jacob replied. "Until now, that has been their way. Soon they will expose themselves in the daylight. Then we will know the beginning of the end is upon us. We must be here, awaiting them with our eyes open."

"But *why*, Herr Freund? Why must we stay here? I don't understand. We Jews can't win—"

"We are Germans first, Miriam," Herr Freund said quietly. "If we run away, they will never learn that."

He moved slowly toward Solomon, clasped his son's hand as if to shake it and put his other hand on Sol's shoulder.

"Every day for twenty-three years we have served this city," Jacob said. "Tomorrow shall be no different."

CHAPTER THIRTY-EIGHT

August 1936

Wondering why anyone would object to taking a ferry across the Havel to Pfaueninsel—Peacock Island—Erich ambled across the pontoon bridge the Wehrmacht had erected for the convenience of Dr. Goebbels' guests.

Achilles tugged at her harness, a firm chest brace such as a blind man might wear. Erich kept her heeled at his side. He felt proud of himself and of the dog, despite her advanced years. Her coat was dull, her ears sagged, and her canines were yellow and crooked, but she was after all over ninety in human years. She was hard of hearing, and every now and then he had to repeat a command which in earlier years would have brought instant obedience. Still, for an old dog she was in superb shape and capable of inflicting enormous damage—sow-bellied or not. Most of the time she was alert and carried herself well. Not as well as Taurus, of course. Nor could she handle his mental commands as easily. Sometimes the messages were obeyed; sometimes not. He knew he should have brought Taurus tonight, but Achilles was his only hope for a connection to Miriam, and to their shared memories of the island.

They had come to the island together once—she sixteen, her head filled with fairy tales; he determined to be her hero. She had played princess to his Prince Charming as they flirted in the Garden of Palms, danced to the music of King Wilhelm's organ, kissed next to a wooden cabinet that one of the court designers had whimsically shaped like a bamboo hut.

Remembering that day, and hoping she would too, he had slipped her name to someone on the entertainment committee. She had refused to see him since the disturbance at Ananas, where she was now waiting tables—she who used to be the stellar attraction. The only time he saw her was during his brief visits to his parents. He went to catch a glimpse of Miri.

Tonight, she would surely talk to him. He would introduce her to Leni Riefenstahl. They had much in common. Both in the arts, both started out as dancers. Leni was making two documentaries about the Olympic Games. Maybe she would use Miri.

He stopped himself. He was dreaming. A woman who said publicly that when the Führer arrived, the rays of the sun crossed the Hitler sky, would hardly employ a Jewess. She was more likely to put a gorilla to work. Her film, *The Eternal Forest*, for example. About survival of the fittest, it starred ancient Gauls born to worship forest gods and die where wild boar roamed. They clothed themselves in animal skins, drank mead from a ram's horn.

A strange but fascinating woman. Erich wondered what Leni would choose to film tonight. This party was slated to be quite a bash. Everyone from Hess to the Duke of Hamilton was coming. Solomon would say: "And how many Jews?"

He had to admit, he missed Solomon's directness. It was getting dangerous to be seen around a Jew, but that would change. Soon. There would be no more mistakes like the one that had nearly killed his father; there would be no more beatings. The Games had seen to that. Only yesterday, he had spent the day taking down *Juden Unerwünscht*—Jews unwanted—signs. For all their racism, some signs were humorous. Like the one, combining official warning with someone's painted scrawl, that he had put in the trunk of the Rathenau limousine, which he was now driving:

SHARP CURVE, DRIVE CAREFULLY
Jews Drive 200

Just a memento. Even Solomon would understand, surely. No matter what Solomon said, those signs would never go up again. Not after what Hitler and his cronies told the foreign press. The press would report that the rumors were nonsense, that the charming and brilliant Adolph Hitler was Germany's savior, that sometimes the Berlin sky was hazy with skywriting proclaiming peace and good will. "Germany's Golden Age," they announced, led by an "astute, gracious, energetic leader."

Thus heralded, Hitler and his people would dare not go back to what they had been. Thank God.

Erich walked slowly across the bridge, strolling so that he did not appear overeager to investigate the fashionable women and the men in serge suits and uniforms who sauntered on the other side. He did not wish to appear unused to mingling with such an assemblage. The guest list was varied enough to have pleased even the eclectic fantasies of King Friedrich Wilhelm II, who had designed the island as a playground for his mistress, the Countess Lichtenau.

Doubtless, the king would have been delighted to find his *Lustschloss*—Pleasure Palace—filled with foreign dignitaries and members of the old nobility. His "Swiss cottage" in the park, among the tulip trees and Weymouth pines he had imported from the United States, was a fitting setting for drink and discussions between foreign diplomats and generals. The "dairy" and "guest house" were perfect for assignations, as was the Greek temple that stood among Lebanon cedars whose girths measured two-and-a-half meters. What better place for Olympic athletes to live out their fantasies?

He stepped off the bridge and onto the island. Thousands of muted yellow lights shaped like tiny flames adorned the trees. Dancing girls carrying flaming torches lit the footpaths; dressed as pages, they guided the guests to their evening of enchantment. Their full-sleeved satin shirts, tight black pants, and powdered wigs were a touch of genius, combining the theme of the Olympics with the aura of aristocracy.

Erich scanned their faces, looking for Miriam. The island's muster of peacocks, so protected by the law that even pocketing a fallen pinfeather was forbidden, preened around three outdoor dance arenas. Couples waltzed and tangoed, applauding each tune with white-gloved hands and applauding again when, as if rehearsed, the peacocks spread their feathers and screeched. Refreshment pavilions offered lobster, pheasant, and caviar. Waiters in red-and-black tuxedos trimmed in gold poured streams of champagne. For those with more plebeian tastes, there were cauldrons of hot beer soup.

He took a glass of champagne and sipped it. Fascinated by the people, he failed to see Goebbels approaching.

"Toasting the Reich, Herr Rittmeister?"

He must have looked guilty, because Goebbels' thin face broke into the smile of a man who had scored a minor victory over someone he disliked. Erich's unit was guarding Nazi headquarters; he had no specific responsibilities on the island. Technically, though, he was still on duty and should not have been drinking.

Before Erich could think of an appropriate response, Magda Goebbels drew her husband away to watch the brewing of the potent punch known colloquially as "Warsaw Death."

Thank you, Magda, Erich thought, watching them walk away. They were one of the least attractive couples he had ever seen: Goebbels with his limp; she, a head taller, with a prominent nose and chin. Her appearance belied the suggestion that she had once been an actress of beauty, much like the women her Josef consorted with on the nights he was not pretending fanatical devotion to her and to their family.

"The hell with you, Herr Doktor!" Erich took a second glass from a silver tray and followed the crowd to a punchbowl filled with boiled brandy, lemon peel, cloves, and cinnamon. Across the top lay two crossed sabers crowned by a large flaming rum-soaked sugar cube.

The flames rose and the military men around him burst into songs of bravery and battlefield chivalry. If this was the new aristocracy, Erich thought, feeling pleased with himself, perhaps he had not been born too late after all.

A passing waiter took his glass and handed him a fresh drink.

The song began. *"Deutschland, Deutschland über Alles."*

The crowd turned, Erich with it, to watch the Führer step off the bridge. His arm was around the shoulders of an Arab dressed in a flowing robe of white silk. Behind them came the rest of Hitler's party—Göring, Himmler, and the former prince whom many considered to be the true heir to Pfaueninsel, Augustus Wilhelm. Like Goebbels, all were dressed in formal evening attire.

"Heil Hitler!" Goebbels' voice rang out.

"Heil Hitler!" the crowd chanted, lifting their hands to salute their Führer.

Forgetting for a moment that he was holding Achilles' leash, Erich started to salute. Choking, the dog growled in protest.

"Sorry, old pal." Erich lowered his hand.

"Not saluting the Führer, Rittmeister?" Goebbels asked. Making the only decision he could, Erich whispered a terse "Stay!" He dropped the leash and saluted.

At the edge of his peripheral vision, he sensed movement. He turned his head slightly.

A peacock, claiming ownership of the territory, fanned

its feathers. It was accustomed to people but not to a German shepherd invading its territory. Dogs were not usually allowed on the island.

Achilles growled and assumed an attack stance.

"Steady, girl." Erich patted the dog and felt for her leash. Achilles did not seem to feel the affection. Her gaze was riveted on the peacock, her ears pricked up, her tail lifted and stiff.

The singing had died down and the Führer's voice could be heard. "I was misquoted by the press. I have nothing against Negroes," he was saying. "By all means let them compete. We are a democracy, are we not? What I did say is that, descended as they are from jungle peoples, they have an unfair physical advantage and a disadvantage emotionally, intellectually, and socially. Instead of representing the United States, they should be sent to Africa, where they belong."

"A simplistic solution, Herr Hitler." The man who had spoken stepped out of the shadows. His voice held an accent, Spanish perhaps, or Latin American, but the most outstanding thing about him was his clothing. He wore a white silk toreador's "suit-of-lights" trimmed with heavy gold brocade. Down his back and pinned to his hair was a long black pigtail and, on his head and drawn down toward his nose, the heavy *montero* of the bullfighter. Pinned to one shoulder and flowing into and over the crook of his arm was a black cape lined with red silk.

Forgetting all about Achilles, Erich stared in fascination. The man was outrageously handsome in a way Erich was sure no woman could resist.

"Simple, but not simplistic, Señor...Péron, is it?"

"Perón." The man corrected the accent and made a slight bow. "And what of the Jews, Herr Hitler? Do you have an equally *simple* solution for the 'Jewish Question,' as I've heard it called?"

"There are many possible solutions."

"Name one I have not yet heard."

"Let me first remind you that the anti-Semitism people have ascribed to us is a thing of the past. You might not know it, but a Jew, one Hauptmann Fürstner, was responsible for building and organizing the Olympic Village."

"Yes," the man said, "but you have not answered me."

Reporters gathered around the two men scribbled furiously.

"Very well. Though I believe I can safely predict that in another decade or two what you call the Jewish Question will no longer concern anyone, I do have several suggestions. For one thing, they could be ordered to choose a homeland."

The "matador" smiled pleasantly. "I believe someone suggested Nigeria. However, the Nigerians might object to being displaced."

"There are other places. Madagascar, for example."

"Madagascar?"

"Why not? We could pack them off in ships and—"

"You are serious about this, Herr Hitler?"

"It would be convenient if they were all gathered in one place, would it not?"

"Convenient? For whom? And what of the Malagasy?"

"A hodgepodge at best. Negroes, Javanese—"

"I take it you would send *them* back to Africa and Java."

"Ja." The Chancellor glanced around, apparently growing bored with the discussion. "You there! Rittmeister...Alois, is it not? Enjoying yourself? I see you brought your old friend." He nodded toward Achilles.

"Ja, mein Führer!" Erich moved forward, pleased at having been singled out.

"That must once have been a fine animal—but might one of our beautiful young Fräuleins not be a more suitable constant companion for a virile young man?" The Chancellor turned to the man he had called Péron. "The Rittmeister is in charge of a special canine corps. You would be amazed at how well his animals are trained. Not so, Herr Rittmeister?" He motioned at the press. "Tell them!"

Erich hesitated, less pleased. He was being patronized—the butt of Hitler's minor annoyance with the foreigner.

"Go on. Tell them!"

"I—" Erich's mind reeled. "Dogs have a number of military uses," he said quickly. "There are sentry-attack dogs, scout dogs, messenger dogs, wire-laying dogs, pack dogs, sledge dogs. We are trying to combine these types into one." He brought his fists slowly together to illustrate his point. "Imagine a single entity, a Gestalt, a team of dogs as capable of acting on their own initiative as they are of—"

"Tell them what you told me about the javelin," Goebbels interjected. "What did you call it—an art form."

"An art aerodynamically," Erich said, gaining confidence. "Thrown well, it arcs clean, without compromise, like an irrefutable argument—"

Goebbels took hold of Hitler's elbow. "The Rittmeister here won several Youth events. He is a local champion, shall we say."

Hitler jerked from Goebbels' hold. "All of Germany's new generation are champions!" He motioned with his fist as if pounding on an imaginary table. "In any other country, the Rittmeister here could easily have been the best! But here, we have a new Germany, of such depth and breadth of skill…"

He was beginning to lose control of his temper, Erich realized. He did tend to do that at parties. With the foreign press here in full force, the Führer would have to be closely watched.

One of the pages, unmindful of her audience, flung her flaming torch into the birdbath and threw herself into the arms of a young officer, who led her away. His attention distracted, Hitler moved on. The press followed him.

A tipsy, middle-aged woman in a pink gown and hair tinted to match gripped Erich's arm. "Seen my husband?"

"What does he look like?" Erich asked, more happy than not at having had the spotlight removed from him.

"Like a lecher!" She stumbled off into the shadows.

Magda Goebbels walked up to Erich. "They are all lechers." She did not look happy. "My husband said he wanted the girls to look svelte, not homespun, but these girls' behavior is indecent! Disgusting!"

Some of the girls were members of the State Opera's *corps de ballet*, but most, Erich knew, came from music halls and cabarets. Their morality seemed as flexible as their bodies. Already, couples headed for more secluded realms. Former torchbearers and officers, former torchbearers and foreign dignitaries, former torchbearers and men—whatever their description.

"If my Paul Josef spent less time with his movie-star harlots, he might be less accepting of this behavior," Frau Goebbels said quietly. "Any time now, the Führer will lose his temper over this situation, you wait and see. It must be stopped. Can you not—"

She stopped talking, her attention diverted toward Achilles. Unleashed, the dog had begun to stalk a peacock standing like a lawn ornament, its long neck lifted and still. Muzzle thrust out and tail out straight, the dog eased forward.

The peacock screeched indignantly, looking for all the world like a false-eyelashed transvestite whose bottom had been pinched by the wrong person.

Quickly Erich tried to fill his mind with light, to visualize the dog's eyes and transfer a command: *Friend!*

Achilles pivoted mechanically toward the bird.

Play!

Achilles' body untensed. Scampering over to the bird, she nudged it as gently as a kitten testing a ball of string. The peacock strutted back, lifted its fan and emitted a sound that was more tease than screech.

Again the dog advanced and again the bird sidestepped, the beauty of its feathers and voice making the dog appear clumsy by contrast.

People began gathering. The Führer, smiling, nodded to the spectators, then toward his retinue of adjutants and aides, who apparently knew what he wanted of them. Without a word, they scurried in all directions, running into bushes and the pavilions, knocking over trays and tables, pulling people in varying states of undress into the open. Fists and feet and bottles flew.

A bottle hit the peacock. Screeching and stabbing with its beak, it attacked Achilles, who backed up, obviously perplexed.

"Those birds are sacrosanct!" the Führer screamed. "You should have commanded the dog to stay away from it!"

"I—" Erich stopped. No one, not even Adolph Hitler, would believe in the kind of communication he had with his animals. He grabbed for the leash. "Down!"

Achilles sat dead still.

Apparently sensing its advantage, the bird circled her.

"Stop that stupid dog!" Goebbels yelled, limping forward.

"Down!" Erich shouted again...too late. Achilles gave in to instinct. Erich could feel the animal's single-minded intensity and knew he had lost control; his only hope was that the peacock would back away.

But the bird was in full motion, protecting its territory from this strange four-legged invader. One more time it darted forward. One time too many.

It never had a chance. There was a squawking, and a flurry of feathers. Achilles' mouth was around its neck.

Goebbels picked up a tray that had fallen to the ground, held it like a moon-burnished shield, then threw it at the dog.

Achilles opened her mouth as if to catch the tray, and dropped the bird, its wings beating feebly and head hanging limply to one side.

"Stay!" Erich commanded.

Growling, the dog stared at Goebbels' groin.

"Somebody shoot that beast!"

Erich grabbed the dog's harness. Achilles, done with her show of strength, became meekly obedient to Erich's command to heel.

"My fault for losing hold of her," Erich said.

"No one is at fault." Hitler stepped forward and leaned down to pet the dog. "She was simply overexcited by this idiotic event."

Erich breathed more easily.

Hitler leaned close to Erich and, smiling at those around him, said softly, "Now, Herr Rittmeister, you will shoot the dog."

Erich stared in disbelief. "But Herr Führer, you said—"

"I know perfectly well what I said. There is no blame. Nonetheless, there are times when the blameless must be destroyed."

Erich knelt next to Hitler and put his hands in Achilles' fur. He could smell the pungent, sour odor of age.

Briefly the tips of Hitler's fingers made contact with Erich's. "I have given you an order," the Führer said, continuing to fondle the dog. "Once I have made up my mind—" He paused. "I have plans for you, Rittmeister, but I must know you are strong enough to accept the fact that there is no room in the Reich for compassion."

Erich stared at the bright stones on the footpath and wondered what the partygoers were thinking. Many were stepping back, aware that something unusual was happening and wanting no part of it.

"Give me a pistol," Goebbels said, fuming.

"No!" Hitler stood up. "The Rittmeister shall do what must be done. His dog has outlived her usefulness." He took hold of Erich's arm. "I will watch. I order you not to look away or to display emotion."

A series of lightning seizures jolted Erich's body as he unholstered his pistol and released the safety. When they subsided, he cocked the pistol and took aim, his vision blurred by angry tears, his thoughts damning himself, Hitler, the Reich.

Forgive me, Achilles. I love you.

Knowing that the pain the dog would feel would seize him as well, he fired.

Achilles gave a cry that sounded like a human child, fell and lay still. Erich lowered the pistol and stared at his old friend. Red, raw muscle showed where the fur was suddenly missing. *Good-bye, old friend.*

He waited for the pain, welcoming it, but it did not come. He experienced neither guilt nor pain, only numbness. There was no room in him for anything except hatred.

"Now let us forget all of this unpleasantness and watch a more pleasant form of entertainment." Goebbels gave a passing glance to the dead animal. "Come, everyone, the bolero is about to begin."

Erich knelt beside Achilles, stroking her warm fur. Taking Magda by the arm, Goebbels led the way to the largest of the three arenas. Only Perón remained near Erich.

In the center of the arena and raised a meter off the ground was a small circular stage surrounded by twenty chairs, their backs toward the stage. Male dancers in tuxedos and white ruffled shirts emerged from behind a screen and straddled each chair. An equal number of violinists took their places beneath a circle of flickering gaslights.

A circular curtain was raised from the middle of the arena. Curled on the floor under a single gaslight was Miriam Rathenau, sheathed in black tights and leotard.

Softly, slowly, Ravel's music began. She uncoiled languorously, her face expressionless. Erich thought her the most desirable creature he had ever seen. She stretched, swayed—and resumed the fetal position.

Almost imperceptibly the music increased in tempo and volume. This time when the woman stretched, she remained on her knees. The audience's breathing quickened and the circle of male dancers half-stood and inched their chairs toward the raised stage.

Stopped.

Sighed.

Miriam raised her head and slowly came to her feet as the tempo of the music picked up. Erich glanced at the audience, then up at Perón, who was smiling. Women eyed their partners who, in turn, ogled Miriam.

The male dancers removed their tuxedo jackets, threw them aside and inched their chairs forward. The music and the audience and the circle of male dancers were a moving articulation of lust. One dancer, kicking over his chair, climbed up onto the stage. Another followed, and another. The three of them crawled toward her as she turned, lifting her leg higher and higher until it seemed she would surely fall or split herself.

And then the music stopped and the gaslight, flickering one last time, went out.

"Brava!" a man called out. "More!"

After a long silence, the applause began. Despite Miriam's bravura performance, it was, at best, restrained.

Perón bent down close to Erich's ear. "You Germans are a strange breed," he whispered. "On the same night, in the same place, you execute your friend and then view this celebration of life. Neither time have you shown emotion. In Buenos Aires, both would move us to tears."

C HAPTER THIRTY-NINE

With the Games a thing of the past, Sol waited for the *Juden Unerwünscht* signs to go up again—like an expectant father waiting for the birth of a child he knows will be deformed. Every evening, before dinner, he went for a walk. Body throbbing with tension, he wandered Berlin, looking, listening, watching. Though he was accustomed to the noise and odor, tonight the city's sounds and smells assailed him as if the honking and engines and exhaust were somehow exaggerated. There seemed to be an undercurrent, an undefined heightening of the usual cacophony and stench, as if the city of which his family had been a part for eleven generations had become an enormous and unfamiliar factory producing machinery he neither recognized nor understood.

Something drove him out of the city. He had refused Erich's repeated offers to pay for a ticket to the Games, saying that if they disbanded the Oranienburg detention center before the Olympics, he would believe that the signs would stay down—that the worst was over. If that happened, he would buy as many tickets as his pockets could hold and hand them out to the Jews of Berlin. They would come to cheer, hold hands and sing *Deutschland über Alles*.

Sweating profusely from the effort, he walked five kilometers to the Olympia Stadium, to see for himself that all was as surely gone as the Olympic village organizer and builder, Captain Wolfgang Fürstner. Replaced at the last moment as village commandant because he was Jewish, he had calmly put a pistol in his mouth and pulled the trigger.

Still, the Games had been good for business. Foreign visitors bought marks at rates set especially low and, for the first time since Friedrich Weisser's beating, the shop made a nice profit.

Sol had avoided seeing the Games but there had been no avoiding the loudspeakers spread throughout the city. The triumphant cry of the predominantly German crowd calling out, "YESSA O-VENS! YESSA O-VENS!" rang in Solomon's ears as he watched the last of the dismantling process taking place at the stadium.

Though personally delighted by Jesse Owens' triumphs, Sol predicted they would bring nothing but trouble. Even a fool could tell that the Führer was livid over the American's victories. The world's cameras and journalists had recorded the festival of color and sound, the long blue banners showing the five Olympic rings, the red banners decorated with swastikas hung from poles fifteen meters high. The world pictured Berlin roped with evergreens and gold. Thanks to Movietone News, they had seen Hitler Youth bands, brown shirts and short pants scrupulously starched, move through Olympia Stadium's arch and onto the dull red cinder track; they had heard snare drums rattling out marches and loudspeakers playing waltzes and quickstep marches. They had laughed at Hitler's heavy-handed architectural approximation of the grandeur of the Roman Coliseum, his unschooled vision of a new Berlin.

None of it meant anything. The truce was transient, the memories fleeting. Temporary—the operative word of the times.

The Games, the memories, the present—all vaguely moving shadows.

"O-VENS!"

"*SIEG HEIL!*"

"O-VENS!"

"*SIEG HEIL!*"

Head pounding, Solomon began the hike home. When his head and chest began to throb so hard that each step took his breath away, he left the Olympic Highway and hurried along the Konigsallee. Pain notwithstanding, he would be home in time for a whispered *Shabbas* Service around his mother's starched white linen tablecloth and candlesticks—his sister's most recent letter propped against them: *Mama's fine, I'm fine, when are you and Miriam coming so that you can be fine, too?*

Near the Imperial Palace, he had to stop. The noise that spilled from adjacent alleys and avenues engulfed him. Deafened him. Buffeted him as if it were alive.

Then, reflected in a department-store window, he saw the sign that had entered his subconscious and registered its effect on his body before his conscious mind could deal with it: JEWS NOT WELCOME.

Crowds surged around him, smiling and unnoticing. Cars growled and windows leered, tall buildings wavered—and the pain worsened.

He walked on, holding his chest.

Heart attack. Twenty-eight years old, and about to drop dead.

By the time he reached Franzosische Strasse, his chest and throat felt constricted and an icy cold had enveloped him, bringing with it sweat and chills. The sidewalk seemed to roll beneath him, burning his feet.

It's really all gone, Sol thought desperately. The banners, the cheers, the drummers and athletes marching in revue, the doves and balloons and the promises of peace…the journalists, parroting Hitler's proclamation of a Golden Age not only for Germany but for the world.

The city had returned to normal.

A worker in a white painter's smock watched Sol curiously, then picked up a second sign. Expertly splaying out the edges with a yellow bristled brush, he slapped it up:

SHOP HERE! JEWS NOT ADMITTED!
WE GUARANTEE JEWISH FILTH
WON'T DEFILE THIS ESTABLISHMENT

The worker smiled and nodded, his face distorted like an image seen through a fisheye lens. Sol took off his glasses and rapidly cleaned them. Sweat stung his eyes.

Around him, unconcerned, people moved at their normal pace.

He leaned against a brick wall that proclaimed DEATH TO ALL JEWS. The pain in his chest was a jackhammer. The city's noise roared in his ears like an animal. He made his way laboriously along the wall, sliding a hand along its rough surface. At the end of the wall he sank to his knees, teeth gritted in agony.

A white-haired shopkeeper dressed in the black robes of orthodoxy was taping a Jewish star on his shop window. "You all right?" He stepped away as though Sol were unclean.

"Must get home," Sol mumbled in Yiddish.

The man looked around furtively and then bent over Solomon. "Are you ill?" he asked anxiously. "In trouble? Get inside, man. Our enemies are everywhere."

Sol struggled to his feet. He stared at the *Mogen David* the man had pasted on the window; the Star of David bulged and receded as he struggled for breath and tried to focus.

"Why?" He pointed at it.

"Orders. They say they'll leave us in peace if we announce our heritage. So what if Gentiles don't buy from us, at least we'll keep our businesses."

"You believe that!"

"Please, be quiet!" Gathering his scissors and roll of tape, the shopkeeper withdrew into his store like a snail into its shell. When the door shut with a click, the city noise again became a carnivore—some ancient god escaped from back alleys.

Suddenly Solomon knew it for what it was.

Half running, half staggering, he reeled down the street, away from the beast of oncoming riot. His breaths came in gasps. His chest felt white-hot with pain. Auto horns roared in warning and people hurried, looking fearful as they made a path for a madman.

Father! Miriam!

Half an hour later Sol burst into the shop and slammed the door, its bell jangling. Clutching the accouterment cabinet, dripping sweat onto its glass, he fought for breath. His father was in the alcove of the basement stairs, holding the open curtain in his hand. He did not turn around.

"Make a star!" Sol cried. "Put it in the window. They're coming now! In the daylight! I can feel it!"

"What use is there in doing anything—now," Jacob muttered.

"I met another shopkeeper. He was—"

"Only two people besides our family knew that combination." Jacob's voice was low and hoarse. With a sweep of his hand, he indicated the open safe set in the alcove wall. It was empty.

Half a minute passed before Sol realized that they had been robbed and that he knew who had done it. Looking toward the ceiling friezes, he made a sound that was a mix of sobbing and laughter. "Should I summon the Weissers?" he asked sarcastically. "They really should be told."

Jacob wheeled around, his face contorted by fury. "Has my son learned so little? You won't find the Weissers home today. They've abandoned us! Taken what they could, sent away and squirreled away what they could, and abandoned us!"

Solomon heard a new sound inside his head. The wailing cry of a mourner. "I knew it!" he said. "I knew our families should have sat down together months ago and divided everything! One pfennig for you, one for us. One for you—"

"Stop it!"

"The Weissers could have had this case." Sol slapped the one that held the accouterments. "They would have liked that, don't you think? We could have had the one with the pipes. They could have taken the cigars, we the cigarettes. We would get Recha, they would get—"

Jacob raised his hand. "I said stop!" As if involuntarily, his hand continued its motion and he slapped Solomon across the cheek. He was staring, horrified, at his hand when Miriam dashed into the shop.

"Sol! I went upstairs to borrow some yeast from the Weissers. Their door is open and they're not home. I'm worried. There's some kind of commotion down near Leipzigerplatz. I heard someone say it's another food riot." She paused for breath and seemed to notice for the first time that something was amiss.

"I slapped my son, and for what?" Jacob said to no one in particular. "May God forgive me."

"It's not a food riot, Miriam." Sol put his hand on his father's shoulder, his other on his cheek. "It's all right, Papa," he whispered. His chest still hurt, but it was a new hurt, one of loss more than of fear. Much more was gone than the four years' meager profits they had not dared place in the bank to be confiscated. So much more. The Weissers had been like second parents to him and Recha. Jacob and Friedrich had worked together for decades; Jacob gave Friedrich not only a start but a career.

What fundamental madness could cause this? The Nazis? Friedrich's beating? The Depression? All too simplistic.

Father and son looked at one another in terror as shouts and gunshots and sirens echoed from all directions. Then they watched from the door as a phalanx of Nazis moved toward them, striding up Friedrich Ebert Strasse with pistols and clubs and the trophies of rampage. A ruddy-faced Goliath, a swastika armband on one sleeve, a Red Cross armband on the other, marched at the apex of the mob. Whenever he signaled to the men and boys behind him, five or six would break off and enter shops. Sol could hear screams and shrieked prayers rise above the sounds of carnage.

"We must get a star up, Papa!" He scrambled for tape and scissors among the low drawers of the accouterment case.

Arms crossed, Miriam stood on the sidewalk, tears marking her cheeks. "They're destroying everything...all that is or might be Jewish."

"Even where there are stars?" Jacob held his glasses slightly away from his face in an effort to see farther.

"Everything."

"It is the end." He stumbled back inside the shop. There was about him the look of a man hollowed by despair. His face was utterly without emotion and his shoulders sagged as though time itself had bent and then broken his back. "I've seen the beginning of the end. Now I shall see the end. We have all become children of darkness."

He walked in a daze toward the alcove and, after wiping his glasses with his Reichsbanner handkerchief and replacing them on his nose, stood staring at the safe. In a monotone, he said, "The basement. Into the cellar, children."

"They'll come there to ransack the inventory," Sol said.

Jacob dug in a drawer and held up a hammer. "Perhaps, but you will be in the sewer."

The hair on the back of Sol's neck bristled. Some inner sense told him that the chest pains he had experienced had as much to do with whatever lay in the cellar as it did with the terror outside. Numb, he followed his father and Miriam downstairs—toward what? he wondered. His boyhood nightmares?

"We'll never break the weld in time, Papa."

"What choice do we have but to try?" Jacob searched along a top shelf and located the boys' crowbar. Miriam held it against the weld while Solomon, using it like a chisel, bashed against its neck with the hammer. Jacob stood guard at the steps, listening between the ringing of metal against metal.

"I think they're at the apartments! Hurry, my son!" Solomon did not waste time replying. Ceasing to worry about the possibility of missing the crowbar neck and hitting Miriam's hands, he smashed down again and again with all his strength. Sparks flew, some scattering across the limestone before dissipating. Like glowworms, he thought, sweat running in rivulets down his temples and face. Fireflies come to dance on the dead.

"They're outside the shop, Solomon! Faster!"

The weld peeled apart in metal curlicues. Miriam's

eyes were filled with fear, but she kept the bar steady, her whitened knuckles as strained as leather about to be pierced by an awl.

From above came laughter, then the sound of splintering glass.

"Break it, Solomon!" Jacob said hoarsely. "Break it now!"

There was the thumping of boots. Shouted orders. More laughter. The thud of a display case crashing to the floor.

"It won't break, Papa! There's not enough time."

"*Baruch ato adonai*," Jacob prayed. He added a prayer of his own. "May you grant my son the strength of Samson and the wisdom of the king whose name he bears."

Sol jammed the crowbar into the weld and, with Miriam's help, pried down. His muscles screamed and he could feel his veins, enlarged and pulsing in his neck and forehead.

Jacob hurried over and together they pushed down.

The weld gave with a crack. The grate faltered and slid sideways in its rim, and Sol thrust the crowbar back under the lip.

"If Erich's among them, he'll know we're in the sewer," Miriam said.

"If Erich's among them," Sol grunted as he used the crowbar to raise the grate enough to grip it with his fingertips, "then life's not worth living anyway."

The grate creaked and fell back against the wall.

"Go!" Jacob said. "Go!"

Sol lowered himself into the hole, found the two-by-four and dropped the final meter, landing on the rotted, dismantled packing crates. Jumping to his feet, he took hold of Miriam's legs as she lowered herself. They fell back together, and he heard her stifle a startled laugh.

"Your turn next, Papa."

On hands and knees, Jacob Freund looked down into the sewer, surveying its bracken walls in what little light the drain hole allowed. "A man of my years should leap down into such a netherworld?" His tone was oddly flippant. "And who would shut the grate? Are we acrobats who can stand on one another's shoulders?"

"There's a board here, Papa!" Sol started to climb up.

The grate clanged down.

"Papa? What're you doing!"

Fingers through the grating, Jacob Freund looked down with kindly, gray, bespectacled eyes that revealed an acceptance of the world's cruelty. "This we do my way, children." He was whispering, yet his voice seemed to fill the sewer. "First I'm going to cover the grate with empty boxes, then I intend to go upstairs and offer those...those...offer them cigars to commemorate their victory over the helpless."

"But Herr Freund—" Miriam peered up into the drain. "Please, Papa! All of us, or none!"

Sol struggled to open the grate again but could not lift it; his father held it down. Even through the small slats, he could see the slight, wry smile on his father's lips.

"I came through the Great War with but a broken nose and an outbreak of cynicism," Jacob said. "I wish to do battle again. Alone. That is my right as head of this family. Now hush, both of you. Let a not-so-young man have his way."

"Papa...I love you."

"And I love you, Solomon Isaac Freund. No man could have asked for a finer son." He moved away from the grate. Moments later, just as Solomon jumped down from the board and shook his head in bewilderment, Jacob's face was above them once again. Poking his glasses between the slats, he let them drop. Solomon, catching them, looked up in confusion. "If I should die, make sure I'm buried wearing my spectacles," his father said. "I wish to see the face of our enemy when I point him out to God."

He looked at Solomon and Miriam and muttered, in Hebrew, "May God provide." He placed the boxes over the grate.

Chapter forty

Residuals of light danced before Solomon's eyes as he tried to accustom himself to the darkness. Clinging to Miriam, he listened to his father ascend the steps.

"Maybe the Nazis won't hurt him when they see that he's old and half blind," Miriam said.

She sounded unconvinced. Knowing words would only betray his own despair, Sol remained silent. Blackness reigned. It swirled around him, enveloping him in its shroud. The *plook...plook* of dripping water resounded through the sewer, and he thought he heard the scuttling of rats.

The place was colder than he remembered. He welcomed Miriam's embrace as much for its warmth as for its comfort. He tried to concentrate, to control his ragged breathing as the shortness of breath that had seized him on the streets returned to deflate his lungs. Pain settled on his chest like a great weight, but this was no heart attack…he knew that now. A sense of such foreboding filled him that he was sure Miriam must feel it too.

He let go of her and stared into the darkness. Waiting for the laughter, the voices, the images.

"I can hear them up there," Miriam whispered. "Why don't they leave!"

As if in answer to her words, the laughter came, rippling through the sewer.

"No! Go away!" Sol shouted.

"Be quiet, Solomon." Miriam placed a hand over Sol's mouth. "What is it? Are you in pain?" She removed her hand.

He shook her off, fighting the explosion of light in his head.

Miriam gripped his shoulder. "Don't let go of me again, Sol. I'm afraid."

"Me too." They embraced. Upstairs, there was faint scuffling. He could barely hear it above the pounding of his heart and the ghostly laughter that he knew did not come from the shop. Laughter that stopped when a cobalt-blue glow appeared at the end of the sewer and an image of a young black man began to take shape—

—*the black man's skin shines with a blue fire.* He is naked except for a small piece of torn blanket that covers his genitals. He sits perfectly still, staring outward, face expressionless. A white man, monocled and wearing a white, bloodstained laboratory smock, moves toward him, scalpel in hand—

"No!" Solomon reached toward the image. "They've come back!" he whispered, transfixed by a second image that materialized at the other end of the sewer.

—a paraffin lamp casts a blue-black shadow across a rude table in the center of a one-roomed wooden shack. Snow blows through gaps in the wall-boards. In one corner, a figure huddles close to a brazier's red coals, its smoke veiling the low ceiling—a man in a ragged army overcoat and woolen scarf; frostbite has scabbed and pockmarked his dark, sunken cheeks. His eyes are dull, his hands wrapped in bloodstained gauze. An emaciated woman wrapped in an old blanket, an ancient carbine slung across her back, leans over him. Carefully she unwraps the gauze from one of his hands. The fingers are gangrenous stumps—

I am losing my mind, Solomon thought. The riot, the emptied safe, the degradation—together they had caused him to snap.

A fit of shivering seized him, and with it came a voice.

—Three days now the clouds have held, an old man says. Standing knee-high in snow, he looks toward the sky. A worker next to him grabs hold of a corpse and flops it down as if it is a sandbag. The old man glances at it, then at a row of fresh bodies. The setting sun has cast ribbons of russet and gold out of congealed blood and military uniforms—

"Try to see it," Sol told Miriam, though he knew he was asking the impossible.

"What are you talking about?"

"Look!" He turned her around forcefully. "There! There is another! Can you not hear the music?"

—gossamer veils of blue dust-moted light filter through a stained-glass window onto a man seated at a pipe organ. He is blond and broad shouldered, and looks as athletic as he is musically talented. The Bach concerto he plays

reverberates throughout the tall reaches of a rococo church that was obviously once a castle—

"Pull yourself together, Sol!" Miriam's voice was taut with terror. "There's nothing down here! Why don't you think about your papa! He's the one upstairs with...with..."

Papa! Sol blinked and drew a sharp breath as the vision vanished. Was that what the images were telling him—that if he stayed hidden down here, he was no better than the dybbuk?

Running his hands along the moss-slimed bricks, he made sure the board was properly emplaced and again boosted himself onto it. "I don't care what Papa said. I must go up and do what I can."

"Don't be a fool, Sol." Miriam tugged at his trousers. "You'll only make matters worse."

"Have you forgotten what those bastards did to Herr Weisser?" Boots clumped down the stairs. Sol stood suspended between the board and the grating, unable to tell if what he was hearing was out there or inside his head.

"That can't be your father," Miriam whispered. "They are heavier boots...."

The footsteps reached the bottom of the stairs, and stopped.

Jars crashed, followed by what Sol supposed were boxes being pulled from shelves. He heard grunts and the tearing of cardboard. The boxes on top of the grate were sure to be next.

Then, from what seemed the top of the stairs came orders. "As much as you can carry...Havanas if you find any, and American cigarettes."

The boots went up the stairs, and down and up a second time. Then, silence.

"Sol, I smell smoke!"

Sol lifted his nose. His sense of smell had already begun to adapt to the sewer's noxious odors. "You sure?"

Miriam sniffed. "I think so."

"They must be burning whatever inventory they've chosen not to steal." The smoke had begun to penetrate his nostrils and sting his eyes. "We're going up." His matter-of-fact tone reflected his relief at having to deal with something tangible, no matter how dreadful. "We are not going to suffocate down here."

He climbed back down and dislodged the board. "If we go up this way we might be climbing right into a fire or…" Or into Nazi arms, he thought. "There's another drain beneath the furrier's. Maybe when the cabaret was sealed up the workmen didn't realize Erich and I had left the padlock open. It's worth a try."

They went along the sewer, fingers against the walls for guidance, and located the large board at the other end. After hoisting himself up, he helped Miriam.

The grating was unlocked.

"Push!" he told her.

As the grate opened, he remembered the time he and Erich had tried to pick the lock on the cabaret door. Sol had said he wanted to leave the place alone in honor of Rathenau's death; Erich had simply laughed and insisted. The lock had proved easy to jimmy, but they'd not been able to open the door. The workmen had apparently bolted it from the inside, for added security, and had exited through the furrier's upstairs, much to Erich's annoyance and Sol's relief.

He crawled out and helped Miriam through the drain. Holding hands, they groped their way through the subbasement and up the stairs to the deserted cabaret. Musty linen covered the tables. The chairs stacked up against them were netted with spider webs, and above them, from street level, the small stained-glass windows cast a green glow across the dance floor.

He felt an odd sense of wanting her to dance with him and pretend for a moment that dancing and music and love were as commonplace as hatred. Instead they hurried across the room, up the metal stairs, and unbolted and unlocked the entrance door.

It had begun to rain. Miriam started up the steps that led to the street. Sol held her back. He waited, listening for the tromp of boots, watching for them to appear at street level. When none appeared, they ascended to the street. It looked like a war zone. Sticks, bricks, and garbage lay everywhere. Glass from shattered windows gleamed in the waning light. From the direction of Unter den Linden came the sounds of ongoing riot.

Good Yomtov—happy holiday—he thought grimly as, heads down against the rain and the fear of being recognized, they raced to the shop. One of the windows had been knocked out, the other was cracked. The door hung lopsided on a single hinge. Smoke filled the room.

Sol pressed his arm against his mouth and nose, and indicated for Miriam to do the same. She stood in the center of the shop, peering over her arm, quietly crying. Her muffled sobs made him realize that despite the day's horror these were the first tears she had shed. She was amazing, he thought, looking at her as he stumbled around in search of his father.

Display cases lay knocked over and shattered. Glass, cigars, cigarettes and smoking accouterments cluttered the floor. He backtracked to the door and, lowering his arm from his face, peered out at the carnage.

"Must have taken him outside," he said.

Miriam wiped her eyes and lowered her hand. "Maybe he's all right and went downstairs to put out the fire." She pointed at the ribbon of smoke seeping beneath the curtain of the alcove to the basement. "Most of the smoke is going out the door, so he shouldn't be suffering too badly from inhalation."

Sol hurried across the room and, with a growing sense of doom, he threw open the curtain.

Jacob Freund hung upside down, his feet attached to the overhead plumbing by a strand of thick wire. His eyes were open. His mouth had been gagged with a Nazi armband, and his Iron Cross dangled from his neck.

"Papa!" Sol felt the blood leave his face. He reached for his father, but his resolve gave way, and he sagged against the wall. "No! Oh, God, no!"

After a moment he took a deep breath and managed to stand upright. He wedged his fingers between the old man's neck and the twisted ribbon that had stopped the breathing. "May it go easier for you in the afterlife," he cried bitterly. "May your soul flourish in *Olam Haba*."

He laid his cheek against his father's flesh. Already it was becoming cold.

Chapter Forty-one

I truly loved Herr Freund. Tears rolled down Miriam's face. She turned from watching the rain—said to be sent by God when a good man died—to watching Solomon. He cut the body down from the rafter and placed it gently on the floor. Pulling up a stool from behind the counter, he removed his shoes, sat down, and wept.

Yes, my Solomon. Cry for your papa, and for us.

Obedient to Jewish tradition, she neither spoke nor attempted to comfort Solomon, allowing him opportunity to give fullest expression to his sorrow. Later, they would reminisce; it would comfort Sol and lend dignity to Papa.

She wiped away her tears; they would have to wait. The Freunds had taught her about life and, when Sol's grandparents passed away during the previous year, about the dignity of death. Her concern now must be for Sol's well-being.

She made a mental list of death rites. How inappropriate—and inconvenient, she thought, with a stab of guilt—that Jacob had died on the eve of one of Judaism's most joyous holidays, the Festival of the Harvest.

Tradition demanded that he be buried quickly, especially since tomorrow was Succot; the interment could not be on the first day of a festival. She would have to find a member of the sacred society organized by the Jewish community to take care of burials. Succot would preempt the traditional observance of *shiva*—the first week of mourning—and the month of mourning that usually followed, but she was not sure if it preempted the twelve Hebrew months of mourning for a parent, after which Sol would be forbidden to mourn overtly. She had to find food for the Meal of Comfort— bread, to differentiate the meal from a snack; an egg, to symbolize life's continuum—and food for tomorrow's Succot meal.

She remembered the year she and her family built a *succah* in the gardens at the estate. They erected the roof of the hut in the ancient way, with roots and plants, trying to make it as exposed and insecure as the huts the Jews had used during their forty years of wandering. Then they celebrated their trust in divine protection— Mama and Papa and her grandparents leading the family processional around the estate, branches of citron, palm, myrtle and willow held aloft to signify God's omnipresence. And now where was God! Hadn't He tested them enough?

She glanced across the street, and shivered. It had grown dark and the lamps were lit. The men who had done this could easily be waiting there, hiding in the darkness inside the apartment entrance.

Rites. Concentrate on rites, not fears. Complete the respect and honor due all people, even the dead. If she could not acquire a white robe for Jacob's burial, she would see to it that he was properly covered with his *tallis*.

She quietly repeated the prayer said upon taking leave of a mourner during *shiva:* May the Lord comfort you with all the mourners of Zion and Jerusalem.

Sol did not raise his head.

Somewhere, in some deep part of him, he would know where she had gone, that she had not deserted him, she thought, walking to the door of the shop. She had not sat *shiva* for Uncle Walther, her parents, or Oma; she was not raised that way. Some rites had made sense to her even then, like covering mirrors to avoid vanity and only reading books or chapters dealing with laws of mourning. Other rituals, though, had seemed irrelevant: bathing only for cleanliness, wearing the same clothes for a week. Having seen the comfort they took from ritual during their week of *shiva* for Sol's grandparents, she had begun to understand.

She reached for the door handle, but stepped back as a siren screamed—a sound as common to Berliners as the linden trees on the Avenue. A Mercedes with the familiar SS insignia painted on the door pulled up at the apartment building, and a tall SS man whose hair shone silver in the lamp light climbed from the car.

He stared at the shop, then turned toward the apartment building, where a Gestapo agent had appeared. The older man pointed at the shop. The younger nodded, returned to the car, and came away with a clipboard which held several sheets of paper. Judging by the way he ran his index finger down page after page, Miriam figured it was some kind of list. When he had flipped the last page over, the younger man nodded to his companion, and they both laughed. They waved as if at somebody in the apartments. Car doors slammed, and they drove away.

Miriam turned back into the shop. "Solomon," she said softly.

He looked up at her, his face stained with tears.

"I'm sorry, Sol. I wouldn't disturb you, but we have to go back." She knew not quite how—or how much—to tell him. "We have to go back into the sewer. They're still out there—the ones who…" She could not go on, despite the urgency.

"We have to take Papa with us." Sol stood up. "We can't leave him here."

"There's no time for that," Miriam said. "He would not want us to die for his body." She searched for the words that Solomon had taught her, the words that described the afterlife, where a man was judged and where his soul thrived. "He is in *Olam Haba*."

The shop's cellar was too smoke-filled to allow them to descend that way, so after furtive glances up and down the street they returned to Kaverne. Like two small frightened children, they helped each other into the sewer. Please, let them not come looking for us, Miriam prayed as Sol closed the grate.

"There's no way to cover the grate, Miri." His voice was hoarse from weeping.

She nodded, though she knew he could not see her

in the dark. When he sat down, she moved beside him and they held each other in silence until, finally, she could hear by his breathing that he had dozed off. Only then did she allow herself the luxury of more tears.

"*Bruqah!*" Sol shouted.

Miriam awakened into blackness. Her skin felt clammy; her clothes clung to her, and the darkness felt like oil against her face. She shifted her weight and soothed Sol, hoping to stop his nightmares.

"What do you want of me!" He shoved himself from her arms.

"*What do you want?*" the sewer echoed. "*You want...*"

"It's Miriam! I'm here, Sol!"

He found her hand and held it fast. "Tell me it isn't true. Any of it."

"Oh God, how I wish I could!"

"Papa!" He began to weep anew.

When the tears subsided, he said, "The images, Miri. They're still here. A voice kept saying, *Bruqah*, and another asked me over and over, 'Do you hold your seasons dear, Solomon Freund? Is this your season of sadness?'"

Letting go of him, she stood up and groped through the dark, trying to get her bearings.

"Go away!" he cried out.

"Solomon?"

"Miriam?"

She heard him sigh in frustration, and she wondered, as she had before, if his fear of the visions was tainted by his longing for them. Lately, when he talked about his childhood visions, he had tried to convince her, and himself, that the horrors of the sewer had been foreknowledge of what Berlin and the Fatherland would become. They were a barrier, he said, against the insanity.

Tonight she could understand his inability to function, but there had been other times when things mystical seemed to call to him more loudly than his need for her. What must it be like, she thought, living with scenes and voices you could not share? She tried to imagine what Sol had described to her, images seen as if through the aperture of a camera, widening until they crystallized into visions of terror. Laughter mingling with the music-box melody of "Glowworm" as an apparition clarified and dissolved—

"I'll be...all right," he said.

When he said nothing else, she found she needed the reassurance of his voice as a buffer against a silence broken only by dripping water. "How long do you think we've been down here?" she asked him.

"Hours. Who knows. What's it matter, anyway?"

The voice came from below her, and she realized he was still sitting down.

"You think they're still out there?" she asked. "They must go home to sleep sometime. I—"

She could hear his breathing, and she made her way back to him. When she touched him, he put his head against her legs, his arms embracing her at the knees. "We will fix up the shop, Miri. And this place. We'll be safe down here. We'll make it comfortable, you'll see—"

Her hands found his chin and she tilted his head back, bent and awkwardly kissed him. "I'm going to go now," she told him. "Sleep while I'm gone. I'll find help for us—for Papa...."

There was no point in finishing her sentence. She would have to do this alone, though for a few moments she would need his help.

He boosted her, and she climbed from the sewer without much difficulty. She did not know exactly what it was she meant to do, only that something needed to be done. They could not hide forever. The apartment was out of bounds until they were certain the men had found some other form of entertainment, she thought grimly. Burying Jacob was out of the question until a member of the sacred society was found or until Sol had calmed down enough to make rational decisions. But...something.

She entered the shop and made her way to the door, averting her eyes to avoid seeing Jacob's body.

The street, swept with driving rain, was deserted. She cursed the bell that jangled as she opened the door and shivered as a blast of rain and night air hit her. Leaving the door ajar, she went back inside to get her coat and the old boa she had taken to the shop in the hopes of selling it. Ever since she had lost her job at Ananas, she had looked at her few possessions as nothing more than eggs and milk and bread. Things had been better during the Games, but she had harbored no illusions about their remaining that way.

There was only one way they could hope to survive for the long term. They had to leave Germany. Any idea of staying and trying to put the shop to rights was crazy—but leaving required papers, or excellent forgeries.

She went out into the rain, walking fast but in no particular direction, not slowing even as she passed

Ananas. The club's new owners had corrected the place's so-called abuses. Symbolic of peace and prosperity, an eagle clutching a swastika medallion in its claws blazed from the marquee like a beacon. Everything about it promised sanctuary—though not for her. Nowadays the place was almost always filled with military revelry.

The door opened and two men came out. One wore the uniform of the Abwehr. For a moment she thought it was Erich, though she knew he never frequented the club anymore. Chilled to the bone, she stepped into the street, silently acknowledging where it was her feet were taking her: to see the Rittmeister.

He was the only one who could help them. He could find a way to call off the SS, a way to bury Jacob Freund, a way to get them out of the country. Or at least the necessary papers. Or—

Angry at her desperation, she strode toward his apartment. He would have to help them! What choice did he have, after his father robbed them blind? He too had loved Jacob Freund, in whatever way he was capable of loving. Surely he could not refuse!

But he could, and she knew it.

After the Olympics, he had legally divested himself of his former surname, due to its association with the Jewish shop. *Erich Alois* he called himself now. If he could do that, she thought, he could certainly refuse to take any responsibility for their safety.

She was across the street from the building where Erich lived when she realized she would be unable to go inside after all. Anything was better than accepting help from Erich or, worse, having him refuse to help them.

Twenty meters away through the fog and drizzle, a rotund, heavy-jowled man wearing a fur-collared overcoat and carrying a walking stick had stopped beneath a street lamp and was staring toward her. Someone she knew? She squinted in his direction.

"*Wie viel!*" he called out. "How much?"

She smiled somberly. Must look quite a sight, she thought—the boa bedraggled, hair rain-soaked and plastered to her head. Small wonder he thought her a prostitute!

He rapidly approached. "Let's not waste time!" His accent clearly pegged him as British. "Answer me! I asked you how much!"

Impatience had turned his tone ugly.

"Sorry, *Schatzie*," Miriam said. "I'm through for the night."

"Not good enough for you?" Putting down the tip of his walking stick to balance himself, he stepped across the water accumulating in the gutter and grabbed hold of her arm.

"Get away!" She tried to shake off his hand, but he tightened his grip.

"Look at you! Why would anyone pay good money for such a tramp! You should pay *me* to take you home."

He shoved her aside. Caught off-balance she stumbled and with a cry fell into the street. She huddled there, head down, sobbing softly and uncaring that she was forming a dam in the drainage.

The man laughed and reached down with his walking stick as if to help her lift herself. "Come on. I'll scrub you down and you can service me while I dine."

Miriam batted away the stick, climbed from the gutter

with the dignity of a dancer recovering from a fall during a performance, and unsteadily gained her feet. Throwing the boa over her shoulder, she started across the street. The heel of her left shoe had been loosened by the fall and she walked awkwardly, but she held her head high and her face was set like stone against the slanting rain.

"A filet of sole for a superior performance."

"I would rather starve."

The man shook his stick. "Come back, or I'll report you to the Gestapo for soliciting! I know you're a Jew! I can smell it."

Miriam quickened her pace. It was enough to cause her heel, already weakened, to collapse. Even her dancer's training did not enable her to stay upright.

She hit the sidewalk clumsily, in a sprawl. She heard the man laugh as she drew herself up with her arms and unsteadily climbed to her feet. She bent over, balancing precariously on one foot as she tried to remove the broken shoe.

"I saw you from my window." Erich stepped into the light and reached to take hold of her shoulders before she toppled again.

She stepped away from him, nearly going down again in the process.

"That little otter's mine by first right, soldier." The man in the overcoat ambled toward them. "Go back to your flat. If you want to fuck her you'll have to wait your turn."

Erich stepped back, poised on the balls of his feet, eyeing the man coldly.

"Anyone can see she's Jewish." The man looked startled by Erich's officer insignia. "First come, first—"

"She doesn't have a trace of Jewish blood in her."

"Oh? Friend of yours, Herr Rittmeister? I'd be more careful of the company I keep if I were you."

"That's enough." Erich's voice was dangerously low.

"Whatever you say, Rittmeister. You want to tarnish your soul by protecting a Jewish whore, that's your business."

Without warning, Erich's foot snapped up. The Briton tried to block with his walking stick, but did not get it horizontal fast enough. The kick struck his abdomen, and the man's eyes bulged. He stared at Erich as though attempting to hold his breath, then bent over, clutching his midriff. Air issued through his lips. Erich hit him in the face with his fist. His ring, with its curled metal center, gouged the man's cheek, and he toppled.

How she'd like to place the stick across that fat neck and strangle the swine, she thought. Strangle them both! "You're quite the gentleman," she said angrily, furious at herself and the whole situation.

"I'll kill him if you want."

"Don't be an ass." She finally got her left shoe off, stepped over the fallen man and clumped through the puddles, hurrying away from Erich.

He caught up as she rounded the corner onto Mauerstrasse. "I don't know what you think you're doing wandering around the streets in the middle of the night," he said, taking her arm. "You'd better come with me before someone worse finds you."

She shook him off. "Leave me alone."

"You may be sure that man will go to the authorities. You'll be detained before you ever reach—"

"I couldn't care less."

"Don't be a fool, Miriam!"

Wheeling, she faced him. "What would you have me do? Register a complaint with the police? Go with you, perhaps even to the home you and your Nazi cronies stole from me?" Clasping her hands as though in prayer, she gazed into his eyes with the overacted, maudlin look that until recently had so characterized romantic films. "Shall we summon a carriage and a team of four to whisk us away to your estate, my love? Maybe while we're there His Highness Gauleiter Goebbels will set our lives aright. Think that if I fuck him, he will give me back what has been stolen from us, or grant me clemency from hunger? Maybe he can do better than that. Maybe he or His Holiness Adolph Hitler can raise Jacob Freund from the dead!"

She broke into sobs.

"Jacob? What about Jacob! Dead?"

She nodded, and the world began to swim. Trying to keep from blacking out, she did not resist when he put an arm across her shoulders. He guided her into the building.

In the smoky Bierstube on the ground floor a trombone was blowing *oom-pah-pah* and people were laughing and clinking glasses. She forced herself up two steep stair flights, Erich holding her to keep her from collapsing. On the third-floor landing he pulled her to face him, clutching her hands with his, against his chest. "What's this about Jacob?"

"They...they hanged him. Oh, God." She felt dizzy again. "Brownshirts broke into the shop and...your parents...I need to lie down."

"My parents! They were attacked *again*?"

"They got away. Got away with—"

"Thank God for that." He inserted the key, kicked open the door, and maneuvered her inside. "And Solomon? Is he okay?"

"What do you care about Solomon!"

Erich helped her onto the bed and, pulling a blanket across her feet, looked at her quizzically. He appeared stunned, and she wondered if he was focused on an issue he had hoped never to have to examine too thoroughly. Then slowly he appeared to regain the control that she knew was as essential to him as breath itself. He finished covering her legs with the blanket, and leaned over her.

"Solomon," he said huskily, "is my brother."

She sensed it was the truth. At least for the moment.

Chapter forty-two

She's beautiful, Erich thought. *Even drenched, she's beautiful.*

Miriam held out her hands as if to stop the world from spinning, exhaled audibly and sat up, blinking. She rubbed her eyes and, shaking her head ruefully, put her hands over her face as if to shield herself from grief.

Gently Erich lifted her hands aside. Her eyes were downcast and her face looked haggard. "Dry your hair." He handed her a towel. "You'll feel better."

She sat with the towel against her left cheek, slowly rocking.

"The man outside. Did he hurt you?"

She shook her head. "Only my pride. At least, what's left of my pride." Her trembling increased. Tears rolled down her cheeks. He lifted the wet boa from her shoulders and threw it in the sink, thinking fleetingly that it looked like a drowned cat. Then he pulled up a chair and sat on it, backward, facing her.

"I knew it would come to this!" He made a fist.

"There was an officer with a list. An SS officer."

"Silver-haired?"

She nodded disconsolately.

"That *bastard!*" He punched the air.

"There is more." From the strain in her face he knew she was on the verge of hysteria. He patted her wrist to calm her, but she jerked away. She took a deep breath. "Late this afternoon, Sol went out for a walk. I was at home. Your parents were minding the shop. Around sundown, Herr Freund and I went across the street to the shop and—and—"

He tilted the chair forward. "Tell me!"

She lifted the towel and began rubbing vigorously, wrathfully, at her hair, her features seized with anger. "Everything had been cleaned out...everything! Is that what you need to hear, Erich Alois? Your parents cleaned out the safe! They took every last pfennig and as many accouterments as they could!"

"Surely there's some mistake...."

Feeling suddenly, strangely empty, he tipped back in the chair.

His parents were imperfect, yes, but...*thieves?* Had all moral values been signed away with the 1918 Armistice? Betrayal, the Führer taught, was the province of Red revolutionaries, republicans...and Jews.

Especially the Jews.

His parents had stabbed the Freunds in the back; in time, they too would find some way to blame their misconduct on the Jews.

"Herr Freund made us hide in the sewer." Miriam's words were tumbling out now, and she was crying. "They destroyed the shop and...and strung him up in his own shop like a criminal, Erich...strangled him with his Iron Cross—"

She broke into convulsive sobs. He wanted to comfort her, but instead he backed away as if from something too hideous to contemplate. He felt as though he, personally, had killed Jacob Freund by provoking Otto Hempel's hatred and by being a part of the larger organization that condoned and encouraged such acts. A murderer, he thought, had no business giving solace to the orphans he had created. And then there were his parents.

"We *have* to get out of Germany," she said. Her voice had taken on a new urgency. "You're the only one who can help us, Erich...."

Angry and frustrated that all his dreaming about her had come to this, he walked to the balcony window and stared at the city's fog-blurred lights. Yes, he had to get them out, but how? Even if he could secure papers for them, getting them out of Germany wasn't enough. Right now there were neutral countries, but for how long?

Ultimately, Adolph Hitler would lay claim to them all.

"I'm deeply sorry, Miriam," he said softly. "Herr Freund was a good man. I wish—" He was about to say he wished his own father had been as moral. "He was...special. I promise I'll find a way to help you, but it's not going to be easy. I have to think about it...find a way, a safe way."

"But you will try to help?"

"As God is my witness. Whatever you need, I'll get. Papers, petitions, money. Whatever it takes. I'm no longer powerless in the Party," he assured her in a choked voice. "There is much I can do behind the scenes. I want to keep you safe."

She looked up at him. "If you're serious, why have you stood by for so long?" she asked between sobs. Her eyes revealed her need to accept his offer, no matter how much she mistrusted him.

He knelt beside her, elbows on the chair, and looked at her closely. "I don't blame you for the way you feel." When he reached out and touched her cheek, he saw her steel herself, but she did not draw away.

Exhausted, her face tear-stained, she still looked beautiful; only an enormous effort of will stopped him from trying to kiss her. Was Solomon, he wondered, similarly enslaved?

"You'll catch pneumonia if you stay in those wet things," he said, standing. He lifted off his desktop and set it against the wall; where the desk had been was a gold-rimmed porcelain bathtub. "You'll feel better after a bath and some food."

"I have to get back to Sol...."

"Solomon can take care of himself. You need to take care of *yourself* for a change. Please—while I think this through."

"I must get back." She no longer sounded defiant. "Herr Freund's body. What are we going to do with the—"

"Just rest. You'll be able to think better after you've had some sleep. I'll get you some food from downstairs. Sol will be all right for now. And he'll be a lot more all right if I can work things out."

He put a large kettle on each of the narrow stove's two burners. After placing a silk shirt and one of his robes on the bed, he gave her the most reassuring smile he could muster and headed down to the Bierstube.

Think! he told himself as he descended the stairs. There had to be some service he could render in exchange for the safety of his friends. Would he ever be rid of Hempel and his need for vengeance? Hempel was no fool; he knew just where and when to inflict pain, as if he had a talent for looking into the soul of his enemy. It was not happenstance that the mob had stormed down Friedrich Ebert Strasse. Brownshirt violence was seemingly random only in the particulars. Hempel, he was sure, had chosen the area carefully.

It would happen again. Unless he could get them out.

Why such emphasis on eradicating the Jews? he thought bitterly. They weren't responsible for what ailed the world, though some facts *were* irrefutable. Only one in a hundred Germans and one in five Berliners was Jewish, yet they dominated the giant Darmstädter, Deutche, and Dresdener banks; owned such huge department stores as Wertheim, Tietz, and KadeWe; and controlled the largest newspaper groups, Ullstein and Mosse. The question was not whether the Jews had power, but whether they wielded power for the good of the Reich.

In his opinion they had. People like Jacob Freund were proof of that. Until Adolph Hitler had insisted otherwise.

I too might have marched to the drum of the Party propaganda, had Pfaueninsel not happened. So perhaps Achilles did not die in vain.

Before entering the Bierstube, he took a deep breath to compose himself, and straightened his uniform.

He returned with a metwurst, a loaf of pumpernickel, a couple of cheeses including a small brie, a bottle of burgundy—hardly the meal he had envisioned serving Miriam the first time she came to his flat, he thought angrily. He found her sleeping, her hair turbaned, more towels on the floor, her shoulders bare and beautiful. No wonder, he thought, unable to stifle a sentimental smile, Lady Venus so easily entrapped Tannhäuser in her web of desire.

Removing his clothes, he slipped into the tub. Perhaps, like Napoleon, he could best contemplate conquests in the bath. What looked like one of her pubic hairs floated in the water. He wound it around his finger and, settling back, watched the lights of a barge moving along Landwehr Kanal, its filthy water a dumping place for refuse—and bodies; during the aborted Bolshevik Revolution, the Freikorps had dumped Rosa Luxemburg there after bludgeoning her to death. Four months in the canal before being found.

That was 1918. The same year he and Solomon found the sewer.

Poor *Spatz*. So naïve, so sure the world was rooted in good and not evil. He himself had known better, even then. They'd been born too late for the war—the real war—the one against moral decline. How he longed, even now, for the imperial purity of the Kaiserzeit, the prewar Old Order. Peace, and respect for traditional values.

Chivalry and the Kaiserzeit had died the moment the Armistice went into effect, the eleventh hour of the

JANET BERLINER AND GEORGE GUTHRIDGE

eleventh day of the eleventh month of the year the Freikorps quelled a revolution and Friedrich Weisser drowned a terrier pup named Bull.

"I've got it!"

He sat up. With a perplexed cry, Miriam jolted upright in bed, the robe clutched against her throat. Smiling at his creativity, he stepped from the tub and wrapped a towel around his waist. How clever, he told himself as he sat down at the table, grinning at her; use that asset which made it so dangerous for her to stay in the Fatherland.

Her name. Her legacy from one of the last of the Old Order.

"I can get you out. Both of you."

"You're certain?"

He nodded. "I *will* help you...and Solomon."

"I know." She was trying to be patient, but he sensed her growing agitation.

"Getting you out of Germany is not enough. You must leave Europe. There's a South American here in Berlin." He hesitated, then decided there was no harm in mentioning the name. "An emissary to Italy—Perón's his name. He'll help. I'm sure he will."

"Juan Perón? I've known him for years. He was a friend of Uncle Walther's. They really liked each other."

"Well, he certainly seems to like you," Erich said, watching her face. Her tension seemed to have lessened. Apparently, he had managed to say the right thing. He wondered, with a pique of jealousy, about the wisdom of having thought of the Argentinean, feeling a vague unease about her exact relationship with the man. "Perón saw you dance at Pfaueninsel. He was enchanted.

If he made an official request to have you perform in his country, Hitler would not refuse. But it will take time—"

"Sol must leave now!" Her voice was edged with panic. "He's cracking up, Erich. If he stays any longer, that sewer could become his tomb—if we're not arrested first."

"Then there's only one answer. Solomon must go to Amsterdam right away and join you in South America later. He's not the problem, you are. Papers for him shouldn't be impossible to arrange—I don't think he's on any list of known enemies of the Party—"

"He's a Jew!" she said bitterly.

"It can be done, Miri. But you're Walther Rathenau's niece—"

"Are you saying I'm on some kind of special list?"

"I don't know, but it's more than likely. Anyhow, the problem's more complicated than that." He looked at her seriously. "What I'm saying is that it will take time to make the arrangements for you. I must be careful, if I am to stay alive myself."

"And in the meantime?"

"In the meantime," he said, "Solomon leaves and you stay with me."

She laughed mirthlessly. "I see. I'm beginning to understand. You've dropped the name *Weisser*, now all you have to do is get rid of Solomon—"

"Stop it!"

"No, *you* stop! If you think I'm coming to live at the estate with you—"

He put a hand on her arm. "You couldn't, even if you...if I wanted you to. Not without renouncing your faith. But you can stay here safely, at least for a while. Fortunately, the landlady doesn't care who lives here, she just cares about the rent money. That way I'll look after you—but only as much as you want me to."

After a moment's silence Miriam nodded in acquiescence. "Thank you, Erich," she said simply. "Now I really must go."

"Stay in bed," Erich said gruffly. "You need to rest. I'll go and find Solomon."

"No." She rose from the bed and scooped up her clothes. "I have to go to him. Tell him myself."

"All right, then. But be ready for me when I come."

"When, Erich? I must know—"

"I told you, I don't know. Today, tomorrow, next week."

He thought for a moment. What he really wanted to say was that he didn't know the answer to that *either*, but as his mind began to reel, he realized he *could* do it. With luck, in a few hours. At least set the thing in motion.

"Tonight," he said definitively. "I'll send Konrad with the limousine. He can take Solomon to the train station and bring you here."

"Konrad," she said softly. The expression on her face told him that she was thinking of the other time Konrad drove her to the station, with Solomon in tow, only that time she was the one leaving, for Paris. "Won't that draw too much attention to us?"

"I don't think so," Erich said, his mind continuing to spin out the scenario and its possibilities. "Once you are living in my flat, it will be assumed that you are my mistress. Making a show of bringing you here at the same time as sending Solomon away will make sense to the Party. They know of your...friendship...with Solomon. My participation in both actions will be understood."

"If you say so," she said quietly. "I have no choice but to trust your judgment. It seems to me, however, that understanding does not necessarily constitute approval. I imagine they would be more likely to approve if you disposed of Sol in some other, less kindly way. Not so?"

"Not so," Erich said. But Miriam's question penetrated to the darkest regions of his soul. To keep from looking her directly in the eye, he turned to stare out the window. He saw the lights of another barge moving through the fog. Probably carrying coal, he reflected, and more than likely headed for the Krupp furnaces. The munitions factories were working at full capacity. War was inevitable, people said, though surely not in *this* decade.

Well, let it come—whenever; he had his own war to wage.

He listened to the sounds from the bathroom, where Miriam was dressing to leave. Someday, somehow, he swore, he would have Adolph Hitler's head on a pike.

And Miriam Rathenau permanently in his bed.

C HAPTER FORTY-THREE

—a sea, blue-black as ink. On a cliff, silhouetted against the ocean, stands a tall man whose hair is the color of foam. A second man squats in the grass, his dark skin deeply pockmarked.

The tall man has one end of a leather strap wound around his wrist; the other end is attached to a boy who crouches at the man's feet like a dog. His back is covered with the furry skin of an animal, and he wears a collar around his neck.

The man who is standing signals for quiet. The boy quivers visibly, shoulders tensed and face set in a fury as he strains against the leash. Kneeling, the tall man puts a hand on the boy's furry back and unhooks the leash clip from the collar.

Solomon! the boy cries. Bruqah!…Miriam!…Solomon! For God's sake, somebody help me!—

"Somebody help me," Sol mumbled as the vision

dissipated and he awoke into the blackness of the sewer. His skin and clothes were soaked with the sweat and smell of terror, and the darkness around him pressed in on him like a live body.

He rolled over on the makeshift flooring and slid his hands up the slimy walls, struggling to stand. Papa! He must go upstairs and pray for Papa, and for himself; he must pray for Miri, and Recha, and Mama. In the darkness he found his old book bag, still hanging from the two-by-twelve after so many years. He hugged it to his chest as he rocked on his heels, crying—

—*the sea roars like a beast in heat as the boy bounds forward toward a corpse that hangs from the branch of a huge palm tree.* Above its head, a simian creature points a long finger.

Mihinana! the white-haired man commands, swacking the boy on the butt. Eat!—

Sol leaned forward, as if seeing more clearly would bring understanding, but the knot in his stomach simply tightened and the fog that clouded his mind thickened—

—*the boy responds to the whip.* First on all fours, then on his feet, now flying through the air as he grips the corpse like a gibbon, legs hugging the waist. He swings upside-down with the body, sinking his teeth into the hip and shaking his head wildly as he fights to tear off a chunk of flesh. His eyes are wide open. Blood curls down his chin.

A guttural voice rings through the darkness: "*There is nowhere to run, Solomon Freund. Watch. Enjoy. As you hold your seasons dear, so you have no choice—*"

"What do you want of me?"

"*What do you want?*" the sewer echoed. "*You want...want ...*"

A light from above erupted against Sol's face, and he jerked up his arms defensively.

"Go away." His voice was a rasp.

A whisper: *Is this your season of madness?*

"Yes!" Sol shouted at the twilight voice of his childhood. "Yes, I am mad. MAD!"

"Solomon, are you all right?"

"Miriam?"

Leaning down, she shone a flashlight around the sewer—like a mother assuring herself there was no tangible cause for her child's nightmare, Sol thought bitterly.

He let go of the book bag, as ashamed of the pleasure it had once brought him as he was of Miriam seeing him like this, and squinted upward, trying to focus. Her face floated behind the light. "I'm fine, I...what time is it?"

"Six o'clock."

"In the morning?"

"Yes." She sounded defensive, as if his question contained an accusation. In a way it had. He needed to know where she had been—and with whom.

"Papa!" he said, remembering. Papa was dead, his body lying in the shop—and he was concerned about where Miriam had been! How long would it take before he fully comprehended Papa's death? A week—a month—a year? And at what cost to his sanity?

What is the price of five sparrows, Solomon?

The voice came to him out of the sewer, as it had done so many years before.

"Eat," he heard again, but this time it was real. "You

must come out of there." Miriam reached down as if to pull him out. "I have brought bread, and here's a hard-boiled egg."

"I'm going to Papa." He took hold of her hand and climbed into the subbasement.

"Papa would wish you to keep up your strength." She had spread out a newspaper on the floor of the subbasement and laid it out like a tablecloth. On top of it, she had placed a metwurst, half a loaf of pumpernickel, a small brie, a half-empty bottle of burgundy.

From her pocket she took a precious egg wrapped in a face-cloth. He took the egg from her, broke it in two, and handed her back half. "This food," he said. "Where did you get it?"

"Eat," she said. "When you are finished we have urgent things to talk about."

In deference to the pain in Miriam's eyes he broke off a small crust of bread and ate it with the egg. "God willing," he said, "whatever we must discuss can wait until sundown. For this one day, I will mourn for my father."

"And I will leave you to mourn in solitude," Miriam said. "But if I must interrupt...if I call out to you to come at once, do as I say."

When Sol did not answer, Miriam became insistent. "Promise me, Solomon," she said.

The urgency in her voice transferred itself to him through his pain. "I will," he said, nodding at her. "Now I must go to Papa."

He made his way up through the cabaret and into the shop. Once inside, he tore down the curtain that separated the shop from the basement steps, and covered his father's body. That done, he sat down on the stool and gave himself up to a day of prayer, and to memories of his father's goodness.

Time slid by, almost tangible, emollient and liquid as he sank ever deeper into dreams that were memories. Light played along the edges of his consciousness and began to turn slowly, a sparkling pinwheel that revolved, broke into shafts, became a world of gently tumbling crystals. "Season of madness," he thought he heard himself mutter, though he was uncertain if the words were outside his head or within it. He felt his chin droop forward and the muscles of his neck and shoulders go slack, and he entered a darkness tinged with gray, moiling fog.

For all the hours of the day, no other reality entered his consciousness. He would have sat there through the night had Miriam not come for him.

"The sun is setting," Miriam said. "You have been here all day, Sol." She took his hand. "It is Succot. Come. We will sanctify this holy day as best we can."

"I love you, Papa," he said softly. He looked at the Iron Cross that lay on his palm. He had been clutching it throughout the day, and its edges had ridged his skin. Turning to Miriam, he did his best to smile. "I love you too," he said.

She watched him find a box, layer it with tissue paper, and lay the medal on top.

"I want you to have this," he told her. "If anything ever happens to me, it is yours."

"Nothing—"

He placed his hand over her mouth. "If I am not here

and you need help," he went on, "you must go to Erich. Despite everything, he is the only brother I have. It is tradition that a man take care of his brother's wife."

She took the box without further protest and gently kissed him on the cheek. There were tears in her eyes, though whether for Papa or because of his words to her, he did not know.

Silently, she led him to the meal she had set up on the floor of the cabaret's subbasement. Covering her head with one of Jacob's old handkerchiefs, she lit a candle she had melted onto a saucer. When she had repeated the traditional blessing, she poured wine into a chipped coffee cup Jacob had kept at the back of the shop.

Sol lifted the wine, placed a hand on his head where his *yarmulke* should have been and sang softly, "*Baruch ato adonai, eluhainu melech ha-olam…*"

Remembering other holidays with his family and choked by tears, he could not finish the prayer.

"Now let us eat." Miriam took the cup from him.

"How can I fill my stomach when my father's body is—"

"Didn't God command us to give thanks, even during mourning?"

A strand of hair had fallen across her eyes. He pushed it back in place. "Is this the time for talking?" he asked. *Is this your season of madness?* he heard, as if in counterpoint to his own words.

"While you were in there," she nodded toward the sewer entry, "I went to see Erich. The food we ate, it came from him."

Sol glanced toward the sewer. While he was in there,

talking to ghosts, had she... He put his hands on her shoulders. "It's all right if you slept with him—"

"It's all right with *you?*" she said sharply.

"Stop it. Please. Not now."

"How can I stop anything, Solomon? In the name of Heaven, how? Sometimes I feel like walking into the Reichschancellery and spitting in the eye of the first SS officer I see, just to get it over with."

"I'm sorry, Miri. I did not mean to offend you." Sol waited a moment before continuing. Taking her hand in his, he said, "You have to come with me to Amsterdam, Miriam. We must find a way to leave together. If you stay here, Erich will never let you go."

She shook her head. "You may be able to get to Amsterdam without too many problems right now," she said, "but even Holland will not always be safe for either of us. Erich came up with a better idea. He's going to suggest to an Argentinean named Juan Perón that he ask Hitler to have me do an official dance tour in South America. He feels that the Führer is unlikely to refuse the request."

"Why would this Perón do you a favor?"

"I've known him longer than I've known you. He was very fond of Uncle Walther—and me. He'll do it. I know he will. Once I'm there you will join me, you and Mama and Recha."

"Like Papa joined them in Holland? If you insist on South America, I'll leave when Hitler grants Perón's request. Not a moment sooner."

"No, Sol. You have to leave as soon as possible!" Suddenly she was in his arms, sobbing. "Why must you fight me, Solomon? Safety—that's all that matters, right now."

"What is Erich's plan for me?"

Quietly, she filled him in.

"And what happens to you in the interim?"

He could feel her stiffen. "Erich says it will be safest for me if I move into his flat while I wait for him to make the arrangements for me to leave."

Sol heard the echo of his own words. *You must go to Erich. Despite everything, he is the only brother I have. It is tradition that a man take care of his brother's wife.*

After a moment he said, trembling, "I will do what you wish on one condition."

"Anything—"

He put his finger to her lips and picked up the candle. Taking her hand, he led her up the stairs and into the cabaret. On the dusty dance floor, amid the pallor of green light beaming down through one of the few small stained-glass windows that remained unbroken, he lifted her knuckles to his lips and closed his eyes.

"There is a season for all things, Miri," he said, once again echoing the twilight voice. "Marry me."

"Here? Tonight? And who will be the rabbi?"

"God."

He opened his eyes and looked into hers, and saw her answer. Though he felt joyous, he held back, denying himself his emotions. If he gave in to his feelings, would God not punish him, what with Papa dead upstairs, Mama unstable, and Recha—

"I have no right to be happy," Miriam said, as if she could hear his thoughts. Her eyes shone with tears. "You say there is a season for all things. Perhaps, too, there is a reason for everything, one only God understands. If so, He will surely forgive me for a moment of joy."

What Sol felt at that moment was akin to the passion of cerebral discovery; he had not believed it possible to feel that way except from what lay between the bindings of a book. He had the impression that if he stood still long enough and stayed silent enough, the cabaret would disappear and they would be transported to some bygone era when the world was whole and where they had a chance for peace and contentment.

They stood among dusty muslin sheets, thrown carelessly over once-new tables and chairs surrounding an abandoned dance floor in a closed cabaret in a world without hope. Berlin, the Reich, their own emotions, Erich: to Sol, they all seemed like spokes of a wheel someone else had set in motion. Like the wheels of Walther Rathenau's limousine, which could even now be headed toward the cabaret. He gave no credence to Miriam's words and hopes concerning the freedom South America afforded. He did not want to leave her, had not really believed she would accept his suggestion—no matter how obvious and necessary his immediate departure.

"The marriage will make the paperwork easier when I get to South America," she said.

"Is that the only reason we should marry?"

"What do you think?" she asked softly.

He slid his arms around her waist. "I think love is a better reason."

"And I do love you," she said.

He kissed her and discovered a new yielding to her

lips. When the embrace ended, he glanced around the room and said, "Didn't I hear something about there being a wedding in here today?"

She squeezed his hands, and smiled. "Make two stacks of three tables each. I will be right back."

Fear touched him. "You're not going outside, are you?"

"Of course not," she said as affably and coyly as a girl at a prom. "Wait and see." She moved across the floor and into the shadows with her dancer's grace.

By the time Sol had the tables piled up in the center of the dance floor, Miriam returned, a rose-colored shawl over her shoulders. "Remember this? I wore it that first night in the cabaret—Miss Debutante, singing and dancing and expecting the world to applaud." She briefly curtsied.

"But where—"

"A different kind of tradition, Sol." She took off the shawl and draped it between the two table stacks. "Every performer leaves something behind in the dressing room, for luck. I was young, rich, and silly…I left the biggest and brightest thing I could think of. It was there, in the costume trunk. It's a bit musty, but at least the fish moths left it alone. Here, give me a hand."

"And do what?"

"We have to have a canopy, don't we? It wouldn't be a wedding without one."

"Does that mean you are accepting my proposal, Fräulein Rathenau?" he asked seriously.

"Let's just say I have given the matter due consideration, and I concur with your idea, Herr Freund."

Before he could say anything else she bounded off

again, this time down the stairs leading to the subbasement. He worked on the canopy, wondering what surprise she now had in store for him.

She returned with the burgundy and three dusty glasses.

Wriggling out of her slip, she wrapped it around one of the glasses and placed it under the canopy. "Now flowers, and…" She looked around in dismay. "Forget it. There's no way."

"Music? I'll be back."

He hurried down the stairs. When he returned, she twirled around to show him the lavender spray she had twisted into her hair. "Lilac. It's silk, but it'll do."

"And here's my contribution." He dug in his pocket and pulled out the harmonica he had retrieved from his old book bag. He blew in the mouth organ to clear it of dust and, with the instrument cupped lovingly in his hands, watched her sway as he softly played a Schubert melody.

When he had finished, he fished in his pocket, pulled out a cigar and removed their gold bands. "I went up through the sewer and…"

She put her fingers to his lips to hush him. "My God, Solomon Freund, you must have shopped for weeks! Don't tell anyone where you bought the rings." Glancing around suspiciously, she added, "Some of the fashionable women in this place might overhear and bribe the jeweler for duplicates."

Taking the wrapper-rings from his hand, she held them in her palm for a moment before returning the smaller of the two to him. The look in her eyes told him that to her it truly was a treasure.

He ushered her beneath the canopy and took her in his arms. "In the eyes of God, from this day on and for as long as we shall live, we are man and wife," he said huskily. Trembling, he slid the cigar band onto her finger. "I love you, Miriam. I always have, I always will."

"And I love you, Solomon Freund."

He held out his hand. As she slipped the ring on his finger, he brought down his heel sharp and hard onto the wrapped glass and felt it splinter underfoot. Then he kissed her.

As dusk faded and shadows lengthened, they held each other like children. When night came, so did Konrad.

"A few more minutes, please, Konnie," Miriam begged.

Sol knew that Konrad had never been able to refuse Miriam anything. Though he frowned and was clearly worried, he did not refuse her now. "It *can* only be a few minutes, Miss Miriam," he said, glancing at the wristwatch Miriam had brought him from America so many years before. "The train for Amsterdam leaves in half an hour, and you are expected at the flat."

He headed up the circular stairs. As he closed the door behind himself, Miriam glided into Solomon's arms. "One dance, my love," she whispered.

He held her so close, he thought she must break in two. Then, warmed by wine and passion, they ignored the storm clouds gathering outside and danced to imaginary violins playing Schubert and Strauss and Brahms for them alone.

But the storm would not be denied. Growing ever more ominous, it continued unabated on its predetermined course.

Afterword

The Madagascar Plan—the basis of *The Madagascar Manifesto*, of which *Child of the Light* is part—was first proposed by Napoleon's staff. The German High Command adopted it in 1938. Shortly thereafter, Eichmann embraced it as the "solution" to the "Jewish Question." The Plan's many supporters—and many agendas—included the U.S. Congress and France's Baron von Rothchild, the Jewish cognac magnate who offered to buy the island in a desperate attempt to help save his people.

The cigar shop is based on a store in what until recently was East Berlin. The beatings resulting from the "mistaken identity" and the robbery by the Gentile co-owners really happened. The Jewish co-owner and his son—modeled on Janet Berliner's grandfather—witnessed Rathenau's assassination. Except for the second nurse and the grenade that kills her, the assassination is presented exactly as it happened. That Rathenau's chauffeur survived without a scratch was probably due less to good luck or miracle than to a weak grenade.

The assassins who went to prison were released after short terms. One of them, Ernst von Salomon, became a successful novelist and playwright; all his writings are based on his association with the conspirators.

A meeting between Hitler and a Gypsy fortune-teller really occurred, as did the wild pre-Olympics party at Peacock Island and the winter solstice celebrations by the SS. The Grünewald synagogue, Wewelsburg Castle, Luna Park, and the Wannsee are real places. The Nazi *"Endlösung"* (the decision to exterminate the Jews through the use of poison gas) was decided at Wannsee in 1943.

The El Dorado was real, though Kaverne is fictitious, as is Ananas. Brecht escaped from Germany and, together with his collaborator Kurt Weill, became a wealthy playwright, mostly from the British production of *The Threepenny Opera*. Werner Fink miraculously survived the Nazi regime.

"Vlad"—Vladimir Nabokov—did teach tennis lessons in Berlin. He emigrated to the United States and became one of this country's top novelists and critics; he was particularly famous for *Lolita*. Whether he ever met Rathenau's niece is a matter of conjecture.

Prince Auwi was killed on the Russian Front. Juan Perón, who became the head of Argentina, was emissary to Italy and was in Berlin at the time of the novel.

The authors strove to reflect language use and rhythms that were prevalent at the time, but for reading ease did take certain small liberties. For example, "suspenders" and "flashlight" were only then replacing the more common *braces* and *hand torch*.

Biography

In 1935, Janet Berliner's parents fled Berlin to escape the Nazi terror. In 1961, Janet left her native South Africa in protest against apartheid. After living and teaching in New York, she moved to San Francisco's Bay Area; started her own business as an editorial consultant, lecturer, and writer; and wrote *Rite of the Dragon*, which got her banned from South Africa. She now lives and works in Las Vegas. She is the coeditor of *Peter S. Beagle's Immortal Unicorn* and *David Copperfield's Tales of the Impossible* (HarperPrism, Fall '95). She is cocreator of Peter S. Beagle's *Unicorn Sonata* (Turner Publishing, Fall '96), and recently completed *The Michael Crichton Companion* for Ballantine Books.

Besides having been named as one of America's top educators, George Guthridge has sold more than fifty short stories and novelettes and has been a Nebula and Hugo finalist. He currently teaches at the University of Alaska Fairbanks, Bristol Bay.

July 1996

BOOK TWO
of the
Madagascar
Manifesto

Child
OF THE JOURNEY

BY JANET BERLINER AND GEORGE GUTHRIDGE

White Wolf Publishing

BOREALIS

continue the journey...